PUFFIN BOOKS
THE ROOM OF MANY COLOURS
A TREASURY OF STORIES FOR CHILDREN

Ruskin Bond's first novel, *The Room on the Roof*, written when he was seventeen, received the John Llewellyn Rhys Memorial Prize in 1957. Since then he has written a number of novellas (including *Vagrants in the Valley, A Flight of Pigeons* and *Mr Oliver's Diary*), essays, poems and children's books, many of which have been published in Puffin Books. He has also written over 500 short stories and articles that have appeared in magazines and anthologies. He received the Sahitya Akademi Award in 1993, the Padma Shri in 1999 and the Padma Bhushan in 2014.

Ruskin Bond was born in Kasauli, Himachal Pradesh, and grew up in Jamnagar, Dehradun, New Delhi and Simla. As a young man, he spent four years in the Channel Islands and London. He returned to India in 1955. He now lives in Landour, Mussoorie, with his adopted f

Also in Puffin by Ruskin Bond

A Treasury of
Stories for
Children

RUSKIN BOND

The Room of Many Colours

ILLUSTRATIONS BY

ARCHANA SREENIVASAN

PUFFIN BOOKS

An imprint of Penguin Random House

PUFFIN BOOKS

USA | Canada | UK | Ireland | Australia
New Zealand | India | South Africa | China

Puffin Books is part of the Penguin Random House group of companies
whose addresses can be found at global.penguinrandomhouse.com

Published by Penguin Random House India Pvt. Ltd
7th Floor, Infinity Tower C, DLF Cyber City,
Gurgaon 122 002, Haryana, India

Penguin
Random House
India

First published as *Ruskin Bond's Treasury of Stories for Children* in Viking by Penguin
Books India 2000
Published in Puffin Books 2001
This edition published 2014

20

ISBN 9780143333371

Typeset in Adobe Garamond Pro by Ram Das Lal, New Delhi
Printed at Replika Press Pvt. Ltd, India

www.penguin.co.in

For Siddharth—
Thanks for the new coat.
But that's another story . . .

Contents

Introduction

IT BEGAN IN a forest rest house. My father died when I was ten, and for the next few years books became a scarce commodity, for my mother and stepfather were not great readers. In my lonely early teens I seized upon almost any printed matter that came my way, whether it was a girls' classic like *Little Women*, a *Hotspur* or *Champion* comic, a detective story or *The Naturalist on the River Amazon* by Henry Walter Bates. The only books I baulked at reading were collections of sermons (amazing how often they turned up in those early years) and self-improvement books, since I hadn't the slightest desire to improve myself in any way.

I think it all began in a forest rest house in the Siwalik Hills, a subtropical range cradling the Doon Valley in northern India. Here my stepfather and his gun-toting friends were given to hunting birds and animals. He was a poor shot, so he cannot really be blamed for the absence of wildlife today; but he did his best to eliminate every creature that came within his sights.

On one of his shikar trips we were staying near the Timli Pass. My stepfather and his friends were after a tiger (you were out of fashion if you weren't after big game) and set out every morning with an army of paid villagers to beat the jungle, that is, to make enough noise with drums, whistles, tin trumpets and empty kerosene tins to disturb the tiger and drive the unwilling beast into the open where he could conveniently be despatched. Truly bored by this form of sport, I stayed behind in the rest house, and in the course of the morning's exploration of the bungalow, discovered a dusty but crowded bookshelf half-hidden in a corner of the back veranda.

Who had left them there? A literary forest officer? A memsahib who'd been bored by her husband's campfire boasting? Or someone like me who had no enthusiasm for the 'manly' sport of slaughtering wild animals, and had brought his library along to pass the time?

Or possibly the poor fellow had gone into the jungle one day as a gesture towards his more bloodthirsty companions, and been trampled by an elephant or gored by a wild boar, or (more likely) accidentally shot by one of his companions—and they had taken his remains away but left his books behind.

Anyway, there they were—a shelf of some fifty volumes, obviously untouched for several years. I wiped the dust off the covers and examined the titles. As my reading tastes had not yet formed, I was ready to try anything. The bookshelf was varied in its contents—and my own interests have remained equally wide-ranging.

On that fateful day in the forest rest house, I discovered two very funny books. One was P.G. Wodehouse's *Love Among the Chickens*, an early Ukridge story and still one of my favourites. The other was *The Diary of a Nobody* by George and Weedon Grossmith, who spent more time on the stage than in the study but are now remembered mainly for this hilarious book. It isn't everyone's cup of tea. Recently, I lent my copy to a Swiss friend, who could see nothing funny about it. I must have read it a dozen times; I pick it up whenever I'm feeling low, and on one occasion it even cured me of a peptic ulcer!

Anyway, back to the rest house. By the time the perspiring hunters came back late in the evening, I'd started on M.R. James's *Ghost Stories of an Antiquary*, which had me hooked on ghost stories for the rest of my life. It kept me awake most of the night, until the oil in the kerosene lamp had finished.

Next morning, fresh and optimistic again, the shikaris set out for a different area, where they hoped to locate the tiger. All day I could hear the beaters' drums throbbing in the distance. This did not prevent me from finishing a collection of stories called *The Big Karoo* by Pauline Smith—wonderfully evocative of the pioneering Boers in South Africa.

My concentration was disturbed only once, when I looked up and saw a spotted deer crossing the open clearing in front of the bungalow. The deer disappeared into the forest and I returned to my book.

Dusk had fallen when I heard the party returning from

the hunt. The great men were talking loudly and seemed excited. Perhaps they had got their tiger! I came out on the veranda to meet them.

'Did you shoot the tiger?' I asked.

'No, Ruskin,' said my stepfather. 'I think we'll catch up with it tomorrow. But you should have been with us—we saw a spotted deer!'

There were three days left and I knew I would never get through the entire bookshelf. So I chose *David Copperfield*—my first encounter with Dickens—and settled down in the veranda armchair to make the acquaintance of Mr Micawber and his family, along with Aunty Betsy Trotwood, Mr Dick, Peggotty and a host of other larger-than-life characters. I think it would be true to say that Copperfield set me off on the road to literature. I identified with young David and wanted to grow up to be a writer like him.

But on my second day with the book an event occurred which interrupted my reading for a little while.

I'd noticed, on the previous day, that a number of stray dogs—some of them belonging to watchmen, villagers and forest rangers—always hung about the bungalow, waiting for scraps of food to be thrown away. It was about ten o'clock in the morning (a time when wild animals seldom come into the open), when I heard a sudden yelp coming from the clearing. Looking up, I saw a large, full-grown leopard making off with one of the dogs. The other dogs, while keeping their distance, set up a furious barking, but the leopard and its victim had soon disappeared. I returned to *David Copperfield*.

It was getting late when the shikaris returned. They

looked dirty, sweaty and disgruntled. Next day, we were to return to the city, and none of them had anything to show for a week in the jungle.

'I saw a leopard this morning,' I said modestly.

No one took me seriously. 'Did you really?' said the leading shikari, glancing at the book in my hands. 'Young Master Copperfield says he saw a leopard!'

'Too imaginative for his age,' said my stepfather. 'Comes from reading so much, I expect.'

I went to bed and left them to their tales of the 'good old days' when rhinos, cheetahs and possibly even unicorns were still available for slaughter. Camp broke up before I could finish *Copperfield*, but the forest ranger said I could keep the book. And so I became the only member of the expedition with a trophy to take home.

After that adventure, I was always looking for books in unlikely places. Although I never went to college, I think I have read as much, if not more, than most collegiates, and it would be true to say that I received a large part of my education in second-hand bookshops. London had many, and Calcutta once had a large number of them, but I think the prize must go to the small town in Wales called Hay-on-Wye, which has twenty-six bookshops and over a million books. It's in the world's quiet corners that book lovers still flourish—a far from dying species!

One of my treasures is a little novel called *Sweet Rocket* by Mary Johnston. It was a failure when first published in 1920. It has only the thinnest outline of a story but the author sets out her ideas in lyrical prose that seduces me at every turn of the page. Miss Johnston was a Virginian. She did not travel outside America. But her little book did. I found it in 1990, buried under a pile of railway timetables at a bookstall in Simla, the old summer capital of India—almost as though it had been waiting for me those seventy years.

Among my souvenirs is a charming little recipe book, small enough to slip into an apron pocket. (You need to be a weightlifter to pick up some of the cookery books that are published today.) This one's charm lies not so much in its recipes for roast lamb and mint sauce (which are very good too) but in the margins of each page, enlivened with little Victorian maxims concerning good food and wise eating. Here are a few chosen at random:

'There is skill in all things, even in making porridge.'
'Dry bread at home is better than curried prawns abroad.'
'Eating and drinking should not keep men from thinking.'
'Better a small fish than an empty dish.'
'Let not your tongue cut your throat.'

I have collected a number of little books, like my father's *Finger Prayer Book*, which is the size of a small finger but is replete with Psalms, and the complete *Book of Common Prayer*. Another is *The Pocket Trivet: An Anthology for Optimists*, published by *The Morning Post* newspaper in 1932 and designed to slip into the waistcoat pocket. But what is a trivet, one might well ask . . .

Introduction

Well, it's a stand for a small pot or kettle, fixed securely over a grate. To be right as a trivet is to be perfectly and thoroughly right—*just* right, like the short sayings in this tiny anthology, which range from Emerson's 'Hitch your wagon to a star!' to the Japanese proverb 'In the marketplace there is money to be made, but under the cherry tree there is rest.'

Books help me to forget the dilapidated old building in which I live and work, and to look instead at the ever-changing cloud patterns as seen from my small bedroom-cum-study window. There is no end to the shapes made by the clouds, or to the stories they set off in my head.

But I can't despise this dilapidated old building. I've lived in it for over twenty years and it's here that I've written most of my stories for children. It has given shelter to me and my extended family. There are ten of us now.

The roof has blown off a couple of times, the walls tremble when heavy vehicles pass below. But I never run short of ideas, and there is never a dull moment in my life. The grandchildren see to that. Sometimes I tell them stories, often they tell me stories. Sometimes stories come in at my window! This is one writer who never suffers from writer's block.

Most of our living has to happen in the mind. And to quote one anonymous sage from my Trivet: 'The world is only the size of each man's head.'

Landour, Mussoorie   Ruskin Bond
November 2000

A Long Walk with Granny

GRANNY COULD HEAR the distant roar of the river and smell the pine needles beneath her feet, and feel the presence of her grandson, Mani; but she couldn't see the river or the trees; and of her grandson she could only make out his fuzzy hair, and sometimes, when he was very close, his blackberry eyes and the gleam of his teeth when he smiled.

Granny wore a pair of old glasses; she'd been wearing them for well over ten years, but her eyes had grown steadily weaker, and the glasses had grown older and were now scratched and spotted, and there was very little she could see through them. Still, they were better than nothing. Without them, everything was just a topsy-turvy blur.

Of course, Granny knew her way about the house and the fields, and on a clear day she could see the mountains— the mighty Himalayan snow peaks—striding away into

1

the sky; but it was felt by Mani and his father that it was high time Granny had her eyes tested and got herself new glasses.

'Well, you know we can't get them in the village,' said Granny.

Mani said, 'You'll have to go to the eye hospital in Mussoorie. That's the nearest town.'

'But that's a two-day journey,' protested Granny. 'First I'd have to walk to Nain Market, twelve miles at least, spend the night there at your Uncle's place, and then catch a bus for the rest of the journey! You know how I hate buses. And it's ten years since I walked all the way to Mussoorie. That was when I had these glasses made.'

'Well, it's still there,' said Mani's father. 'What is?'

'Mussoorie.'

'And the eye hospital?'

'That too.'

'Well, my eyes are not too bad, really,' said Granny, looking for excuses. She did not feel like going far from the village; in particular she did not want to be parted from Mani. He was eleven and quite capable of looking after himself, but Granny had brought him up ever since his mother had died when he was only a year old. She was his Nani (maternal grandmother), and had cared for boy and father, and cows and hens and household, all these years, with great energy and devotion.

'I can manage quite well,' she said. 'As long as I can see what's right in front of me, there's no problem. I know you got a ball in your hand, Mani; please don't bounce it off the cow.'

'It's not a ball, Granny; it's an apple.'

'Oh, is it?' said Granny, recovering quickly from her mistake. 'Never mind. Just don't bounce it off the cow. And don't eat too many apples!'

'Now listen,' said Mani's father sternly, 'I know you don't want to go anywhere. But we're not sending you off on your own. I'll take you to Mussoorie.'

'And leave Mani here by himself? How could you even think of doing that?'

'Then *I'll* take you to Mussoorie,' said Mani eagerly. 'We can leave Father on his own, can't we? I've been to Mussoorie before, with my school friends. I know where we can stay. But . . .' He paused a moment and looked doubtfully from his father to his grandmother. 'You wouldn't be able to walk *all* the way to Nain, would you, Granny?'

'Of course I can walk,' said Granny. 'I may be going blind, but there's nothing wrong with my legs!'

That was true enough. Only day before they'd found Granny in the walnut tree, tossing walnuts, not very accurately, into a large basket on the ground.

'But you're seventy, Granny.'

'What has that got to do with it? And besides, it's downhill to Nain.'

'And uphill coming back.'

'Uphill's easier!' said Granny.

Now that she knew Mani might be accompanying her, she was more than ready to make the journey.

The monsoon rains had begun, and in front of the small stone house a cluster of giant dahlias reared their heads. Mani had seen them growing in Nain and had brought some bulbs home. 'These are big flowers, Granny,' he'd said. 'You'll be able to see them better.'

She could indeed see the dahlias, splashes of red and yellow against the old stone of the cottage walls.

Looking at them now, Granny said, 'While we're in Mussoorie, we'll get some seeds and bulbs. And a new bell for the white cow. And a pullover for your father. And shoes for you. Look, there's nothing much left of the ones you're wearing.'

'Now just a minute,' said Mani's father. 'Are you going there to have your eyes tested, or are you going on a shopping expedition? I've got only a hundred rupees to spare. You'll have to manage with that.'

'We'll manage,' said Mani. 'We'll sleep at the bus shelter.'

'No, we won't,' said Granny. 'I've got fifty rupees of my own. We'll stay at a hotel!'

Early next morning, in a light drizzle, Granny and Mani set out on the path to Nain.

Mani carried a small bedding-roll on his shoulder; Granny carried a large cloth shopping bag and an umbrella.

The path went through fields and around the brow of the hill and then began to wind here and there, up and down and around, as though it had a will of its own and no

4

intention of going anywhere in particular. Travellers new to the area often left the path, because they were impatient or in a hurry, and thought there were quicker, better ways of reaching their destinations. Almost immediately they found themselves lost. For it was a wise path and a good path, and had found the right way of crossing the mountains after centuries of trial and error.

'Whenever you feel tired, we'll take a rest,' said Mani. 'We've only just started out,' said Granny. 'We'll rest when you're hungry!'

They walked at a steady pace, without talking too much. A flock of parrots whirled overhead, flashes of red and green against the sombre sky. High in a spruce tree a barbet called monotonously. But there were no other sounds, except for the hiss and gentle patter of the rain.

Mani stopped to pick wild blackberries from a bush. Granny wasn't fond of berries and did not slacken her pace. Mani had to run to catch up with her. Soon his lips were purple with the juice from the berries.

The rain stopped and the sun came out. Below them, the light green of the fields stood out against the dark green of the forests, and the hills were bathed in golden sunshine.

Mani ran ahead.

'Can you see all right, Granny?' he called.

'I can see the path and I can see your white shirt. That's enough for just now.'

'Well, watch out, there are some mules coming down the road.'

Granny stepped aside to allow the mules to pass. They clattered by, the mule driver urging them on with a romantic song; but the last mule veered towards Granny and appeared to be heading straight for her. Granny saw it just in time. She knew that mules and ponies always preferred going around objects if they could see what lay ahead of them, so she held out her open umbrella and the mule cantered round it without touching her.

Granny and Mani ate their light meal on the roadside, in the shade of a whispering pine, and drank from a spring a little further down the path.

By late afternoon they were directly above Nain.

'We're almost there,' said Mani. 'I can see the temple near Uncle's house.'

'I can't see a thing,' said Granny.

'That's because of the mist. There's a thick mist coming up the valley.'

It began raining heavily as they entered the small market town on the banks of the river. Granny's umbrella was leaking badly. But they were soon drying themselves in Uncle's house, and drinking glasses of hot, sweet milky tea.

Mani got up early the next morning and ran down the narrow street to bathe in the river. The swift but shallow mountain river was a tributary of the sacred Ganga, and its waters were held sacred too. As the sun rose, people thronged the steps leading down to the river, to bathe or pray or float flower-offerings downstream.

As Mani dressed, he heard the blare of a bus horn.

There was only one bus to Mussoorie. He scampered up the slope, wondering if they'd miss it. But Granny was waiting for him at the bus stop. She had already bought their tickets. The motor road followed the course of the river, which thundered a hundred feet below. The bus was old and rickety, and rattled so much that the passengers could barely hear themselves speaking.

One of them was pointing to a spot below, where another bus had gone off the road a few weeks back, resulting in many casualties.

The driver appeared to be unaware of the accident. He drove at some speed, and whenever he went round a bend, everyone in the bus was thrown about. In spite of all the noise and confusion, Granny fell asleep, her head resting against Mani's shoulder.

Suddenly, the bus came to a grinding halt. People were thrown forward in their seats. Granny's glasses fell off and had to be retrieved from the folds of someone else's umbrella.

'What's happening?' she asked. 'Have we arrived?'

'No, something is blocking the road,' said Mani.

'It's a landslide!' exclaimed someone, and all the passengers put their heads out of the windows to take a look.

It was a big landslide. Sometime in the night, during the heavy rain, earth and trees and bushes had given way and come crashing down, completely blocking the road. Nor was it over yet. Debris was still falling. Mani saw rocks hurtling down the hill and into the river.

'Not a suitable place for a bus stop,' observed Granny, who couldn't see a thing.

Even as she spoke, a shower of stones and small rocks came clattering down on the roof of the bus. Passengers cried out in alarm. The driver began reversing, as more rocks came crashing down.

'I never did trust motor roads,' said Granny.

The driver kept backing until they were well away from the landslide. Then everyone tumbled out of the bus. Granny and Mani were the last to get down.

They could tell it would take days to clear the road, and most of the passengers decided to return to Nain with the bus. But a few bold spirits agreed to walk to Mussoorie, taking a short cut up the mountain which would bypass the landslide.

'It's only ten miles from here by the footpath,' said one of them. 'A stiff climb, but we can make it by evening.'

Mani looked at Granny. 'Shall we go back?'

'What's ten miles?' said Granny. 'We did that yesterday.'

So they started climbing a narrow path, little more than a goat track, which went steeply up the mountainside. But there was much huffing and puffing and pausing for breath, and by the time they got to the top of the mountain, Granny and Mani were on their own. They could see a few stragglers far below; the rest had retreated to Nain.

Granny and Mani stood on the summit of the mountain. They had it all to themselves. Their village was hidden by the range to the north. Far below rushed the river. Far above circled a golden eagle.

In the distance, on the next mountain, the houses of Mussoorie were white specks on the dark green hillside.

'Did you bring any food from Uncle's house?' asked Mani.

'Naturally,' said Granny. 'I knew you'd soon be hungry. There are pakoras and buns, and peaches from Uncle's garden.'

'Good!' said Mani, forgetting his tiredness. 'We'll eat as we go along. There's no need to stop.' 'Eating or walking?'

'Eating, of course. We'll stop when you're tired, Granny.'

'Oh, I can walk forever,' said Granny, laughing. 'I've been doing it all my life. And one day I'll just walk over the mountains and into the sky. But not if it's raining. This umbrella leaks badly.'

Down again they went, and up the next mountain, and over bare windswept hillsides, and up through a dark gloomy deodar forest. And then just as it was getting dark, they saw the lights of Mussoorie twinkling ahead of them.

As they came nearer, the lights increased, until presently they were in a brightly lit bazaar, swallowed up by crowds of shoppers, strollers, tourists and merrymakers. Mussoorie seemed a very jolly sort of place for those who had money to spend. Jostled in the crowd, Granny kept one hand firmly on Mani's shoulder so that she did not lose him.

They asked around for the cheapest hotel. But there were no cheap hotels. So they spent the night in a dharamsala adjoining the temple, where other pilgrims had taken shelter.

Next morning, at the eye hospital, they joined a long queue of patient patients. The eye specialist, a portly man in a suit and tie who himself wore glasses, dealt with the patients in a brisk but kind manner. After an hour's wait, Granny's turn came.

The doctor took one horrified look at Granny's glasses and dropped them in a wastebasket. Then he fished them out and placed them on his desk and said, 'On second thought, I think I'll send them to a museum. You should have changed your glasses years ago. They've probably done more harm than good.'

He examined Granny's eyes with a strong light, and said, 'Your eyes are very weak, but you're not going blind. We'll fit you up with a stronger pair of glasses.' Then he placed her in front of a board covered with letters in English and Hindi, large and small, and asked Granny if she could make them out.

'I can't even see the board,' said Granny.

'Well, can you see me?' asked the doctor.

'Some of you,' said Granny.

'I want you to see all of me,' said the doctor, and he balanced a wire frame on Granny's nose and began trying out different lenses.

Suddenly, Granny could see much better. She saw the board and the biggest letters on it.

'Can you see me now?' asked the doctor.

'*Most of you,*' said Granny. And then added, by way of being helpful, 'There's quite a lot of you to see.'

'Thank you,' said the doctor. 'And now turn around and tell me if you can see your grandson.'

Granny turned, and saw Mani clearly for the first time in many years.

'Mani!' she exclaimed, clapping her hands with joy. 'How nice you look! What a fine boy I've brought up! But you *do* need a haircut. And a wash. And buttons on your shirt. And a new pair of shoes. Come along to the bazaar!'

'First have your new glasses made,' said Mani, laughing. 'Then we'll go shopping!'

A day later, they were in a bus again, although no one knew how far it would be able to go. Sooner or later they would have to walk.

Granny had a window seat, and Mani sat beside her. He had new shoes and Granny had a new umbrella and they had also bought a thick woollen Tibetan pullover for Mani's father. And seeds and bulbs and a cowbell.

As the bus moved off, Granny looked eagerly out of the window. Each bend in the road opened up new vistas for her, and she could see many things that she hadn't seen for a long time—distant villages, people working in the fields, milkmen on the road, two dogs rushing along beside the bus, monkeys in the trees, and, most wonderful of all, a rainbow in the sky.

She couldn't see perfectly, of course, but she was very pleased with the improvement.

'What a large cow!' she remarked, pointing at a beast grazing on the hillside.

'It's not a cow, Granny,' said Mani. 'It's a buffalo.'

Granny was not to be discouraged. 'Anyway, I saw it,' she insisted.

While most of the people on the bus looked weary and bored, Granny continued to gaze out of the window, discovering new sights.

Mani watched for a time and listened to her excited chatter. Then his head began to nod. It dropped against Granny's shoulder, and remained there, comfortably supported. The bus swerved and jolted along the winding mountain road, but Mani was fast asleep.

Animals on the Track

'ALL ABOARD!' SHRIEKED Popeye, Grandmother's pet parrot, as the family climbed aboard the Lucknow Express. We were moving from Dehra to Lucknow, in northern India, and as Grandmother had insisted on taking her parrot along, Grandfather and I had insisted on bringing our pets—a teenaged tiger (Grandfather's) and a small squirrel (mine). But we thought it prudent to leave the python behind.

In those days the trains in India were not so crowded and it was possible to travel with a variety of creatures. Grandfather had decided to do things in style by travelling first-class, so we had a four-berth compartment of our own, and Timothy, the tiger, had an entire berth to himself. Later, everyone agreed that Timothy behaved perfectly throughout the journey. Even the guard admitted that he could not have asked for a better passenger: no stealing from vendors, no shouting at coolies, no breaking of railway property, no spitting on the platform.

All the same, the journey was not without incident. Before we reached Lucknow, there was excitement enough for everyone.

To begin with, Popeye objected to vendors and other people poking their hands in at the windows. Before the train had moved out of the Dehra station, he had nipped two fingers and tweaked a ticket-inspector's ear.

No sooner had the train started moving than Chips, my squirrel, emerged from my pocket to examine his surroundings. Before I could stop him, he was out of the compartment door, scurrying along the corridor.

Chips discovered that the train was a squirrel's paradise, almost all the passengers having bought large quantities of roasted peanuts before the train pulled out. He had no difficulty in making friends with both children and grown-ups, and it was an hour before he returned to our compartment, his tummy almost bursting.

'I think I'll go to sleep,' said Grandmother, covering herself with a blanket and stretching out on the berth opposite Timothy's. 'It's been a tiring day.'

'Aren't you going to eat anything?' asked Grandfather.

'I'm not hungry—I had some soup before we left. You two help yourselves from the tiffin-basket.'

Grandmother dozed off, and even Popeye started nodding, lulled to sleep by the clackety-clack of the wheels and the steady puffing of the steam engine.

'Well, I'm hungry,' I said. 'What did Granny make for us?'

'Ham sandwiches, boiled eggs, a roast chicken, gooseberry pie. It's all in the tiffin-basket under your berth.'

I tugged at the large basket and dragged it into the centre of the compartment. The straps were loosely tied. No sooner had I undone them than the lid flew open, and I let out a gasp of surprise.

In the basket was Grandfather's pet python, curled up contentedly on the remains of our dinner. Grandmother had insisted that we leave the python behind, and Grandfather had let it loose in the garden. Somehow, it had managed to snuggle itself into the tiffin-basket.

'Well, what are you staring at?' asked Grandfather from his corner.

'It's the python!' I said. 'And its finished all our dinner.'

Grandfather joined me, and together we looked down at what remained of the food. Pythons don't chew, they swallow: outlined along the length of the large snake's sleek body were the distinctive shapes of a chicken, a pie, and six boiled eggs. We couldn't make out the ham sandwiches, but presumably these had been eaten too because there was no sign of them in the basket. Only a few apples remained. Evidently, the python did not care for apples.

Grandfather snapped the basket shut and pushed it back beneath the berth.

'We mustn't let Grandmother see him,' he said. 'She might think we brought him along on purpose.'

'Well, I'm hungry,' I complained. Just then Chips returned from one of his forays and presented me with a peanut.

'Thanks,' I said. 'If you keep bringing me peanuts all night, I might last until morning.'

But it was not long before I felt sleepy. Grandfather had begun to nod and the only one who was wide awake was the squirrel, still intent on investigating distant compartments.

A little after midnight there was a great clamour at the end of the corridor. Grandfather and I woke up. Timothy growled in his sleep, and Popeye made complaining noises.

Suddenly there were cries of 'Saap, saap!' (Snake, snake!)

Grandfather was on his feet in a moment. He looked under the berth. The tiffin-basket was empty.

'The python's out,' he said, and dashed out of our compartment in his pyjamas. I was close behind.

About a dozen passengers were bunched together outside the washroom door.

'Anything wrong?' asked Grandfather casually.

'We can't get into the toilet,' said someone. 'There's a huge snake inside.'

'Let me take a look,' said Grandfather. 'I know all about snakes.'

The passengers made way for him, and he entered the washroom to find the python curled up in the washbasin. After its heavy meal it had become thirsty and, finding the lid of the tiffin-basket easy to pry up, had set out in search of water.

Grandfather gathered up the sleepy, overfed python and stepped out of the washroom. The passengers hastily made way for them.

'Nothing to worry about,' said grandfather cheerfully. 'It's just a harmless young python. He's had his dinner already, so no one is in any danger!' And he marched back to our compartment with the python in his arms. As soon as I was inside, he bolted the door.

Grandmother was sitting up on her berth.

'I knew you'd do something foolish behind my back,' she scolded. 'You told me you'd got rid of that creature, and all the time you've been hiding it from me.'

Grandfather tried to explain that we had nothing to do with it, that the python had snuggled itself into the tiffin-basket, but Grandmother was unconvinced. She declared that Grandfather couldn't live without the creature and that he had deliberately brought it along.

'What will Mabel do when she sees it!' cried Grandmother despairingly.

My Aunt Mabel was a schoolteacher in Lucknow. She was going to share our new house, and she was terrified of all reptiles, particularly snakes.

'We won't let her see it,' said Grandfather. 'Back it goes into the tiffin-basket.'

Early next morning the train steamed into Lucknow. Aunt Mabel was on the platform to receive us.

Grandfather let all the other passengers get off before he emerged from the compartment with Timothy on a chain. I had Chips in my pocket, suitcase in both hands. Popeye stayed perched on Grandmother's shoulder, eyeing the busy platform with considerable distrust.

Aunt Mabel, a lover of good food, immediately spotted

the tiffin-basket, picked it up and said, 'It's not very heavy. I'll carry it out to the taxi. I hope you've kept something for me.'

'A whole chicken,' I said.

'We hardly ate anything,' said Grandfather. 'It's all yours, Aunty!' I added.

'Oh, good!' exclaimed Aunt Mabel. 'Its been ages since I tasted something cooked by your grandmother.' And after that there was no getting the basket away from her.

Glancing at it, I thought I saw the lid bulging, but Grandfather had tied it down quite firmly this time and there was little likelihood of its suddenly bursting open.

An enormous 1950 Chevrolet taxi was waiting outside the station, and the family tumbled into it. Timothy got on to the back seat, leaving enough room for Grandfather and me. Aunt Mabel sat up in front with Grandmother, the tiffin-basket on her lap.

'I'm dying to see what's inside,' she said. 'Can't I take just a little peek?'

'Not now,' said Grandfather. 'First let's enjoy the breakfast you've got waiting for us.'

'Yes, wait until we get home,' said Grandmother. 'Now tell the taxi driver where to take us, dear. He's looking rather nervous.'

Aunt Mabel gave instructions to the driver and the taxi shot off in a cloud of dust.

'Well, here we go!' said Grandfather. 'I'm looking forward to settling into the new house.'

Popeye, perched proudly on Grandmother's shoulder, kept one suspicious eye on the quivering tiffin-basket.

'All aboard!' he squawked. 'All aboard!'

When we got to our new house, we found a light breakfast waiting for us on the dining table.

'It isn't much,' said Aunt Mabel. 'But we'll supplement it with the contents of your hamper.' And placing the basket on the table, she removed the lid.

The python was half-asleep, with an apple in its mouth. Aunt Mabel was no Eve, to be tempted. She fainted away.

Grandfather promptly picked up the python, took it into the garden, and draped it over a branch of a guava tree.

When Aunt Mabel recovered, she insisted that there was a huge snake in the tiffin-basket. We showed her the empty basket.

'You're seeing things,' said Grandfather. 'It must be the heat,' I said.

Grandmother said nothing. But Popeye broke into shrieks of maniacal laughter, and soon everyone, including a slightly hysterical Aunt Mabel, was doubled up with laughter.

A Tiger in the House

TIMOTHY, THE TIGER-CUB, was discovered by Grandfather on a hunting expedition in the Terai jungle near Dehra.

Grandfather was no shikari, but as he knew the forests of the Siwalik hills better than most people, he was persuaded to accompany the party—it consisted of several Very Important Persons from Delhi—to advise on the terrain and the direction the beaters should take once a tiger had been spotted.

The camp itself was sumptuous—seven large tents (one for each shikari), a dining tent, and a number of servants' tents. The dinner was very good, as Grandfather admitted afterwards; it was not often that one saw hot-water plates, finger-glasses, and seven or eight courses, in a tent in the jungle! But that was how things were done in the days of the Viceroys . . . There were also some fifteen elephants, four of them with howdahs for the shikaris, and the others specially trained for taking part in the beat.

The sportsmen never saw a tiger, nor did they shoot anything else, though they saw a number of deer, peacock, and wild boar. They were giving up all hope of finding a tiger, and were beginning to shoot at jackals, when Grandfather, strolling down the forest path at some distance from the rest of the party, discovered a little tiger about eighteen inches long, hiding among the intricate roots of a banyan tree. Grandfather picked him up, and brought him home after the camp had broken up. He had the distinction of being the only member of the party to have bagged any game, dead or alive.

At first the tiger cub, who was named Timothy by Grandmother, was brought up entirely on milk given to him in a feeding bottle by our cook, Mahmoud. But the milk proved too rich for him, and he was put on a diet of raw mutton and cod liver oil, to be followed later by a more tempting diet of pigeons and rabbits.

Timothy was provided with two companions—Toto the monkey, who was bold enough to pull the young tiger by the tail, and then climb up the curtains if Timothy lost his temper; and a small mongrel puppy, found on the road by Grandfather. At first Timothy appeared to be quite afraid of the puppy, and darted back with a spring if it came too near. He would make absurd dashes at it with his large forepaws, and then retreat to a ridiculously safe distance. Finally, he allowed the puppy to crawl on his back and rest there!

One of Timothy's favourite amusements was to stalk

anyone who would play with him, and so, when I came to live with Grandfather, I became one of the tiger's favourites. With a crafty look in his glittering eyes, and his body crouching, he would creep closer and closer to me, suddenly making a dash for my feet, rolling over on his back and kicking with delight, and pretending to bite my ankles.

He was by this time the size of a full-grown retriever, and when I took him out for walks, people on the road would give us a wide berth. When he pulled hard on his chain, I had difficulty in keeping up with him. His favourite place in the house was the drawing room, and he would make himself comfortable on the long sofa, reclining there with great dignity, and snarling at anybody who tried to get him off.

Timothy had clean habits, and would scrub his face with his paws exactly like a cat. He slept at night in the cook's quarters, and was always delighted at being let out by him in the morning.

'One of these days,' declared Grandmother in her prophetic manner, 'we are going to find Timothy sitting on Mahmoud's bed, and no sign of the cook except his clothes and shoes!'

Of course, it never came to that, but when Timothy was about six months old a change came over him; he grew steadily less friendly. When out for a walk with me, he would try to steal away to stalk a cat or someone's pet Pekinese. Sometimes at night we would hear frenzied cackling from the poultry house, and in the morning there would be feathers lying all over the veranda. Timothy had to be

chained up more often. And, finally, when he began to stalk
Mahmoud about the house with what looked like villainous
intent, Grandfather decided it was time to transfer him to
a zoo.

The nearest zoo was at Lucknow, two hundred miles
away. Reserving a first-class compartment for himself
and Timothy—no one would share a compartment with
them—Grandfather took him to Lucknow where the zoo
authorities were only too glad to receive as a gift a well-fed
and fairly civilized tiger.

About six months later, when my grandparents were visiting
relatives in Lucknow, Grandfather took the opportunity of
calling at the zoo to see how Timothy was getting on. I was
not there to accompany him, but I heard all about it when
he returned to Dehra.

Arriving at the zoo, Grandfather made straight for the
particular cage in which Timothy had been interned. The
tiger was there, crouched in a corner, full-grown and with a
magnificent striped coat.

'Hello Timothy!' said Grandfather and, climbing the
railing with ease, he put his arm through the bars of the
cage.

The tiger approached the bars, and allowed Grandfather to
put both hands around his head. Grandfather stroked the tiger's
forehead and tickled his ear, and, whenever he growled, smacked
him across the mouth, which was his old way of keeping him
quiet.

He licked Grandfather's hands and only sprang away

when a leopard in the next cage snarled at him. Grandfather 'shooed' the leopard away, and the tiger returned to lick his hands; but every now and then the leopard would rush at the bars, and the tiger would slink back to his corner.

A number of people had gathered to watch the reunion when a keeper pushed his way through the crowd and asked Grandfather what he was doing.

'I'm talking to Timothy,' said Grandfather. 'Weren't you here when I gave him to the zoo six months ago?'

'I haven't been here very long,' said the surprised keeper. 'Please continue your conversation. But I have never been able to touch him myself, he is always very bad tempered.'

'Why don't you put him somewhere else?' suggested Grandfather. 'That leopard keeps frightening him. I'll go and see the Superintendent about it.'

Grandfather went in search of the Superintendent of the zoo, but found that he had gone home early; and so, after wandering about the zoo for a little while, he returned to Timothy's cage to say goodbye. It was beginning to get dark.

He had been stroking and slapping Timothy for about five minutes when he found another keeper observing him with some alarm. Grandfather recognized him as the keeper who had been there when Timothy had first come to the zoo.

'*You* remember me,' said Grandfather. 'Now why don't you transfer Timothy to another cage, away from this stupid leopard?'

'But—sir—' stammered the keeper, 'it is not your tiger.'

'I know, I know,' said Grandfather testily. 'I realize he is no longer mine. But you might at least take a suggestion or two from me.'

'I remember your tiger very well,' said the keeper. 'He died two months ago.'

'Died!' exclaimed Grandfather.

'Yes, sir, of pneumonia. This tiger was trapped in the hills only last month, and he is very dangerous!'

Grandfather could think of nothing to say. The tiger was still licking his arm, with increasing relish. Grandfather took what seemed to him an age to withdraw his hand from the cage.

With his face near the tiger's he mumbled, 'Goodnight, Timothy,' and giving the keeper a scornful look, walked briskly out of the zoo.

The Playing Fields of Simla

IT HAD BEEN a lonely winter for a twelve-year-old boy.

I hadn't really got over my father's untimely death two years previously; nor had I as yet reconciled myself to my mother's marriage to the Punjabi gentleman who dealt in second-hand cars. The three-month winter break over, I was almost happy to return to my boarding school in Simla—that elegant hill station once celebrated by Kipling and soon to lose its status as the summer capital of the Raj in India.

It wasn't as though I had many friends at school. I had always been a bit of a loner, shy and reserved, looking out only for my father's rare visits—on his brief leaves from RAF duties—and to my sharing his tent or Air Force hutment outside Delhi or Karachi. Those unsettled but happy days would not come again. I needed a friend but it was not easy to find one among a horde of rowdy, pea-shooting fourth formers, who carved their names on desks and stuck chewing gum on the class teacher's chair. Had I grown up with other children, I might have developed a taste for schoolboy anarchy; but, in sharing my father's loneliness after his separation from my mother, I had turned into a premature adult. The mixed nature of my reading—Dickens, Richmal Crompton, Tagore and *Champion* and *Film Fun* comics—probably reflected the confused state of my life. A book reader was rare even in those pre-electronic times. On rainy days most boys played cards or Monopoly, or listened to Artie Shaw on the wind-up gramophone in the common room.

After a month in the fourth form I began to notice a new boy, Omar, and then only because he was a quiet, almost taciturn person who took no part in the form's feverish attempts to imitate the Marx Brothers at the circus. He showed no resentment at the prevailing anarchy: nor did he make a move to participate in it. Once he caught me looking at him, and he smiled ruefully, tolerantly. Did I sense another adult in the class? Someone who was a little older than his years?

Even before we began talking to each other, Omar and I developed an understanding of sorts, and we'd nod almost respectfully to each other when we met in the classroom corridors or the environs of dining hall or dormitory. We were not in the same house. The house System practised its own form of apartheid, whereby a member of, say, Curzon House was not expected to fraternize with someone belonging to Rivaz or Lefroy! Those public schools certainly knew how to clamp you into compartments. However, these barriers vanished when Omar and I found ourselves selected for the School Colts' hockey team—Omar as a full-back, I as goalkeeper. I think a defensive position suited me by nature. In all modesty I have to say that I made a good goalkeeper, both at hockey and football. And fifty years on, I am still keeping goal. Then I did it between goalposts, now I do it off the field—protecting a family, protecting my independence as a writer . . .

The taciturn Omar now spoke to me occasionally, and we combined well on the field of play. A good understanding is needed between goalkeeper and full-back. We were on the same wavelength. I anticipated his moves, he was familiar with mine. Years later, when I read Conrad's *The Secret Sharer*, I thought of Omar.

It wasn't until we were away from the confines of school, classroom and dining hall that our friendship flourished. The hockey team travelled to Sanawar on the next mountain range, where we were to play a couple of matches against our old rivals, the Lawrence Royal Military School. This had been my father's old school, but I did not know that in his time it had also been a military orphanage. Grandfather, who had been a private foot soldier—of the likes of Kipling's Mulvaney, Otheris and Learoyd—had joined the Scottish Rifles after leaving home at the age of seventeen. He had died while his children were still very young, but my father's more rounded education had enabled him to become an officer.

Omar and I were thrown together a good deal during the visit to Sanawar, and in our more leisurely moments, strolling undisturbed around a school where we were guests and not pupils, we exchanged life histories and other confidences. Omar, too, had lost his father—had I sensed that before?—shot in some tribal encounter on the Frontier, for he hailed from the lawless lands beyond Peshawar. A wealthy uncle was seeing to Omar's education. The RAF was now seeing to mine.

We wandered into the school chapel, and there I found my father's name—A.A. Bond—on the school's roll of honour board: old boys who had lost their lives while serving during the two World Wars.

'What did his initials stand for?' asked Omar. 'Aubrey Alexander.'

'Unusual names, like yours. Why did your parents call you Ruskin?'

'I am not sure. I think my father liked the works of John Ruskin, who wrote on serious subjects like art and architecture. I don't think anyone reads him now. They'll read *me*, though!' I had already started writing my first book. It was called *Nine Months* (the length of the school term, not a pregnancy), and it described some of the happenings at school and lampooned a few of our teachers. I had filled three slim exercise books with this premature literary project, and I allowed Omar to go through them. He must have been my first reader and critic. 'They're very interesting,' he said, 'but you'll get into trouble if someone finds them. Specially Mr Oliver.' And he read out an offending verse— Olly, Olly, Olly, with his balls on a trolley, And his arse all painted green!

I have to admit it wasn't great literature. I was better

at hockey and football. I made some spectacular saves, and we won our matches against Sanawar. When we returned to Simla, we were school heroes for a couple of days and lost some of our reticence; we were even a little more forthcoming with other boys. And then Mr Fisher, my housemaster, discovered my literary opus, *Nine Months*, under my mattress, and took it away and read it (as he told me later) from cover to cover. Corporal punishment then being in vogue, I was given six of the best with a springy malacca cane, and my manuscript was torn up and deposited in Fisher's waste-paper basket. All I had to show for my efforts were some purple welts on my bottom. These were proudly displayed to all who were interested, and I was a hero for another two days.

'Will you go away too when the British leave India?' Omar asked me one day.

'I don't think so,' I said. 'My stepfather is Indian.'

'Everyone is saying that our leaders and the British are going to divide the country. Simla will be in India, Peshawar in Pakistan!'

'Oh, it won't happen,' I said glibly. 'How can they cut up such a big country?' But even as we chatted about the possibility, Nehru and Jinnah and Mountbatten and all those who mattered were preparing their instruments for major surgery.

Before their decision impinged on our lives and everyone else's, we found a little freedom of our own—in an underground tunnel that we discovered below the third flat.

It was really part of an old, disused drainage system, and

when Omar and I began exploring it, we had no idea just how far it extended. After crawling along on our bellies for some twenty feet, we found ourselves in complete darkness. Omar had brought along a small pencil torch, and with its help we continued writhing forward (moving backwards would have been quite impossible) until we saw a glimmer of light at the end of the tunnel. Dusty, musty, very scruffy, we emerged at last on to a grassy knoll, a little way outside the school boundary.

It's always a great thrill to escape beyond the boundaries that adults have devised. Here we were in unknown territory. To travel without passports—that would be the ultimate in freedom!

But more passports were on their way—and more boundaries.

Lord Mountbatten, viceroy and governor-general-to-be, came for our Founder's Day and gave away the prizes. I had won a prize for something or the other, and mounted the rostrum to receive my book from this towering, handsome man in his pinstripe suit. Bishop Cotton's was then the premier school of India, often referred to as the 'Eton of the East'. Viceroys and governors had graced its functions. Many of its boys had gone on to eminence in the civil services and armed forces. There was one 'old boy' about whom they maintained a stolid silence—General Dyer, who had ordered the massacre at Amritsar and destroyed the trust that had been building up between Britain and India.

Now Mountbatten spoke of the momentous events that were happening all around us—the War had just come to an end, the United Nations held out the promise of a world living in peace and harmony, and India, an equal partner with Britain, would be among the great nations . . .

A few weeks later, Bengal and Punjab provinces were bisected. Riots flared up across northern India, and there was a great exodus of people crossing the newly drawn frontiers of Pakistan and India. Homes were destroyed, thousands lost their lives.

The common-room radio and the occasional newspaper kept us abreast of events, but in our tunnel, Omar and I felt immune from all that was happening, worlds away from all the pillage, murder and revenge. And outside the tunnel, on the pine knoll below the school, there was fresh untrodden grass, sprinkled with clover and daisies, the only sounds the hammering of a woodpecker, the distant insistent call of the Himalayan barbet. Who could touch us there?

'And when all the wars are done,' I said, 'a butterfly will still be beautiful.'

'Did you read that somewhere?'

'No, it just came into my head.'

'Already you're a writer.'

'No, I want to play hockey for India or football for Arsenal. Only winning teams!'

'You can't win forever. Better to be a writer.'

When the monsoon rains arrived, the tunnel was flooded, the drain choked with rubble. We were allowed out to the cinema to see Lawrence Olivier's *Hamlet*, a film that did nothing to raise our spirits on a wet and gloomy afternoon—but it was our last picture that year, because communal riots suddenly broke out in Simla's Lower Bazaar, an area that was still much as Kipling had described it—'a man who knows his way there can defy all the police of India's summer capital'—and we were confined to school indefinitely.

One morning after chapel, the headmaster announced that the Muslim boys—those who had their homes in what was now Pakistan—would have to be evacuated, sent to their homes across the border with an armed convoy.

The tunnel no longer provided an escape for us. The bazaar was out of bounds. The flooded playing field was deserted. Omar and I sat on a damp wooden bench and talked about the future in vaguely hopeful terms; but we didn't solve any problems. Mountbatten and Nehru and Jinnah were doing all the solving.

It was soon time for Omar to leave—he along with some fifty other boys from Lahore, Pindi and Peshawar. The rest of us—Hindus, Christians, Parsis—helped them load their luggage into the waiting trucks. A couple of boys broke down and wept. So did our departing school captain, a Pathan who had been known for his stoic and unemotional demeanour. Omar waved cheerfully to me and I waved back. We had vowed to meet again some day.

The convoy got through safely enough. There was only one casualty—the school cook, who had strayed into an off-limits area in the foothills town of Kalka and been set upon by a mob. He wasn't seen again.

Towards the end of the school year, just as we were all getting ready to leave for the school holidays, I received a letter from Omar. He told me something about his new school and how he missed my company and our games and our tunnel to freedom. I replied and gave him my home address, but I did not hear from him again. The land, though divided, was still a big one, and we were very small.

Some seventeen or eighteen years later I did get news of Omar, but in an entirely different context. India and Pakistan were at war and in a bombing raid over Ambala, not far from Simla, a Pakistani plane was shot down. Its crew died in the crash. One of them, I learnt later, was Omar.

Did he, I wonder, get a glimpse of the playing fields we knew so well as boys?

Perhaps memories of his schooldays flooded back as he flew over the foothills. Perhaps he remembered the tunnel through which we were able to make our little escape to freedom.

But there are no tunnels in the sky.

The Wind on Haunted Hill

WHO—WHOO—WHOOO, cried the wind as it swept down from the Himalayan snows. It hurried over the hills and passes, and hummed and moaned in the tall pines and deodars.

On Haunted Hill there was little to stop the wind—only a few stunted trees and bushes, and the ruins of what had once been a small settlement.

On the slopes of the next hill there was a small village. People kept large stones on their tin roofs to prevent them from blowing away. There was nearly always a wind in these parts. Even on sunny days, doors and windows rattled, chimneys choked, clothes blew away.

Three children stood beside a low stone wall, spreading clothes out to dry. On each garment they placed a rock. Even then the clothes fluttered like flags and pennants.

Usha, dark-haired, rose-cheeked, struggled with her

grandfather's long, loose shirt. She was eleven or twelve. Her younger brother, Suresh, was doing his best to hold down a bedsheet while Binya, a slightly older girl, Usha's friend and neighbour, was handing them the clothes, one at a time.

Once they were sure everything was on the wall, firmly held down by rocks, they climbed up on the flat stones and sat there for a while, in the wind and the sun, staring across the fields at the ruins on Haunted Hill.

'I must go to the bazaar today,' said Usha.

'I wish I could come too,' said Binya. 'But I have to help with the cows and the housework. Mother isn't well.'

'I can come!' said Suresh. He was always ready to visit the bazaar, which was three miles away on the other side of Haunted Hill.

'No, you can't,' said Usha. 'You must help Grandfather chop wood.'

Their father was in the army, posted in a distant part of the country, and Suresh and his grandfather were the only men in the house. Suresh was eight, chubby and almond-eyed.

'Won't you be afraid to come back alone?' he asked.

'Why should I be afraid?'

'There are ghosts on the hill.'

'I know, but I will be back before it gets dark. Ghosts don't appear during the day.'

'Are there many ghosts in the ruins?' asked Binya.

'Grandfather says so. He says that many years ago—over a hundred years ago—English people lived on the hill.

But it was a bad spot, always getting struck by lightning,

39

and they had to move to the next range and build another place.'

'But if they went away, why should there be any ghosts?'

'Because—Grandfather says—during a terrible storm one of the houses was hit by lightning and everyone in it was killed. Everyone, including the children.'

'Were there many children?'

'There were two of them. A brother and sister. Grandfather says he has seen them many times, when he has passed through the ruins late at night. He has seen them playing in the moonlight.'

'Wasn't he frightened?'

'No. Old people don't mind seeing ghosts.'

Usha set out on her walk to the bazaar at two in the afternoon. It was about an hour's walk. She went through the fields, now turning yellow with flowering mustard, then along the saddle of the hill, and up to the ruins.

The path went straight through the ruins. Usha knew it well; she had often taken it while going to the bazaar to do the weekly shopping, or to see her aunt who lived in the town.

Wild flowers grew in the crumbling walls. A wild plum tree grew straight out of the floor of what had once been a large hall. Its soft white blossoms had begun to fall. Lizards scuttled over the stones, while a whistling-thrush, its deep purple plumage glistening in the soft sunshine, sat in an empty window and sang its heart out.

Usha sang to herself, as she tripped lightly along the path. Soon she had left the ruins behind. The path dipped steeply down to the valley and the little town with its straggling bazaar.

Usha took her time in the bazaar. She bought soap and matches, spices and sugar (none of these things could be had in the village, where there was no shop), and a new pipe stem for her grandfather's hookah, and an exercise book for Suresh to do his sums in. As an afterthought, she bought him some marbles. Then she went to a mochi's shop to have her mother's slippers repaired. The mochi was busy, so she left the slippers with him and said she'd be back in half an hour.

She had two rupees of her own saved up, and she used the money to buy herself a necklace of amber-coloured beads from the old Tibetan lady who sold charms and trinkets from a tiny shop at the end of the bazaar.

There she met her Aunt Lakshmi, who took her home for tea.

Usha spent an hour in Aunt Lakshmi's little flat above the shops, listening to her aunt talk about the ache in her left shoulder and the stiffness in her joints. She drank two cups of sweet hot tea, and when she looked out of the window she saw that dark clouds had gathered over the mountains.

Usha ran to the cobbler's and collected her mother's slippers. The shopping bag was full. She slung it over her shoulder and set out for the village.

Strangely, the wind had dropped. The trees were still, not a leaf moved. The crickets were silent in the grass. The crows flew round in circles, then settled down for the night in an oak tree.

'I must get home before dark,' said Usha to herself, as she

hurried along the path. But already the sky was darkening. The clouds, black and threatening, loomed over Haunted Hill. This was March, the month for storms.

A deep rumble echoed over the hills, and Usha felt the first heavy drop of rain hit her cheek.

She had no umbrella with her; the weather had seemed so fine just a few hours ago. Now all she could do was tie an old scarf over her head, and pull her shawl tight across her shoulders. Holding the shopping bag close to her body, she quickened her pace. She was almost running. But the raindrops were coming down faster now. Big, heavy pellets of rain.

A sudden flash of lightning lit up the hill. The ruins stood out in clear outline. Then all was dark again. Night had fallen.

'I won't get home before the storm breaks,' thought Usha. 'I'll have to shelter in the ruins.' She could only see a few feet ahead, but she knew the path well and she began to run.

Suddenly, the wind sprang up again and brought the rain with a rush against her face. It was cold, stinging rain. She could hardly keep her eyes open.

The wind grew in force. It hummed and whistled. Usha did not have to fight against it. It was behind her now, and helped her along, up the steep path and on to the brow of the hill.

There was another flash of lightning, followed by a peal of thunder. The ruins loomed up before her, grim and forbidding.

She knew there was a corner where a piece of old roof remained. It would give some shelter. It would be better than trying to go on. In the dark, in the howling wind, she had only to stray off the path to go over a rocky cliff edge.

Who—whoo—whooo, howled the wind. She saw the wild plum tree swaying, bent double, its foliage thrashing against the ground. The broken walls did little to stop the wind.

Usha found her way into the ruined building, helped by her memory of the place and the constant flicker of lightning. She began moving along the wall, hoping to reach the sheltered corner. She placed her hands flat against the stones and moved sideways. Her hand touched something soft and furry. She gave a startled cry and took her hand away. Her cry was answered by another cry—half snarl, half screech—and something leapt away in the darkness.

It was only a wild cat. Usha realized this when she heard it. The cat lived in the ruins, and she had often seen it. But for a moment she had been very frightened. Now, she moved quickly along the wall until she heard the rain drumming on the remnant of the tin roof.

Once under it, crouching in the corner, she found some shelter from the wind and the rain. Above her, the tin sheets groaned and clattered, as if they would sail away at any moment. But they were held down by the solid branch of a straggling old oak tree.

Usha remembered that across this empty room stood an old fireplace and that there might be some shelter under the blocked-up chimney. Perhaps it would be drier than it was

43

in her corner; but she would not attempt to find it just now. She might lose her way altogether.

Her clothes were soaked and the water streamed down from her long, black hair to form a puddle at her feet. She stamped her feet to keep them warm. She thought she heard a faint cry—was it the cat again, or an owl?—but the sound of the storm blotted out all other sounds.

There had been no time to think of ghosts, but now that she was in one place, without any plans for venturing out again, she remembered Grandfather's story about the lightning-blasted ruins. She hoped and prayed that lightning would not strike *her* as she sheltered there.

Thunder boomed over the hills, and the lightning came quicker now, only a few seconds between each burst of lightning.

Then there was a bigger flash than most, and for a second or two the entire ruin was lit up. A streak of blue sizzled along the floor of the building, in at one end and out at the other. Usha was staring straight ahead. As the opposite wall was lit up, she saw, crouching in the disused fireplace, two small figures—they could only have been children!

The ghostly figures looked up, staring back at Usha. And then everything was dark again.

Usha's heart was in her mouth. She had seen, without a shadow of a doubt, two ghostly creatures at the other side of the room, and she wasn't going to remain in that ruined building a minute longer.

She ran out of her corner, ran towards the big gap in

the wall through which she had entered. She was halfway across the open space when something—someone—fell against her. She stumbled, got up and again bumped into something. She gave a frightened scream. Someone else screamed. And then there was a shout, a boy's shout, and Usha instantly recognized the voice.

'Suresh!'

'Usha!'

'Binya!'

'It's me!'

'It's us!'

They fell into each other's arms, so surprised and relieved that all they could do was laugh and giggle and repeat each other's names.

Then Usha said, 'I thought you were ghosts.'

'We thought *you* were a ghost!' said Suresh.

'Come back under the roof,' said Usha.

They huddled together in the corner chattering excitedly. 'When it grew dark, we came looking for you,' said Binya.

'And then the storm broke.'

'Shall we run back together?' asked Usha. 'I don't want to stay here any longer.'

'We'll have to wait,' said Binya. 'The path has fallen away at one place. It won't be safe in the dark, in all this rain.'

'Then we may have to wait till morning,' said Suresh. 'And I'm feeling hungry!'

The wind and rain continued, and so did the thunder

45

and lightning, but they were not afraid now. They gave each other warmth and confidence. Even the ruins did not seem so forbidding.

After an hour the rain stopped, and although the wind continued to blow, it was now taking the clouds away, so that the thunder grew more distant. Then the wind too, moved on, and all was silent.

Towards dawn the whistling-thrush began to sing. Its sweet broken notes flooded the rainwashed ruins with music.

'Let's go,' said Usha.

'Come on,' said Suresh. 'I'm hungry.'

As it grew lighter, they saw that the plum tree stood upright again, although it had lost all its blossoms.

They stood outside the ruins, on the brow of the hill, watching the sky grow pink. A light breeze had sprung up.

When they were some distance from the ruins, Usha looked back and said, 'Can you see something there, behind the wall? It's like a hand waving.'

'I can't see anything,' said Suresh.

'It's just the top of the plum tree,' said Binya.

They were on the path leading across the saddle of the hill. 'Goodbye, goodbye . . .'

Voices on the wind.

'Who said goodbye?' asked Usha.

'Not I,' said Suresh.

'Not I,' said Binya.

'I heard someone calling.'

'It's only the wind.'

Usha looked back at the ruins. The sun had come up

and was touching the top of the walls. The leaves of the plum tree shone. The thrush sat there, singing.

'Come on,' said Suresh. *I'm hungry.*

'Goodbye, goodbye, goodbye, goodbye . . .'

Usha heard them calling. Or was it just the wind?

Riding Through the Flames

I

AS ROMI WAS about to mount his bicycle, he saw smoke rising from behind the distant line of trees.

'It looks like a forest fire,' said Prem, his friend and classmate.

'It's well to the east,' said Romi. 'Nowhere near the road.'

'There's a strong wind,' said Prem, looking at the dry leaves swirling across the road.

It was the middle of May, and it hadn't rained for several weeks. The grass was brown, the leaves of the trees covered with dust. Even though it was getting on to six o'clock in the evening, the boys' shirts were damp with sweat.

'It will be getting dark soon,' said Prem. 'You'd better spend the night at my house.'

'No, I said I'd be home tonight. My father isn't keeping well. The doctor has given me some pills for him.'

'You'd better hurry, then. That fire seems to be spreading.'

'Oh, it's far off. It will take me only forty minutes to ride through the forest. Bye, Prem—see you tomorrow!'

Romi mounted his bicycle and pedalled off down the main road of the village, scattering stray hens, stray dogs and stray villagers.

'Hey, look where you're going!' shouted an angry villager, leaping out of the way of the oncoming bicycle. 'Do you think you own the road?'

'Of course I own it,' called Romi cheerfully, and cycled on.

His own village lay about seven miles distant, on the other side of the forest; but there was only a primary school in his village, and Romi was now at High School. His father, who was a fairly wealthy sugar cane farmer, had only recently bought him the bicycle. Romi didn't care too much for school and felt there weren't enough holidays but he enjoyed the long rides, and he got on well with his classmates.

He might have stayed the night with Prem had it not been for the pills which the Vaid—the village doctor—had given him for his father.

Romi's father was having back trouble, and the pills had been specially prepared from local herbs.

Having been given such a fine bicycle, Romi felt that the least he could do in return was to get those pills to his father as early as possible.

He put his head down and rode swiftly out of the village. Ahead of him, the smoke rose from the burning forest and the sky glowed red.

II

He had soon left the village far behind. There was a slight climb, and Romi had to push harder on the pedals to get over the rise. Once over the top, the road went winding down to the edge of the forest.

This was the part Romi enjoyed the most. He relaxed, stopped pedalling, and allowed the bicycle to glide gently down the slope. Soon the wind was rushing past him, blowing his hair about his face and making his shirt billow out behind him. He burst into song.

A dog from the village ran beside him, barking furiously.

Romi shouted to the dog, encouraging him in the race.

Then the road straightened out, and Romi began pedalling again.

The dog, seeing the forest ahead, turned back to the village. It was afraid of the forest.

The smoke was thicker now, and Romi caught the smell of burning timber. But ahead of him the road was clear. He rode on.

It was a rough, dusty road, cut straight through the forest. Tall trees grew on either side, cutting off the last of the daylight. But the spreading glow of the fire on the right lit up the road, and giant tree-shadows danced before the boy on the bicycle.

Usually the road was deserted. This evening it was alive with wild creatures fleeing from the forest fire.

The first animal that Romi saw was a hare, leaping across the road in front of him. It was followed by several more hares. Then a band of monkeys streamed across, chattering excitedly.

They'll be safe on the other side, thought Romi. The fire won't cross the road.

But it was coming closer. And realizing this, Romi pedalled harder. In half an hour he should be out of the forest.

Suddenly, from the side of the road, several pheasants rose in the air, and with a *whoosh*, flew low across the path, just in front of the oncoming bicycle. Taken by surprise, Romi fell off. When he picked himself up and began brushing his clothes, he saw that his knee was bleeding. It wasn't a deep cut, but he allowed it to bleed a little, took out his handkerchief and bandaged his knee. Then he mounted the bicycle again.

He rode a bit slower now, because birds and animals kept coming out of the bushes.

Not only pheasants but smaller birds too were streaming across the road—parrots, jungle crows, owls, magpies—and the air was filled with their cries.

Everyone's on the move, thought Romi. It must be a really big fire.

He could see the flames now, reaching out from behind the trees on his right, and he could hear the crackling as the dry leaves caught fire. The air was hot on his face. Leaves, still alight or turning to cinders, floated past.

A herd of deer crossed the road and Romi had to stop until they had passed. Then he mounted again and rode on; but now, for the first time, he was feeling afraid.

III

From ahead came a faint clanging sound. It wasn't an animal sound, Romi was sure of that. A fire engine? There were no fire engines within fifty miles.

The clanging came nearer and Romi discovered that the noise came from a small boy who was running along the forest path, two milk cans clattering at his side.

'Teju!' called Romi, recognizing a boy from a neighbouring village. 'What are you doing out here?'

'Trying to get home, of course,' said Teju, panting along beside the bicycle.

'Jump on,' said Romi, stopping for him.

Teju was only eight or nine—a couple of years younger than Romi. He had come to deliver milk to some road-workers, but the workers had left at the first signs of the fire, and Teju was hurrying home with his cans still full of milk.

He got up on the crossbar of the bicycle, and Romi moved on again. He was quite used to carrying friends on the crossbar.

'Keep beating your milk cans,' said Romi. 'Like that, the animals will know we are coming. My bell doesn't make enough noise. I'm going to get a horn for my cycle!'

'I never knew there were so many animals in the jungle,'

53

said Teju. 'I saw a python in the middle of the road. It stretched right across!'

'What did you do?'

'Just kept running and jumped right over it!'

Teju continued to chatter but Romi's thoughts were on the fire, which was much closer now. Flames shot up from the dry grass and ran up the trunks of trees and along the branches. Smoke billowed out above the forest.

Romi's eyes were smarting and his hair and eyebrows felt scorched. He was feeling tired but he couldn't stop now, he had to get beyond the range of the fire. Another ten or fifteen minutes of steady riding would get them to the small wooden bridge that spanned the little river separating the forest from the sugar cane fields.

Once across the river, they would be safe. The fire could not touch them on the other side because the forest ended at the river's edge. But could they get to the river in time?

IV

Clang, clang, clang, went Teju's milk cans. But the sounds of the fire grew louder too.

A tall silk-cotton tree, its branches leaning across the road, had caught fire. They were almost beneath it when there was a crash and a burning branch fell to the ground a few yards in front of them.

The boys had to get off the bicycle and leave the road, forcing their way through a tangle of thorny bushes on the left, dragging and pushing at the bicycle and only returning to the road some distance ahead of the burning tree.

'We won't get out in time,' said Teju, back on the crossbar but feeling disheartened.

'Yes, we will,' said Romi, pedalling with all his might. 'The fire hasn't crossed the road as yet.'

Even as he spoke, he saw a small flame leap up from the grass on the left. It wouldn't be long before more sparks and burning leaves were blown across the road to kindle the grass on the other side.

'Oh, look!' exclaimed Romi, bringing the bicycle to a sudden stop.

'What's wrong now?' asked Teju, rubbing his sore eyes. And then, through the smoke, he saw what was stopping them.

An elephant was standing in the middle of the road.

Teju slipped off the crossbar, his cans rolling on the ground, bursting open and spilling their contents.

The elephant was about forty feet away. It moved about restlessly, its big ears flapping as it turned its head from side to side, wondering which way to go.

From far to the left, where the forest was still untouched, a herd of elephants moved towards the river. The leader of the herd raised his trunk and trumpeted a call. Hearing it, the elephant on the road raised its own trunk and trumpeted a reply. Then it shambled off into the forest, in the direction of the herd, leaving the way clear.

'Come, Teju, jump on!' urged Romi. 'We can't stay here much longer!'

V

Teju forgot about his milk cans and pulled himself up on the crossbar. Romi ran forward with the bicycle, to gain speed, and mounted swiftly. He kept as far as possible to the left of the road, trying to ignore the flames, the crackling, the smoke and the scorching heat.

It seemed that all the animals who could get away had done so. The exodus across the road had stopped.

'We won't stop again,' said Romi, gritting his teeth. 'Not even for an elephant!'

'We're nearly there!' said Teju. He was perking up again.

A jackal, overcome by the heat and smoke, lay in the middle of the path, either dead or unconscious. Romi did not stop. He swerved round the animal. Then he put all his strength into one final effort.

He covered the last hundred yards at top speed, and then they were out of the forest, freewheeling down the sloping road to the river.

'Look!' shouted Teju. 'The bridge is on fire!'

Burning embers had floated down on to the small wooden bridge and the dry, ancient timber had quickly caught fire. It was now burning fiercely.

Romi did not hesitate. He left the road, riding the bicycle over sand and pebbles. Then with a rush they went down the river bank and into the water.

The next thing they knew they were splashing around, trying to find each other in the darkness.

'Help!' cried Teju. 'I'm drowning!'

VI

'Don't be silly,' said Romi. 'The water isn't deep—it's only up to the knees. Come here and grab hold of me.'

Teju splashed across and grabbed Romi by the belt. 'The water's so cold,' he said, his teeth chattering.

'Do you want to go back and warm yourself?' asked Romi. 'Some people are never satisfied. Come on, help me get the bicycle up. It's down here, just where we are standing.'

Together they managed to heave the bicycle out of the water and stand it upright.

'Now sit on it,' said Romi. 'I'll push you across.'

'We'll be swept away,' said Teju.

'No, we won't. There's not much water in the river at this time of the year. But the current is quite strong in the middle, so sit still. All right?'

'All right,' said Teju nervously.

Romi began guiding the bicycle across the river, one hand on the seat and one hand on the handlebar. The river was shallow and sluggish in midsummer; even so, it was quite swift in the middle. But having got safely out of the burning forest, Romi was in no mood to let a little river defeat him.

He kicked off his shoes, knowing they would be lost, and then gripping the smooth stones of the riverbed with his toes, he concentrated on keeping his balance and getting the bicycle and Teju through the middle of the stream. The water here came up to his waist, and the current would have been too strong for Teju. But when they reached the shallows, Teju got down and helped Romi push the bicycle.

They reached the opposite bank and sank down on the grass.

'We can rest now,' said Romi. 'But not all night—I've got some medicine to give my father.' He felt in his pockets and found that the pills, in their envelope, had turned to a soggy mess. 'Oh well, he has to take them with water anyway,' he said.

They watched the fire as it continued to spread through the forest. It had crossed the road down which they had come. The sky was a bright red, and the river reflected the colour of the sky.

Several elephants had found their way down to the river. They were cooling off by spraying water on each other with their trunks. Further downstream there were deer and other animals.

Romi and Teju looked at each other in the glow from the fire. They hadn't known each other very well before. But now they felt they had been friends for years.

'What are you thinking about?' asked Teju.

'I'm thinking,' said Romi, 'that even if the fire is out in a day or two, it will be a long time before the bridge is repaired. So I'm thinking it will be a nice long holiday from school!'

'But you can walk across the river,' said Teju. 'You just did it.'

'Impossible,' said Romi. 'It's much too swift.'

A Rupee Goes a Long Way

RANJI HAD A one-rupee coin. He'd had it since morning, and now it was afternoon—and that was far too long to keep a rupee. It was time he spent the money, or some of it, or most of it.

Ranji had made a list in his head of all the things he wanted to buy and all the things he wanted to eat. But he knew that with only one rupee in his pocket the list wouldn't get much shorter. His tummy, he decided, should be given first choice. So he made his way to the Jumna Sweet Shop, tossed the coin on the counter, and asked for a rupee's worth of jalebi—those spangled, golden sweets made of flour and sugar that are so popular in India.

The shopkeeper picked up the coin, looked at it carefully, and set it back on the counter. 'That coin's no good,' he said.

'Are you sure?' Ranji asked.

'Look,' said the shopkeeper, holding up the coin. 'It's got

England's King George on one side. These coins went out of use long ago. If it was one of the older ones—like Queen Victoria's, made of silver—it would be worth something for the silver, much more than a rupee. But this isn't a silver rupee. So, you see, it isn't old enough to be valuable, and it isn't new enough to buy anything.'

Ranji looked from the coin to the shopkeeper to the chains of hot jalebis sizzling in a pan. He shrugged, took the coin back, and turned on to the road. There was no one to blame for the coin.

Ranji wandered through the bazaar. He gazed after the passing balloon man, whose long pole was hung with balloons of many colours. They were only twenty paise each—he could have had five for a rupee—but he didn't have any more change.

He was watching some boys playing marbles and wondering whether he should join them, when he heard a familiar voice behind him. 'Where are you going, Ranji?'

It was Mohinder Singh, Ranji's friend. Mohinder's turban was too big for him and was almost falling over his eyes. In one hand he held a home-made fishing rod, complete with hook and line.

'I'm not going anywhere,' said Ranji. 'Where are you going?'

'I'm not going, I've *been*,' Mohinder said. 'I was fishing in the canal all morning.'

Ranji stared at the fishing rod. 'Will you lend it to me?' he asked.

'You'll only lose it or break it,' Mohinder said. 'But I

don't mind selling it to you. Two rupees. Is that too much?'

'I've got one rupee,' said Ranji, showing his coin. 'But it's an old one. The sweet-seller would not take it.'

'Please let me see it,' said Mohinder.

He took the coin and looked it over as though he knew all about coins. 'Hmmm . . . I don't suppose it's worth much, but my uncle collects old coins. Give it to me and I'll give you the rod.'

'All right,' said Ranji, only too happy to make the exchange. He took the fishing rod, waved goodbye to Mohinder, and set off. Soon he was on the main road leading out of town.

After some time a truck came along. It was on its way to the quarries near the riverbed, where it would be loaded with limestone. Ranji knew the driver and waved and shouted to him until he stopped.

'Will you take me to the river?' Ranji asked. 'I'm going fishing.'

There was already someone sitting up in the front with the driver. 'Climb up in the back,' he said. 'And don't lean over the side.'

Ranji climbed into the back of the open truck. Soon he was watching the road slide away from him. They quickly passed bullock carts, cyclists and a long line of camels. Motorists honked their horns as dust from the truck whirled up in front of them.

Soon the truck stopped near the riverbed. Ranji got down, thanked the driver, and began walking along the bank. It was the dry season, and the river was just a shallow, muddy stream. Ranji walked up and down without finding water deep enough for the smallest of fish.

'No wonder Mohinder let me have his rod,' he muttered.

And with a shrug he turned back towards the town.

It was a long, hot walk back to the bazaar. Ranji walked slowly along the dusty road, swiping at bushes with his fishing rod. There were ripe mangoes on the trees, and Ranji tried to get at a few of them with the tip of the rod, but they were well out of reach. The sight of all those mangoes made his mouth water, and he thought again of the jalebis that he hadn't been able to buy.

He had reached a few scattered houses when he saw a barefoot boy playing a flute. In the stillness of the hot afternoon the cheap flute made a cheerful sound.

Ranji stopped walking. The boy stopped playing. They stood there, sizing each other up. The boy had his eye on Ranji's fishing rod; Ranji had his eye on the flute.

'Been fishing?' asked the flute player.

'Yes,' said Ranji.

'Did you catch anything?'

'No,' said Ranji. 'I didn't stay very long.'

'Did you see any fish?'

'The water was very muddy.'

There was a long silence. Then Ranji said, 'It's a good rod.' 'This is a good flute,' said the boy.

Ranji took the flute and examined it. He put it to his lips and blew hard. There was a shrill, squeaky noise, and a startled magpie flew out of a mango tree.

'Not bad,' said Ranji.

The boy had taken the rod from Ranji and was looking it over. 'Not bad,' he said.

Ranji hesitated no longer. 'Let's exchange.'

A trade was made, and the barefoot boy rested the fishing rod on his shoulder and went on his way, leaving Ranji with the flute.

Ranji began playing the flute, running up and down the scale. The notes sounded lovely to him, but they startled people who were passing on the road.

After a while Ranji felt thirsty and drank water from a roadside tap. When he came to the clock tower, where the bazaar began, he sat on the low wall and blew vigorously on the flute. Several children gathered around, thinking he might be a snake charmer. When no snake appeared, they went away.

'I can play better than that,' said a boy who was carrying several empty milk cans.

'Let's see,' Ranji said.

The boy took the flute and put it to his lips and played a lovely little tune.

'You can have it for a rupee,' said Ranji.

'I don't have any money to spare,' said the boy. 'What I get for my milk, I have to take home. But you can have this necklace.'

He showed Ranji a pretty necklace of brightly coloured stones.

'I'm not a girl,' said Ranji.

'I didn't say you had to wear it. You can give it to your sister.'

63

'I don't have a sister.'

'Then you can give it to your mother,' said the boy. 'Or your grandmother. The stones are very precious. They were found in the mountains near Tibet.'

Ranji was tempted. He knew the stones had little value, but they were pretty. And he was tired of the flute.

They made the exchange, and the boy went off playing the flute. Ranji was about to thrust the necklace into his pocket when he noticed a girl staring at him. Her name was Koki and she lived close to his house.

'Hello, Koki,' he said, feeling rather silly with the necklace still in his hands.

'What's that you've got, Ranji?'

'A necklace. It's pretty, isn't it? Would you like to have it?'

'Oh, thank you,' said Koki, clapping her hands with pleasure.

'One rupee,' said Ranji. 'Oh,' said Koki.

She made a face, but Ranji was looking the other way and humming. Koki kept staring at the necklace. Slowly she opened a little purse, took out a shining new rupee, and held it out to Ranji.

Ranji handed her the necklace. The coin felt hot in his hand. It wasn't going to stay there for long. Ranji's stomach was rumbling. He ran across the street to the Jumna Sweet Shop and tossed the coin on the counter. 'Jalebis for a rupee,' he said.

The sweet-seller picked up the coin, studied it carefully, then gave Ranji a toothy smile and said, 'Always at your service, sir.' He filled a paper bag with hot jalebis and handed them over.

When Ranji reached the clock tower, he found Koki waiting.

'Oh, I'm so hungry,' she said, giving him a shy smile.

So they sat side by side on the low wall, and Koki helped Ranji finish the jalebis.

The Flute Player

DOWN THE MAIN road passed big yellow buses, cars, pony-drawn tongas, motorcycles and bullock-carts. This steady flow of traffic seemed, somehow, to form a barrier between the city on one side of the Trunk Road, and the distant sleepy villages on the other. It seemed to cut India in half—the India Kamla knew slightly, and the India she had never seen.

Kamla's grandmother lived on the outskirts of the city of Jaipur, and just across the road from the house there were fields and villages stretching away for hundreds of miles. But Kamla had never been across the main road. This separated the busy city from the flat green plains stretching endlessly towards the horizon.

Kamla was used to city life. In England, it was London and Manchester. In India, it was Delhi and Jaipur. Rainy Manchester was, of course, different in many ways from sun-drenched Jaipur, and Indian cities had stronger smells and more vibrant colours than their English counterparts. Nevertheless, they had much in common: busy people always on the move, money constantly changing hands, buses to catch, schools to attend, parties to go to, TV to watch. Kamla had seen very little of the English countryside, even less of India outside the cities.

Her parents lived in Manchester where her father was a doctor in a large hospital. She went to school in England. But this year, during the summer holidays, she had come to India to stay with her grandmother. Apart from a maidservant and a grizzled old nightwatchman, Grandmother lived quite alone in a small house on the outskirts of Jaipur. During the winter months, Jaipur's climate was cool and bracing but in the summer, a fierce sun poured down upon the city from a cloudless sky.

None of the other city children ventured across the main road into the fields of millet, wheat and cotton, but Kamla was determined to visit the fields before she returned to England. From the flat roof of the house she could see them stretching away for miles, the ripening wheat swaying in the hot wind. Finally, when there were only two days left before she went to Delhi to board a plane for London, she made up her mind and crossed the main road.

She did this in the afternoon, when Grandmother was asleep and the servants were in the bazaar. She slipped out of the back door and her slippers kicked up the dust as she ran down the path to the main road. A bus roared past and more dust rose from the road and swirled about her. Kamla ran through the dust, past the jacaranda trees that lined the road, and into the fields.

Suddenly, the world became an enormous place, bigger and more varied than it had seemed from the air, also mysterious and exciting—and just a little frightening.

The sea of wheat stretched away till it merged with the hot blinding blue of the sky. Far to her left were a few trees and the low white huts of a village. To her right lay hollow pits of red dust and a blackened chimney where bricks used to be made. In front, some distance away, Kamla could see a camel moving round a well, drawing up water for the fields. She set out in the direction of the camel.

Her grandmother had told her not to wander off on her own in the city; but this wasn't the city, and as far as she knew, camels did not attack people.

It took her a long time to get to the camel. It was about half a mile away, though it seemed much nearer. And when Kamla reached it, she was surprised to find that there was no one else in sight. The camel was turning the wheel by itself, moving round and round the well, while the water kept gushing up in little trays to run down the channels into the fields. The camel took no notice of Kamla, did not look at her even once, just carried on about its business.

There must be someone here, thought Kamla, walking towards a mango tree that grew a few yards away. Ripe mangoes dangled like globules of gold from its branches. Under the tree, fast asleep, was a boy.

All he wore was a pair of dirty white shorts. His body

had been burnt dark by the sun; his hair was tousled, his feet chalky with dust. In the palm of his outstretched hand was a flute. He was a thin boy, with long bony legs, but Kamla felt that he was strong too, for his body was hard and wiry.

Kamla came nearer to the sleeping boy, peering at him with some curiosity, for she had not seen a village boy before. Her shadow fell across his face. The coming of the shadow woke the boy. He opened his eyes and stared at Kamla. When she did not say anything, he sat up, his head a little to one side, his hands clasping his knees, and stared at her.

'Who are you?' he asked a little gruffly. He was not used to waking up and finding strange girls staring at him.

'I'm Kamla. I've come from England, but I'm really from India. I mean I've come home to India, but I'm really from England.' This was getting to be rather confusing, so she countered with an abrupt, 'Who are *you*?'

'I'm the strongest boy in the village,' said the boy, deciding to assert himself without any more ado. 'My name is Romi. I can wrestle and swim and climb any tree.'

'And do you sleep a lot?' asked Kamla innocently. Romi scratched his head and grinned.

'I must look after the camel,' he said. 'It is no use staying awake for the camel. It keeps going round the well until it is tired, and then it stops. When it has rested, it starts going round again. It can carry on like that all day. But it eats a lot.'

Mention of the camel's food reminded Romi that he was hungry. He was growing fast these days and was nearly always hungry. There were some mangoes lying beside him, and he offered one to Kamla. They were silent for a few minutes. You cannot suck mangoes and talk at the same time. After they had finished, they washed their hands in the water from one of the trays.

'There are parrots in the tree,' said Kamla, noticing three or four green parrots conducting a noisy meeting in the topmost branches. They reminded her a bit of a pop group she had seen and heard at home.

'They spoil most of the mangoes,' said Romi.

He flung a stone at them, missing, but they took off with squawks of protest, flashes of green and gold wheeling in the sunshine.

'Where do you swim?' asked Kamla. 'Down in the well?'

'Of course not. I'm not a frog. There is a canal not far from here. Come, I will show you!'

As they crossed the fields, a pair of blue jays flew out of a bush, rockets of bright blue that dipped and swerved, rising and falling as they chased each other.

Remembering a story that Grandmother had told her, Kamla said, 'They are sacred birds, aren't they? Because of their blue throats.' She told him the story of the god Shiva having a blue throat because he had swallowed a poison that would have destroyed the world; he had kept the poison in his throat and would not let it go further. 'And so his throat is blue, like the blue jay's.'

Romi liked this story. His respect for Kamla was greatly increased. But he was not to be outdone, and when a small grey squirrel dashed across the path he told her that squirrels, too, were sacred. Krishna, the god who had been born into a farmer's family like Romi's, had been fond of squirrels and would take them in his arms and stroke them. 'That is why squirrels have four dark lines down their backs,' said Romi. 'Krishna was very dark, as dark as I am, and the stripes are the marks of his fingers.'

'Can you catch a squirrel?' asked Kamla.

'No, they are too quick. But I caught a snake once. I caught it by its tail and dropped it in the old well. That well is full of snakes. Whenever we catch one, instead of killing it, we drop it in the well! They can't get out.'

Kamla shuddered at the thought of all those snakes swimming and wriggling about at the bottom of the deep well. She wasn't sure that she wanted to return to the well with him. But she forgot about the snakes when they reached the canal.

It was a small canal, about ten metres wide, and only waist-deep in the middle, but it was very muddy at the bottom. She had never seen such a muddy stream in her life.

'Would you like to get in?' asked Romi.

'No,' said Kamla. 'You get in.'

Romi was only too ready to show off his tricks in the water. His toes took a firm hold on the grassy bank, the muscles of his calves tensed, and he dived into the water with a loud splash, landing rather awkwardly on his belly. It was a poor dive, but Kamla was impressed.

Romi swam across to the opposite bank and then back again. When he climbed out of the water, he was covered with mud. It made him look quite fierce. 'Come on in,' he invited. 'It's not deep.'

71

'It's dirty,' said Kamla, but felt tempted all the same.

'It's only mud,' said Romi. 'There's nothing wrong with mud. Camels like mud. Buffaloes love mud.'

'I'm not a camel—or a buffalo.'

'All right. You don't have to go right in. Just walk along the sides of the channel.'

After a moment's hesitation, Kamla slipped her feet out of her slippers, and crept cautiously down the slope till her feet were in the water. She went no further, but even so, some of the muddy water splashed on to her clean white skirt. What would she tell Grandmother? Her feet sank into the soft mud and she gave a little squeal as the water reached her knees. It was with some difficulty that she got each foot out of the sticky mud.

Romi took her by the hand, and they went stumbling along the side of the channel while little fish swam in and out of their legs, and a heron, one foot raised, waited until they had passed before snapping a fish out of the water. The little fish glistened in the sun before it disappeared down the heron's throat.

Romi gave a sudden exclamation and came to a stop.

Kamla held on to him for support.

'What is it?' she asked, a little nervously.

'It's a tortoise,' said Romi. 'Can you see it?'

He pointed to the bank of the canal, and there, lying quite still, was a small tortoise. Romi scrambled up the bank and, before Kamla could stop him, had picked up the tortoise. As soon as he touched it, the animal's head and legs disappeared into its shell. Romi turned it over, but from behind the breastplate only the head and a spiky tail were visible.

'Look!' exclaimed Kamla, pointing to the ground where the tortoise had been lying. 'What's in that hole?'

They peered into the hole. It was about half a metre deep, and at the bottom were five or six white eggs, a little smaller than a hen's eggs.

'Put it back,' said Kamla. 'It was sitting on its eggs.'

Romi shrugged and dropped the tortoise back on its hole. It peeped out from behind its shell, saw the children were still present, and retreated into its shell again.

'I must go,' said Kamla. 'It's getting late. Granny will wonder where I have gone.'

They walked back to the mango tree, and washed their hands and feet in the cool clear water from the well; but only after Romi had assured Kamla that there weren't any snakes in the well—he had been talking about an old disused well on the far side of the village. Kamla told Romi she would take him to her house one day, but it would have to be next year, or perhaps the year after, when she came to India again.

'Is it very far, where you are going?' asked Romi.

'Yes, England is across the seas. I have to go back to my parents. And my school is there, too. But I will take the plane from Delhi. Have you ever been to Delhi?'

'I have not been further than Jaipur,' said Romi. 'What is England like? Are there canals to swim in?'

'You can swim in the sea. Lots of people go swimming in the sea. But it's too cold most of the year. Where I live,

73

there are shops and cinemas and places where you can eat anything you like. And people from all over the world come to live there. You can see red faces, brown faces, black faces, white faces!'

'I saw a red face once,' said Romi. 'He came to the village to take pictures. He took one of me sitting on the camel. He said he would send me the picture, but it never came.'

Kamla noticed the flute lying on the grass. 'Is it your flute?' she asked.

'Yes,' said Romi. 'It is an old flute. But the old ones are best. I found it lying in a field last year. Perhaps it was god Krishna's! He was always playing the flute.'

'And who taught you to play it?'

'Nobody. I learnt by myself. Shall I play it for you?'

Kamla nodded, and they sat down on the grass, leaning against the trunk of the mango tree, and Romi put the flute to his lips and began to play.

It was a slow, sweet tune, a little sad, a little happy, and the notes were taken up by the breeze and carried across the fields. There was no one to hear the music except the birds and the camel and Kamla. Whether the camel liked it or not, we shall never know; it just kept going round and round the well, drawing up water for the fields. And whether the birds liked it or not, we cannot say, although it is true that they were all suddenly silent when Romi began to play. But Kamla was charmed by the music, and she watched Romi while he played, and the boy smiled at her with his eyes and ran his fingers along the flute. When he stopped playing, everything was still, everything silent, except for the soft wind sighing in the wheat and the gurgle of water coming up from the well.

Kamla stood up to leave.

'When will you come again?' asked Romi.

'I will try to come next year,' said Kamla.

'That is a long time. By then you will be quite old. You may not want to come.'

'I will come,' said Kamla.

'Promise?'

'Promise.'

Romi put the flute in her hands and said, 'You keep it. I can get another one.'

'But I don't know how to play it,' said Kamla.

'It will play by itself,' said Romi.

She took the flute and put it to her lips and blew on it, producing a squeaky little note that startled a lone parrot out of the mango tree. Romi laughed, and while he was laughing, Kamla turned and ran down the path through the fields. And when she had gone some distance, she turned and waved to Romi with the flute. He stood near the well and waved back to her.

Cupping his hands to his mouth, he shouted across the fields, 'Don't forget to come next year!'

And Kamla called back, 'I won't forget.' But her voice was faint, and the breeze blew the words away and Romi did not hear them.

Was England home? wondered Kamla. Or was this Indian city home? Or was her true home in that other India, across the busy Trunk Road? Perhaps she would find out one day.

Romi watched her until she was just a speck in the distance, and then he turned and shouted at the camel, telling it to move faster. But the camel did not even glance at him, it just carried on as before, as India had carried on for thousands of years, round and round and round the well, while the water gurgled and splashed over the smooth stones.

The Night the Roof Blew Off

LOOKING BACK AT the experience, I suppose it was the sort of thing that should have happened in a James Thurber story, like the dam that burst or the ghost who got in. But I wasn't thinking of Thurber at the time, although a few of his books were among the many I was trying to save from the icy rain and sleet pouring into my bedroom and study.

We have grown accustomed to sudden storms up here at 7,000 feet in the Himalayan foothills, and the old building in which I live has, for over a hundred years, received the brunt of the wind and the rain as they sweep across the hills from the east.

We'd lived in the building for over ten years without any untoward happening. It had even taken the shock of an earthquake without sustaining any major damage: it is difficult to tell the new cracks from the old.

It's a three-storey building, and I live on the top floor with my adopted family—three children and their parents. The roof consists of corrugated tin sheets, the ceiling, of wooden boards. That's the traditional hill station roof.

Ours had held fast in many a storm, but the wind that night was stronger than we'd ever known it. It was cyclonic in its intensity, and it came rushing at us with a high-pitched eerie wail. The old roof groaned and protested at the unrelieved pressure. It took this battering for several hours while the rain lashed against the windows, and the lights kept coming and going.

There was no question of sleeping, but we remained in bed for warmth and comfort. The fire had long since gone out, the chimney stack having collapsed, bringing down a shower of sooty rainwater.

After about four hours of buffeting, the roof could take it no longer. My bedroom faces east, so my portion of the roof was the first to go.

The wind got under it and kept pushing, until, with a ripping, groaning sound, the metal sheets shifted from their moorings, some of them dropping with claps like thunder on to the road below.

So that's it, I thought, nothing worse can happen. As long as the ceiling stays on, I'm not getting out of my bed. We'll pick up the roof in the morning.

Icy water cascading down on my face made me change my mind in a hurry. Leaping from my bed, I found that much of the ceiling had gone too. Water was pouring on to my open typewriter—the typewriter that had been my trusty companion for almost thirty years!—and on to the bedside radio, bed covers, and clothes' cupboard. The only object that wasn't receiving any rain was the potted philodendron, which could have done with a little watering.

Picking up my precious typewriter and abandoning the rest, I stumbled into the front sitting-room (cum library), only to find that a similar situation had developed there. Water was pouring through the wooden slats, raining down on the bookshelves.

By now I had been joined by the children, who had come to rescue me. Their section of the roof hadn't gone as yet. Their parents were struggling to close a window that had burst open, letting in lashings of wind and rain.

'Save the books!' shouted Dolly, the youngest, and that became our rallying cry for the next hour or two.

I have open shelves, vulnerable to borrowers as well as to floods. Dolly and her brother picked up armfuls of books and carried them into their room. But the floor was now awash all over the apartment, so the books had to be piled on the beds. Dolly was helping me gather up some of my manuscripts when a large field rat leapt on to the desk in front of her. Dolly squealed and ran for the door.

'It's all right,' said Mukesh, whose love of animals extends even to field rats. 'He's only sheltering from the storm.'

Big brother Rakesh whistled for our mongrel, Toby, but Toby wasn't interested in rats just then. He had taken shelter in the kitchen, the only dry spot in the house.

At this point, two rooms were practically roofless, and the sky was frequently lighted up for us by flashes of lightning. There were fireworks inside too, as water sputtered and crackled along a damaged electric wire. Then the lights went out altogether, which in some ways made the house a safer place.

Prem, the children's father, is at his best in an emergency, and he had already located and lit two kerosene lamps; so we continued to transfer books, papers, and clothes to the children's room.

We noticed that the water on the floor was beginning to subside a little.

'Where is it going?' asked Dolly, for we could see no outlet.

'Through the floor,' said Mukesh. 'Down to the rooms below.' He was right, too. Cries of consternation from our neighbours told us that they were now having their share of the flood.

Our feet were freezing because there hadn't been time to put on enough protective footwear, and in any case, shoes and slippers were awash. Tables and chairs were also piled high with books. I hadn't realized the considerable size of my library until that night!

The available beds were pushed into the driest corner of the children's room and there, huddled in blankets and quilts, we spent the remaining hours of the night, while the storm continued to threaten further mayhem.

But then the wind fell, and it began to snow. Through the door to the sitting-room I could see snowflakes drifting through the gaps in the ceiling, settling on picture frames, statuettes and miscellaneous ornaments. Mundane things like a glue bottle and a plastic doll took on a certain beauty when covered with soft snow. The clock on the wall had stopped and with its covering of snow reminded me of a painting by Salvador Dali. And my shaving brush looked ready for use!

Most of us dozed off.

I sensed that the direction of the wind had changed, and that it was now blowing from the west; it was making a rushing sound in the trees rather than in what remained of our roof. The clouds were scurrying away.

When the dawn broke, we found the windowpanes encrusted with snow and icicles. Then the rising sun struck through the gaps in the ceiling and turned everything to gold. Snow crystals glinted like diamonds on the empty bookshelves. I crept into my abandoned bedroom to find the philodendron looking like a Christmas tree.

Prem went out to find a carpenter and a tinsmith, while the rest of us started putting things in the sun to dry out. And by evening, we'd put much of the roof on again. Vacant houses are impossible to find in Mussoorie, so there was no question of moving.

But it's a much-improved roof now, and I look forward to approaching storms with some confidence!

Faraway Places

ANIL AND HIS parents lived in a small coastal town on the Kathiawar peninsula, where Anil's father was an engineer in the Public Works Department. The boy attended the local school but as his home was some way out of town, he hadn't the opportunity of making many friends.

Sometimes he went for a walk with his father or mother, but most of the time they were busy, his mother in the house, his father in the office, and as a result he was usually left to his own resources. However, one day Anil's father took him down to the docks, about two miles from the house. They drove down in a car, and took the car right up to the pier.

It was a small port, with a cargo steamer in dock, and a few fishing vessels in the harbour. But the sight of the sea and the ships put a strange longing in Anil's heart.

The fishing vessels plied only up and down the Gulf.

But the little steamer, with its black hull and red and white funnel held romance, the romance of great distances and faraway ports of call, with magic names like Yokohama, Valparaiso, San Diego, London . . .

Anil's father knew the captain of the steamer, and took his son aboard. The captain was a Scotsman named MacWhirr, a very jolly person with a thunderous laugh that showed up a set of dirty yellow teeth. Captain MacWhirr liked to chew tobacco and spit it all over the deck, but he offered Anil's father the best of cigarettes and produced a bar of chocolate for Anil.

'Well, young man,' he said to the boy with a wink, 'how would you like to join the crew of my ship, and see the world?'

'I'd like to, very much, captain sir,' said Anil, looking up uncertainly at his father.

The captain roared with laughter, patted Anil on the shoulder, and spat tobacco on the floor.

'You'd like to, eh? I wonder what your father has to say to that!'

But Anil's father had nothing to say.

Anil visited the ship once again with his father, and got to know the captain a little better; and the captain said, 'Well, boy, whenever you've nothing to do, you're welcome aboard my ship. You can have a look at the engines, if you like, or at anything else that takes your fancy.'

The next day Anil walked down to the docks alone, and the captain lowered the gangplank specially for him. Anil spent the entire day on board, asking questions of the captain and the crew. He made friends quickly, and the following day, when he came aboard, they greeted him as though he was already one of them.

'Can I come with you on your next voyage?' he asked the captain. 'I can scrub the deck and clean the cabins, and you don't have to pay me anything.'

Captain MacWhirr was taken aback, but a twinkle came into his eye, and he put his head back and laughed indulgently. 'You're just the person we want! We sail any day now, my boy, so you'd better get yourself ready. A little more cargo, and we'll be steaming into the Arabian Sea. First call Aden, then Suez, and up the Canal!'

'Will you tell me one or two days before we sail, so that I can get my things ready?' asked Anil.

'I'll do that,' said the captain. 'But don't you think you should discuss this with your father? Your parents might not like being left alone so suddenly.'

'Oh no, sir, I can't tell them; they wouldn't like it at all. You won't tell them, will you, captain sir?'

'No, of course not, my boy,' said Captain MacWhirr, with a huge wink.

During the next two days Anil remained at home, feverishly excited, busily making preparations for the voyage. He filled a pillowcase with some clothes, a penknife and a bar of chocolate, and hid the bundle in an old cupboard.

At dinner, one evening, the conversation came around to the subject of ships, and Anil's mother spoke to her husband, 'I understand your friend, the captain of the cargo ship, sails tonight.'

'That's right,' said the boy's father. 'We won't see him again for sometime.'

Anil wanted to interrupt and inform them that Captain MacWhirr wouldn't be sailing yet, but he did not want to arouse his parents' suspicions. And yet, the more he pondered over his mother's remark, the less certain he felt. Perhaps the ship was sailing that night; perhaps the captain had mentioned the fact to Anil's parents so that the information could be passed on. After all, Anil hadn't been down to the docks for two days, and the captain couldn't have had the opportunity of notifying Anil of the ship's imminent departure.

Anyway, Anil decided there was no time to lose. He went to his room and, collecting the bundle of clothes, slipped out of the house. His parents were sitting out on the veranda and for awhile Anil stood outside in the gathering dusk, watching them. He felt a pang of regret at having to leave them alone for so long, perhaps several months; he would like to take them along, too, but he knew that wouldn't be practical. Perhaps, when he had a ship of his own . . .

He hurried down the garden path, and as soon as he was on the road to the docks, he broke into a run. He felt sure he had heard the hoot of a steamer.

Anil ran down the pier, breathing heavily, his bundle of clothes beginning to come undone. He saw the steamer, but it was moving. It was moving slowly out of the harbour, sending the waves rippling back to the pier.

'Captain!' shouted Anil. 'Wait for me!'

A sailor, standing in the bow, waved to Anil; but that was all. Anil stood at the end of the pier, waving his hands and shouting desperately.

'Captain, oh captain sir, wait for me!'

Nobody answered him. The sea gulls, wheeling in the wake of the ship, seemed to take up his cry. 'Captain, captain . . .'

The ship drew further away, gathering speed. Still Anil shouted, in a hoarse, pleading voice. Yokohama, Valparaiso, San Diego, London, all were slipping away forever . . .

He stood alone on the pier, his bundle at his feet, the harbour lights beginning to twinkle, the gulls wheeling around him. 'First call Aden, then Suez, and up the Canal.' But for Anil there was only the empty house and the boredom of the schoolroom.

Next year, sometime, he told himself, Captain MacWhirr would return. He would be back, and then Anil wouldn't make a mistake. He'd be on the ship long before it sailed. Captain MacWhirr had promised to take him along, and wasn't an adult's word to be trusted? And so he remained for a long time on the pier, staring out to sea until the steamer went over the horizon. Then he picked up his bundle and made for home. This year, next year, sometime . . . Yokohama, Valparaiso, San Diego, London!

The Tree Lover

I WAS NEVER able to get over the feeling that plants and trees loved Grandfather with as much tenderness as he loved them. I was sitting beside him on the veranda steps one morning, when I noticed the tendril of a creeping vine that was trailing near my feet. As we sat there, in the soft sunshine of a north Indian winter, I saw that the tendril was moving very slowly away from me and towards Grandfather. Twenty minutes later it had crossed the veranda step and was touching Grandfather's feet.

There is probably a scientific explanation for the plant's behaviour—something to do with light and warmth—but I like to think that it moved that way simply because it was fond of Grandfather. One felt like drawing close to him. Sometimes when I sat alone beneath a tree I would feel a little lonely or lost; but as soon as Grandfather joined me, the garden would become a happy place, the tree itself more friendly.

Grandfather had served many years in the Indian Forest Service, and so it was natural that he should know and understand and like trees. On his retirement from the Service, he had built a bungalow on the outskirts of Dehra, planting trees all round it: limes, mangoes, oranges and guavas; also eucalyptus, jacaranda and the Persian lilac. In the fertile Doon valley, plants and trees grew tall and strong.

There were other trees in the compound before the house was built, including an old peepul which had forced its way through the walls of an abandoned outhouse, knocking the bricks down with its vigorous growth. Peepul trees are great show-offs. Even when there is no breeze, their broad-chested, slim-waisted leaves will spin like tops, determined to attract your attention and invite you into the shade.

Grandmother had wanted the peepul tree cut down, but Grandfather had said, 'Let it be. We can always build another outhouse.'

The gardener, Dukhi, who was a Hindu, was pleased that we had allowed the tree to live. Peepul trees are sacred to Hindus, and some people believe that ghosts live in the branches. 'If we cut the tree down, wouldn't the ghosts go away?' I asked.

'I don't know,' said Grandfather. 'Perhaps they'd come into the house.'

Dukhi wouldn't walk under the tree at night. He said that once, when he was a youth, he had wandered beneath a peepul tree late at night, and that something heavy had fallen with a thud on his shoulders. Since then he had always walked with a slight stoop, he explained.

'Nonsense,' said Grandmother, who didn't believe in ghosts. 'He got his stoop from squatting on his haunches year after year, weeding with that tiny spade of his!'

I never saw any ghosts in our peepul tree. There are peepul trees all over India, and people sometimes leave offerings of milk and flowers beneath them to keep the spirits happy. But since no one left any offerings under our tree, I expect the ghosts left in disgust, to look for peepul trees where there was both board and lodging.

Grandfather was about sixty, a lean active man who still rode his bicycle at great speed. He had stopped climbing trees a year previously, when he had got to the top of the jackfruit tree and had been unable to come down again. We had to fetch a ladder for him.

Grandfather bathed quite often but got back into his gardening clothes immediately after the bath. During meals, ladybirds or caterpillars would sometimes walk off his shirtsleeves and wander about on the tablecloth, and this always annoyed Grandmother.

She grumbled at Grandfather a lot, but he didn't mind, because he knew she loved him.

My favourite tree was the banyan which grew behind the house. Its spreading branches, which hung to the ground and took root again, formed a number of twisting passageways. The tree was older than the house, older than my grandparents; I could hide in its branches, behind a screen of thick green leaves, and spy on the world below.

The banyan tree was a world in itself, populated with small animals and large insects. While the leaves were still pink and tender, they would be visited by the delicate map butterfly, who left her eggs in their care. The 'honey' on the leaves—a sweet, sticky smear—also attracted the little striped squirrels, who soon grew used to having me in the tree and became quite bold, accepting gram from my hand.

At night the tree was visited by the hawk cuckoo. Its shrill, nagging cry kept us awake on hot summer nights. Indians called the bird 'Paos-ala', which means 'Rain is coming!' But according to Grandfather, when the bird was in full cry, it seemed to be shouting, 'Oh dear, oh dear! How very hot it's getting! We feel it . . . we feel it . . . WE FEEL IT!'

Grandfather wasn't content with planting trees in our garden. During the rains we would walk into the jungle beyond the riverbed, armed with cuttings and saplings, and these we would plant in the forest, beside the tall sal and shisham trees.

'But no one ever comes here,' I protested, the first time we did this. 'Who is going to see them?'

'We're not planting for people only,' said Grandfather. 'We're planting for the forest—and for the birds and animals who live here and need more food and shelter.'

He told me how men, and not only birds and animals, needed trees—for keeping the desert away, for attracting rain, for preventing the banks of rivers from being washed away, and for wild plants and grasses to grow beneath.

'And for timber?' I asked, pointing to the sal and shisham trees.

'Yes, and for timber. But men are cutting down the trees

without replacing them. For every tree that's felled, we must plant *two*. Otherwise, one day there'll be no forests at all, and the world will become one great desert.'

The thought of a world without trees became a sort of nightmare for me—it's one reason why I shall never want to live on the treeless Moon—and I helped Grandfather in his tree planting with even greater enthusiasm. He taught me a poem by George Morris, and we would recite it together:

> Woodman, spare that tree!
> Touch not a single bough!
> In youth it sheltered me,
> And I'll protect it now.

'One day the trees will move again,' said Grandfather. 'They've been standing still for thousands of years, but one day they'll move again. There was a time when trees could walk about like people, but along came the Devil and cast a spell over them, rooting them to one place. But they're always trying to move—see how they reach out with their arms!—and some of them, like the banyan tree with its travelling roots, manage to get quite far!'

In the autumn, Grandfather took me to the hills. The deodars (Indian cedars), oaks, chestnuts and maples were very different from the trees I had grown up with in Dehra. The broad leaves of the horse chestnut had turned yellow, and smooth brown chestnuts lay scattered on the roads. Grandfather and I filled our pockets with them, then climbed the slope of a bare hill and started planting the chestnuts in the ground.

I don't know if they ever came up, because I never went there again. Goats and cattle grazed freely on the hill, and, if the trees did come up in the spring, they may well have been eaten; but I like to think that somewhere in the foothills of the Himalayas there is a grove of chestnut trees, and that birds and flying foxes and cicadas have made their homes in them.

Back in Dehra, we found an island, a small rocky island in the middle of a dry riverbed. It was one of those riverbeds, so common in the Doon valley, which are completely dry in summer but flooded during the monsoon rains. A small mango tree was growing in the middle of the island, and Grandfather said, 'If a mango can grow here, so can other trees.'

As soon as the rains set in—and while the river could still be crossed—we set out with a number of tamarind, laburnum and coral tree saplings and cuttings, and spent the day planting them on the island.

When the monsoon set in, the trees appeared to be flourishing.

The monsoon season was the time for rambling about. At every turn there was something new to see. Out of earth and rock and leafless bough, the magic touch of the monsoon rains had brought life and greenness. You could almost see the broad-leaved vines grow. Plants sprang up in the most unlikely places. A peepul would take root in the ceiling, a

mango would sprout on the window sill. We did not like to remove them; but they had to go, if the house was to be kept from falling down. 'If you want to live in a tree, it's all right by me,' said Grandmother. 'But I like having a roof over my head, and I'm not going to have it brought down by the jungle!'

The common monsoon sights along the Indian roads were always picturesque—the wide plains, with great herds of smoke-coloured, delicate-limbed cattle being driven slowly home for the night, accompanied by several ungainly buffaloes, and flocks of goats and black long-tailed sheep. Then you came to a pond, where some buffaloes were enjoying themselves, with no part of them visible but the tips of their noses, while on their backs were a number of merry children, perfectly and happily naked.

The banyan tree really came to life during the monsoon, when the branches were thick with scarlet figs. Humans couldn't eat the berries, but the many birds that gathered in the tree—gossipy rosy pastors, quarrelsome mynahs, cheerful bulbuls and coppersmiths, and sometimes a noisy, bullying crow—feasted on them. And when night fell and the birds were resting, the dark flying foxes flapped heavily about the tree, chewing and munching loudly as they clambered over the branches.

The tree crickets were a band of willing artists who started their singing at almost any time of the day but preferably in the evenings. Delicate pale green creatures with transparent wings, they were hard to find amongst the lush monsoon foliage; but once found, a tap on the bush or leaf on which one of them sat would put an immediate end to its performance.

At the height of the monsoon, the banyan tree was like an orchestra with the musicians constantly tuning up. Birds, insects and squirrels welcomed the end of the hot weather and the cool quenching relief of the monsoon.

A toy flute in my hands, I would try adding my shrill piping to theirs. But they must have thought poorly of my piping, for, whenever I played, the birds and the insects kept a pained and puzzled silence.

I wonder if they missed me when I went away—for when the War came, followed by the Independence of India, I was sent to a boarding school in the hills. Grandfather's house was put up for sale. During the holidays I went to live with my parents in Delhi, and it was from them I learnt that my grandparents had gone to England.

When I finished school, I too went to England with my parents, and was away from India for several years. But recently I was in Dehra again, and after first visiting the old house—where I found that the banyan tree had grown over the wall and along part of the pavement, almost as though it had tried to follow Grandfather—I walked out of town towards the riverbed.

It was February, and as I looked across the dry watercourse, my eye was caught by the spectacular red plumes of the coral blossom. In contrast to the dry riverbed, the island was a small green paradise. When I walked across to the trees, I noticed that a number of squirrels had come to live in them. And a koel (a sort of crow-pheasant) challenged me with a mellow 'who-are-you, who-are-you . . .'

But the trees seemed to know me. They whispered among themselves and beckoned me nearer. And looking around, I noticed that other small trees and wild plants and grasses had sprung up under the protection of the trees we had placed there.

The trees had multiplied! They were moving. In one small corner of the world, Grandfather's dream was coming true, and the trees were moving again.

How Far Is the River?

BETWEEN THE BOY and the river was a mountain. I was a small boy, and it was a small river, but the mountain was big.

The thickly forested mountain hid the river, but I knew it was there and what it looked like; I had never seen the river with my own eyes, but from the villagers I had heard of it, of the fish in its waters, of its rocks and currents and waterfalls, and it only remained for me to touch the water and know it personally.

I stood in front of our house on the hill opposite the mountain, and gazed across the valley, dreaming of the river. I was barefooted; not because I couldn't afford shoes, but because I felt free with my feet bare, because I liked the feel of warm stones and cool grass, because not wearing shoes saved me the trouble of taking them off.

It was eleven o'clock and I knew my parents wouldn't

be home till evening. There was a loaf of bread I could take with me, and on the way I might find some fruit. Here was the chance I had been waiting for: it would not come again for a long time, because it was seldom that my father and mother visited friends for the entire day. If I came back before dark, they wouldn't know where I had been.

I went into the house and wrapped the loaf of bread in a newspaper. Then I closed all the doors and windows.

The path to the river dropped steeply into the valley, then rose and went round the big mountain. It was frequently used by the villagers, woodcutters, milkmen, shepherds, mule-drivers—but there were no villages beyond the mountain or near the river.

I passed a woodcutter and asked him how far it was to the river. He was a short, powerful man, with a creased and weathered face, and muscles that stood out in hard lumps.

'Seven miles,' he said. 'Why do you want to know?'

'I am going there,' I said.

'Alone?'

'Of course.'

'It will take you three hours to reach it, and then you have to come back. It will be getting dark, and it is not an easy road.'

'But I'm a good walker,' I said, though I had never walked further than the two miles between our house and my school. I left the woodcutter on the path, and continued down the hill.

It was a dizzy, winding path, and I slipped once or twice and slid into a bush or down a slope of slippery pine-needles. The hill was covered with lush green ferns, the trees were entangled in creepers, and a great wild dahlia would suddenly rear its golden head from the leaves and ferns.

Soon I was in the valley, and the path straightened out and then began to rise. I met a girl who was coming from the opposite direction. She held a long curved knife with which she had been cutting grass, and there were rings in her nose and ears and her arms were covered with heavy bangles. The bangles made music when she moved her wrists. It was as though her hands spoke a language of their own.

'How far is it to the river?' I asked.

The girl had probably never been to the river, or she may have been thinking of another one, because she said, 'Twenty miles,' without any hesitation.

I laughed and ran down the path. A parrot screeched suddenly, flew low over my head, a flash of blue and green. It took the course of the path, and I followed its dipping flight, running until the path rose and the bird disappeared amongst the trees.

A trickle of water came down the hillside, and I stopped to drink. The water was cold and sharp but very refreshing. But I was soon thirsty again. The sun was striking the side of the hill, and the dusty path became hotter, the stones scorching my feet. I was sure I had covered half the distance: I had been walking for over an hour.

Presently, I saw another boy ahead of me driving a few goats down the path.

'How far is the river?' I asked.

The village boy smiled and said, 'Oh, not far, just round the next hill and straight down.'

Feeling hungry, I unwrapped my loaf of bread and broke it in two, offering one half to the boy. We sat on the hillside and ate in silence.

When we had finished, we walked on together and began talking; and talking, I did not notice the smarting of my feet, and the heat of the sun, the distance I had covered and the distance I had yet to cover. But after some time my companion had to take another path, and once more I was on my own.

I missed the village boy; I looked up and down the mountain path but no one else was in sight. My own home was hidden from view by the side of the mountain, and there was no sign of the river. I began to feel discouraged. If someone had been with me, I would not have faltered; but alone, I was conscious of my fatigue and isolation.

But I had come more than half way, and I couldn't turn back; I had to see the river. If I failed, I would always be a little ashamed of the experience. So I walked on, along the hot, dusty, stony path, past stone huts and terraced fields, until there were no more fields or huts, only forest and sun and loneliness. There were no men, and no sign of man's influence—only trees and rocks and grass and small flowers—and silence . . . The silence was impressive and a little frightening. There was no movement, except for the bending of grass beneath my feet, and the circling of a hawk against the blind blue of the sky.

Then, as I rounded a sharp bend, I heard the sound of water. I gasped with surprise and happiness, and began to run. I slipped and stumbled, but I kept on running, until I was able to plunge into the snow-cold mountain water.

And the water was blue and white and wonderful.

The Haunted Bicycle

I WAS LIVING at the time in a village about five miles out of Shahganj, a district in east Uttar Pradesh, and my only means of transport was a bicycle. I could of course have gone into Shahganj on any obliging farmer's bullock-cart, but, in spite of bad roads and my own clumsiness as a cyclist, I found the bicycle a trifle faster. I went into Shahganj almost every day, collected my mail, bought a newspaper, drank innumerable cups of tea, and gossiped with the tradesmen. I cycled back to the village at about six in the evening, along a quiet, unfrequented forest road. During the winter months it was dark by six, and I would have to use a lamp on the bicycle.

One evening, when I had covered about half the distance to the village, I was brought to a halt by a small boy who was standing in the middle of the road. The forest at that late hour was no place for a child: wolves and hyenas were common in

101

the district. I got down from my bicycle and approached the boy, but he didn't seem to take much notice of me.

'What are you doing here on your own?' I asked.

'I'm waiting,' he said, without looking at me.

'Waiting for whom? Your parents?'

'No, I am waiting for my sister.'

'Well, I haven't passed her on the road,' I said. 'She may be further ahead. You had better come along with me, we'll soon find her.'

The boy nodded and climbed silently on to the crossbar in front of me. I have never been able to recall his features. Already it was dark and besides, he kept his face turned away from me.

The wind was against us, and as I cycled on, I shivered with the cold, but the boy did not seem to feel it. We had not gone far when the light from my lamp fell on the figure of another child who was standing by the side of the road. This time it was a girl. She was a little older than the boy, and her hair was long and windswept, hiding most of her face.

'Here's your sister,' I said. 'Let's take her along with us.' The girl did not respond to my smile, and she did no more than nod seriously to the boy. But she climbed up on to my back carrier, and allowed me to pedal off again. Their replies to my friendly questions were monosyllabic, and I gathered that they were wary of strangers. Well, when I got to the village, I would hand them over to the headman, and he could locate their parents.

The road was level, but I felt as though I was cycling uphill. And then I noticed that the boy's head was much closer to my face, that the girl's breathing was loud and heavy, almost as though she was doing the riding. Despite the cold wind, I began to feel hot and suffocated.

'I think we'd better take a rest,' I suggested.

'No!' cried the boy and girl together. 'No rest!'

I was so surprised that I rode on without any argument; and then, just as I was thinking of ignoring their demand and stopping, I noticed that the boy's hands, which were resting on the handlebar, had grown long and black and hairy.

My hands shook and the bicycle wobbled about on the road.

'Be careful!' shouted the children in unison. 'Look where you're going!'

Their tone now was menacing and far from childlike. I took a quick glance over my shoulder and had my worst fears confirmed. The girl's face was huge and bloated. Her legs, black and hairy, were trailing along the ground.

'Stop!' ordered the terrible children. 'Stop near the stream!' But before I could do anything, my front wheel hit a stone and the bicycle toppled over. As I sprawled in the dust, I felt something hard, like a hoof, hit me on the back of the head, and then there was total darkness.

When I recovered consciousness, I noticed that the moon had risen and was sparkling on the waters of a stream. The children were not to be seen anywhere. I got up from the ground and began to brush the dust from my clothes. And then, hearing the sound of splashing and churning in the stream, I looked up again.

Two small black buffaloes gazed at me from the muddy, moonlit water.

Whistling in the Dark

THE MOON WAS almost at the full. Bright moonlight flooded the road. But I was stalked by the shadows of the trees, by the crooked oak branches reaching out towards me—some threateningly, others as though they needed companionship.

Once I dreamt that the trees could walk. That on moonlit nights like this they would uproot themselves for a while, visit each other, talk about old times—for they had seen many men and happenings, specially the older ones. And then, before dawn, they would return to the places where they had been condemned to grow. Lonely sentinels of the night. And this was a good night for them to walk. They appeared eager to do so: a restless rustling of leaves, the creaking of branches—these were sounds that came from within them in the silence of the night . . .

Occasionally, other strollers passed me in the dark. It was

still quite early, just eight o'clock, and some people were on their way home. Others were walking into town for a taste of the bright lights, shops and restaurants. On the unlit road I could not recognize them. They did not notice me. I was reminded of an old song from my childhood. Softly, I began humming the tune, and soon the words came back to me:

> We three,
> We're not a crowd;
> We're not even company—
> My echo,
> My shadow,
> And me . . .

I looked down at my shadow, moving silently beside me. We take our shadows for granted, don't we? There they are, the uncomplaining companions of a lifetime, mute and helpless witnesses to our every act of commission or omission. On this bright moonlit night I could not help noticing you, Shadow, and I was sorry that you had to see so much that I was ashamed of; but glad, too, that you were around when I had my small triumphs. And what of my echo? I thought of calling out to see if my call came back to me; but I refrained from doing so, as I did not wish to disturb the perfect stillness of the mountains or the conversations of the trees.

The road wound up the hill and levelled out at the top, where it became a ribbon of moonlight entwined between tall deodars. A flying squirrel glided across the road, leaving one tree for another. A nightjar called. The rest was silence.

The old cemetery loomed up before me. There were many old graves—some large and monumental—and there were a few recent graves too, for the cemetery was still in use. I could see flowers scattered on one of them—a few late dahlias and scarlet salvia. Further on, near the boundary wall, part of the cemetery's retaining wall had collapsed in the heavy monsoon rains. Some of the tombstones had come down with the wall. One grave lay exposed. A rotting coffin and a few scattered bones were the only relics of someone who had lived and loved like you and me.

Part of the tombstone lay beside the road, but the lettering had worn away. I am not normally a morbid person, but something made me stoop and pick up a smooth round shard of bone, probably part of a skull. When my hand closed over it, the bone crumbled into fragments. I let them fall to the grass. Dust to dust.

And from somewhere, not too far away, came the sound of someone whistling.

At first I thought it was another late-evening stroller, whistling to himself much as I had been humming my old song. But the whistler approached quite rapidly; the whistling was loud and cheerful. A boy on a bicycle sped past. I had only a glimpse of him, before his cycle went weaving through the shadows on the road.

But he was back again in a few minutes. And this time he stopped a few feet away from me, and gave me a quizzical half-smile. A slim dusky boy of fourteen or fifteen. He wore a school blazer and a yellow scarf. His eyes were pools of liquid moonlight.

'You don't have a bell on your cycle,' I said.

He said nothing, just smiled at me with his head a little to one side. I put out my hand, and I thought he was going to take it. But then, quite suddenly, he was off again, whistling cheerfully though rather tunelessly. A whistling schoolboy. A bit late for him to be out, but he seemed an independent sort.

The whistling grew fainter, then faded away altogether. A deep sound-denying silence fell upon the forest. My shadow and I walked home.

Next morning I woke to a different kind of whistling—the song of the thrush outside my window.

It was a wonderful day, the sunshine warm and sensuous, and I longed to be out in the open. But there was work to be done, proofs to be corrected, letters to be written. And it was several days before I could walk to the top of the hill, to that lonely tranquil resting place under the deodars. It seemed to me ironic that those who had the best view of the glistening snow-capped peaks were all buried several feet underground.

Some repair work was going on. The retaining wall of the cemetery was being shored up, but the overseer told me that there was no money to restore the damaged grave. With the help of the chowkidar, I returned the scattered bones to a little hollow under the collapsed masonry, and I left some money with him so that he could have the open grave bricked up. The name on the gravestone had worn away, but I could make out a date—20 November 1950—some fifty years ago, but not too long ago as gravestones go . . .

I found the burial register in the church vestry and turned back the yellowing pages to 1950, when I was just a schoolboy myself. I found the name there—Michael Dutta, aged fifteen—and the cause of death: road accident.

Well, I could only make guesses. And to turn conjecture into certainty, I would have to find an old resident who might remember the boy or the accident.

There was old Miss Marley at Pine Top. A retired teacher from Woodstock, she had a wonderful memory, and she had lived in the hill station for more than half a century.

White-haired and smooth-cheeked, her bright blue eyes full of curiosity, she gazed benignly at me through her old-fashioned pince-nez.

'Michael was a charming boy—full of exuberance, always ready to oblige. I had only to mention that I needed a newspaper or an Aspirin, and he'd be off on his bicycle, swooping down these steep roads with great abandon. But these hills roads, with their sudden corners, weren't meant for racing around on a bicycle. They were widening our road for motor traffic, and a truck was coming uphill, loaded with rubble, when Michael came round a bend and smashed headlong into it. He was rushed to the hospital, and the doctors did their best, but he did not recover consciousness. Of course you must have seen his grave. That's why you're here. His parents? They left shortly afterwards. Went abroad, I think . . . A charming boy, Michael, but just a bit too reckless. You'd have liked him, I think.'

I did not see the phantom bicycle-rider again for some time, although I felt his presence on more than one occasion. And when, on a cold winter's evening, I walked past that lonely cemetery, I thought I heard him whistling far away. But he did not manifest himself. Perhaps it was only the echo of a whistle, in communion with my insubstantial shadow.

It was several months before I saw that smiling face again. And then it came at me out of the mist as I was walking home in drenching monsoon rain. I had been to a dinner party at the old community centre, and I was returning home along a very narrow, precipitous path known as the Eyebrow. A storm had been threatening all evening. A heavy mist had settled on the hillside. It was so thick that the light from my torch simply bounced off it. The sky blossomed with sheet lightning and thunder rolled over the mountains. The rain became heavier. I moved forward slowly, carefully, hugging the hillside. There was a clap of thunder, and then I saw him emerge from the mist and stand in my way—the same slim dark youth who had materialized near the cemetery. He did not smile. Instead, he put up his hand and waved me back. I hesitated, stood still. The mist lifted a little, and I saw that the path had disappeared. There was a gaping emptiness a few feet in front of me. And then a drop of over a hundred feet to the rocks below.

As I stepped back, clinging to a thorn bush for support, the boy vanished. I stumbled back to the community centre and spent the night on a chair in the library.

I did not see him again.

But weeks later, when I was down with a severe bout

of flu, I heard him from my sickbed, whistling beneath my window. Was he calling to me to join him, I wondered, or was he just trying to reassure me that all was well? I got out of bed and looked out, but I saw no one. From time to time I heard his whistling; but as I got better, it grew fainter until it ceased altogether.

Fully recovered, I renewed my old walks to the top of the hill. But although I lingered near the cemetery until it grew dark, and paced up and down the deserted road, I did not see or hear the whistler again. I felt lonely, in need of a friend, even if it was only a phantom bicycle-rider. But there were only the trees.

And so every evening I walk home in the darkness, singing the old refrain:

> We three,
> We're not alone,
> We're not even company—
> My echo,
> My shadow,
> And me . . .

Four Boys on a Glacier

ON A DAY that promised rain we bundled ourselves into the bus that was to take us to Kapkote (where people lost their caps and coats, punned Anil), the starting point of our Himalayan trek. I was seventeen at the time, and Anil and Somi were sixteen. Each of us carried a haversack, and we had also brought along a good-sized bedding-roll which, apart from blankets, contained bags of rice and flour, thoughtfully provided by Anil's mother. We had no idea how we would carry the bedding-roll once we started walking, but we didn't worry too much about details.

We were soon in the hills of Kumaon, on a winding road that took us up and up, until we saw the valley and our small town spread out beneath us, the river a silver ribbon across the plain. We took a sharp bend, the valley disappeared, and the mountains towered above us.

At Kapkote we had refreshments and the shopkeeper

told us we could spend the night in one of his rooms. The surroundings were pleasant, the hills wooded with deodars, the lower slopes planted with fresh green paddy. At night there was a wind moaning in the trees and it found its way through the cracks in the windows and eventually through our blankets.

Next morning we washed our faces at a small stream near the shop and filled our water bottles for the day's march. A boy from the nearby village approached us, and asked where we were going.

'To the glacier,' said Somi.

'I'll come with you,' said the boy. 'I know the way.'

'You're too small,' said Anil. 'We need someone who can carry our bedding-roll.'

'I'm small but I'm strong,' said the boy, who certainly looked sturdy. He had pink cheeks and a well-knit body.

'See!' he said, and, picking up a rock the size of a football, he heaved it across the stream.

'I think he can come with us,' I said.

And then, we were walking—at first above the little Sarayu river, then climbing higher along the rough mule track, always within sound of the water, which we glimpsed now and then, swift, green and bubbling.

We were at the forest rest house by six in the evening, after covering fifteen miles. Anil found the watchman asleep in a patch of fading sunlight and roused him. The watchman, who hadn't been bothered by visitors for weeks, grumbled at our intrusion but opened a room for us. He also produced some potatoes from his store, and these were roasted for dinner.

Just as we were about to get into our beds we heard a thud on the corrugated tin roof, and then the sound of someone—or something—scrambling about on the roof. Anil, Somi and I were alarmed but Bisnu, who was already under the blankets, merely yawned, and turned over on his side.

'It's only a bear,' he said. 'Didn't you see the pumpkins on the roof? Bears love pumpkins.'

For half an hour we had to listen to the bear as it clambered about on the roof, feasting on the watchman's ripe pumpkins. At last there was silence. Anil and I crawled out of our blankets and went to the window. And through the frosted glass we saw a black Himalayan bear ambling across the slope in front of the house.

Our next rest house lay in a narrow valley, on the banks of the rushing Pindar river, which twisted its way through the mountains. We walked on, past terraced fields and small stone houses, until there were no more fields or houses, only forest and sun and silence.

It was different from the silence of a room or an empty street.

And then, the silence broke into sound—the sound of the river.

Far down in the valley, the Pindar tumbled over itself in its impatience to reach the plains. We began to run; slipped and stumbled, but continued running.

The rest house stood on a ledge just above the river, and the sound of the water rushing down the mountain-defile could be heard at all times. The sound of the birds, which we had grown used to, was drowned by the sound of the water, but the birds themselves could be seen, many-coloured, standing out splendidly against the dark green forest foliage—the red crowned jay, the paradise flycatcher, the purple whistling thrush and others we could not recognize.

Higher up the mountain, above some terraced land where oats and barley were grown, stood a small cluster of huts. This, we were told by the watchman, was the last village on the way to the glacier. It was, in fact, one of the last villages in India, because if we crossed the difficult passes beyond the glacier, we would find ourselves in Tibet.

Anil asked the watchman about the Abominable Snowman. The Nepalese believe in the existence of the Snowman, and our watchman was Nepalese.

'Yes, I have seen the yeti,' he told us. 'A great shaggy, flat-footed creature. In the winter, when it snows heavily, he passes the bungalow at night. I have seen his tracks the next morning.'

'Does he come this way in the summer?' asked Somi, anxiously.

'No,' said the watchman. 'But sometimes I have seen the *lidini*. You have to be careful of her.'

'And who is the *lidini*?' asked Anil.

'She is the snow-woman, and far more dangerous. She has the same height as the yeti—about seven feet when her back is straight—and her hair is much longer. Also, she has very long teeth. Her feet face inwards, but she can run very fast, specially downhill. If you see a *lidini*, and she chases you, always run in an uphill direction. She tires quickly because of her crooked feet. But when running downhill she has no trouble at all, and you want to be very fast to escape her!'

'Well, we are quite fast,' said Anil with a nervous laugh. 'But it's just a fairy story, I don't believe a word of it.'

The watchman was most offended, and refused to tell us anything more about snowmen and snow-women. But he helped Bisnu make a fire, and presented us with a black, sticky sweet, which we ate with relish.

It was a fine, sunny morning when we set out to cover the last seven miles to the glacier. We had expected a stiff climb, but the rest house was 11,000 feet above sea level, and the rest of the climb was fairly gradual.

Suddenly, abruptly, there were no more trees. As the bungalow dropped out of sight, the trees and bushes gave way to short grass and little pink and blue alpine flowers. The snow peaks were close now, ringing us in on every side. We passed white waterfalls, cascading hundreds of feet down precipitous rock faces, thundering into the little river. A great white eagle hovered over us.

The hill fell away, and there, confronting us, was a great white field of snow and ice, cradled between two shining peaks. We were speechless for several minutes. Then we proceeded cautiously on to the snow, supporting each other on the slippery surface. We could not go far, because we were quite unequipped for any high-altitude climbing. But it was a satisfying feeling to know that we were the only young men from our town who had walked so far and so high.

The sun was reflected sharply from the snow and we felt surprisingly warm. It was delicious to feel the sun crawling over our bodies, sinking deep into our bones. Meanwhile, almost imperceptibly, clouds had covered some of the peaks, and white mist drifted down the mountain slopes. It was time to return: we would barely make it to the bungalow before it grew dark.

We took our time returning to Kapkote; stopped by the Sarayu river; bathed with the village boys we had seen on the way up; collected strawberries and ferns and wild flowers; and finally said goodbye to Bisnu.

Anil wanted to take Bisnu along with us, but the boy's parents refused to let him go, saying that he was too young for the life of a city.

'Never mind,' said Somi. 'We'll go on another trek next year, and we'll take you with us, Bisnu.'

This promise pleased Bisnu, and he saw us off at the bus stop, shouldering our bedding-roll to the end. Then he climbed a pine tree to have a better view of us leaving. We saw him waving to us from the tree as the bus went round the bend from Kapkote, and then the hills were left behind and the plains stretched out below.

The Cherry Tree

ONE DAY, WHEN Rakesh was six, he walked home from the Mussoorie bazaar eating cherries. They were a little sweet, a little sour; small, bright red cherries, which had come all the way from the Kashmir Valley.

Here in the Himalayan foothills where Rakesh lived, there were not many fruit trees. The soil was stony, and the dry cold winds stunted the growth of most plants. But on the more sheltered slopes there were forests of oak and deodar.

Rakesh lived with his grandfather on the outskirts of Mussoorie, just where the forest began. His father and mother lived in a small village fifty miles away, where they grew maize and rice and barley in narrow terraced fields on the lower slopes of the mountain. But there were no schools in the village, and Rakesh's parents were keen that he should go to school. As soon as he was of school-going age, they sent him to stay with his grandfather in Mussoorie.

Grandfather was a retired forest ranger. He had a little cottage outside the town.

Rakesh was on his way home from school when he bought the cherries. He paid fifty paise for the bunch. It took him about half an hour to walk home, and by the time he reached the cottage there were only three cherries left.

'Have a cherry, Grandfather,' he said, as soon as he saw his grandfather in the garden.

Grandfather took one cherry and Rakesh promptly ate the other two. He kept the last seed in his mouth for some time, rolling it round and round on his tongue until all the tang had gone. Then he placed the seed on the palm of his hand and studied it.

'Are cherry seeds lucky?' asked Rakesh.

'Of course.'

'Then I'll keep it.'

'Nothing is lucky if you put it away. If you want luck, you must put it to some use.'

'What can I do with a seed?'

'Plant it.'

So Rakesh found a small spade and began to dig up a flower bed.

'Hey, not there,' said Grandfather. 'I've sown mustard in that bed. Plant it in that shady corner, where it won't be disturbed.'

Rakesh went to a corner of the garden where the earth was soft and yielding. He did not have to dig. He pressed the seed into the soil with his thumb and it went right in.

Then he had his lunch and ran off to play cricket with

his friends and forgot all about the cherry seed.

When it was winter in the hills, a cold wind blew down from the snows and went *whoo-whoo-whoo* in the deodar trees, and the garden was dry and bare. In the evenings Grandfather told Rakesh stories—stories, about people who turned into animals, and ghosts who lived in trees, and beans that jumped and stones that wept—and, in turn, Rakesh would read to him from the newspaper, Grandfather's eyesight being rather weak. Rakesh found the newspaper very dull—specially after the stories—but Grandfather wanted all the news . . .

They knew it was spring when the wild duck flew north again, to Siberia. Early in the morning, when he got up to chop wood and light a fire, Rakesh saw the V-shaped formation streaming northwards, the calls of the birds carrying clearly through the thin mountain air.

One morning in the garden he bent to pick up what he thought was a small twig and found to his surprise that it was well rooted. He stared at it for a moment, then ran to fetch Grandfather, calling, 'Dada, come and look, the cherry tree has come up!'

'What cherry tree?' asked Grandfather, who had forgotten about it.

'The seed we planted last year—look, it's come up!'

Rakesh went down on his haunches, while Grandfather bent almost double and peered down at the tiny tree. It was about four inches high.

'Yes, it's a cherry tree,' said Grandfather. 'You should water it now and then.'

Rakesh ran indoors and came back with a bucket of water. 'Don't drown it!' said Grandfather.

Rakesh gave it a sprinkling and circled it with pebbles. 'What are the pebbles for?' asked Grandfather.

'For privacy,' said Rakesh.

He looked at the tree every morning but it did not seem to be growing very fast. So he stopped looking at it—except quickly, out of the corner of his eye. And, after a week or two, when he allowed himself to look at it properly, he found that it had grown—at least an inch!

That year the monsoon rains came early and Rakesh plodded to and from school in raincoat and gumboots. Ferns sprang from the trunks of trees, strange looking lilies came up in the long grass, and even when it wasn't raining, the trees dripped and mist came curling up the valley. The cherry tree grew quickly in this season.

It was about two feet high when a goat entered the garden and ate all the leaves. Only the main stem and two thin branches remained.

'Never mind,' said Grandfather, seeing that Rakesh was upset. 'It will grow again, cherry trees are tough.'

Towards the end of the rainy season new leaves appeared on the tree. Then a woman cutting grass scrambled down the hillside, her scythe swishing through the heavy monsoon foliage. She did not try to avoid the tree: one sweep, and the cherry tree was cut in two.

When Grandfather saw what had happened, he went after the woman and scolded her; but the damage could not be repaired.

'Maybe it will die now,' said Rakesh.

'Maybe,' said Grandfather.

But the cherry tree had no intention of dying.

By the time summer came round again, it had sent out several new shoots with tender green leaves. Rakesh had grown taller too. He was eight now, a sturdy boy with curly black hair and deep black eyes. Blackberry eyes, Grandfather called them.

That monsoon Rakesh went home to his village, to help his father and mother with the planting and ploughing and sowing. He was thinner but stronger when he came back to Grandfather's house at the end of the rains, to find that the cherry tree had grown another foot. It was now up to his chest.

Even when there was rain, Rakesh would sometimes water the tree. He wanted it to know that he was there.

One day he found a bright green praying mantis perched on a branch, peering at him with bulging eyes. Rakesh let it remain there. It was the cherry tree's first visitor.

The next visitor was a hairy caterpillar, who started making a meal of the leaves. Rakesh removed it quickly and dropped it on a heap of dry leaves.

'They're pretty leaves,' said Rakesh. 'And they are always ready to dance. If there's a breeze.'

After Grandfather had come indoors, Rakesh went into the garden and lay down on the grass beneath the tree. He gazed up through the leaves at the great blue sky; and turning on his side, he could see the mountain striding away into the clouds. He was still lying beneath the tree when the evening shadows crept across the garden. Grandfather came back and sat down beside Rakesh, and they waited in silence until the stars came out and the nightjar began to call. In the forest below, the crickets and cicadas began tuning up; and suddenly the tree was full of the sound of insects.

'There are so many trees in the forest,' said Rakesh. 'What's so special about this tree? Why do we like it so much?'

'We planted it ourselves,' said Grandfather. 'That's why it's special.'

'Just one small seed,' said Rakesh, and he touched the smooth bark of the tree that had grown. He ran his hand along the trunk of the tree and put his finger to the tip of a leaf. 'I wonder,' he whispered, 'is this what it feels to be God?'

Picnic at Fox-Burn

IN SPITE OF the frenetic building activity in most hill stations, there are still a few ruins to be found on the outskirts—neglected old bungalows that have fallen or been pulled down, and which now provide shelter for bats, owls, stray goats, itinerant sadhus, and sometimes the restless spirits of those who once dwelt in them.

One such ruin is Fox-Burn, but I won't tell you exactly where it can be found, because I visit the place for purposes of meditation (or just plain contemplation) and I would hate to arrive there one morning to find about fifty people picnicking on the grass.

And yet it did witness a picnic of sorts the other day, when the children accompanied me to the ruin. They had heard it was haunted, and they wanted to see the ghost.

Rakesh is twelve, Mukesh is six, and Dolly is four, and they are not afraid of ghosts.

I should mention here that before Fox-Burn became a ruin, back in the 1940s, it was owned by an elderly English woman, Mrs Williams, who ran it as a boarding house for several years. In the end, poor health forced her to give up this work, and during her last years, she lived alone in the huge house, with just a chowkidar to help. Her children, who had grown up on the property, had long since settled in faraway lands.

When Mrs Williams died, the chowkidar stayed on for some time until the property was disposed of; but he left as soon as he could. Late at night there would be a loud rapping on his door, and he would hear the old lady calling out, 'Shamsher Singh, open the door! Open the door, I say, and let me in!'

Needless to say, Shamsher Singh kept the door firmly closed. He returned to his village at the first opportunity. The hill station was going through a slump at the time, and the new owners pulled the house down and sold the roof and beams as scrap.

'What does Fox-Burn mean?' asked Rakesh, as we climbed the neglected, overgrown path to the ruin.

'Well, Burn is a Scottish word meaning stream or spring. Perhaps there was a spring here, once. If so, it dried up long ago.'

'And did a fox live here?'

'Maybe a fox came to drink at the spring. There are still foxes living on the mountain. Sometimes you can see them dancing in the moonlight.'

Passing through a gap in a wall, we came upon the ruins

of the house. In the bright light of a summer morning it did not look in the least spooky or depressing. A line of Doric pillars were all that remained of what must have been an elegant porch and veranda. Beyond them, through the deodars, we could see the distant snows. It must have been a lovely spot in which to spend the better part of one's life. No wonder Mrs Williams wanted to come back.

The children were soon scampering about on the grass, while I sought shelter beneath a huge chestnut tree.

There is no tree so friendly as the chestnut, specially in summer when it is in full leaf.

Mukesh discovered an empty water tank and Rakesh suggested that it had once fed the burn that no longer existed. Dolly busied herself making nosegays with the daisies that grew wild in the grass.

Rakesh looked up suddenly. He pointed to a path on the other side of the ruin, and exclaimed: 'Look, what's that? Is it Mrs Williams?'

'A ghost!' said Mukesh excitedly.

But it turned out to be the local washerwoman, a large white bundle on her head, taking a short cut across the property.

A more peaceful place could hardly be imagined, until a large black dog, a spaniel of sorts, arrived on the scene. He wanted someone to play with—indeed, he insisted on playing—and ran circles round us until we threw sticks for him to fetch and gave him half our sandwiches.

'Whose dog is it?' asked Rakesh.

'I've no idea.'

'Did Mrs Williams keep a black dog?'

'Is it a *ghost* dog?' asked Mukesh.

'It looks real to me,' I said.

'And it's eaten all my biscuits,' said Dolly.

'Don't ghosts have to eat?' asked Mukesh.

'I don't know. We'll have to ask one.'

'It can't be any fun being a ghost if you can't eat,' declared Mukesh.

The black dog left us as suddenly as he had appeared, and as there was no sign of an owner, I began to wonder if he had not, after all, been an apparition.

A cloud came over the sun, the air grew chilly.

'Let's go home,' said Mukesh.

'I'm hungry,' said Rakesh.

'Come along, Dolly,' I called.

But Dolly couldn't be seen.

We called out to her, and looked behind trees and pillars, certain that she was hiding from us. Almost five minutes passed in searching for her, and a sick feeling of apprehension was coming over me, when Dolly emerged from the ruins and ran towards us.

'Where have you been?' we demanded, almost with one voice.

'I was playing—in there—in the old house. Hide-and-seek.'

'On your own?'

'No, there were two children. A boy and a girl. They were playing too.'

'I haven't seen any children,' I said.

'They've gone now.'

'Well, it's time we went too.'

We set off down the winding path, with Rakesh leading the way, and then we had to wait because Dolly had stopped and was waving to someone.

'Who are you waving to, Dolly?'

'To the children.'

'Where are they?'

'Under the chestnut tree.'

'I can't see them. Can you see them, Rakesh? Can you Mukesh?'

Rakesh and Mukesh said they couldn't see any children.

But Dolly was still waving. 'Goodbye,' she called. 'Goodbye!'

Were there voices on the wind? Faint voices calling goodbye?

Could Dolly see something we couldn't see? 'We can't see anyone,' I said.

'No,' said Dolly. 'But they can see me!'

Then she left off her game and joined us, and we ran home laughing. Mrs Williams may not have revisited her old house that day but perhaps her children had been there, playing under the chestnut tree they had known so long ago.

Panther's Moon

I

IN THE ENTIRE village, he was the first to get up. Even the dog, a big hill mastiff called Sheroo, was asleep in a corner of the dark room, curled up near the cold embers of the previous night's fire. Bisnu's tousled head emerged from his blanket. He rubbed the sleep from his eyes and sat up on his haunches. Then, gathering his wits, he crawled in the direction of the loud ticking that came from the battered little clock which occupied the second-most honoured place in a niche in the wall. The most honoured place belonged to a picture of Ganesh, the god of learning, who had an elephant's head and a fat boy's body.

Bringing his face close to the clock, Bisnu could just make out the hands. It was five o'clock. He had half an hour in which to get ready and leave.

He got up, in vest and underpants, and moved quietly towards the door. The soft tread of his bare feet woke Sheroo, and the big, black dog rose silently and padded behind the boy. The door opened and closed, and then the boy and the dog were outside in the early dawn. The month was June, and the nights were warm, even in the Himalayan valleys; but there was fresh dew on the grass. Bisnu felt the dew beneath his feet. He took a deep breath and began walking down to the stream.

The sound of the stream filled the small valley. At that early hour of the morning, it was the only sound; but Bisnu was hardly conscious of it. It was a sound he lived with and took for granted. It was only when he has crossed the hill, on his way to the town—and the sound of the stream grew distant—that he really began to notice it. And it was only when the stream was too far away to be heard that he really missed its sound.

He slipped out of his underclothes, gazed for a few moments at the goose pimples rising on his flesh, and then dashed into the shallow stream. As he went further in, the cold mountain water reached his loins and navel, and he gasped with shock and pleasure. He drifted slowly with the current, swam across to a small inlet which formed a fairly deep pool, and plunged beneath the water. Sheroo hated cold water at this early hour. Had the sun been up, he would not have hesitated to join Bisnu. Now he contented himself with sitting on a smooth rock and gazing placidly at the slim brown boy splashing about in the clear water, in the widening light of dawn.

Bisnu did not stay long in the water. There wasn't time. When he returned to the house, he found his mother up, making tea and chapattis. His sister, Puja, was still asleep. She was a little older than Bisnu, a pretty girl with large black eyes, good teeth and strong arms and legs. During the day, she helped her mother in the house and in the fields. She did not go to the school with Bisnu. But when he came home in the evenings, he would try teaching her some of the things he had learnt. Their father was dead. Bisnu, at twelve, considered himself the head of the family.

He ate two chapattis, after spreading butter-oil on them. He drank a glass of hot sweet tea. His mother gave two thick chapattis to Sheroo, and the dog wolfed them down in a few minutes. Then she wrapped two chapattis and a gourd curry in some big green leaves, and handed these to Bisnu. This was his lunch packet. His mother and Puja would take their meal afterwards.

When Bisnu was dressed, he stood with folded hands before the picture of Ganesh. Ganesh is the god who blesses all beginnings. The author who begins to write a new book, the banker who opens a new ledger, the traveller who starts on a journey, all invoke the kindly help of Ganesh. And as Bisnu made a journey every day, he never left without the goodwill of the elephant-headed god.

How, one might ask, did Ganesh get his elephant's head? When born, he was a beautiful child. Parvati, his mother, was so proud of him that she went about showing him to everyone. Unfortunately, she made the mistake of showing the child to that envious planet, Saturn, who promptly burnt off poor Ganesh's head. Parvati, in despair, went to Brahma, the Creator, for a new head for her son. He had no head to give her but advised her to search for some man or animal caught in a sinful or wrong act. Parvati wandered about until she came upon an elephant sleeping with its head the wrong way, that is, to the south. She promptly removed the elephant's head and planted it on Ganesh's shoulders, where it took root.

Bisnu knew this story. He had heard it from his mother.

Wearing a white shirt and black shorts, and a pair of worn white keds, he was ready for his long walk to school, five miles up the mountain.

His sister woke up just as he was about to leave. She pushed the hair away from her face and gave Bisnu one of her rare smiles.

'I hope you have not forgotten,' she said.

'Forgotten?' said Bisnu, pretending innocence. 'Is there anything I am supposed to remember?'

'Don't tease me. You promised to buy me a pair of bangles, remember? I hope you won't spend the money on sweets, as you did last time.'

'Oh yes, your bangles,' said Bisnu. 'Girls have nothing better to do than waste money on trinkets. Now, don't lose your temper! I'll get them for you. Red and gold are the colours you want?'

'Yes, brother,' said Puja gently, pleased that Bisnu had remembered the colours. 'And for your dinner tonight we'll make you something special. Won't we, Mother?'

'Yes. But hurry up and dress. There is some ploughing

133

to be done today. The rains will soon be here, if the gods are kind.'

'The monsoon will be late this year,' said Bisnu. 'Mr Nautiyal, our teacher, told us so. He said it had nothing to do with the gods.'

'Be off, you are getting late,' said Puja, before Bisnu could begin an argument with his mother. She was diligently winding the old clock. It was quite light in the room. The sun would be up any minute.

Bisnu shouldered his school-bag, kissed his mother, pinched his sister's cheeks, and left the house. He started climbing the steep path up the mountainside. Sheroo bounded ahead; for he, too, always went with Bisnu to school.

Five miles to school. Every day, except Sunday, Bisnu walked five miles to school; and in the evening, he walked home again. There was no school in his own small village of Manjari, for the village consisted of only five families. The nearest school was at Kemptee, a small township on the bus route through the district of Garhwal. A number of boys walked to school, from distances of two or three miles; their villages were not quite as remote as Manjari. But Bisnu's village lay right at the bottom of the mountain, a drop of over two thousand feet from Kemptee. There was no proper road between the village and the town.

In Kemptee, there was a school, a small mission hospital, a post office and several shops. In Manjari village there were none of these amenities. If you were sick, you stayed at home until you got well; if you were *very* sick, you walked or were carried to the hospital, up the five-mile path. If you wanted to buy something, you went without it; but if you wanted it very badly, you could walk the five miles to Kemptee.

Manjari was known as the Five-mile Village.

Twice a week, if there were any letters, a postman came to the village. Bisnu usually passed the postman on his way to and from school.

There were other boys in Manjari village, but Bisnu was the only one who went to school. His mother would not have fussed if he had stayed at home and worked in the fields. That was what the other boys did; all except lazy Chittru, who preferred fishing in the stream or helping himself to the fruit off other people's trees. But Bisnu went to school. He went because he wanted to. No one could force him to go; and no one could stop him from going. He had set his heart on receiving a good schooling. He wanted to read and write as well as anyone in the big world, the world that seemed to begin only where the mountains ended. He felt cut off from the world in his small valley. He would rather live at the top of a mountain than at the bottom of one. That was why he liked climbing to Kemptee, it took him to the top of the mountain; and from its ridge he could look down on his own valley, to the north, and on the wide endless plains stretching towards the south.

The plainsman looks to the hills for the needs of his spirit but the hill man looks to the plains for a living.

Leaving the village and the fields below him, Bisnu climbed steadily up the bare hillside, now dry and brown. By the time the sun was up, he had entered the welcome shade of an oak and rhododendron forest. Sheroo went bounding ahead, chasing squirrels and barking at langurs.

A colony of langurs lived in the oak forest. They fed on oak leaves, acorns, and other green things, and usually remained in the trees, coming down to the ground only to play or bask in the sun. They were beautiful, supple-limbed animals, with black faces and silver-grey coats and long, sensitive tails. They leapt from tree to tree with great agility. The young ones wrestled on the grass like boys.

A dignified community, the langurs did not have the cheekiness or dishonest habits of the red monkeys of the plains; they did not approach dogs or humans. But they had grown used to Bisnu's comings and goings, and did not fear him. Some of the older ones would watch him quietly, a little puzzled. They did not go near the town, because the Kemptee boys threw stones at them. And, anyway, the oak forest gave them all the food they required.

Emerging from the trees, Bisnu crossed a small brook. Here he stopped to drink the fresh clean water of a spring. The brook tumbled down the mountain and joined the river a little below Bisnu's village. Coming from another direction was a second path, and at the junction of the two paths Sarru was waiting for him.

Sarru came from a small village about three miles from Bisnu's and closer to the town. He had two large milk cans slung over his shoulders. Every morning he carried this milk to town, selling one can to the school and the other to Mrs Taylor, the lady doctor at the small mission hospital. He was a little older than Bisnu but not as well-built.

They hailed each other, and Sarru fell into step beside Bisnu. They often met at this spot, keeping each other company for the remaining two miles to Kemptee.

'There was a panther in our village last night,' said Sarru.

This information interested but did not excite Bisnu. Panthers were common enough in the hills and did not usually present a problem except during the winter months, when their natural prey was scarce. Then, occasionally, a panther would take to haunting the outskirts of a village, seizing a careless dog or a stray goat.

'Did you lose any animals?' asked Bisnu.

'No. It tried to get into the cowshed but the dogs set up an alarm. We drove it off.'

'It must be the same one which came around last winter. We lost a calf and two dogs in our village.'

'Wasn't that the one the shikaris wounded? I hope it hasn't become a cattle-lifter.'

'It could be the same. It has a bullet in its leg. These hunters are the people who cause all the trouble. They think it's easy to shoot a panther. It would be better if they missed altogether, but they usually wound it.'

'And then the panther's too slow to catch the barking-deer, and starts on our own animals.'

'We're lucky it didn't become a maneater. Do you remember the maneater six years ago? I was very small then. My father told me all about it. Ten people were killed in our valley alone. What happened to it?'

'I don't know. Some say it poisoned itself when it ate the headman of another village.'

Bisnu laughed. 'No one liked that old villain. He must have been a maneater himself in some previous existence!' They linked arms and scrambled up the stony path. Sheroo began barking and ran ahead. Someone was coming down the path.

It was Mela Ram, the postman.

II

'Any letters for us?' asked Bisnu and Sarru together.

They never received any letters but that did not stop them from asking. It was one way of finding out who had received letters.

'You're welcome to all of them,' said Mela Ram, 'if you'll carry my bag for me.'

'Not today,' said Sarru. 'We're busy today. Is there a letter from Corporal Ghanshyam for his family?'

'Yes, there is a postcard for his people. He is posted on the Ladakh border now and finds it very cold there.'

Postcards, unlike sealed letters, were considered public property and were read by everyone. The senders knew that too, and so Corporal Ghanshyam Singh was careful to mention that he expected a promotion very soon. He wanted everyone in his village to know it.

Mela Ram, complaining of sore feet, continued on his way, and the boys carried on up the path. It was eight o'clock when they reached Kemptee. Dr Taylor's outpatients were just beginning to trickle in at the hospital gate. The doctor was trying to prop up a rose creeper which had blown down during the night. She liked attending to her plants in the mornings, before starting on her patients. She found this helped her in her work. There was a lot in common between ailing plants and ailing people.

Dr Taylor was fifty, white-haired but fresh in the face and full of vitality. She had been in India for twenty years, and ten of these had been spent working in the hill regions.

She saw Bisnu coming down the road. She knew about the boy and his long walk to school and admired him for his keenness and sense of purpose. She wished there were more like him.

Bisnu greeted her shyly. Sheroo barked and put his paws up on the gate.

'Yes, there's a bone for you,' said Dr Taylor. She often put aside bones for the big, black dog, for she knew that Bisnu's people could not afford to give the dog a regular diet of meat—though he did well enough on milk and chapattis.

She threw the bone over the gate and Sheroo caught it before it fell. The school bell began ringing and Bisnu broke into a run. Sheroo loped along behind the boy.

When Bisnu entered the school gate, Sheroo sat down on the grass of the compound. He would remain there until the lunchbreak. He knew of various ways of amusing himself during school hours and had friends among the bazaar dogs. But just then he didn't want company. He had his bone to get on with.

Mr Nautiyal, Bisnu's teacher, was in a bad mood. He was a keen rose grower and only that morning on getting up and looking out of his bedroom window, had been horrified to see a herd of goats in his garden. He had chased them down the road with a stick but the damage had already been done. His prize roses had all been consumed.

Mr Nautiyal had been so upset that he had gone without his breakfast. He had also cut himself whilst shaving. Thus, his mood had gone from bad to worse. Several times during the day he brought down his ruler on the knuckles of any boy who irritated him. Bisnu was one of his best pupils. But even Bisnu irritated him by asking too many questions about a new sum which Mr Nautiyal didn't feel like explaining.

That was the kind of day it was for Mr Nautiyal. Most schoolteachers know similar days.

'Poor Mr Nautiyal,' thought Bisnu. 'I wonder why he's so upset. It must be because of his pay. He doesn't get much money. But he's a good teacher. I hope he doesn't take another job.'

But after Mr Nautiyal had eaten his lunch, his mood improved (as it always did after a meal), and the rest of the day passed serenely. Armed with a bundle of homework, Bisnu came out from the school compound at four o'clock, and was immediately joined by Sheroo. He proceeded down the road in the company of several of his classfellows. But he did not linger long in the bazaar. There were five miles to walk and he did not like to get home too late. Usually, he reached his house just as it was beginning to get dark.

Sarru had gone home long ago and Bisnu had to make the return journey on his own. It was a good opportunity to memorize the words of an English poem he had been asked to learn.

Bisnu had reached the little brook when he remembered the bangles he had promised to buy for his sister.

'Oh, I've forgotten them again,' he said aloud. 'Now I'll catch it—and she's probably made something special for my dinner!'

Sheroo, to whom these words were addressed, paid no attention but bounded off into the oak forest. Bisnu looked around for the monkeys but they were nowhere to be seen.

'Strange,' he thought, 'I wonder why they have disappeared.' He was startled by a sudden sharp cry, followed by a fierce yelp. He knew at once that Sheroo was in trouble. The noise came from the bushes down the khud, into which the dog had rushed but a few seconds previously.

Bisnu jumped off the path and ran down the slope towards the bushes. There was no dog and not a sound. He whistled and called but there was no response. Then he saw something lying on the dry grass. He picked it up. It was a portion of a dog's collar, stained with blood. It was Sheroo's collar and Sheroo's blood.

Bisnu did not search further. He knew, without a doubt, that Sheroo had been seized by a panther. No other animal could have attacked so silently and swiftly and carried off a big dog without a struggle. Sheroo was dead—must have been dead within seconds of being caught and flung into the air. Bisnu knew the danger that lay in wait for him if he followed the blood trail through the trees. The panther would attack anyone who interfered with its meal.

With tears starting in his eyes, Bisnu carried on down the path to the village. His fingers still clutched the little bit of bloodstained collar that was all that was left to him of his dog.

III

Bisnu was not a very sentimental boy but he sorrowed for his dog who had been his companion on many a hike into the hills and forests. He did not sleep that night, but turned restlessly from side to side moaning softly. After some time he felt Puja's hand on his head. She began stroking his brow. He took her hand in his own and the clasp of her rough, warm, familiar hand gave him a feeling of comfort and security.

Next morning, when he went down to the stream to bathe, he missed the presence of his dog. He did not stay long in the water. It wasn't as much fun when there was no Sheroo to watch him.

When Bisnu's mother gave him his food she told him to be careful and hurry home that evening. A panther, even if it is only a cowardly lifter of sheep or dogs, is not to be trifled with. And this particular panther had shown some daring by seizing the dog even before it was dark.

Still, there was no question of staying away from school. If Bisnu remained at home every time a panther put in an appearance, he might just as well stop going to school altogether.

He set off even earlier than usual and reached the meeting of the paths long before Sarru. He did not wait for his friend because he did not feel like talking about the loss of his dog. It was not the day for the postman and so Bisnu reached Kemptee without meeting anyone on the way. He tried creeping past the hospital gate unnoticed but Dr Taylor saw him and the first thing she said was, 'Where's Sheroo? I've got something for him.'

When Dr Taylor saw the boy's face, she knew at once that something was wrong.

'What is it, Bisnu?' she asked. She looked quickly up and down the road. 'Is it Sheroo?'

He nodded gravely.

'A panther took him,' he said.

'In the village?'

'No, while we were walking home through the forest. I did not see anything—but I heard.'

Dr Taylor knew that there was nothing she could say that would console him and she tried to conceal the bone which she had brought out for the dog, but Bisnu noticed her hiding it behind her back and tears welled up in his eyes. He turned away and began running down the road.

His schoolfellows noticed Sheroo's absence and questioned Bisnu. He had to tell them everything. They were full of sympathy but they were also quite thrilled at what had happened and kept pestering Bisnu for all the details. There was a lot of noise in the classroom and Mr Nautiyal had to call for order. When he learnt what had happened, he patted Bisnu on the head and told him that he need not attend school for the rest of the day. But Bisnu did not want to go home. After school, he got into a fight with one of the boys and that helped him forget.

IV

The panther that plunged the village into an atmosphere of gloom and terror may not have been the same panther that took Sheroo. There was no way of knowing, and it would have made no difference, because the panther that came by night and struck at the people of Manjari was that most feared of wild creatures, a maneater.

Nine-year-old Sanjay, son of Kalam Singh, was the first child to be attacked by the panther.

Kalam Singh's house was the last in the village and nearest the stream. Like the other houses, it was quite small, just a room above and a stable below, with steps leading up from outside the house. He lived there with his wife, two sons (Sanjay was the youngest), and his little daughter, Basanti, who had just turned three.

Sanjay had brought his father's cows home after grazing them on the hillside in the company of other children. He had also brought home an edible wild plant which his mother cooked into a tasty dish for their evening meal. They had their food at dusk, sitting on the floor of their single room, and soon after settled down for the night. Sanjay curled up in his favourite spot, with his head near the door, where he got a little fresh air. As the nights were warm, the door was usually left a little ajar. Sanjay's mother piled ash on the embers of the fire and the family was soon asleep.

No one heard the stealthy padding of a panther approaching the door, pushing it wider open. But suddenly there were sounds of a frantic struggle and Sanjay's stifled cries were mixed with the grunts of the panther. Kalam Singh leapt to his feet with a shout. The panther had dragged Sanjay out of the door and was pulling him down the steps when Kalam Singh started battering at the animal with a large stone. The rest of the family screamed in terror, rousing the entire village. A number of men came to Kalam Singh's assistance and the panther was driven off. But Sanjay lay unconscious.

Someone brought a lantern and the boy's mother screamed when she saw her small son with his head lying in a pool of blood. It looked as if the side of his head had been eaten off by the panther. But he was still alive and as Kalam Singh plastered ash on the boy's head to stop the bleeding, he found that though the scalp had been torn off one side of the head, the bare bone was smooth and unbroken.

'He won't live through the night,' said a neighbour. 'We'll have to carry him down to the river in the morning.'

The dead were always cremated on the banks of a small river which flowed past Manjari village.

Suddenly the panther, still prowling about the village, called out in rage and frustration and the villagers rushed to their homes in panic and barricaded themselves in for the night.

Sanjay's mother sat by the boy for the rest of the night, weeping and watching. Towards dawn, he started to moan and show signs of coming round. At this sign of returning consciousness, Kalam Singh rose determinedly and looked around for his stick.

He told his elder son to remain behind with the mother

and daughter as he was going to take Sanjay to Dr Taylor at the hospital.

'See, he is moaning and in pain,' said Kalam Singh. 'That means he has a chance to live if he can be treated at once.'

With a stout stick in his hand, and Sanjay on his back, Kalam Singh set off on the two miles of hard mountain track to the hospital at Kemptee. His son, a blood-stained cloth around his head, was moaning but still unconscious. When at last Kalam Singh climbed up through the last fields below the hospital, he asked for the doctor and stammered out an account of what had happened.

It was a terrible injury, as Dr Taylor discovered. The bone over almost one-third of the head was bare and the scalp was torn all round. As the father told his story, the doctor cleaned and dressed the wound and then gave Sanjay a shot of penicillin to prevent sepsis. Later, Kalam Singh carried the boy home again.

V

After this, the panther went away for some time. But the people of Manjari could not be sure of its whereabouts. They kept to their houses after dark and shut their doors. Bisnu had to stop going to school because there was no one to accompany him and it was dangerous to go alone. This worried him, because his final exam was only a few weeks off and he would be missing important classwork. When he wasn't in the fields, helping with the sowing of rice and maize, he would be sitting in the shade of a chestnut tree, going through his well-thumbed second-hand school books. He had no other reading, except for a copy of the Ramayana and a Hindi translation of *Alice in Wonderland.* These were well preserved, read only in fits and starts, and usually kept locked in his mother's old tin trunk.

Sanjay had nightmares for several nights and woke up screaming. But with the resilience of youth, he quickly recovered. At the end of the week, he was able to walk to the hospital, though his father always accompanied him. Even a desperate panther will hesitate to attack a party of two. Sanjay, with his thin little face and huge bandaged head, looked a pathetic figure but he was getting better and the wound looked healthy.

Bisnu often went to see him and the two boys spent long hours together near the stream. Sometimes Chittru would join them and they would try catching fish with a home-made net. They were often successful in taking home one or two mountain trout. Sometimes Bisnu and Chittru wrestled in the shallow water or on the grassy banks of the stream. Chittru was a chubby boy with a broad chest, strong legs and thighs and when he used his weight, he got Bisnu under him. But Bisnu was hard and wiry and had very strong wrists and fingers. When he had Chittru in a vice, the bigger boy would cry out and give up the struggle. Sanjay could not join in these games.

He had never been a very strong boy and he needed plenty of rest if his wounds were to heal well.

The panther had not been seen for over a week and the

people of Manjari were beginning to hope that it might have moved on over the mountain or further down the valley.

'I think I can start going to school again,' said Bisnu. 'The panther has gone away.'

'Don't be too sure,' said Puja. 'The moon is full these days and perhaps it is only being cautious.'

'Wait a few days,' said their mother. 'It is better to wait. Perhaps you could go the day after tomorrow when Sanjay goes to the hospital with his father. Then you will not be alone.'

And so, two days later, Bisnu went up to Kemptee with Sanjay and Kalam Singh. Sanjay's wound had almost healed over. Little islets of flesh had grown over the bone. Dr Taylor told him that he need come to see her only once a fortnight, instead of every third day.

Bisnu went to his school and was given a warm welcome by his friends and by Mr Nautiyal.

'You'll have to work hard,' said his teacher. 'You have to catch up with the others. If you like, I can give you some extra time after classes.'

'Thank you sir, but it will make me late,' said Bisnu. 'I must get home before it is dark, otherwise my mother will worry. I think the panther has gone but nothing is certain.'

'Well, you mustn't take risks. Do your best, Bisnu. Work hard and you'll soon catch up with your lessons.'

Sanjay and Kalam Singh were waiting for him outside the school. Together they took the path down to Manjari, passing the postman on the way. Mela Ram said he had heard that the panther was in another district and that there was nothing to fear. He was on his rounds again.

Nothing happened on the way. The langurs were back in their favourite part of the forest. Bisnu got home just as the kerosene lamp was being lit. Puja met him at the door with a winsome smile.

'Did you get the bangles?' she asked. But Bisnu had forgotten again.

VI

There had been a thunderstorm and some rain—a short, sharp shower which gave the villagers hope that the monsoon would arrive on time. It brought out the thunder-lilies—pink, crocus-like flowers which sprang up on the hillsides immediately after a summer shower.

Bisnu, on his way home from school, was caught in the rain. He knew the shower would not last so he took shelter in a small cave and, to pass the time, began doing sums, scratching figures in the damp earth with the end of a stick.

When the rain stopped, he came out from the cave and continued down the path. He wasn't in a hurry. The rain had made everything smell fresh and good. The scent from fallen pine needles rose from wet earth. The leaves of the oak trees had been washed clean and a light breeze turned them about, showing their silver undersides. The birds, refreshed and high-spirited, set up a terrific noise. The worst offenders were the yellow-bottomed bulbuls who squabbled and fought in the blackberry bushes. A barbet, high up in the branches of a deodar, set up its querulous, plaintive call. And a flock of bright green parrots came swooping down the hill to settle in a wild plum tree and feast on the unripe fruit. The langurs, too, had been revived by the rain. They leapt friskily from tree to tree greeting Bisnu with little grunts.

He was almost out of the oak forest when he heard a faint bleating. Presently, a little goat came stumbling up the path towards him. The kid was far from home and must have strayed from the rest of the herd. But it was not yet conscious of being lost. It came to Bisnu with a hop, skip and a jump and started nuzzling against his legs like a cat.

'I wonder who you belong to,' mused Bisnu, stroking the little creature. 'You'd better come home with me until someone claims you.'

He didn't have to take the kid in his arms. It was used to humans and followed close at his heels. Now that darkness was coming on, Bisnu walked a little faster.

He had not gone very far when he heard the sawing grunt of a panther.

The sound came from the hill to the right and Bisnu judged the distance to be anything from a hundred to two hundred yards. He hesitated on the path, wondering what to do. Then he picked the kid up in his arms and hurried on in the direction of home and safety.

The panther called again, much closer now. If it was an ordinary panther, it would go away on finding that the kid was with Bisnu. If it was the maneater, it would not hesitate to attack the boy, for no maneater fears a human. There was no time to lose and there did not seem much point in running. Bisnu looked up and down the hillside. The forest was far behind him and there were only a few trees in his vicinity. He chose a spruce.

The branches of the Himalayan spruce are very brittle and snap easily beneath a heavy weight. They were strong enough to support Bisnu's light frame. It was unlikely they would take the weight of a full-grown panther. At least that was what Bisnu hoped.

Holding the kid with one arm, Bisnu gripped a low branch and swung himself up into the tree. He was a good climber. Slowly but confidently he climbed halfway up the tree, until he was about twelve feet above the ground. He couldn't go any higher without risking a fall.

He had barely settled himself in the crook of a branch when the panther came into the open, running into the clearing at a brisk trot. This was no stealthy approach, no wary stalking of its prey. It was the maneater, all right. Bisnu felt a cold shiver run down his spine. He felt a little sick.

The panther stood in the clearing with a slight thrusting forward of the head. This gave it the appearance of gazing intently and rather short-sightedly at some invisible object in the clearing. But there is nothing short-sighted about a panther's vision. Its sight and hearing are acute.

Bisnu remained motionless in the tree and sent up a prayer to all the gods he could think of. But the kid began bleating. The panther looked up and gave its deep-throated, rasping grunt—a fearsome sound, calculated to strike terror in any tree-borne animal. Many a monkey, petrified by a panther's roar, has fallen from its perch to make a meal for Mr Spots. The maneater was trying the same technique on Bisnu. But though the boy was trembling with fright, he clung firmly to the base of the spruce tree.

The panther did not make any attempt to leap into the tree. Perhaps it knew instinctively that this was not the type of tree that it could climb. Instead it described a semicircle round the tree, keeping its face turned towards Bisnu. Then it disappeared into the bushes.

The maneater was cunning. It hoped to put the boy off his guard, perhaps entice him down from the tree. For, a few seconds later, with a half-humorous growl, it rushed back into the clearing and then stopped, staring up at the boy in some surprise. The panther was getting frustrated. It snarled and putting its forefeet up against the tree trunk began scratching at the bark in the manner of an ordinary domestic cat. The tree shook at each thud of the beast's paw.

Bisnu began shouting for help.

The moon had not yet come up. Down in Manjari village, Bisnu's mother and sister stood in their lighted doorway, gazing anxiously up the pathway. Every now and then Puja would turn to take a look at the small clock.

Sanjay's father appeared in a field below. He had a kerosene lantern in his hand.

'Sister, isn't your boy home as yet?' he asked.

'No, he hasn't arrived. We are very worried. He should have been home an hour ago. Do you think the panther will be about tonight? There's going to be a moon.'

'True, but it will be dark for another hour. I will fetch

the other menfolk and we will go up the mountain for your boy. There may have been a landslide during the rain. Perhaps the path has been washed away.'

'Thank you, brother. But arm yourselves, just in case the panther is about.'

'I will take my spear,' said Kalam Singh. 'I have sworn to spear that devil when I find him. There is some evil spirit dwelling in the beast and it must be destroyed!'

'I am coming with you,' said Puja.

'No, you cannot go,' said her mother. 'It's bad enough that Bisnu is in danger. You stay at home with me. This is work for men.'

'I shall be safe with them,' insisted Puja. 'I am going, Mother!' And she jumped down the embankment into the field and followed Sanjay's father through the village.

Ten minutes later, two men armed with axes had joined Kalam Singh in the courtyard of his house and the small party moved silently and swiftly up the mountain path. Puja walked in the middle of the group, holding the lantern. As soon as the village lights were hidden by a shoulder of the hill, the men began to shout—both to frighten the panther, if it was about, and to give themselves courage.

Bisnu's mother closed the front door and turned to the image of Ganesh, for comfort and help.

Bisnu's calls were carried on the wind, and Puja and the men heard him while they were still half a mile away. Their own shouts increased in volume and, hearing their voices, Bisnu felt strength return to his shaking limbs. Emboldened by the approach of his own people, he began shouting insults at the snarling panther, then throwing twigs and small branches at the enraged animal. The kid added its bleats to the boy's shouts, the birds took up the chorus. The langurs squealed and grunted, the searchers shouted themselves hoarse, and the panther howled with rage. The forest had never before been so noisy.

As the search party drew near, they could hear the panther's savage snarls, and hurried, fearing that perhaps Bisnu had been seized. Puja began to run.

'Don't rush ahead, girl,' said Kalam Singh. 'Stay between us.'

The panther, now aware of the approaching humans, stood still in the middle of the clearing, head thrust forward in a familiar stance. There seemed too many men for one panther. When the animal saw the light of the lantern dancing between the trees, it turned, snarled defiance and hate, and without another look at the boy in the tree, disappeared into the bushes. It was not yet ready for a showdown.

VII

Nobody turned up to claim the little goat so Bisnu kept it. A goat was a poor substitute for a dog but, like Mary's lamb, it followed Bisnu wherever he went and the boy couldn't help being touched by its devotion. He took it down to the stream where it would skip about in the shallows and nibble the sweet grass that grew on the banks.

As for the panther, frustrated in its attempt on Bisnu's life, it did not wait long before attacking another human.

It was Chittru who came running down the path one afternoon, babbling excitedly about the panther and the postman.

Chittru, deeming it safe to gather ripe bilberries in the daytime, had walked about half a mile up the path from the village when he had stumbled across Mela Ram's mailbag lying on the ground. Of the postman himself there was no sign. But a trail of blood led through the bushes.

Once again, a party of men headed by Kalam Singh and accompanied by Bisnu and Chittru, went out to look for the postman. But though they found Mela Ram's bloodstained clothes, they could not find his body. The panther had made no mistake this time.

It was to be several weeks before Manjari had a new postman.

A few days after Mela Ram's disappearance, an old woman was sleeping with her head near the open door of her house. She had been advised to sleep inside with the door closed but the nights were hot and anyway the old woman was a little deaf and in the middle of the night, an hour before moonrise, the panther seized her by the throat. Her strangled cry woke her grown-up son and all the men in the village woke up at his shouts and came running.

The panther dragged the old woman out of the house and down the steps but left her when the men approached with their axes and spears and made off into the bushes. The old woman was still alive and the men made a rough stretcher of bamboo and vines and started carrying her up the path. But they had not gone far when she began to cough and because of her terrible throat wounds her lungs collapsed and she died.

It was the 'dark of the month'—the week of the new moon when nights are darkest.

Bisnu, closing the front door and lighting the kerosene lantern, said, 'I wonder where that panther is tonight!'

The panther was busy in another village: Sarru's village.

A woman and her daughter had been out in the evening bedding the cattle down in the stable. The girl had gone into the house and the woman was following. As she bent down to go in at the low door, the panther sprang from the bushes. Fortunately, one of its paws hit the doorpost and broke the force of the attack, or the woman would have been killed. When she cried out, the men came round shouting and the panther slunk off. The woman had deep scratches on her back and was badly shocked.

The next day a small party of villagers presented themselves in front of the magistrate's office at Kemptee and demanded that something be done about the panther. But the magistrate was away on tour and there was no one else in Kemptee who had a gun. Mr Nautiyal met the villagers and promised to write to a well-known shikari, but said that it would be at least a fortnight before the shikari would be able to come.

Bisnu was fretting because he could not go to school. Most boys would be only too happy to miss school but when you are living in a remote village in the mountains and having an education is the only way of seeing the world, you look forward to going to school, even if it is five miles from home. Bisnu's exams were only two weeks off and he didn't want to remain in the same class while the others were promoted. Besides, he knew he could pass even though he had missed a number of lessons. But he had to sit for the exams. He couldn't miss them.

'Cheer up, Bhaiya,' said Puja, as they sat drinking glasses of hot tea after their evening meal. 'The panther may go away once the rains break.'

'Even the rains are late this year,' said Bisnu. 'It's so hot and dry. Can't we open the door?'

'And be dragged down the steps by the panther?' said his mother. 'It isn't safe to have the window open, let alone the door.' And she went to the small window—through which a cat would have found difficulty in passing—and bolted it firmly.

With a sigh of resignation Bisnu threw off all his clothes except his underwear and stretched himself out on the earthen floor.

'We will be rid of the beast soon,' said his mother. 'I know it in my heart. Our prayers will be heard and you shall go to school and pass your exams.'

To cheer up her children, she told them a humorous story which had been handed down to her by her grandmother. It was all about a tiger, a panther and a bear, the three of whom were made to feel very foolish by a thief hiding in the hollow trunk of a banyan tree. Bisnu was sleepy and did not listen very attentively. He dropped off to sleep before the story was finished.

When he woke, it was dark and his mother and sister

were asleep on the cot. He wondered what it was that had woken him. He could hear his sister's easy breathing and the steady ticking of the clock. Far away an owl hooted—an unlucky sign, his mother would have said; but she was asleep and Bisnu was not superstitious.

And then he heard something scratching at the door and the hair on his head felt tight and prickly. It was like a cat scratching, only louder. The door creaked a little whenever it felt the impact of the paw—a heavy paw, as Bisnu could tell from the dull sound it made.

'It's the panther,' he muttered under his breath, sitting up on the hard floor.

The door, he felt, was strong enough to resist the panther's weight. And if he set up an alarm, he could rouse the village. But the middle of the night was no time for the bravest of men to tackle a panther.

In a corner of the room stood a long bamboo stick with a sharp knife tied to one end which Bisnu sometimes used for spearing fish. Crawling on all fours across the room, he grasped the home-made spear and then, scrambling on to a cupboard, he drew level with the skylight window. He could get his head and shoulders through the window.

'What are you doing up there?' said Puja, who had woken up at the sound of Bisnu shuffling about the room. 'Be quiet,' said Bisnu. 'You'll wake Mother.'

Their mother was awake by now. 'Come down from there, Bisnu. I can hear a noise outside.'

'Don't worry,' said Bisnu, who found himself looking down on the wriggling animal which was trying to get its paw in under the door. With his mother and Puja awake, there was no time to lose. He had got the spear through the window, and though he could not manoeuvre it so as to strike the panther's head, he brought the sharp end down with considerable force on the animal's rump.

With a roar of pain and rage the maneater leapt down from the steps and disappeared into the darkness. It did not pause to see what had struck it. Certain that no human could have come upon it in that fashion, it ran fearfully to its lair, howling until the pain subsided.

VIII

A panther is an enigma. There are occasions when he proves himself to be the most cunning animal under the sun and yet the very next day he will walk into an obvious trap that no self-respecting jackal would ever go near. One day a panther will prove himself to be a complete coward and run like a hare from a couple of dogs and the very next he will dash in amongst half a dozen men sitting round a campfire and inflict terrible injuries on them.

It is not often that a panther is taken by surprise, as his power of sight and hearing are very acute. He is a master in the art of camouflage and his spotted coat is admirably suited for the purpose. He does not need heavy jungle to hide in. A couple of bushes and the light and shade from surrounding trees are enough to make him almost invisible.

Because the Manjari panther had been fooled by Bisnu, it did not mean that he was a stupid panther. It simply meant that he had been a little careless. And Bisnu and Puja, growing in confidence since their midnight encounter with the animal, became a little careless themselves.

Puja was hoeing the last field above the house and Bisnu, at the other end of the same field, was chopping up several branches of green oak, prior to leaving the wood to dry in the loft. It was late afternoon and the descending sun glinted in patches on the small river. It was a time of day when only the most desperate and daring of maneaters would be likely to show itself.

Pausing for a moment to wipe the sweat from his brow, Bisnu glanced up at the hillside and his eye caught sight of a rock on the brow of the hill which seemed unfamiliar to him. Just as he was about to look elsewhere, the round rock began to grow and then alter its shape and Bisnu, watching in fascination, was at last able to make out the head and forequarters of the panther. It looked enormous from the angle at which he saw it and for a moment he thought it was a tiger. But Bisnu knew instinctively that it was the maneater.

Slowly the wary beast pulled itself to its feet and began to walk round the side of the great rock. For a second it disappeared and Bisnu wondered if it had gone away. Then it reappeared and the boy was all excitement again. Very slowly and silently the panther walked across the face of the rock until it was in direct line with the corner of the field where Puja was working.

With a thrill of horror Bisnu realized that the panther was stalking his sister. He shook himself free from the spell which had woven itself round him and shouting hoarsely ran forward.

'Run, Puja, run!' he called. 'It's on the hill above you!'

Puja turned to see what Bisnu was shouting about. She saw him gesticulate to the hill behind her, looked up just in time to see the panther crouching for his spring.

With great presence of mind, she leapt down the banking of the field and tumbled into an irrigation ditch.

The springing panther missed its prey, lost its foothold on the slippery shale banking and somersaulted into the ditch a few feet away from Puja. Before the animal could recover from its surprise, Bisnu was dashing down the slope, swinging his axe and shouting 'Maro, maro!' (Kill, kill!).

Two men came running across the field. They, too, were armed with axes. Together with Bisnu they made a half-circle around the snarling animal which turned at bay and plunged at them in order to get away. Puja wriggled along the ditch on her stomach. The men aimed their axes at the panther's head and Bisnu had the satisfaction of getting in a well-aimed blow between the eyes. The animal then charged straight at one of the men, knocked him over, and tried to get at his throat. Just then Sanjay's father arrived with his long spear. He plunged the end of the spear into the panther's neck.

The panther left its victim and ran into the bushes, dragging the spear through the grass and leaving a trail of blood on the ground. The men followed cautiously—all except the man who had been wounded and who lay on the ground while Puja and the other womenfolk rushed up to help him.

The panther had made for the bed of the stream and Bisnu, Sanjay's father, and their companion were able to follow it quite easily. The water was red where the panther had crossed the stream, and the rocks were stained with blood. After they had gone downstream for about a furlong, they found the panther lying still on its side at the edge of the water. It was mortally wounded but it continued to wave its tail like an angry cat. Then even the tail lay still.

'It is dead,' said Bisnu. 'It will not trouble us again in this body.'

'Let us be certain,' said Sanjay's father and he bent down and pulled the panther's tail.

There was no response.

'It is dead,' said Kalam Singh. 'No panther would suffer such an insult were it alive!'

They cut down a long piece of thick bamboo and tied the panther to it by its feet. Then, with their enemy hanging upside down from the bamboo pole, they started back for the village.

'There will be a feast at my house tonight,' said Kalam Singh. 'Everyone in the village must come. And tomorrow we will visit all the villages in the valley and show them the dead panther so that they may move about again without fear.'

'We can sell the skin in Kemptee,' said their companion. 'It will fetch a good price.'

'But the claws we will give to Bisnu,' said Kalam Singh, putting his arm around the boy's shoulders. 'He has done a man's work today. He deserves the claws.'

A panther's or tiger's claws are considered to be lucky charms.

'I will take only three claws,' said Bisnu. 'One each for my mother and sister, and one for myself. You may give the others to Sanjay and Chittru and the smaller children.'

As the sun set, a big fire was lit in the middle of the village of Manjari and the people gathered round it, singing and laughing. Kalam Singh killed his fattest goat and there was meat for everyone.

IX

Bisnu was on his way home. He had just handed in his first paper, arithmetic, which he had found quite easy. Tomorrow, it would be algebra and when he got home he would have to practise square roots and cube roots and fractional coefficients. Mr Nautiyal and the entire class had been happy that he had been able to sit for the exams. He was also a hero to them for his part in killing the panther. The story had spread through the villages with the rapidity of a forest fire, a fire which was now raging in Kemptee town.

When he walked past the hospital, he was whistling cheerfully. Dr Taylor waved to him from the veranda steps.

'How is Sanjay now?' she asked.

'He is well,' said Bisnu.

'And your mother and sister?'

'They are well,' said Bisnu.

'Are you going to get yourself a new dog?'

'I am thinking about it,' said Bisnu. 'At present I have a baby goat—I am teaching it to swim!'

He started down the path to the valley. Dark clouds had gathered and there was a rumble of thunder. A storm was imminent.

'Wait for me!' shouted Sarru, running down the path behind Bisnu, his milk pails clanging against each other. He fell into step beside Bisnu.

'Well, I hope we don't have any more maneaters for some time,' he said. 'I've lost a lot of money by not being able to take milk up to Kemptee.'

'We should be safe as long as a shikari doesn't wound another panther. There was an old bullet wound in the maneater's thigh. That's why it couldn't hunt in the forest. The deer were too fast for it.'

'Is there a new postman yet?'

'He starts tomorrow. A cousin of Mela Ram's.'

When they reached the parting of their ways, it had begun to rain a little.

'I must hurry,' said Sarru. 'It's going to get heavier any minute.'

'I feel like getting wet,' said Bisnu. 'This time it's the monsoon, I'm sure.'

Bisnu entered the forest on his own and at the same time the rain came down in heavy opaque sheets. The trees shook in the wind and the langurs chattered with excitement.

It was still pouring when Bisnu emerged from the forest, drenched to the skin. But the rain stopped suddenly, just as the village of Manjari came in view. The sun appeared through a rift in the clouds. The leaves and the grass gave out a sweet, fresh smell.

Bisnu could see his mother and sister in the field transplanting the rice seedlings. The menfolk were driving the yoked oxen through the thin mud of the fields, while the children hung on to the oxen's tails, standing on the plain wooden harrows, and with weird cries and shouts sending the animals almost at a gallop along the narrow terraces.

Bisnu felt the urge to be with them, working in the fields. He ran down the path, his feet falling softly on the wet earth. Puja saw him coming and waved to him. She met him at the edge of the field.

'How did you find your paper today?' she asked.

'Oh, it was easy.' Bisnu slipped his hand into hers and together they walked across the field. Puja felt something smooth and hard against her fingers and before she could see what Bisnu was doing, he had slipped a pair of bangles over her wrist.

'I remembered,' he said with a sense of achievement.

Puja looked at the bangles and burst out, 'But they are blue, Bhai, and I wanted red and gold bangles!' And then, when she saw him looking crestfallen, she hurried on, 'But they are very pretty and you did remember . . . Actually, they're just as nice as red and gold bangles! Come into the house when you are ready. I have made something special for you.'

'I am coming,' said Bisnu, turning towards the house. 'You don't know how hungry a man gets, walking five miles to reach home!'

The Leopard

I FIRST SAW the leopard when I was crossing the small stream at the bottom of the hill.

The ravine was so deep that for most of the day it remained in shadow. This encouraged many birds and animals to emerge from cover during the daylight hours. Few people ever passed that way: only milkmen and charcoal-burners from the surrounding villages. As a result, the ravine had become a little haven of wildlife, one of the few natural sanctuaries left near Mussoorie, a hill station in northern India.

Below my cottage was a forest of oak and maple and Himalayan rhododendron. A narrow path twisted its way down through the trees, over an open ridge where red sorrel grew wild, and then steeply down through a tangle of wild raspberries, creeping vines and slender bamboo. At the bottom of the hill the path led on to a grassy verge, surrounded by wild dog roses. (It is surprising how closely the flora of the lower Himalayas, between 5,000 and 8,000 feet, resembles that of the English countryside.)

The stream ran close by the verge, tumbling over smooth pebbles, over rocks worn yellow with age, on its way to the plains and to the little Song River and, finally, to the sacred Ganga.

When I first discovered the stream it was early April and the wild roses were flowering—small white blossoms lying in clusters.

I walked down to the stream almost every day after two or three hours of writing. I had lived in cities too long and had returned to the hills to renew myself, both physically and mentally. Once you have lived with mountains for any length of time you belong to them, and must return again and again.

Nearly every morning, and sometimes during the day, I heard the cry of the barking deer. And in the evening, walking through the forest, I disturbed parties of pheasant. The birds went gliding down the ravine on open, motionless wings. I saw pine martens and a handsome red fox, and I recognized the footprints of a bear.

As I had not come to take anything from the forest, the birds and animals soon grew accustomed to my presence; or possibly they recognized my footsteps. After some time, my approach did not disturb them.

The langurs in the oak and rhododendron trees, who would at first go leaping through the branches at my approach, now watched me with some curiosity as they munched the tender green shoots of the oak. The young ones scuffled and wrestled like boys while their parents groomed each other's coats, stretching themselves out on the sunlit hillside.

But one evening, as I passed, I heard them chattering in the trees, and I knew I was not the cause of their excitement. As I crossed the stream and began climbing the hill, the grunting and chattering increased, as though the langurs were trying to warn me of some hidden danger. A shower of pebbles came rattling down the steep hillside, and I looked up to see a sinewy, orange-gold leopard poised on a rock about twenty feet above me.

It was not looking towards me but had its head thrust attentively forward, in the direction of the ravine. Yet it must have sensed my presence because it slowly turned its head and looked down at me.

It seemed a little puzzled at my presence there; and when, to give myself courage, I clapped my hands sharply, the leopard sprang away into the thickets, making absolutely no sound as it melted into the shadows.

I had disturbed the animal in its quest for food. But a little later I heard the quickening cry of a barking-deer as it fled through the forest. The hunt was still on.

The leopard, like other members of the cat family, is nearing extinction in India, and I was surprised to find one so close to Mussoorie. Probably the deforestation that had been taking place in the surrounding hills had driven the deer into this green valley; and the leopard, naturally, had followed.

It was some weeks before I saw the leopard again,

although I was often made aware of its presence. A dry, rasping cough sometimes gave it away. At times I felt almost certain that I was being followed.

Once, when I was late getting home, and the brief twilight gave way to a dark moonless night, I was startled by a family of porcupines running about in a clearing. I looked around nervously and saw two bright eyes staring at me from a thicket. I stood still, my heart banging away against my ribs. Then the eyes danced away and I realized that they were only fireflies.

In May and June, when the hills were brown and dry, it was always cool and green near the stream, where ferns and maidenhair and long grasses continued to thrive.

Downstream, I found a small pool where I could bathe, and a cave with water dripping from the roof, the water spangled gold and silver in the shafts of sunlight that pushed through the slits in the cave roof.

'He maketh me to lie down in green pastures: he leadeth me beside the still waters.' Perhaps David had discovered a similar paradise when he wrote those words; perhaps I, too, would write good words. The hill station's summer visitors had not discovered this haven of wild and green things. I was beginning to feel that the place belonged to me, that dominion was mine.

The stream had at least one other regular visitor, a spotted forktail, and though it did not fly away at my approach, it became restless if I stayed too long, and then it would move from boulder to boulder uttering a long complaining cry.

I spent an afternoon trying to discover the bird's nest,

which I was certain contained young ones, because I had seen the forktail carrying grubs in her bill. The problem was that when the bird flew upstream I had difficulty in following her rapidly enough as the rocks were sharp and slippery.

Eventually, I decorated myself with bracken fronds and, after slowly making my way upstream, hid myself in the hollow stump of a tree at a spot where the forktail often disappeared. I had no intention of robbing the bird. I was simply curious to see its home.

By crouching down, I was able to command a view of a small stretch of the stream and the side of the ravine; but I had done little to deceive the forktail, who continued to object strongly to my presence so near her home.

I summoned up my reserves of patience and sat perfectly still for about ten minutes. The forktail quietened down. Out of sight, out of mind. But where had she gone? Probably into the walls of the ravine where, I felt sure, she was guarding her nest.

I decided to take her by surprise and stood up suddenly, in time to see not the forktail on her doorstep but the leopard bounding away with a grunt of surprise! Two urgent springs, and it had crossed the stream and plunged into the forest.

I was as astonished as the leopard, and forgot all about the forktail and her nest. Had the leopard been following me again? I decided against this possibility. Only maneaters follow humans and, as far as I knew, there had never been a maneater in the vicinity of Mussoorie.

During the monsoon the stream became a rushing

torrent, bushes and small trees were swept away, and the friendly murmur of the water became a threatening boom. I did not visit the place too often as there were leeches in the long grass.

One day I found the remains of a barking deer which had only been partly eaten. I wondered why the leopard had not hidden the rest of his meal, and decided that it must have been disturbed while eating.

Then, climbing the hill, I met a party of hunters resting beneath the oaks. They asked me if I had seen a leopard. I said I had not. They said they knew there was a leopard in the forest.

Leopard skins, they told me, were selling in Delhi at over 1,000 rupees each. Of course there was a ban on the export of skins, but they gave me to understand that there were ways and means . . . I thanked them for their information and walked on, feeling uneasy and disturbed.

The hunters had seen the carcass of the deer, and they had seen the leopard's pug-marks, and they kept coming to the forest. Almost every evening I heard their guns banging away; for they were ready to fire at almost anything.

'There's a leopard about,' they always told me. 'You should carry a gun.'

'I don't have one,' I said.

There were fewer birds to be seen, and even the langurs had moved on. The red fox did not show itself; and the pine martens, who had become quite bold, now dashed into hiding at my approach. The smell of one human is like the smell of any other.

And then the rains were over and it was October; I could lie in the sun, on sweet-smelling grass, and gaze up through a pattern of oak leaves into a blinding blue heaven. And I would praise God for leaves and grass and the smell of things—the smell of mint and bruised clover—and the touch of things—the touch of grass and air and sky, the touch of the sky's blueness.

I thought no more of the men. My attitude towards them was similar to that of the denizens of the forest. These were men, unpredictable, and to be avoided if possible.

On the other side of the ravine rose Pari Tibba, Hill of the Fairies; a bleak, scrub-covered hill where no one lived.

It was said that in the previous century Englishmen had tried building their houses on the hill, but the area had always attracted lightning, due to either the hill's location or due to its mineral deposits; after several houses had been struck by lightning, the settlers had moved on to the next hill, where the town now stands.

To the hillmen it is Pari Tibba, haunted by the spirits of a pair of ill-fated lovers who perished there in a storm; to others it is known as Burnt Hill, because of its scarred and stunted trees.

One day, after crossing the stream, I climbed Pari Tibba—a stiff undertaking, because there was no path to the top and I had to scramble up a precipitous rock face with the help of rocks and roots that were apt to come loose in my groping hand.

But at the top was a plateau with a few pine trees, their upper branches catching the wind and humming softly.

There I found the ruins of what must have been the houses of the first settlers—just a few piles of rubble, now overgrown with weeds, sorrel, dandelions and nettles.

As I walked through the roofless ruins, I was struck by the silence that surrounded me, the absence of birds and animals, the sense of complete desolation.

The silence was so absolute that it seemed to be ringing in my ears. But there was something else of which I was becoming increasingly aware: the strong feline odour of one of the cat family. I paused and looked about. I was alone. There was no movement of dry leaf or loose stone.

The ruins were for the most part open to the sky. Their rotting rafters had collapsed, jamming together to form a low passage like the entrance to a mine and this dark cavern seemed to lead down into the ground. The smell was stronger when I approached this spot, so I stopped again and waited there, wondering if I had discovered the lair of the leopard, wondering if the animal was now at rest after a night's hunt. Perhaps he was crouching there in the dark, watching me, recognizing me, knowing me as the man who walked alone in the forest without a weapon.

I like to think that he was there, that he knew me, and that he acknowledged my visit in the friendliest way: by ignoring me altogether.

Perhaps I had made him confident—too confident, too careless, too trusting of the human in his midst. I did not venture any further; I was not out of my mind. I did not seek physical contact, or even another glimpse of that beautiful sinewy body, springing from rock to rock. It was his trust I wanted, and I think he gave it to me.

But did the leopard, trusting one man, make the mistake of bestowing his trust on others? Did I, by casting out all fear—my own fear, and the leopard's protective fear—leave him defenceless?

Because next day, coming up the path from the stream, shouting and beating drums, were the hunters. They had a long bamboo pole across their shoulders; and slung from the pole, feet up, head down, was the lifeless body of the leopard, shot in the neck and in the head.

'We told you there was a leopard!' they shouted, in great good humour. 'Isn't he a fine specimen?'

'Yes,' I said. 'He was a beautiful leopard.'

I walked home through the silent forest. It was very silent, almost as though the birds and animals knew that their trust had been violated.

I remembered the lines of a poem by D.H. Lawrence; and, as I climbed the steep and lonely path to my home, the words beat out their rhythm in my mind: 'There was room in the world for a mountain lion and me.'

The Thief

I WAS STILL a thief when I met Arun and though I was only fifteen, I was an experienced and fairly successful hand.

Arun was watching the wrestlers when I approached him. He was about twenty, a tall, lean fellow, and he looked kind and simple enough for my purpose. I hadn't had much luck of late and thought I might be able to get into this young person's confidence. He seemed quite fascinated by the wrestling. Two well-oiled men slid about in the soft mud, grunting and slapping their thighs. When I drew Arun into conversation, he didn't seem to realize I was a stranger.

'You look like a wrestler yourself,' I said.

'So do you,' he replied, which put me out of my stride for a moment because at the time I was rather thin and bony and not very impressive physically.

'Yes,' I said. 'I wrestle sometimes.'

'What's your name?'

'Deepak,' I lied.

Deepak was about my fifth name. I had earlier called myself Ranbir, Sudhir, Trilok and Surinder.

After this preliminary exchange, Arun confined himself to comments on the match, and I didn't have much to say. After a while he walked away from the crowd of spectators. I followed him.

'Hello,' he said. 'Enjoying yourself?'

I gave him my most appealing smile. 'I want to work for you,' I said.

He didn't stop walking. 'And what makes you think I want someone to work for me?'

'Well,' I said, 'I've been wandering about all day looking for the best person to work for. When I saw you, I knew that no one else had a chance.'

'You flatter me,' he said. 'That's all right.'

'But you can't work for me.'

'Why not?'

'Because I can't pay you.'

I thought that over for a minute. Perhaps I had misjudged my man.

'Can you feed me?' I asked.

'Can you cook?' he countered.

'I can cook,' I lied.

'If you can cook,' he said, 'I'll feed you.'

He took me to his room and told me I could sleep in the veranda. But I was nearly back on the street that night. The meal I cooked must have been pretty awful because Arun gave it to the neighbour's cat and told me to be off. But I just hung around smiling in my most appealing way and then he couldn't help laughing. He sat down on the bed and laughed for a full five minutes and later patted me on the head and said, never mind, he'd teach me to cook in the morning.

Not only did he teach me to cook but he taught me to write my name and his and said he would soon teach me to write whole sentences and add money on paper when you didn't have any in your pocket!

It was quite pleasant working for Arun. I made the tea in the morning and later went out shopping. I would take my time buying the day's supplies and make a profit of about twenty-five paise a day. I would tell Arun that rice was fifty-six paise a pound (it generally was), but I would get it at fifty paise a pound. I think he knew I made a little this way but he didn't mind. He wasn't giving me a regular wage.

I was really grateful to Arun for teaching me to write. I knew that once I could write like an educated man, there would be no limit to what I could achieve. It might even be an incentive to be honest.

Arun made money by fits and starts. He would be borrowing one week, lending the next. He would keep worrying about his next cheque but as soon as it arrived, he would go out and celebrate lavishly.

One evening he came home with a wad of notes and at night, I saw him tuck the bundles under his mattress at the head of the bed.

I had been working for Arun for nearly a fortnight and, apart from the shopping, hadn't done much to exploit him. I had every opportunity for doing so. I had a key to the front door which meant I had access to the room whenever Arun was out. He was the most trusting person I had ever met. And that was why I couldn't make up my mind to rob him.

It's easy to rob a greedy man because he deserves to be robbed. It's easy to rob a rich man because he can afford to be robbed. But it's difficult to rob a poor man, even one who really doesn't care if he's robbed. A rich man or a greedy man or a careful man wouldn't keep his money under a pillow or mattress. He'd lock it up in a safe place. Arun had put his money where it would be child's play for me to remove it without his knowledge.

It's time I did some real work, I told myself. I'm getting out of practice . . . If I don't take the money, he'll only waste it on his friends . . . He doesn't even pay me . . .

Arun was asleep. Moonlight came in from the veranda and fell across the bed. I sat up on the floor, my blanket wrapped round me, considering the situation. There was quite a lot of money in that wad and if I took it, I would have to leave town—I might take the 10.30 express to Amritsar . . .

Slipping out of the blanket, I crept on all fours through the door and up to the bed and peeped at Arun. He was sleeping peacefully with a soft and easy breathing. His face was clear and unlined. Even I had more markings on my face, though mine were mostly scars.

My hand took on an identity of its own as it slid around under the mattress, the fingers searching for the notes. They found them and I drew them out without a crackle.

Arun sighed in his sleep and turned on his side, towards me. My free hand was resting on the bed and his hair touched my fingers.

I was frightened when his hair touched my fingers, and crawled quickly and quietly out of the room.

When I was in the street, I began to run. I ran down the bazaar road to the station. The shops were all closed but a few lights were on in the upper windows. I had the notes at my waist, held there by the string of my pyjamas. I felt I had to stop and count the notes though I knew it might make me late for the train. It was already 10.20 by the clock tower. I slowed down to a walk and my fingers flicked through the notes. There were about a hundred rupees in fives. A good haul. I could live like a prince for a month or two.

When I reached the station I did not stop at the ticket office (I had never bought a ticket in my life) but dashed straight onto the platform. The Amritsar Express was just moving out. It was moving slowly enough for me to be able to jump on the footboard of one of the carriages but I hesitated for some urgent, unexplainable reason.

I hesitated long enough for the train to leave without me.

When it had gone and the noise and busy confusion of the platform had subsided, I found myself standing alone on the deserted platform. The knowledge that I had a hundred stolen rupees in my pyjamas only increased my feeling of isolation and loneliness. I had no idea where to spend the night. I had never kept any friends because sometimes friends can be one's undoing. I didn't want to make myself conspicuous by staying at a hotel. And the only person I knew really well in town was the person I had robbed!

Leaving the station, I walked slowly through the bazaar keeping to dark, deserted alleys. I kept thinking of Arun. He would still be asleep, blissfully unaware of his loss.

I have made a study of men's faces when they have lost something of material value. The greedy man shows panic, the rich man shows anger, the poor man shows fear. But I knew that neither panic nor anger nor fear would show on Arun's face when he discovered the theft; only a terrible sadness, not for the loss of the money but for my having betrayed his trust.

I found myself on the maidan and sat down on a bench with my feet tucked up under my haunches. The night was a little cold and I regretted not having brought Arun's blanket along. A light drizzle added to my discomfort. Soon it was raining heavily. My shirt and pyjamas stuck to my skin and a cold wind brought the rain whipping across my face. I told myself that sleeping on a bench was something I should have been used to by now but the veranda had softened me.

I walked back to the bazaar and sat down on the steps of a closed shop. A few vagrants lay beside me, rolled up tight in thin blankets. The clock showed midnight. I felt for the notes. They were still with me but had lost their crispness and were damp with rainwater.

Arun's money. In the morning he would probably have given me a rupee to go to the pictures but now I had it all. No more cooking his meals, running to the bazaar, or learning to write whole sentences. Whole sentences . . .

They were something I had forgotten in the excitement of a hundred rupees. Whole sentences, I knew, could one day bring me more than a hundred rupees. It was a simple matter to steal (and sometimes just as simple to be caught) but to be a really big man, a wise and successful man, that was something. I should go back to Arun, I told myself, if only to learn how to write.

Perhaps it was also concern for Arun that drew me back. A sense of sympathy is one of my weaknesses, and through hesitation over a theft I had often been caught. A successful thief must be pitiless. I was fond of Arun. My affection for him, my sense of sympathy, but most of all my desire to write whole sentences, drew me back to the room.

I hurried back to the room extremely nervous, for it is easier to steal something than to return it undetected. If I was caught beside the bed now, with the money in my hand, or with my hand under the mattress, there could be only one explanation: that I was actually stealing. If Arun woke up, I would be lost.

I opened the door clumsily and stood in the doorway in clouded moonlight. Gradually, my eyes became accustomed to the darkness of the room. Arun was still asleep. I went on all fours again and crept noiselessly to the head of the bed. My hand came up with the notes. I felt his breath on my fingers. I was fascinated by his tranquil features and easy breathing and remained motionless for a minute. Then my hand explored the mattress, found the edge, slipped under it with the notes.

I awoke late next morning to find that Arun had already

made the tea. I found it difficult to face him in the harsh light of day. His hand was stretched out towards me. There was a five-rupee note between his fingers. My heart sank.

'I made some money yesterday,' he said. 'Now you'll get paid regularly.' My spirit rose as rapidly as it had fallen. I congratulated myself on having returned the money.

But when I took the note, I realized that he knew everything.

The note was still wet from last night's rain.

'Today I'll teach you to write a little more than your name,' he said.

He knew but neither his lips nor his eyes said anything about their knowing.

I smiled at Arun in my most appealing way. And the smile came by itself, without my knowing it.

The Fight

RANJI HAD BEEN less than a month in Rajpur when he discovered the pool in the forest. It was the height of summer, and his school had not yet opened, and, having as yet made no friends in this semi-hill station, he wandered about a good deal by himself into the hills and forests that stretched away interminably on all sides of the town. It was hot, very hot, at that time of the year, and Ranji walked about in his vest and shorts, his brown feet white with the chalky dust that flew up from the ground. The earth was parched, the grass brown, the trees listless, hardly stirring, waiting for a cool wind or a refreshing shower of rain.

It was on such a day—a hot, tired day—that Ranji found the pool in the forest. The water had a gentle translucency, and you could see the smooth round pebbles at the bottom of the pool. A small stream emerged from a cluster of rocks to feed the pool. During the monsoon, this stream would be a gushing torrent, cascading down from the hills, but during the summer, it was barely a trickle. The rocks, however, held the water in the pool, and it did not dry up like the pools in the plains.

When Ranji saw the pool, he did not hesitate to get into it.

He had often gone swimming, alone or with friends, when he had lived with his parents in a thirsty town in the middle of the Rajputana desert. There, he had known only sticky, muddy pools, where buffaloes wallowed and women washed clothes. He had never seen a pool like this—so clean and cold and inviting. He threw off all his clothes, as he had done when he went swimming in the plains, and leapt into the water. His limbs were supple, free of any fat, and his dark body glistened in patches of sunlit water.

The next day he came again to quench his body in the cool waters of the forest pool. He was there for almost an hour, sliding in and out of the limpid green water, or lying stretched out on the smooth yellow rocks in the shade of broad-leaved sal trees. It was while he lay thus, naked on a rock, that he noticed another boy standing a little distance away, staring at him in a rather hostile manner. The other boy was a little older than Ranji, taller, thickset, with a broad nose and thick, red lips. He had only just noticed Ranji, and he stood at the edge of the pool, wearing a pair of bathing shorts, waiting for Ranji to explain himself.

When Ranji did not say anything, the other called out, 'What are you doing here, Mister?'

Ranji, who was prepared to be friendly, was taken aback at the hostility of the other's tone.

'I am swimming,' he replied. 'Why don't you join me?'

'I always swim alone,' said the other. 'This is my pool, I did not invite you here. And why are you not wearing any clothes?'

'It is not your business if I do not wear clothes. I have nothing to be ashamed of.'

'You skinny fellow, put on your clothes.'

'Fat fool, take yours off.'

This was too much for the stranger to tolerate. He strode up to Ranji, who still sat on the rock and, planting his broad feet firmly on the sand, said (as though this would settle the matter once and for all), 'Don't you know I am a Punjabi? I do not take replies from villagers like you!'

'So you like to fight with villagers?' said Ranji. 'Well, I am not a villager. I am a Rajput!'

'I am a Punjabi!'

'I am a Rajput!'

They had reached an impasse. One had said he was a Punjabi, the other had proclaimed himself a Rajput. There was little else that could be said.

'You understand that I am a Punjabi?' said the stranger, feeling that perhaps this information had not penetrated Ranji's head.

'I have heard you say it three times,' replied Ranji. 'Then why are you not running away?'

'I am waiting for *you* to run away!'

'I will have to beat you,' said the stranger, assuming a

violent attitude, showing Ranji the palm of his hand.

'I am waiting to see you do it,' said Ranji.

'You will see me do it,' said the other boy.

Ranji waited. The other boy made a strange, hissing sound. They stared each other in the eye for almost a minute. Then the Punjabi boy slapped Ranji across the face with all the force he could muster. Ranji staggered, feeling quite dizzy. There were thick red finger marks on his cheek.

'There you are!' exclaimed his assailant. 'Will you be off now?'

For answer, Ranji swung his arm up and pushed a hard, bony fist into the other's face.

And then they were at each other's throats, swaying on the rock, tumbling on to the sand, rolling over and over, their legs and arms locked in a desperate, violent struggle. Gasping and cursing, clawing and slapping, they rolled right into the shallows of the pool.

Even in the water the fight continued as, spluttering and covered with mud, they groped for each other's head and throat. But after five minutes of frenzied, unscientific struggle, neither boy had emerged victorious. Their bodies heaving with exhaustion, they stood back from each other, making tremendous efforts to speak.

'Now—now do you realize—I am a Punjabi?' gasped the stranger.

'Do you know I am a Rajput?' said Ranji with difficulty.

They gave a moment's consideration to each other's answers and, in that moment of silence, there was only their heavy breathing and the rapid beating of their hearts.

'Then you will not leave the pool?' said the Punjabi boy.

'I will not leave it,' said Ranji.

'Then we shall have to continue the fight,' said the other.

'All right,' said Ranji.

But neither boy moved, neither took the initiative. The Punjabi boy had an inspiration.

'We will continue the fight tomorrow,' he said. 'If you dare to come here again tomorrow, we will continue this fight, and I will not show you mercy as I have done today.'

'I will come tomorrow,' said Ranji. 'I will be ready for you.'

They turned from each other then and, going to their respective rocks, put on their clothes, and left the forest by different routes.

When Ranji got home, he found it difficult to explain the cuts and bruises that showed on his face, leg and arms. It was difficult to conceal the fact that he had been in an unusually violent fight, and his mother insisted on his staying at home for the rest of the day. That evening, though, he slipped out of the house and went to the bazaar, where he found comfort and solace in a bottle of vividly coloured lemonade and a banana-leaf full of hot, sweet jalebis. He had just finished the lemonade when he saw his adversary coming down the road. His first impulse was to turn away and look elsewhere, his second to throw the lemonade bottle at his enemy. But he did neither of these things. Instead, he stood his ground and scowled at his passing adversary. And the Punjabi boy said nothing either, but scowled back with equal ferocity.

The next day was as hot as the previous one. Ranji felt weak and lazy and not at all eager for a fight. His body was stiff and sore after the previous day's encounter. But he could not refuse the challenge. Not to turn up at the pool would be an acknowledgement of defeat. From the way he felt just then, he knew he would be beaten in another fight. But he could not acquiesce in his own defeat. He must defy his enemy to the last, or outwit him, for only then could he gain his respect. If he surrendered now, he would be beaten for all time; but to fight and be beaten today left him free to fight and be beaten again. As long as he fought, he had a right to the pool in the forest.

He was half hoping that the Punjabi boy would have forgotten the challenge, but these hopes were dashed when he saw his opponent sitting, stripped to the waist, on a rock on the other side of the pool. The Punjabi boy was rubbing oil on his body, massaging it into his broad thighs. He saw Ranji beneath the sal trees, and called a challenge across the waters of the pool.

'Come over on this side and fight!' he shouted.

But Ranji was not going to submit to any conditions laid down by his opponent.

'Come *this* side and fight!' he shouted back with equal vigour.

'Swim across and fight me here!' called the other. 'Or perhaps you cannot swim the length of this pool?'

But Ranji could have swum the length of the pool a dozen times without tiring, and here he would show the

Punjabi boy his superiority. So, slipping out of his vest and shorts, he dived straight into the water, cutting through it like a knife, and surfaced with hardly a splash. The Punjabi boy's mouth hung open in amazement.

'You can dive!' he exclaimed.

'It is easy,' said Ranji, treading water, waiting for a further challenge. 'Can't you dive?'

'No,' said the other. 'I jump straight in. But if you will tell me how, I will make a dive.'

'It is easy,' said Ranji. 'Stand on the rock, stretch your arms out and allow your head to displace your feet.'

The Punjabi boy stood up, stiff and straight, stretched out his arms, and threw himself into the water. He landed flat on his belly, with a crash that sent the birds screaming out of the trees.

Ranji dissolved into laughter.

'Are you trying to empty the pool?' he asked, as the Punjabi boy came to the surface, spouting water like a small whale.

'Wasn't it good?' asked the boy, evidently proud of his feat.

'Not very good,' said Ranji. 'You should have more practice.

See, I will do it again.'

And pulling himself up on a rock, he executed another perfect dive. The other boy waited for him to come up, but, swimming under water, Ranji circled him and came upon him from behind.

'How did you do that?' asked the astonished youth.

'Can't you swim under water?' asked Ranji.

'No, but I will try it.'

The Punjabi boy made a tremendous effort to plunge to the bottom of the pool and indeed he thought he had gone right down, though his bottom, like a duck's, remained above the surface.

Ranji, however, did not discourage him.

'It was not bad,' he said. 'But you need a lot of practice.'

'Will you teach me?' asked his enemy.

'If you like, I will teach you.'

'You must teach me. If you do not teach me, I will beat you. Will you come here every day and teach me?'

'If you like,' said Ranji. They had pulled themselves out of the water, and were sitting side by side on a smooth grey rock.

'My name is Suraj,' said the Punjabi boy. 'What is yours?'

'It is Ranji.'

'I am strong, am I not?' asked Suraj, bending his arm so that a ball of muscle stood up stretching the white of his flesh.

'You are strong,' said Ranji. 'You are a real pahelwan.'

'One day I will be the world's champion wrestler,' said Suraj, slapping his thighs, which shook with the impact of his hand. He looked critically at Ranji's hard, thin body. 'You are quite strong yourself,' he conceded. 'But you are too bony. I know, you people do not eat enough. You must come and have your food with me. I drink one seer of milk every day. We have got our own cow! Be my friend, and I will make you a pahelwan like me! I know—if you teach me to dive and swim underwater, I will make you a pahelwan! That is fair, isn't it?'

'That is fair!' said Ranji, though he doubted if he was getting the better of the exchange.

Suraj put his arm around the younger boy and said, 'We are friends now, yes?'

They looked at each other with honest, unflinching eyes, and in that moment love and understanding were born.

'We are friends,' said Ranji.

The birds had settled again in their branches, and the pool was quiet and limpid in the shade of the sal trees.

'It is our pool,' said Suraj. 'Nobody else can come here without our permission. Who would dare?'

'Who would dare?' said Ranji, smiling with the knowledge that he had won the day.

The Boy Who Broke the Bank

NATHU GRUMBLED TO himself as he swept the steps of the Pipalnagar Bank, owned by Seth Govind Ram. He used the small broom hurriedly and carelessly, and the dust, after rising in a cloud above his head, settled down again on the steps. As Nathu was banging his pan against a dustbin, Sitaram, the washerman's son, passed by.

Sitaram was on his delivery round. He had a bundle of freshly pressed clothes balanced on his head.

'Don't raise such dust!' he called out to Nathu. 'Are you annoyed because they are still refusing to pay you an extra two rupees a month?'

'I don't wish to talk about it,' complained the sweeper boy. 'I haven't even received my regular pay. And this is the twentieth of the month. Who would think a bank would hold up a poor man's salary? As soon as I get my money, I'm off! Not another week do I work in this place.' And Nathu

194

banged the pan against the dustbin several times, just to emphasize his point and give himself confidence.

'Well, I wish you luck,' said Sitaram. 'I'll keep a lookout for any jobs that might suit you.' And he plodded barefoot along the road, the big bundle of clothes hiding most of his head and shoulders.

At the fourth home he visited, Sitaram heard the lady of the house mention that she was in need of a sweeper. Tying his bundle together, he said, 'I know of a sweeper boy who's looking for work. He can start from next month. He's with the bank just now but they aren't giving him his pay, and he wants to leave.'

'Is that so?' said Mrs Srivastava. 'Well, tell him to come and see me tomorrow.'

And Sitaram, glad that he had been of service to both a customer and his friend, hoisted his bag on his shoulders and went his way.

Mrs Srivastava had to do some shopping. She gave instructions to the ayah about looking after the baby, and told the cook not to be late with the midday meal. Then she set out for the Pipalnagar marketplace, to make her customary tour of the cloth shops.

A large, shady tamarind tree grew at one end of the bazaar, and it was here that Mrs Srivastava found her friend, Mrs Bhushan, sheltering from the heat. Mrs Bhushan was fanning herself with a large handkerchief. She complained of the summer which, she affirmed, was definitely the hottest in the history of Pipalnagar. She then showed Mrs Srivastava a sample of the cloth she was going to buy, and for five minutes they discussed its shade, texture and design. Having exhausted this topic, Mrs Srivastava said, 'Do you know, my dear, that Seth Govind Ram's bank can't even pay its employees? Only this morning I heard a complaint from their sweeper, who hasn't received his wages for over a month!'

'Shocking!' remarked Mrs Bhushan. 'If they can't pay the sweeper, they must be in a bad way. None of the others could be getting paid either.'

She left Mrs Srivastava at the tamarind tree and went in search of her husband, who was sitting in front of Kamal Kishore's photographic shop, talking to the owner.

'So there you are!' cried Mrs Bhushan. 'I've been looking for you for almost an hour. Where did you disappear?'

'Nowhere,' replied Mr Bhushan. 'Had you remained stationary in one shop, I might have found you. But you go from one shop to another, like a bee in a flower garden.'

'Don't start grumbling. The heat is trying enough. I don't know what's happening to Pipalnagar. Even the bank's about to go bankrupt.'

'What's that?' said Kamal Kishore, sitting up suddenly. 'Which bank?'

'Why, the Pipalnagar Bank, of course. I hear they have stopped paying employees. Don't tell me you have an account there, Mr Kishore?'

'No, but my neighbour has!' he exclaimed; and he called out over the low partition to the keeper of the barber shop next door. 'Deep Chand, have you heard the latest? The Pipalnagar Bank is about to collapse. You'd better get your money out as soon as you can!'

Deep Chand, who was cutting the hair of an elderly gentleman, was so startled that his hand shook and he nicked his customer's right ear. The customer yelped in pain and distress: pain, because of the cut and distress because of the awful news he had just heard. With one side of his neck still unshaven, he sped across the road to the general merchant's store where there was a telephone. He dialled Seth Govind Ram's number. The Seth was not at home. Where was he, then? The Seth was holidaying in Kashmir. Oh, was that so? The elderly gentleman did not believe it. He hurried back to the barber's shop and told Deep Chand, 'The bird has flown! Seth Govind Ram has left town. Definitely, it means a collapse.' And then he dashed out of the shop, making a beeline for his office and chequebook.

The news spread through the bazaar with the rapidity of a forest fire. At the general merchant's it circulated amongst the customers, and then spread with them in various directions, to the betel-seller, the tailor, the free vendor, the jeweller, the beggar sitting on the pavement.

Old Ganpat, the beggar, had a crooked leg. He had been squatting on the pavement for years, calling for alms. In the evening someone would come with a barrow and take him away. He had never been known to walk. But now, on learning that the bank was about to collapse, Ganpat astonished everyone by leaping to his feet and actually running at top speed in the direction of the bank. It soon became known that he had a thousand rupees in savings!

Men stood in groups at street corners discussing the situation. Pipalnagar seldom had a crisis, seldom or never had floods, earthquakes or drought; and the imminent crash of the Pipalnagar Bank set everyone talking and speculating and rushing about in a frenzy. Some boasted of their far-sightedness, congratulating themselves on having already taken out their money, or on never having put any in; others speculated on the reasons for the crash, putting it all down to excesses indulged in by Seth Govind Ram. The Seth had fled the state, said one. He had fled the country, said another. He was hiding in Pipalnagar, said a third. He had hanged himself from the tamarind tree, said a fourth, and had been found that morning by the sweeper boy.

By noon the small bank had gone through all its ready cash, and the harassed manager was in a dilemma. Emergency funds could only be obtained from another bank some thirty miles distant, and he wasn't sure he could persuade the crowd to wait until then. And there was no way of contacting Seth Govind Ram on his houseboat in Kashmir.

People were turned back from the counters and told to return the following day. They did not like the sound of that.

And so they gathered outside, on the steps of the bank, shouting, 'Give us our money or we'll break in!' and 'Fetch the Seth, we know he's hiding in a safe deposit locker!' Mischief-makers who didn't have a paisa in the bank joined the crowd and aggravated the mood. The manager stood at the door and tried to placate them. He declared that the bank had plenty of money but no immediate means of collecting it; he urged them to go home and come back the next day.

'We want it now!' chanted some of the crowd. 'Now, now, now!'

And a brick hurtled through the air and crashed through the plate glass window of the Pipalnagar Bank.

Nathu arrived next morning to sweep the steps of the bank. He saw the refuse and the broken glass and the stones cluttering the steps. Raising his hands in a gesture of horror and disgust he cried, 'Hooligans! Sons of donkeys! As though it isn't bad enough to be paid late, it seems my work has also to be increased!' He smote the steps with his broom, scattering the refuse.

'Good morning, Nathu,' said the washerman's boy, getting down from his bicycle. 'Are you ready to take up a new job from the first of next month? You'll have to, I suppose, now that the bank is going out of business.'

'How's that?' said Nathu.

'Haven't you heard? Well you'd better wait here until half the population of Pipalnagar arrives to claim their money.' And he waved cheerfully—he did not have a bank account—and sped away on his cycle.

Nathu went back to sweeping the steps, muttering to himself. When he had finished his work, he sat down on the highest step, to await the arrival of the manager. He was determined to get his pay.

'Who would have thought the bank would collapse!' he said to himself, and looked thoughtfully into the distance. 'I wonder how it could have happened . . .'

Chachi's Funeral

CHACHI DIED AT 6 p.m. on Wednesday the 5th of April, and came to life again exactly twenty minutes later. This is how it happened.

Chachi was, as a rule, a fairly tolerant, easygoing person, who waddled about the house without paying much attention to the swarms of small sons, daughters, nephews and nieces who poured in and out of the rooms. But she had taken a particular aversion to her ten-year-old nephew, Sunil. She was a simple woman and could not understand Sunil. He was a little brighter than her own sons, more sensitive, and inclined to resent a scolding or a cuff across the head. He was better looking than her own children. All this, in addition to the fact that she resented having to cook for the boy while both his parents went out to office jobs, led her to grumble at him a little more than was really necessary.

Sunil sensed his aunt's jealousy and fanned its flames. He

was a mischievous boy, and did little things to annoy her, like bursting paperbags behind her while she dozed, or commenting on the width of her pyjamas when they were hung out to dry. On the evening of the 5th of April, he had been in particularly high spirits and, feeling hungry, entered the kitchen with the intention of helping himself to some honey. But the honey was on the top shelf, and Sunil wasn't quite tall enough to grasp the bottle. He got his fingers to it but as he tilted it towards him, it fell to the ground with a crash.

Chachi reached the scene of the accident before Sunil could slip away. Removing her slipper, she dealt him three or four furious blows across the head and shoulders. This done, she sat down on the floor and burst into tears.

Had the beating come from someone else, Sunil might have cried; but his pride was hurt and, instead of weeping, he muttered something under his breath and stormed out of the room.

Climbing the steps to the roof, he went to his secret hiding place, a small hole in the wall of the unused barsati, where he kept his marbles, kite-string, tops, and a clasp-knife. Opening the knife, he plunged it thrice into the soft wood of the window frame.

'I'll kill her!' he whispered fiercely, 'I'll kill her, I'll kill her!' 'Whom are you going to kill, Sunil?'

It was his cousin Madhu, a dark, slim girl of twelve, who aided and abetted him in most of his exploits. Sunil's Chachi was her 'Mammi'. It was a very big family.

'Chachi,' said Sunil. 'She hates me, I know. Well, I hate her too. This time I'll kill her.'

'How are you going to do it?'

'I'll stab with this.' He showed her the knife. 'Three times, in the heart.'

'But you'll be caught. The C.I.D. is very clever. Do you want to go to jail?'

'Won't they hang me?'

'They don't hang small boys. They send them to boarding schools.'

'I don't want to go to a boarding school.'

'Then better not kill your Chachi. At least not this way. I'll show you how.'

Madhu produced pencil and paper, went down on her hands and knees, and screwing up her face in sharp concentration, made a rough drawing of Chachi. Then, with a red crayon, she sketched in a big heart in the region of Chachi's stomach.

'Now,' she said, 'stab her to death!'

Sunil's eyes shone with excitement. Here was a great new game. You could always depend on Madhu for something original. He held the drawing against the woodwork, and plunged his knife three times into Chachi's pastel breast.

'You have killed her,' said Madhu.

'Is that all?'

'Well, if you like, we can cremate her.'

'All right.'

She took the torn paper, crumpled it up, produced a box of matches from Sunil's hiding place, lit a match, and set fire to the paper. In a few minutes all that remained of Chachi was a few ashes.

'Poor Chachi,' said Madhu.

'Perhaps we shouldn't have done it,' said Sunil beginning to feel sorry.

'I know, we'll put her ashes in the river!'

'What river?'

'Oh the drain will do.'

Madhu gathered the ashes together, and leant over the balcony of the roof. She threw out her arms and the ashes drifted downwards. Some of them settled on the pomegranate tree, a few reached the drain and were carried away by a sudden rush of kitchen water. She turned to face Sunil.

Big tears were rolling down Sunil's cheeks. 'What are you crying for?' asked Madhu.

'Chachi. I didn't hate her so much.'

'Then why did you want to kill her?'

'Oh, that was different.'

'Come on, then, let's go down. I have to do my homework.'

As they came down the steps from the roof, Chachi emerged from the kitchen.

'Oh Chachi!' shouted Sunil. He rushed to her and tried to get his arms around her ample waist.

'Now what's up?' grumbled Chachi. 'What is it this time?'

'Nothing, Chachi. I love you so much. Please don't leave us.'

A look of suspicion crossed Chachi's face. She frowned down at the boy. But she was reassured by the look of genuine affection that she saw in his eyes.

'Perhaps he *does* care for me, after all,' she thought and patted him gently on the head. She took him by the hand and led him back to the kitchen.

The Tunnel

IT WAS ALMOST noon, and the jungle was very still, very silent. Heat waves shimmered along the railway embankment where it cut a path through the tall evergreen trees. The railway lines were two straight black serpents disappearing into the tunnel in the hillside.

Ranji stood near the cutting, waiting for the midday train. It wasn't a station and he wasn't catching a train. He was waiting so he could watch the steam engine come roaring out of the tunnel.

He had cycled out of town and taken the jungle path until he had come to a small village. He had left the cycle there, and walked over a low, scrub-covered hill and down to the tunnel exit.

Now he looked up. He had heard, in the distance, the shrill whistle of the engine. He couldn't see anything, because the train was approaching from the other side of the hill, but presently a sound like distant thunder came from the tunnel, and he knew the train was coming through.

A second or two later the steam engine shot out of the tunnel, snorting and puffing like some green, black and gold dragon, some beautiful monster out of Ranji's dreams. Showering sparks right and left, it roared a challenge to the jungle.

Instinctively, Ranji stepped back a few paces. Waves of hot steam struck him in the face. Even the trees seemed to flinch from the noise and heat. And then the train had gone, leaving only a plume of smoke to drift lazily over the tall shisham trees.

The jungle was still again. No one moved.

Ranji turned from watching the drifting smoke and began walking along the embankment towards the tunnel. It grew darker the further he walked, and when he had gone about twenty yards, it became pitch black. He had to turn and look back at the opening to make sure that there was a speck of daylight in the distance.

Ahead of him, the tunnel's other opening was also a small round circle of light.

The walls of the tunnel were damp and sticky. A bat flew past. A lizard scuttled between the lines. Coming straight from the darkness into the light, Ranji was dazzled by the sudden glare. He put a hand up to shade his eyes and looked up at the scrub-covered hillside, and he thought he saw something moving between the trees.

It was just a flash of gold and black, and a long swishing

tail. It was there between the trees for a second or two, and then it was gone.

About fifty feet from the entrance to the tunnel stood the watchman's hut. Marigolds grew in front of the hut, and at the back there was a small vegetable patch. It was the watchman's duty to inspect the tunnel and keep it clear of obstacles.

Every day, before the train came through, he would walk the length of the tunnel. If all was well, he would return to his hut and take a nap. If something was wrong, he would walk back up the line and wave a red flag and the engine-driver would slow down.

At night, the watchman lit an oil lamp and made a similar inspection. If there was any danger to the train, he'd go back up the line and wave his lamp to the approaching engine. If all was well, he'd hang his lamp at the door of his hut and go to sleep.

He was just settling down on his cot for an afternoon nap when he saw the boy come out of the tunnel. He waited until the boy was only a few feet away and then said, 'Welcome, welcome. I don't often get visitors. Sit down for a while, and tell me why you were inspecting my tunnel.'

'Is it your tunnel?' asked Ranji.

'It is,' said the watchman. 'It is truly my tunnel, since no one else will have anything to do with it. I have only lent it to the Government.'

Ranji sat down on the edge of the cot.

'I wanted to see the train come through,' he said. 'And then, when it had gone, I decided to walk through the tunnel.'

'And what did you find in it?'

'Nothing. It was very dark. But when I came out, I thought I saw an animal—up on the hill—but I'm not sure, it moved off very quickly.'

'It was a leopard you saw,' said the watchman. 'My leopard.'

'Do you own a leopard too?'

'I do.'

'And do you lend it to the Government?'

'I do not.'

'Is it dangerous?'

'Not if you leave it alone. It comes this way for a few days every month, because there are still deer in this jungle, and the deer is its natural prey. It keeps away from people.'

'Have you been here a long time?' asked Ranji.

'Many years. My name is Kishan Singh.'

'Mine is Ranji.'

'There is one train during the day. And there is one train during the night. Have you seen the Night Mail come through the tunnel?'

'No. At what time does it come?'

'About nine o'clock, if it isn't late. You could come and sit here with me, if you like. And, after it has gone, I will take you home.'

'I'll ask my parents,' said Ranji. 'Will it be safe?'

'It is safer in the jungle than in the town. No rascals out here. Only last week, when I went into the town, I had my pocket picked! Leopards don't pick pockets.'

Kishan Singh stretched himself out on his cot. 'And now

I am going to take a nap, my friend. It is too hot to be up and about in the afternoon.'

'Everyone goes to sleep in the afternoon,' complained Ranji. 'My father lies down as soon as he's had his lunch.'

'Well, the animals also rest in the heat of the day. It is only the tribe of boys who cannot, or will not, rest.'

Kishan Singh placed a large banana leaf over his face to keep away the flies, and was soon snoring gently. Ranji stood up, looking up and down the railway tracks. Then he began walking back to the village.

The following evening, towards dusk, as the flying-foxes swooped silently out of the trees, Ranji made his way to the watchman's hut.

It had been a long hot day, but now the earth was cooling and a light breeze was moving through the trees. It carried with it the scent of mango blossom, the promise of rain.

Kishan Singh was waiting for Ranji. He had watered his small garden and the flowers looked cool and fresh. A kettle was boiling on an oil-stove.

'I am making tea,' he said. 'There is nothing like a glass of hot, sweet tea while waiting for a train.'

They drank their tea, listening to the sharp notes of the tailor-bird and the noisy chatter of the seven-sisters. As the brief twilight faded, most of the birds fell silent. Kishan lit his oil-lamp and said it was time for him to inspect the tunnel. He moved off towards the dark entrance, while Ranji sat on the cot, sipping tea.

In the dark, the trees seemed to move closer. And the night life of the forest was conveyed on the breeze—the sharp call of a barking-deer, the cry of a fox, the quaint tonk-tonk of a nightjar.

There were some sounds that Ranji would not recognize—sounds that came from the trees. Creakings, and whisperings, as though the trees were coming alive, stretching their limbs in the dark, shifting a little, flexing their fingers.

Kishan Singh stood outside the tunnel, trimming his lamp. The night sounds were familiar to him and he did not give them much thought; but something else—a padded footfall, a rustle of dry leaves—made him stand still for a few seconds, peering into the darkness. Then, humming softly, he returned to where Ranji was waiting. Ten minutes remained for the Night Mail to arrive.

As the watchman sat down on the cot beside Ranji, a new sound reached both of them quite distinctly—a rhythmic sawing sound, as of someone cutting through the branch of a tree.

'What's that?' whispered Ranji.

'It's the leopard,' said Kishan Singh. 'I think it's in the tunnel.'

'The train will soon be here.'

'Yes, my friend. And if we don't drive the leopard out of the tunnel, it will be run over by the engine.'

'But won't it attack us if we try to drive it out?' asked Ranji, beginning to share the watchman's concern.

'It knows me well. We have seen each other many times. I don't think it will attack. Even so, I will take my axe along. You had better stay here, Ranji.'

'No, I'll come too. It will be better than sitting here alone in the dark.'

'All right, but stay close behind me. And, remember, there is nothing to fear.'

Raising his lamp, Kishan Singh walked into the tunnel, shouting at the top of his voice to try and scare away the animal. Ranji followed close behind. But he found he was unable to do any shouting; his throat had gone quite dry.

They had gone about twenty paces into the tunnel when the light from the lamp fell upon the leopard. It was crouching between the tracks, only fifteen feet away from them. Baring its teeth and snarling, it went down on its belly, tail twitching. Ranji felt sure it was going to spring at them.

Kishan Singh and Ranji both shouted together. Their voices rang through the tunnel. And the leopard, uncertain as to how many terrifying humans were there in front of him, turned swiftly and disappeared into the darkness.

To make sure it had gone, Ranji and the watchman walked the length of the tunnel. When they returned to the entrance, the rails were beginning to hum. They knew the train was coming.

Ranji put his hand to one of the rails and felt its tremor. He heard the distant rumble of the train. And then the engine came round the bend, hissing at them, scattering sparks into the darkness, defying the jungle as it roared through the steep sides of the cutting. It charged straight into the tunnel, thundering past Ranji like the beautiful dragon of his dreams.

And when it had gone, the silence returned and the

forest seemed to breathe, to live again. Only the rails still trembled with the passing of the train.

They trembled again to the passing of the same train, almost a week later, when Ranji and his father were both travelling in it.

Ranji's father was scribbling in a notebook, doing his accounts. How boring of him, thought Ranji as he sat near an open window staring out at the darkness. His father was going to Delhi on a business trip and had decided to take the boy along.

'It's time you learnt something about the business,' he had said, to Ranji's dismay.

The Night Mail rushed through the forest with its hundreds of passengers. The carriage wheels beat out a steady rhythm on the rails. Tiny flickering lights came and went, as they passed small villages on the fringe of the jungle.

Ranji heard the rumble as the train passed over a small bridge. It was too dark to see the hut near the cutting, but he knew they must be approaching the tunnel. He strained his eyes, looking out into the night; and then, just as the engine let out a shrill whistle, Ranji saw the lamp.

He couldn't see Kishan Singh, but he saw the lamp, and he knew that his friend was out there.

The train went into the tunnel and out again, it left the jungle behind and thundered across the endless plains. And Ranji stared out at the darkness, thinking of the lonely cutting in the forest, and the watchman with the lamp who would always remain a firefly for those travelling thousands, as he lit up the darkness for steam engines and leopards.

The Prospect of Flowers

FERN HILL, THE Oaks, Hunter's Lodge, The Parsonage, The Pines, Dumbarnie, Mackinnon's Hall and Windermere. These are the names of some of the old houses that still stand on the outskirts of one of the smaller Indian hill stations. Most of them have fallen into decay and ruin. They are very old, of course—built over a hundred years ago by Britishers who sought relief from the searing heat of the plains. Today's visitors to the hill stations prefer to live near the markets and cinemas and many of the old houses, set amidst oak and maple and deodar, are inhabited by wild cats, bandicoots, owls, goats, and the occasional charcoal-burner or mule-driver.

But amongst these neglected mansions stands a neat, whitewashed cottage called Mulberry Lodge. And in it, up to a short time ago, lived an elderly English spinster named Miss Mackenzie.

In years, Miss Mackenzie was more than 'elderly,' being well over eighty. But no one would have guessed it. She was clean, sprightly, and wore old-fashioned but well-preserved dresses. Once a week, she walked the two miles to town to buy butter and jam and soap and sometimes a small bottle of eau-de-Cologne.

She had lived in the hill station since she had been a girl in her teens, and that had been before the First World War. Though she had never married, she had experienced a few love affairs and was far from being the typical frustrated spinster of fiction. Her parents had been dead thirty years; her brother and sister were also dead. She had no relatives in India, and she lived on a small pension of forty rupees a month and the gift parcels that were sent out to her from New Zealand by a friend of her youth.

Like other lonely old people, she kept a pet, a large black cat with bright yellow eyes. In her small garden she grew dahlias, chrysanthemums, gladioli and a few rare orchids. She knew a great deal about plants, and about wild flowers, trees, birds and insects. She had never made a serious study of these things, but having lived with them for so many years, had developed an intimacy with all that grew and flourished around her.

She had few visitors. Occasionally, the padre from the local church called on her, and once a month the postman came with a letter from New Zealand or her pension papers. The milkman called every second day with a litre of milk for the lady and her cat. And sometimes she received a couple of eggs free, for the egg-seller remembered a time when Miss Mackenzie, in her earlier prosperity, bought eggs from him in large quantities. He was a sentimental man. He remembered her as a ravishing beauty in her twenties when he had gazed at her in round-eyed, nine-year-old wonder and consternation.

Now it was September and the rains were nearly over and Miss Mackenzie's chrysanthemums were coming into their own. She hoped the coming winter wouldn't be too severe because she found it increasingly difficult to bear the cold.

One day, as she was pottering about in her garden, she saw a schoolboy plucking wild flowers on the slope about the cottage.

'Who's that?' she called. 'What are you up to, young man?'

The boy was alarmed and tried to dash up the hillside, but he slipped on pine needles and came slithering down the slope into Miss Mackenzie's nasturtium bed.

When he found there was no escape, he gave a bright disarming smile and said, 'Good morning, Miss.'

He belonged to the local English-medium school, and wore a bright red blazer and a red and black striped tie. Like most polite Indian schoolboys, he called every woman 'Miss.'

'Good morning,' said Miss Mackenzie severely. 'Would you mind moving out of my flower bed?'

The boy stepped gingerly over the nasturtiums and looked up at Miss Mackenzie with dimpled cheeks and appealing eyes. It was impossible to be angry with him.

'You're trespassing,' said Miss Mackenzie.

'Yes, Miss.'

'And you ought to be in school at this hour.'

'Yes, Miss.'

'Then what are you doing here?'

'Picking flowers, Miss.' And he held up a bunch of ferns and wild flowers.

'Oh,' Miss Mackenzie was disarmed. It was a long time since she had seen a boy taking an interest in flowers, and, what was more, playing truant from school in order to gather them.

'Do you like flowers?' she asked.

'Yes, Miss. I'm going to be a botan—a botantist?'

'You mean a botanist.'

'Yes, Miss.'

'Well, that's unusual. Most boys at your age want to be pilots or soldiers or perhaps engineers. But you want to be a botanist. Well, well. There's still hope for the world, I see. And do you know the names of these flowers?'

'This is a bukhilo flower,' he said, showing her a small golden flower. 'That's a Pahari name. It means puja, or prayer. The flower is offered during prayers. But I don't know what this is . . .'

He held out a pale pink flower with a soft, heart-shaped leaf.

'It's a wild begonia,' said Miss Mackenzie. 'And that purple stuff is salvia, but it isn't wild. It's a plant that escaped from my garden. Don't you have any books on flowers?'

'No, Miss.'

'All right, come in and I'll show you a book.'

She led the boy into a small front room, which was crowded with furniture and books and vases and jam jars and offered him a chair. He sat awkwardly on its edge. The black cat immediately leapt on to his knees, and settled down on them, purring loudly.

'What's your name?' asked Miss Mackenzie, as she rummaged among her books.

'Anil, Miss.'

'And where do you live?'

'When school closes, I go to Delhi. My father has a business.'

'Oh, and what's that?'

'Bulbs, Miss.'

'Flower bulbs?'

'No, electric bulbs.'

'Electric bulbs! You might send me a few, when you get home. Mine are always fusing, and they're so expensive, like everything else these days. Ah, here we are!' She pulled a heavy volume down from the shelf and laid it on the table. '*Flora Himaliensis*, published in 1892, and probably the only copy in India. This is a very valuable book, Anil. No other naturalist has recorded so many wild Himalayan flowers. And let me tell you this; there are many flowers and plants which are still unknown to the fancy botanists who spend all their time with microscopes instead of in the mountains. But perhaps, *you'll* do something about that, one day.'

'Yes, Miss.'

They went through the book together, and Miss Mackenzie pointed out many flowers that grew in and around the hill station, while the boy made notes of their names and seasons. She lit a stove, and put the kettle on for tea. And then the old English lady and the small Indian boy sat side by side over cups of hot sweet tea, absorbed in a book of wild flowers.

'May I come again?' asked Anil, when finally he rose to go.

'If you like,' said Miss Mackenzie. 'But not during school hours. You mustn't miss your classes.'

After that, Anil visited Miss Mackenzie about once a week, and nearly always brought a wildflower for her to identify. She found herself looking forward to the boy's visits—and sometimes, when more than a week passed and he didn't come, she was disappointed and lonely and would grumble at the black cat.

Anil reminded her of her brother, when the latter had been a boy. There was no physical resemblance. Andrew had been fair-haired and blue-eyed. But it was Anil's eagerness, his alert, bright look and the way he stood—legs apart, hands on hips, a picture of confidence—that reminded her of the boy who had shared her own youth in these same hills.

And why did Anil come to see her so often?

Partly because she knew about wild flowers, and he really did want to become a botanist. And partly because she smelt of freshly baked bread, and that was a smell his own grandmother had possessed. And partly because she was lonely and sometimes a boy of twelve can sense loneliness better than an adult. And partly because he was a little different from other children.

By the middle of October, when there was only a fortnight left for the school to close, the first snow had fallen on the distant mountains. One peak stood high above the rest, a white pinnacle against the azure-blue sky. When the sun set, this peak turned from orange to gold to pink to red.

'How high is that mountain?' asked Anil.

'It must be over 12,000 feet,' said Miss Mackenzie. 'About thirty miles from here, as the crow flies. I always wanted to go there, but there was no proper road. At that height, there'll be flowers that you don't get here—the blue gentian and the purple columbine, the anemone and the edelweiss.'

'I'll go there one day,' said Anil.

'I'm sure you will, if you really want to.'

The day before his school closed, Anil came to say goodbye to Miss Mackenzie.

'I don't suppose you'll be able to find many wild flowers in Delhi,' she said. 'But have a good holiday.'

'Thank you, Miss.'

As he was about to leave, Miss Mackenzie, on an impulse, thrust the *Flora Himaliensis* into his hands.

'You keep it,' she said. 'It's a present for you.'

'But I'll be back next year, and I'll be able to look at it then. It's so valuable.'

'I know it's valuable and that's why I've given it to you. Otherwise it will only fall into the hands of the junk-dealers.'

'But, Miss . . .'

'Don't argue. Besides, I may not be here next year.'

'Are you going away?'

'I'm not sure. I may go to England.'

She had no intention of going to England; she had not seen the country since she was a child, and she knew she would not fit in with the life of post-war Britain. Her home was in these hills, among the oaks and maples and deodars. It was lonely, but at her age it would be lonely anywhere.

The boy tucked the book under his arm, straightened his tie, stood stiffly to attention, and said, 'Goodbye, Miss Mackenzie.'

It was the first time he had spoken her name.

Winter set in early, and strong winds brought rain and sleet, and soon there were no flowers in the garden or on the hillside. The cat stayed indoors, curled up at the foot of Miss Mackenzie's bed.

Miss Mackenzie wrapped herself up in all her old shawls and mufflers, but still she felt the cold. Her fingers grew so stiff that she took almost an hour to open a can of baked beans. And then it snowed and for several days the milkman did not come. The postman arrived with her pension papers, but she felt too tired to take them up to town to the bank.

She spent most of the time in bed. It was the warmest place. She kept a hot-water bottle at her back, and the cat kept her feet warm. She lay in bed, dreaming of the spring and summer months. In three months' time, the primroses would be out and with the coming of spring, the boy would return.

One night the hot-water bottle burst and the bedding

was soaked through. As there was no sun for several days, the blanket remained damp. Miss Mackenzie caught a chill and had to keep to her cold, uncomfortable bed. She knew she had a fever but there was no thermometer with which to take her temperature. She had difficulty in breathing.

A strong wind sprang up one night, and the window flew open and kept banging all night. Miss Mackenzie was too weak to get up and close it, and the wind swept the rain and sleet into the room. The cat crept into the bed and snuggled close to its mistress's warm body. But towards morning that body had lost its warmth and the cat left the bed and started scratching about on the floor.

As a shaft of sunlight streamed through the open window, the milkman arrived. He poured some milk into the cat's saucer on the doorstep and the cat leapt down from the window sill and made for the milk.

The milkman called a greeting to Miss Mackenzie, but received no answer. Her window was open and he had always known her to be up before sunrise. So he put his head in at the window and called again. But Miss Mackenzie did not answer. She had gone away to the mountain where the blue gentian and purple columbine grew.

A Face in the Dark

MR OLIVER, AN Anglo-Indian teacher, was returning to his school late one night, on the outskirts of the hill station of Simla. From before Kipling's time, the school had been run on English public school lines and the boys, most of them from wealthy Indian families, wore blazers, caps and ties. *Life* magazine, in a feature on India, had once called it the 'Eton of the East'. Mr Oliver had been teaching in the school for several years.

The Simla Bazaar, with its cinemas and restaurants, was about three miles from the school and Mr Oliver, a bachelor, usually strolled into the town in the evening, returning after dark, when he would take a short cut through the pine forest.

When there was a strong wind, the pine trees made sad, eerie sounds that kept most people to the main road. But Mr Oliver was not a nervous or imaginative man. He carried a torch and its gleam—the batteries were running down—moved fitfully down the narrow forest path. When its flickering light fell on the figure of a boy, who was sitting alone on a rock, Mr Oliver stopped. Boys were not supposed to be out after dark.

'What are you doing out here, boy?' asked Mr Oliver sharply, moving closer so that he could recognize the miscreant. But even as he approached the boy, Mr Oliver sensed that something was wrong. The boy appeared to be crying. His head hung down, he held his face in his hands, and his body shook convulsively. It was a strange, soundless weeping and Mr Oliver felt distinctly uneasy.

'Well, what's the matter?' he asked, his anger giving way to concern. 'What are you crying for?' The boy would not answer or look up. His body continued to be racked with silent sobbing. 'Come on, boy, you shouldn't be out here at this hour. Tell me the trouble. Look up!' The boy looked up. He took his hands from his face and looked up at his teacher. The light from Mr Oliver's torch fell on the boy's face—if you could call it a face.

It had no eyes, ears, nose or mouth. It was just a round smooth head—with a school cap on top of it! And that's where the story should end. But for Mr Oliver it did not end here.

The torch fell from his trembling hand. He turned and scrambled down the path, running blindly through the trees and calling for help. He was still running towards the school buildings when he saw a lantern swinging in the middle of the path. Mr Oliver stumbled up to the watchman, gasping for breath. 'What is it, sahib?' asked the watchman. 'Has there been an accident? Why are you running?'

'I saw something—something horrible—a boy weeping in the forest—and he had no face!'

'No face, sahib?'

'No eyes, nose, mouth—nothing!'

'Do you mean it was like this, sahib?' asked the watchman and raised the lamp to his own face. The watchman had no eyes, no ears, no features at all—not even an eyebrow! And that's when the wind blew the lamp out.

The Room of Many Colours

LAST WEEK I wrote a story, and all the time I was writing it I thought it was a good story; but when it was finished and I had read it through, I found that there was something missing, that it didn't ring true. So I tore it up. I wrote a poem, about an old man sleeping in the sun, and this was true, but it was finished quickly, and once again I was left with the problem of what to write next. And I remembered my father, who taught me to write; and I thought, why not write about my father, and about the trees we planted, and about the people I knew while growing up and about what happened on the way to growing up . . .

And so, like Alice, I must begin at the beginning, and in the beginning there was this red insect, just like a velvet button, which I found on the front lawn of the bungalow. The grass was still wet with overnight rain.

I placed the insect on the palm of my hand and took it into the house to show my father.

'Look, Dad,' I said, 'I haven't seen an insect like this before. Where has it come from?'

'Where did you find it?' he asked.

'On the grass.'

'It must have come down from the sky,' he said. 'It must have come down with the rain.'

Later, he told me how the insect really happened but I preferred his first explanation. It was more fun to have it dropping from the sky.

I was seven at the time, and my father was thirty-seven, but, right from the beginning, he made me feel that I was old enough to talk to him about everything—insects, people, trees, steam engines, King George, comics, crocodiles, the Mahatma, the Viceroy, America, Mozambique and Timbuctoo. We took long walks together, explored old ruins, chased butterflies and waved to passing trains.

My mother had gone away when I was four, and I had very dim memories of her. Most other children had their mothers with them, and I found it a bit strange that mine couldn't stay. Whenever I asked my father why she'd gone, he'd say, 'You'll understand when you grow up.' And if I asked him *where* she'd gone, he'd look troubled and say, 'I really don't know.' This was the only question of mine to which he didn't have an answer.

But I was quite happy living alone with my father; I had never known any other kind of life.

We were sitting on an old wall, looking out to sea at a

couple of Arab dhows and a tram steamer, when my father said, 'Would you like to go to sea one day?'

'Where does the sea go?' I asked.

'It goes everywhere.'

'Does it go to the end of the world?'

'It goes right round the world. It's a round world.'

'It can't be.'

'It is. But it's so big, you can't see the roundness. When a fly sits on a watermelon, it can't see right round the melon, can it? The melon must seem quite flat to the fly. Well, in comparison to the world, we're much, much smaller than the tiniest of insects.'

'Have you been around the world?' I asked.

'No, only as far as England. That's where your grandfather was born.'

'And my grandmother?'

'She came to India from Norway when she was quite small. Norway is a cold land, with mountains and snow, and the sea cutting deep into the land. I was there as a boy. It's very beautiful, and the people are good and work hard.'

'I'd like to go there.'

'You will, one day. When you are older, I'll take you to Norway.'

'Is it better than England?'

'It's quite different.'

'Is it better than India?'

'It's quite different.'

'Is India like England?'

'No, it's different.'

227

'Well, what does "different" mean?'

'It means things are not the same. It means people are different. It means the weather is different. It means tree and birds and insects are different.'

'Are English crocodiles different from Indian crocodiles?'

'They don't have crocodiles in England.'

'Oh, then it must be different.'

'It would be a dull world if it was the same everywhere,' said my father.

He never lost patience with my endless questioning. If he wanted a rest, he would take out his pipe and spend a long time lighting it. If this took very long, I'd find something else to do. But sometimes I'd wait patiently until the pipe was drawing, and then return to the attack.

'Will we always be in India?' I asked.

'No, we'll have to go away one day. You see, it's hard to explain, but it isn't really our country.'

'Ayah says it belongs to the King of England, and the jewels in his crown were taken from India, and that when the Indians get their jewels back, the King will lose India! But first they have to get the crown from the King, but this is very difficult, she says, because the crown is always on his head. He even sleeps wearing his crown!'

Ayah was my nanny. She loved me deeply, and was always filling my head with strange and wonderful stories.

My father did not comment on Ayah's views. All he said was, 'We'll have to go away some day.'

'How long have we been here?' I asked.

'Two hundred years.'

'No, I mean *us.*'

'Well, you were born in India, so that's seven years for you.'

'Then can't I stay here?'

'Do you want to?'

'I want to go across the sea. But can we take Ayah with us?'

'I don't know, son. Let's walk along the beach.'

We lived in an old palace beside a lake. The palace looked like a ruin from the outside, but the rooms were cool and comfortable. We lived in one wing, and my father organized a small school in another wing. His pupils were the children of the Raja and the Raja's relatives. My father had started life in India as a tea planter, but he had been trained as a teacher and the idea of starting a school in a small state facing the Arabian Sea had appealed to him. The pay wasn't much, but we had a palace to live in, the latest 1938-model Hillman to drive about in, and a number of servants. In those days, of course, everyone had servants (although the servants did not have any!). Ayah was our own; but the cook, the bearer, the gardener, and the bhisti were all provided by the state.

Sometimes I sat in the schoolroom with the other children (who were all much bigger than me), sometimes I remained in the house with Ayah, sometimes I followed the gardener, Dukhi, about the spacious garden.

Dukhi means 'sad', and though I never could discover if the gardener had anything to feel sad about, the name certainly suited him. He had grown to resemble the drooping weeds that he was always digging up with a tiny spade. I seldom saw him standing up. He always sat on the ground with his knees well up to his chin, and attacked the weeds from this position. He could spend all day on his haunches, moving about the garden simply by shuffling his feet along the grass.

I tried to imitate his posture, sitting down on my heels and putting my knees into my armpits, but could never hold the position for more than five minutes.

Time had no meaning in a large garden, and Dukhi never hurried. Life, for him, was not a matter of one year succeeding another, but of five seasons—winter, spring, hot weather, monsoon and autumn—arriving and departing. His seedbeds had always to be in readiness for the coming season, and he did not look any further than the next monsoon. It was impossible to tell his age. He may have been thirty-six or eighty-six. He was either very young for his years or very old for them.

Dukhi loved bright colours, specially reds and yellows. He liked strongly scented flowers, like jasmine and honeysuckle. He couldn't understand my father's preference for the more delicately perfumed petunias and sweet peas. But I shared Dukhi's fondness for the common bright orange marigold, which is offered in temples and is used to make garlands and nosegays. When the garden was bare of all colour, the marigold would still be there, gay and flashy, challenging the sun.

Dukhi was very fond of making nosegays, and I liked to watch him at work. A sunflower formed the centrepiece. It was surrounded by roses, marigolds and oleander, fringed with green leaves, and bound together with silver thread. The perfume was overpowering. The nosegays were presented to me or my father on special occasions, that is, on a birthday or to guests of my father's who were considered important.

One day I found Dukhi making a nosegay, and said, 'No one is coming today, Dukhi. It isn't even a birthday.'

'It is a birthday, chhota sahib,' he said. 'Little sahib' was the title he had given me. It wasn't much of a title compared to Raja sahib, Diwan sahib or Burra sahib, but it was nice to have a title at the age of seven.

'Oh,' I said. 'And is there a party, too?'

'No party.'

'What's the use of a birthday without a party? What's the use of a birthday without presents?'

'This person doesn't like presents—just flowers.'

'Who is it?' I asked, full of curiosity.

'If you want to find out, you can take these flowers to her. She lives right at the top of that far side of the palace. There are twenty-two steps to climb. Remember that, chhota sahib, you take twenty-three steps and you will go over the edge and into the lake!'

I started climbing the stairs.

It was a spiral staircase of wrought iron, and it went round and round and up and up, and it made me quite dizzy and tired.

At the top, I found myself on a small balcony which looked out over the lake and another palace, at the crowded city and the distant harbour. I heard a voice, a rather high,

231

musical voice, saying (in English), 'Are you a ghost?' I turned to see who had spoken but found the balcony empty. The voice had come from a dark room.

I turned to the stairway, ready to flee, but the voice said, 'Oh, don't go, there's nothing to be frightened of!'

And so I stood still, peering cautiously into the darkness of the room.

'First, tell me—are you a ghost?'

'I'm a boy,' I said.

'And I'm a girl. We can be friends. I can't come out there, so you had better come in. Come along, I'm not a ghost either—not yet, anyway!'

As there was nothing very frightening about the voice, I stepped into the room. It was dark inside, and, coming in from the glare, it took me some time to make out the tiny, elderly lady seated on a cushioned gilt chair. She wore a red sari, lots of coloured bangles on her wrists, and golden earrings. Her hair was streaked with white, but her skin was still quite smooth and unlined, and she had large and very beautiful eyes.

'You must be Master Bond!' she said. 'Do you know who I am?'

'You're a lady with a birthday,' I said, 'but that's all I know. Dukhi didn't tell me any more.'

'If you promise to keep it secret, I'll tell you who I am. You see, everyone thinks I'm mad. Do you think so too?'

'I don't know.'

'Well, you must tell me if you think so,' she said with a chuckle. Her laugh was the sort of sound made by the gecko, a little wall-lizard, coming from deep down in the throat. 'I have a feeling you are a truthful boy. Do you find it very difficult to tell the truth?'

'Sometimes.'

'Sometimes. Of course, there are times when I tell lies— lots of little lies—because they're such fun! But would you call me a liar? I wouldn't, if I were you, but *would* you?'

'Are you a liar?'

'I'm asking you! If I were to tell you that I was a queen— that I *am* a queen—would you believe me?'

I thought deeply about this, and then said, 'I'll try to believe you.'

'Oh, but you *must* believe me. I'm a real queen, I'm a rani! Look, I've got diamonds to prove it!' And she held out her hands, and there was a ring on each finger, the stones glowing and glittering in the dim light. 'Diamonds, rubies, pearls and emeralds! Only a queen can have these!' She was most anxious that I should believe her.

'You must be a queen,' I said.

'Right!' she snapped. 'In that case, would you mind calling me "Your Highness"?'

'Your Highness,' I said.

She smiled. It was a slow, beautiful smile. Her whole face lit up.

'I could love you,' she said. 'But better still, I'll give you something to eat. Do you like chocolates?'

'Yes, Your Highness.'

'Well,' she said, taking a box from the table beside her, 'these have come all the way from England. Take two. Only two, mind, otherwise the box will finish before Thursday, and I don't want that to happen because I won't get any more till Saturday. That's when Captain MacWhirr's ship gets in, the *S.S. Lucy*, loaded with boxes and boxes of chocolates!'

'All for you?' I asked in considerable awe.

'Yes, of course. They have to last at least three months. I get them from England. I get only the best chocolates. I like them with pink, crunchy fillings, don't you?'

'Oh, yes!' I exclaimed, full of envy.

'Never mind,' she said. 'I may give you one, now and then—if you're very nice to me! Here you are, help yourself . . .' She pushed the chocolate box towards me.

I took a silver-wrapped chocolate, and then just as I was thinking of taking a second, she quickly took the box away.

'No more!' she said. 'They have to last till Saturday.'

'But I took only *one*,' I said with some indignation.

'Did you?' She gave me a sharp look, decided I was telling the truth, and said graciously, 'Well, in that case, you can have another.'

Watching the rani carefully, in case she snatched the box away again, I selected a second chocolate, this one with a green wrapper. I don't remember what kind of day it was outside, but I remember the bright green of the chocolate wrapper.

I thought it would be rude to eat the chocolates in front of a queen, so I put them in my pocket and said, 'I'd better go now. Ayah will be looking for me.'

'And when will you be coming to see me again?'

'I don't know,' I said.

'Your Highness.'

'Your Highness.'

'There's something I want you to do for me,' she said, placing one finger on my shoulder and giving me a conspiratorial look. 'Will you do it?'

'What is it, Your Highness?'

'What is it? Why do you ask? A real prince never asks where or why or whatever, he simply does what the princess asks of him. When I was a princess—before I became a queen, that is—I asked a prince to swim across the lake and fetch me a lily growing on the other bank.'

'And did he get it for you?'

'He drowned half way across. Let *that* be a lesson to you. Never agree to do something without knowing what it is.'

'But I thought you said . . .'

'Never mind what I *said*. It's what I *say* that matters!'

'Oh, all right,' I said, fidgeting to be gone. 'What is it you want me to do?'

'Nothing.' Her tiny rosebud lips pouted and she stared sullenly at a picture on the wall. Now that my eyes had grown used to the dim light in the room, I noticed that the walls were hung with portraits of stout rajas and ranis turbaned and bedecked in fine clothes. There were also portraits of Queen Victoria and King George V of England. And, in the centre of all this distinguished company, a large picture of Mickey Mouse.

'I'll do it if it isn't too dangerous,' I said.

'Then listen.' She took my hand and drew me towards

her—what a tiny hand she had!—and whispered, 'I want a *red* rose. From the palace garden. But be careful! Don't let Dukhi, the gardener, catch you. He'll know it's for me. He knows I love roses. And he hates me! I'll tell you why, one day. But if he catches you, he'll do something terrible.'

'To me?'

'No, to himself. That's much worse, isn't it? He'll tie himself into knots, or lie naked on a bed of thorns, or go on a long fast with nothing to eat but fruit, sweets and chicken! So you will be careful, won't you?'

'Oh, but he doesn't hate you,' I cried in protest, remembering the flowers he'd sent for her, and looking around I found that I'd been sitting on them. 'Look, he sent these flowers for your birthday!'

'Well, if he sent them for my birthday, you can take them back,' she snapped. 'But if he sent them for *me . . .*' and she suddenly softened and looked coy, 'then I might keep them. Thank you, my dear, it was a very sweet thought.' And she leant forward as though to kiss me.

'It's late, I must go!' I said in alarm, and turning on my heels, ran out of the room and down the spiral staircase.

Father hadn't started lunch, or rather tiffin, as we called it then. He usually waited for me if I was late. I don't suppose he enjoyed eating alone.

For tiffin, we usually had rice, a mutton curry (koftas or meat balls, with plenty of gravy, was my favourite curry), fried dal and a hot lime or mango pickle. For supper, we had English food—a soup, roast pork and fried potatoes, a rich gravy made by my father, and a custard or caramel pudding.

My father enjoyed cooking, but it was only in the morning that he found time for it. Breakfast was his own creation. He cooked eggs in a variety of interesting ways, and favoured some Italian recipes which he had collected during a trip to Europe, long before I was born.

In deference to the feelings of our Hindu friends, we did not eat beef; but, apart from mutton and chicken, there was a plentiful supply of other meats—partridge, venison, lobster, and even porcupine!

'And where have you been?' asked my father, helping himself to the rice as soon as he saw me come in.

'To the top of the old palace,' I said.

'Did you meet anyone there?'

'Yes, I met a tiny lady who told me she was a rani. She gave me chocolates.'

'As a rule, she doesn't like visitors.'

'Oh, she didn't mind me. But is she really a queen?'

'Well, she's the daughter of a maharaja. That makes her a princess. She never married. There's a story that she fell in love with a commoner, one of the palace servants, and wanted to marry him, but of course they wouldn't allow that. She became very melancholic, and started living all by herself in the old palace. They give her everything she needs, but she doesn't go out or have visitors. Everyone says she's mad.'

'How do they know?' I asked.

'Because she's different from other people, I suppose.'

'Is that being mad?'

'No. Not really, I suppose, madness is not *seeing* things as others see them.'

'Is that very bad?'

'No,' said Father, who for once was finding it very difficult to explain something to me. 'But people who are like that—people whose minds are so different that they don't think, step by step, as we do, whose thoughts jump all over the place—such people are very difficult to live with . . .'

'Step by step,' I repeated. 'Step by step . . .'

'You aren't eating,' said my father. 'Hurry up, and you can come with me to school today.'

I always looked forward to attending my father's classes. He did not take me to the schoolroom very often, because he wanted school to be a treat, to begin with, and then, later, the routine wouldn't be so unwelcome.

Sitting there with older children, understanding only half of what they were learning, I felt important and part grown-up. And of course I did learn to read and write, although I first learnt to read upside down, by means of standing in front of the others' desks and peering across at their books. Later, when I went to school, I had some difficulty in learning to read the right way up; and even today I sometimes read upside down, for the sake of variety. I don't mean that I read standing on my head; simply that I held the book upside down.

I had at my command a number of rhymes and jingles, the most interesting of these being 'Solomon Grundy'.

Solomon Grundy,
Born on a Monday,
Christened on Tuesday,
Married on Wednesday,

Took ill on Thursday,
Worse on Friday,
Died on Saturday,
Buried on Sunday:
This is the end of
Solomon Grundy.

Was that all that life amounted to, in the end? And were we all Solomon Grundies? These were questions that bothered me at the time.

Another puzzling rhyme was the one that went:

Hark, hark,
The dogs do bark,
The beggars are coming to town;
Some in rags,
Some in bags,
And some in velvet gowns.

This rhyme puzzled me for a long time. There were beggars aplenty in the bazaar, and sometimes they came to the house, and some of them did wear rags and bags (and some nothing at all) and the dogs did bark at them, but the beggar in the velvet gown never came our way.

'Who's this beggar in a velvet gown?' I asked my father.

'Not a beggar at all,' he said.

'Then why call him one?'

And I went to Ayah and asked her the same question, 'Who is the beggar in the velvet gown?'

'Jesus Christ,' said Ayah.

Ayah was a fervent Christian and made me say my prayers at night, even when I was very sleepy. She had, I think, Arab and Negro blood in addition to the blood of the Koli fishing community to which her mother had belonged. Her father, a sailor on an Arab dhow, had been a convert to Christianity. Ayah was a large, buxom woman, with heavy hands and feet and a slow, swaying gait that had all the grace and majesty of a royal elephant. Elephants for all their size are nimble creatures; and Ayah, too, was nimble, sensitive, and gentle with her big hands. Her face was always sweet and childlike.

Although a Christian, she clung to many of the beliefs of her parents, and loved to tell me stories about mischievous spirits and evil spirits, humans who changed into animals, and snakes who had been princes in their former lives.

There was the story of the snake who married a princess. At first the princess did not wish to marry the snake, whom she had met in a forest, but the snake insisted, saying, 'I'll kill you if you won't marry me,' and of course that settled the question. The snake led his bride away and took her to a great treasure. 'I was a prince in my former life,' he explained. 'This treasure is yours.' And then the snake very gallantly disappeared.

'Snakes,' declared Ayah, 'are very lucky omens if seen early in the morning.'

'But what if the snake bites the lucky person?' I asked.

'He will be lucky all the same,' said Ayah with a logic that was all her own.

Snakes! There were a number of them living in the big garden, and my father had advised me to avoid the long grass. But I had seen snakes crossing the road (a lucky omen, according to Ayah) and they were never aggressive.

'A snake won't attack you,' said Father, 'provided you leave it alone. Of course, if you step on one, it will probably bite.'

'Are all snakes poisonous?'

'Yes, but only a few are poisonous enough to kill a man. Others use their poison on rats and frogs. A good thing, too, otherwise during the rains the house would be taken over by the frogs.'

One afternoon, while Father was at school, Ayah found a snake in the bathtub. It wasn't early morning and so the snake couldn't have been a lucky one. Ayah was frightened and ran into the garden calling for help. Dukhi came running. Ayah ordered me to stay outside while they went after the snake.

And it was while I was alone in the garden—an unusual circumstance, since Dukhi was nearly always there—that I remembered the rani's request. On an impulse, I went to the nearest rose bush and plucked the largest rose, pricking my thumb in the process.

And then, without waiting to see what had happened to the snake (it finally escaped), I started up the steps to the top of the old palace.

When I got to the top, I knocked on the door of the rani's room. Getting no reply, I walked along the balcony until I reached another doorway. There were wooden panels around the door, with elephants, camels and turbaned warriors carved into it. As the door was open, I walked boldly into the room, then stood still in astonishment. The room was filled with a strange light.

There were windows going right round the room, and each small windowpane was made of a different coloured glass. The sun that came through one window flung red and green and purple colours on the figure of the little rani who stood there with her face pressed to the glass.

She spoke to me without turning from the window. 'This is my favourite room. I have all the colours here. I can see a different world through each pane of glass. Come, join me!' And she beckoned to me, her small hand fluttering like a delicate butterfly.

I went up to the rani. She was only a little taller than me, and we were able to share the same windowpane.

'See, it's a red world!' she said.

The garden below, the palace and the lake were all tinted red. I watched the rani's world for a little while and then touched her on the arm and said, 'I have brought you a rose!'

She started away from me, and her eyes looked frightened.

She would not look at the rose.

'Oh, why did you bring it?' she cried, wringing her hands. 'He'll be arrested now!'

'Who'll be arrested?'

'The prince, of course!'

'But *I* took it,' I said. 'No one saw me. Ayah and Dukhi were inside the house, catching a snake.'

'Did they catch it?' she asked, forgetting about the rose.

'I don't know. I didn't wait to see!'

'They should follow the snake, instead of catching it. It may lead them to a treasure. All snakes have treasures to guard.'

This seemed to confirm what Ayah had been telling me, and I resolved that I would follow the next snake that I met.

'Don't you like the rose, then?' I asked.

'Did you steal it?'

'Yes.'

'Good. Flowers should always be stolen. They're more fragrant then.'

Because of a man called Hitler war had been declared in Europe and Britain was fighting Germany.

In my comic papers, the Germans were usually shown as blundering idiots; so I didn't see how Britain could possibly lose the war, nor why it should concern India, nor why it should be necessary for my father to join up. But I remember his showing me a newspaper headline which said:

BOMBS FALL ON BUCKINGHAM PALACE—KING AND QUEEN SAFE

I expect that had something to do with it.

He went to Delhi for an interview with the RAF and I was left in Ayah's charge.

It was a week I remember well, because it was the first time I had been left on my own. That first night I was afraid—afraid of the dark, afraid of the emptiness of the house, afraid of the howling of the jackals outside. The loud ticking of the clock was the only reassuring sound: clocks really made themselves heard in those days! I tried concentrating on the ticking, shutting out other sounds and the menace of the dark, but it wouldn't work. I thought I heard a faint hissing near the bed, and sat up, bathed in perspiration, certain that a snake was in the room. I shouted for Ayah and she came running, switching on all the lights.

'A snake!' I cried. 'There's a snake in the room!'

'Where, baba?'

'I don't know where, but I *heard* it.'

Ayah looked under the bed, and behind the chairs and tables, but there was no snake to be found. She persuaded me that I must have heard the breeze whispering in the mosquito curtains.

But I didn't want to be left alone.

'I'm coming to you,' I said and followed her into her small room near the kitchen.

Ayah slept on a low string cot. The mattress was thin, the blanket worn and patched up; but Ayah's warm and solid body made up for the discomfort of the bed. I snuggled up to her and was soon asleep.

I had almost forgotten the rani in the old palace and was about to pay her a visit when, to my surprise, I found her in the garden.

I had risen early that morning, and had gone running barefoot over the dew-drenched grass. No one was about, but I startled a flock of parrots and the birds rose screeching from a banyan tree and wheeled away to some other corner of the palace grounds. I was just in time to see a mongoose scurrying across the grass with an egg in its mouth. The mongoose must have been raiding the poultry farm at the palace.

I was trying to locate the mongoose's hideout, and was on all fours in a jungle of tall cosmos plants when I heard the rustle of clothes, and turned to find the rani staring at me.

She didn't ask me what I was doing there, but simply said, 'I don't think he could have gone in there.'

'But I saw him go this way,' I said.

'Nonsense! He doesn't live in this part of the garden. He lives in the roots of the banyan tree.'

'But that's where the snake lives,' I said.

'You mean the snake who was a prince. Well, that's who I'm looking for!'

'A snake who was a prince!' I gaped at the rani.

She made a gesture of impatience with her butterfly hands, and said, 'Tut, you're only a child, you can't *understand*. The prince lives in the roots of the banyan tree, but he comes out early every morning. Have you seen him?'

'No. But I saw a mongoose.'

The rani became frightened. 'Oh dear, is there a mongoose in the garden? He might kill the prince!'

'How can a mongoose kill a prince?' I asked.

'You don't understand, Master Bond. Princes, when they die, are born again as snakes.'

'*All* princes?'

'No, only those who die before they can marry.'

'Did your prince die before he could marry you?'

'Yes. And he returned to this garden in the form of a beautiful snake.'

'Well,' I said, 'I hope it wasn't the snake the water-carrier killed last week.'

'He killed a snake!' The rani looked horrified. She was quivering all over. 'It might have been the prince!'

'It was a brown snake,' I said.

'Oh, then it wasn't him.' She looked very relieved. 'Brown snakes are only ministers and people like that. It has to be a green snake to be a prince.'

'I haven't seen any green snakes here.'

'There's one living in the roots of the banyan tree. You won't kill it, will you?'

'Not if it's really a prince.'

'And you won't let others kill it?'

'I'll tell Ayah.'

'Good. You're on my side. But be careful of the gardener. Keep him away from the banyan tree. He's always killing snakes. I don't trust him at all.'

She came nearer and, leaning forward a little, looked into my eyes.

'Blue eyes—I trust them. But don't trust green eyes. And yellow eyes are evil.'

'I've never seen yellow eyes.'

'That's because you're pure,' she said, and turned away and hurried across the lawn as though she had just remembered a very urgent appointment.

The sun was up, slanting through the branches of the

246

banyan tree, and Ayah's voice could be heard calling me for breakfast.

'Dukhi,' I said, when I found him in the garden later that day, 'Dukhi, don't kill the snake in the banyan tree.'

'A snake in the banyan tree!' he exclaimed, seizing his hose.

'No, no!' I said. 'I haven't seen it. But the rani says there's one. She says it was a prince in its former life, and that we shouldn't kill it.'

'Oh,' said Dukhi, smiling to himself. 'The rani says so. All right, you tell her we won't kill it.'

'Is it true that she was in love with a prince but that he died before she could marry him?'

'Something like that,' said Dukhi. 'It was a long time ago—before I came here.'

'My father says it wasn't a prince, but a commoner. Are you a commoner, Dukhi?'

'A commoner? What's that, chhota sahib?'

'I'm not sure. Someone very poor, I suppose.'

'Then I must be a commoner,' said Dukhi.

'Were *you* in love with the rani?' I asked.

Dukhi was so startled that he dropped his hose and lost his balance; the first time I'd seen him lose his poise while squatting on his haunches.

'Don't say such things, chhota sahib!'

'Why not?'

'You'll get me into trouble.'

'Then it must be true.'

Dukhi threw up his hands in mock despair and started collecting his implements.

'It's true, it's true!' I cried, dancing round him, and then I ran indoors to Ayah and said, 'Ayah, Dukhi was in love with the rani!'

Ayah gave a shriek of laughter, then looked very serious and put her finger against my lips.

'Don't say such things,' she said. 'Dukhi is of a very low caste. People won't like it if they hear what you say. And besides, the rani told you her prince died and turned into a snake. Well, Dukhi hasn't become a snake as yet, has he?'

True, Dukhi didn't look as though he could be anything but a gardener; but I wasn't satisfied with his denials or with Ayah's attempts to still my tongue. Hadn't Dukhi sent the rani a nosegay?

When my father came home, he looked quite pleased with himself.

'What have you brought for me?' was the first question I asked.

He had brought me some new books, a dartboard, and a train set; and in my excitement over examining these gifts, I forgot to ask about the result of his trip.

It was during tiffin that he told me what had happened—and what was going to happen.

'We'll be going away soon,' he said. 'I've joined the Royal Air Force. I'll have to work in Delhi.'

'Oh! Will you be in the war, Dad? Will you fly a plane?'

'No, I'm too old to be flying planes. I'll be forty years in July. The RAF will be giving me what they call intelligence work—decoding secret messages and things like that and I don't suppose I'll be able to tell you much about it.'

This didn't sound as exciting as flying planes, but it sounded important and rather mysterious.

'Well, I hope it's interesting,' I said. 'Is Delhi a good place to live in?'

'I'm not sure. It will be very hot by the middle of April. And you won't be able to stay with me, Ruskin—not at first, anyway, not until I can get married quarters and then, only if your mother returns . . . Meanwhile, you'll stay with your grandmother in Dehra.' He must have seen the disappointment in my face, because he quickly added, 'Of course I'll come to see you often. Dehra isn't far from Delhi—only a night's train journey.'

But I was dismayed. It wasn't that I didn't want to stay with my grandmother, but I had grown so used to sharing my father's life and even watching him at work, that the thought of being separated from him was unbearable.

'Not as bad as going to boarding school,' he said. 'And that's the only alternative.'

'Not boarding school,' I said quickly. 'I'll run away from boarding school.'

'Well, you won't want to run away from your grandmother. She's very fond of you. And if you come with me to Delhi, you'll be alone all day in a stuffy little hut while I'm away at work. Sometimes I may have to go on tour—then what happens?'

'I don't mind being on my own.' And this was true. I had already grown accustomed to having my own room and my own trunk and my own bookshelf and I felt as though I was about to lose these things.

'Will Ayah come too?' I asked.

My father looked thoughtful. 'Would you like that?'

'Ayah must come,' I said firmly. 'Otherwise, I'll run away.'

'I'll have to ask her,' said my father.

Ayah, it turned out, was quite ready to come with us. In fact, she was indignant that Father should have considered leaving her behind. She had brought me up since my mother went away, and she wasn't going to hand over charge to any upstart aunt or governess. She was pleased and excited at the prospect of the move, and this helped to raise my spirits.

'What is Dehra like?' I asked my father.

'It's a green place,' he said. 'It lies in a valley in the foothills of the Himalayas, and it's surrounded by forests. There are lots of trees in Dehra.'

'Does Grandmother's house have trees?'

'Yes. There's a big jackfruit tree in the garden. Your grandmother planted it when I was a boy. And there's an old banyan tree, which is good to climb. And there are fruit trees, litchis, mangoes, papayas.'

'Are there any books?'

'Grandmother's books won't interest you. But I'll be bringing you books from Delhi whenever I come to see you.'

I was beginning to look forward to the move. Changing houses had always been fun. Changing towns ought to be fun, too.

A few days before we left, I went to say goodbye to the rani.

'I'm going away,' I said.

'How lovely!' said the rani. 'I wish I could go away!'

'Why don't you?'

'They won't let me. They're afraid to let me out of the palace.'

'What are they afraid of, Your Highness?'

'That I might run away. Run away, far far away, to the land where the leopards are learning to pray.'

Gosh, I thought, she's really quite crazy . . . But then she was silent, and started smoking a small hookah.

She drew on the hookah, looked at me, and asked, 'Where is your mother?'

'I haven't one.'

'Everyone has a mother. Did yours die?'

'No. She went away.'

She drew on her hookah again and then said, very sweetly, 'Don't go away . . .'

'I must,' I said. 'It's because of the war.'

'What war? Is there a war on? You see, no one tells me anything.'

'It's between us and Hitler,' I said.

'And who is Hitler?'

'He's a German.'

'I knew a German once, Dr Schreinherr, he had beautiful hands.'

'Was he an artist?'

'He was a dentist.'

The rani got up from her couch and accompanied me out on to the balcony. When we looked down at the garden, we could see Dukhi weeding a flower bed. Both of us gazed down at him in silence, and I wondered what the rani would say if I asked her if she had ever been in love with the palace gardener. Ayah had told me it would be an insulting question, so I held my peace. But as I walked slowly down the spiral staircase, the rani's voice came after me.

'Thank him,' she said. 'Thank him for the beautiful rose.'

The Last Tonga Ride

IT WAS A warm spring day in Dehra Dun, and the walls of the bungalow were aflame with flowering bougainvillaea. The papayas were ripening. The scent of sweet peas drifted across the garden. Grandmother sat in an easy chair in a shady corner of the veranda, her knitting needles clicking away, her head nodding now and then. She was knitting a pullover for my father. 'Delhi has cold winters,' she had said, and although the winter was still eight months away, she had set to work on getting our woollens ready.

In the Kathiawar states touched by the warm waters of the Arabian Sea, it had never been cold. But Dehra lies at the foot of the first range of the Himalayas.

Grandmother's hair was white and her eyes were not very strong, but her fingers moved quickly with the needles and the needles kept clicking all morning.

When Grandmother wasn't looking, I picked geranium

leaves, crushed them between my fingers and pressed them to my nose.

I had been in Dehra with my grandmother for almost a month and I had not seen my father during this time. We had never before been separated for so long. He wrote to me every week, and sent me books and picture postcards, and I would walk to the end of the road to meet the postman as early as possible to see if there was any mail for us.

We heard the jingle of tonga bells at the gate and a familiar horse-buggy came rattling up the drive.

'I'll see who's come,' I said, and ran down the veranda steps and across the garden.

It was Bansi Lal in his tonga. There were many tongas and tonga-drivers in Dehra but Bansi was my favourite driver. He was young and handsome and always wore a clean white shirt and pyjamas. His pony, too, was bigger and faster than the other tonga ponies.

Bansi didn't have a passenger, so I asked him, 'What have you come for, Bansi?'

'Your grandmother sent for me, dost.' He did not call me 'chhota sahib' or 'baba', but 'dost' and this made me feel much more important. Not every small boy could boast of a tonga-driver for his friend!

'Where are you going, Granny?' I asked, after I had run back to the veranda.

'I'm going to the bank.'

'Can I come too?'

'Whatever for? What will you do in the bank?'

'Oh, I won't come inside, I'll sit in the tonga with Bansi.'

'Come along, then.'

We helped Grandmother into the back seat of the tonga, and then I joined Bansi in the driver's seat. He said something to his pony and the pony set off at a brisk trot, out of the gate and down the road.

'Now, not too fast, Bansi,' said Grandmother, who didn't like anything that went too fast—tonga, motor car, train, or bullock-cart.

'Fast?' said Bansi. 'Have no fear, memsahib. This pony has never gone fast in its life. Even if a bomb went off behind us, we could go no faster. I have another pony which I use for racing when customers are in a hurry. This pony is reserved for you, memsahib.'

There was no other pony, but Grandmother did not know this, and was mollified by the assurance that she was riding in the slowest tonga in Dehra.

A ten-minute ride brought us to the bazaar. Grandmother's bank, the Allahabad Bank, stood near the clock tower. She was gone for about half-an-hour and, during this period, Bansi and I sauntered about in front of the shops. The pony had been left with some green stuff to munch.

'Do you have any money on you?' asked Bansi.

'Four annas,' I said.

'Just enough for two cups of tea,' said Bansi, putting his arm round my shoulders and guiding me towards a tea stall. The money passed from my palm to his.

'You can have tea, if you like,' I said. 'I'll have a lemonade.'

'So be it, friend. A tea and a lemonade, and be quick about it,' said Bansi to the boy in the tea shop and presently the drinks were set before us and Bansi was making a sound rather like his pony when it drank, while I burped my way through some green, gaseous stuff that tasted more like soap than lemonade.

When Grandmother came out of the bank, she looked pensive and did not talk much during the ride back to the house except to tell me to behave myself when I leant over to pat the pony on its rump. After paying off Bansi, she marched straight indoors.

'When will you come again?' I asked Bansi.

'When my services are required, dost. I have to make a living, you know. But I tell you what, since we are friends, the next time I am passing this way after leaving a fare, I will jingle my bells at the gate and if you are free and would like a ride—a fast ride!—you can join me. It won't cost you anything. Just bring some money for a cup of tea.'

'All right—since we are friends,' I said.

'Since we are friends.'

And touching the pony very lightly with the handle of his whip, he sent the tonga rattling up the drive and out of the gate. I could hear Bansi singing as the pony cantered down the road.

Ayah was waiting for me in the bedroom, her hands resting on her broad hips—sure sign of an approaching storm.

'So you went off to the bazaar without telling me,' she said. (It wasn't enough that I had Grandmother's permission!) 'And all this time I've been waiting to give you your bath.'

'It's too late now, isn't it?' I asked hopefully.

'No, it isn't. There's still an hour left for lunch. Off with your clothes!'

While I undressed, Ayah berated me for keeping the company of tonga-drivers like Bansi. I think she was a little jealous.

'He is a rogue, that man. He drinks, gambles, and smokes opium. He has T.B. and other terrible diseases. So don't you be too friendly with him, understand, baba?'

I nodded my head sagely but said nothing. I thought Ayah was exaggerating as she always did about people and, besides, I had no intention of giving up free tonga rides.

As my father had told me, Dehra was a good place for trees, and Grandmother's house was surrounded by several kinds—peepul, neem, mango, jackfruit, papaya, and an ancient banyan tree. Some of the trees had been planted by my father and grandfather.

'How old is the jackfruit tree?' I asked Grandmother.

'Now let me see,' said Grandmother, looking very thoughtful. 'I should remember the jackfruit tree. Oh yes, your grandfather put it down in 1927. It was during the rainy season. I remember because it was your father's birthday and we celebrated it by planting a tree—14 July 1927. Long before you were born!'

The banyan tree grew behind the house. Its spreading branches, which hung to the ground and took root again, formed a number of twisting passageways in which I liked to wander. The tree was older than the house, older than my grandparents, as old as Dehra. I could hide myself in its branches behind thick, green leaves and spy on the world below.

It was an enormous tree, about sixty feet high, and the first time I saw it, I trembled with excitement because I had never seen such a marvellous tree before. I approached it slowly, even cautiously, as I wasn't sure the tree wanted my friendship. It looked as though it had many secrets. There were sounds and movements in the branches but I couldn't see who or what made the sounds.

The tree made the first move, the first overture of friendship.

It allowed a leaf to fall.

The leaf brushed against my face as it floated down, but before it could reach the ground, I caught and held it. I studied the leaf, running my fingers over its smooth, glossy texture. Then I put out my hand and touched the rough bark of the tree and this felt good to me. So I removed my shoes and socks as people do when they enter a holy place; and finding first a foothold and then a handhold on that broad trunk, I pulled myself up with the help of the tree's aerial roots.

As I climbed, it seemed as though someone was helping me. Invisible hands, the hands of the spirit in the tree, touched me and helped me climb.

But although the tree wanted me, there were others who were disturbed and alarmed by my arrival. A pair of parrots suddenly shot out of a hole in the trunk and with shrill cries, flew across the garden—flashes of green and red and gold. A squirrel looked out from behind a branch, saw me, and went scurrying away to inform his friends and relatives.

I climbed higher, looked up, and saw a red beak poised above my head. I shrank away, but the hornbill made no attempt to attack me. He was relaxing in his home, which was a great hole in the tree trunk. Only the bird's head and great beak were showing. He looked at me in rather a bored way, drowsily opening and shutting his eyes.

'So many creatures live here,' I said to myself. 'I hope none of them is dangerous!'

At that moment the hornbill lunged at a passing cricket.

Bill and tree trunk met with a loud and resonant 'Tonk!'

I was so startled that I nearly fell out of the tree. But it was a difficult tree to fall out of! It was full of places where one could sit or even lie down. So I moved away from the hornbill, crawled along a branch which had sent out supports, and so moved quite a distance from the main body of the tree. I left its cold, dark depths for an area penetrated by shafts of sunlight.

No one could see me. I lay flat on the broad branch hidden by a screen of leaves. People passed by on the road below. A sahib in a sun-helmet, his memsahib twirling a coloured silk sun-umbrella. Obviously, she did not want to get too brown and be mistaken for a country-born person. Behind them, a pram wheeled along by a nanny.

Then there were a number of Indians—some in white dhotis, some in western clothes, some in loincloths. Some with baskets on their heads. Others with coolies to carry their baskets for them.

A cloud of dust, the blare of a horn, and down the road, like an out-of-condition dragon, came the latest Morris touring car. Then cyclists. Then a man with a basket of papayas balanced on his head. Following him, a man with a performing monkey. This man rattled a little hand-drum, and children followed man and monkey along the road. They stopped in the shade of a mango tree on the other side of the road. The little red monkey wore a frilled dress and a baby's bonnet. It danced for the children, while the man sang and played his drum.

The clip-clop of a tonga pony, and Bansi's tonga came rattling down the road. I called down to him and he reined in with a shout of surprise, and looked up into the branches of the banyan tree.

'What are you doing up there?' he cried.

'Hiding from Grandmother,' I said.

'And when are you coming for that ride?'

'On Tuesday afternoon,' I said.

'Why not today?'

'Ayah won't let me. But she has Tuesdays off.'

Bansi spat red paan-juice across the road. 'Your ayah is jealous,' he said.

'I know,' I said. 'Women are always jealous, aren't they? I suppose it's because she doesn't have a tonga.'

'It's because she doesn't have a tonga-driver,' said Bansi, grinning up at me. 'Never mind. I'll come on Tuesday—that's the day after tomorrow, isn't it?'

I nodded down to him, and then started backing along my branch, because I could hear Ayah calling in the distance.

Bansi leant forward and smacked his pony across the rump, and the tonga shot forward.

'What were you doing up there?' asked Ayah a little later.

'I was watching a snake cross the road,' I said. I knew she couldn't resist talking about snakes. There weren't as many in Dehra as there had been in Kathiawar and she was thrilled that I had seen one.

'Was it moving towards you or away from you?' she asked.

'It was going away.'

Ayah's face clouded over. 'That means poverty for the beholder,' she said gloomily.

Later, while scrubbing me down in the bathroom, she began to air all her prejudices, which included drunkards ('they die quickly, anyway'), misers ('they get murdered sooner or later') and tonga-drivers ('they have all the vices').

'You are a very lucky boy,' she said suddenly, peering closely at my tummy.

'Why?' I asked. 'You just said I would be poor because I saw a snake going the wrong way.'

'Well, you won't be poor for long. You have a mole on your tummy and that's very lucky. And there is one under your armpit, which means you will be famous. Do you have one on the neck? No, thank God! A mole on the neck is the sign of a murderer!'

'Do you have any moles?' I asked.

Ayah nodded seriously, and pulling her sleeve up to her shoulder, showed me a large mole high on her arm.

'What does that mean?' I asked.

'It means a life of great sadness,' said Ayah gloomily.

'Can I touch it?' I asked.

'Yes, touch it,' she said, and taking my hand, she placed it against the mole.

'It's a nice mole,' I said, wanting to make Ayah happy. 'Can I kiss it?'

'You can kiss it,' said Ayah. I kissed her on the mole.

'That's nice,' she said.

Tuesday afternoon came at last, and as soon as Grandmother was asleep and Ayah had gone to the bazaar, I was at the gate, looking up and down the road for Bansi and his tonga. He was not long in coming. Before the tonga turned into the road, I could hear his voice, singing to the accompaniment of the carriage bells.

He reached down, took my hand, and hoisted me on to the seat beside him. Then we went off down the road at a steady jog-trot. It was only when we reached the outskirts of the town that Bansi encouraged his pony to greater efforts. He rose in his seat, leaned forward and slapped the pony across the haunches. From a brisk trot we changed to a carefree canter. The tonga swayed from side to side. I clung to Bansi's free arm, while he grinned at me, his mouth red with paan-juice.

'Where shall we go, dost?' he asked.

'Nowhere,' I said.

'Anywhere.'

'We'll go to the river,' said Bansi.

The 'river' was really a swift mountain stream that ran

through the forests outside Dehra, joining the Ganga about fifteen miles away. It was almost dry during the winter and early summer; in flood during the monsoon.

The road out of Dehra was a gentle decline and soon we were rushing headlong through the tea gardens and eucalyptus forests, the pony's hoofs striking sparks off the metalled road, the carriage wheels groaning and creaking so loudly that I feared one of them would come off and that we would all be thrown into a ditch or into the small canal that ran beside the road. We swept through mango groves, through guava and litchi orchards, past broad-leaved sal and shisham trees. Once in the sal forest, Bansi turned the tonga on to a rough cart-track, and we continued along it for about a furlong, until the road dipped down to the stream bed.

'Let us go straight into the water,' said Bansi. 'You and I and the pony!' And he drove the tonga straight into the middle of the stream, where the water came up to the pony's knees.

'I am not a great one for baths,' said Bansi, 'but the pony needs one, and why should a horse smell sweeter than its owner?' saying which, he flung off his clothes and jumped into the water.

'Better than bathing under a tap!' he cried, slapping himself on the chest and thighs. 'Come down, dost, and join me!'

After some hesitation I joined him, but had some difficulty in keeping on my feet in the fast current. I grabbed at the pony's tail and hung on to it, while Bansi began sloshing water over the patient animal's back.

After this, Bansi led both me and the pony out of the stream and together we gave the carriage a good washing down. I'd had a free ride and Bansi got the services of a free helper for the long overdue spring-cleaning of his tonga. After we had finished the job, he presented me with a packet of aam papad—a sticky toffee made from mango pulp—and for some time I tore at it as a dog tears at a bit of old leather. Then I felt drowsy and lay down on the brown, sun-warmed grass. Crickets and grasshoppers were telephoning each other from tree and bush and a pair of bluejays rolled, dived, and swooped acrobatically overhead.

Bansi had no watch. He looked at the sun and said, 'It is past three. When will that ayah of yours be home? She is more frightening than your grandmother!'

'She comes at four.'

'Then we must hurry back. And don't tell her where we've been, or I'll never be able to come to your house again. Your grandmother's one of my best customers.'

'That means you'd be sorry if she died.'

'I would indeed, my friend.'

Bansi raced the tonga back to town. There was very little motor traffic in those days, and tongas and bullock-carts were far more numerous than they are today.

We were back five minutes before Ayah returned. Before Bansi left, he promised to take me for another ride the following week.

The house in Dehra had to be sold. My father had not left any money; he had never realized that his health would deteriorate so rapidly from the malarial fevers which had grown in frequency. He was still planning for the future when he died. Now that my father was gone, Grandmother saw no point in staying on in India; there was nothing left in the bank and she needed money for our passages to England, so the house had to go. Dr Ghose, who had a thriving medical practice in Dehra, made her a reasonable offer, which she accepted.

Then things happened very quickly. Grandmother sold most of our belongings, because as she said, we wouldn't be able to cope with a lot of luggage. The kabaris came in droves, buying up crockery, furniture, carpets and clocks at throwaway prices. Grandmother hated parting with some of her possessions such as the carved giltwood mirror, her walnut-wood armchair and her rosewood writing desk, but it was impossible to take them with us. They were carried away in a bullock-cart.

Ayah was very unhappy at first but cheered up when Grandmother got her a job with a tea planter's family in Assam. It was arranged that she could stay with us until we left Dehra.

We went at the end of September, just as the monsoon clouds broke up, scattered, and were driven away by soft breezes from the Himalayas. There was no time to revisit the island where my father and I had planted our trees. And in the urgency and excitement of the preparations for our departure, I forgot to recover my small treasures from the hole in the banyan tree. It was only when we were in Bansi's tonga, on the way to the station, that I remembered my top, catapult, and Iron Cross. Too late! To go back for them would mean missing the train.

'Hurry!' urged Grandmother nervously. 'We mustn't be late for the train, Bansi.'

Bansi flicked the reins and shouted to his pony, and for once in her life Grandmother submitted to being carried along the road at a brisk trot.

'It's five to nine,' she said, 'and the train leaves at nine.'

'Do not worry, memsahib. I have been taking you to the station for fifteen years, and you have never missed a train!'

'No,' said Grandmother. 'And I don't suppose you'll ever take me to the station again, Bansi.'

'Times are changing, memsahib. Do you know that there is now a taxi—a *motor car*—competing with the tongas of Dehra? You are lucky to be leaving. If you stay, you will see me starve to death!'

'We will all starve to death if we don't catch that train,' said Grandmother.

'Do not worry about the train, it never leaves on time, and no one expects it to. If it left at nine o'clock, everyone would miss it.'

Bansi was right. We arrived at the station at five minutes past nine, and rushed on to the platform, only to find that the train had not yet arrived.

The platform was crowded with people waiting to catch the same train or to meet people arriving on it. Ayah was there already, standing guard over a pile of miscellaneous luggage. We sat down on our boxes and became part of the platform life at an Indian railway station.

Moving among piles of bedding and luggage were

sweating, cursing coolies; vendors of magazines, sweetmeats, tea and betel-leaf preparations; also stray dogs, stray people and sometimes a stray stationmaster. The cries of the vendors mixed with the general clamour of the station and the shunting of a steam engine in the yards. 'Tea, hot tea!' Sweets, papads, hot stuff, cold drinks, toothpowder, pictures of film stars, bananas, balloons, wooden toys, clay images of the gods. The platform had become a bazaar.

Ayah was giving me all sorts of warnings.

'Remember, baba, don't lean out of the window when the train is moving. There was that American boy who lost his head last year! And don't eat rubbish at every station between here and Bombay. And see that no strangers enter the compartment. Mr Wilkins was murdered and robbed last year!'

The station bell clanged, and in the distance there appeared a big, puffing steam engine, painted green and gold and black. A stray dog with a lifetime's experience of trains, darted away across the railway lines. As the train came alongside the platform, doors opened, window shutters fell, faces appeared in the openings, and even before the train had come to a stop, people were trying to get in or out.

For a few moments there was chaos. The crowd surged backward and forward. No one could get out. No one could get in. A hundred people were leaving the train, two hundred were getting into it. No one wanted to give way.

The problem was solved by a man climbing out of a window. Others followed his example and the pressure at the doors eased and people started squeezing into their compartments.

Grandmother had taken the precaution of reserving berths in a first-class compartment, and assisted by Bansi and half-a-dozen coolies, we were soon inside with all our luggage. A whistle blasted and we were off! Bansi had to jump from the running train.

As the engine gathered speed, I ignored Ayah's advice and put my head out of the window to look back at the receding platform. Ayah and Bansi were standing on the platform waving to me, and I kept waving to them until the train rushed into the darkness and the bright lights of Dehra were swallowed up in the night. New lights, dim and flickering, came into existence as we passed small villages. The stars too were visible and I saw a shooting star streaking through the heavens.

I remembered something that Ayah had once told me, that stars are the spirits of good men, and I wondered if that shooting star was a sign from my father that he was aware of our departure and would be with us on our journey. And I remembered something else that Ayah had said—that if one wished on a shooting star, one's wish would be granted, provided, of course, that one thrust all five fingers into the mouth at the same time!

'What on earth are you doing?' asked Grandmother staring at me as I thrust my hand into my mouth.

'Making a wish,' I said.

'Oh,' said Grandmother.

She was preoccupied, and didn't ask me what I was wishing for; nor did I tell her.

The Funeral

'I DON'T THINK he should go,' said Aunt M.

'He's too small,' concurred Aunt B. 'He'll get upset, and probably throw a tantrum. And you know Padre Lal doesn't like having children at funerals.'

The boy said nothing. He sat in the darkest corner of the darkened room, his face revealing nothing of what he thought and felt. His father's coffin lay in the next room, the lid fastened forever over the tired, wistful countenance of the man who had meant so much to the boy. Nobody else had mattered—neither uncles nor aunts nor fond grandparents. Least of all the mother who was hundreds of miles away with another husband. He hadn't seen her since he was four—that was just over five years ago—and he did not remember her very well.

The house was full of people—friends, relatives, neighbours. Some had tried to fuss over him but had been discouraged by his silence, the absence of tears. The more understanding of them had kept their distance.

Scattered words of condolence passed back and forth like dragonflies on the wind. 'Such a tragedy!' . . . 'Only forty'. . .

'No one realized how serious it was . . .' 'Devoted to the child' . . .

It seemed to the boy that everyone who mattered in the hill station was present. And for the first time they had the run of the house for his father had not been a sociable man. Books, music, flowers and his stamp collection had been his main preoccupations, apart from the boy.

A small hearse, drawn by a hill pony, was led in at the gate and several able-bodied men lifted the coffin and manoeuvred it into the carriage. The crowd drifted away. The cemetery was about a mile down the road and those who did not have cars would have to walk the distance.

The boy stared through a window at the small procession passing through the gate. He'd been forgotten for the moment—left in care of the servants, who were the only ones to stay behind. Outside, it was misty. The mist had crept up the valley and settled like a damp towel on the face of the mountain. Everyone was wet although it hadn't rained.

The boy waited until everyone had gone and then he left the room and went out on the veranda. The gardener, who had been sitting in a bed of nasturtiums, looked up and asked the boy if he needed anything. But the boy shook his head and retreated indoors. The gardener, looking aggrieved because of the damage done to the flower beds by the mourners, shambled off to his quarters. The sahib's death meant that he would be out of a job very soon. The house would pass into other hands. The boy would go to an orphanage. There weren't many people who kept gardeners these days. In the kitchen, the cook was busy preparing the only big meal ever served in the house. All those relatives, and the Padre too, would come back famished, ready for a sombre but nevertheless substantial meal. He too would be out of a job soon; but cooks were always in demand.

The boy slipped out of the house by a back door and made his way into the lane through a gap in a thicket of dog-roses. When he reached the main road, he could see the mourners wending their way round the hill to the cemetery. He followed at a distance.

It was the same road he had often taken with his father during their evening walks. The boy knew the name of almost every plant and wildflower that grew on the hillside. These, and various birds and insects, had been described and pointed out to him by his father.

Looking northwards, he could see the higher ranges of the Himalayas and the eternal snows. The graves in the cemetery were so laid out that if their incumbents did happen to rise one day, the first thing they would see would be the glint of the sun on those snow-covered peaks. Possibly the site had been chosen for the view. But to the boy it did not seem as if anyone would be able to thrust aside those massive tombstones and rise from their graves to enjoy the view. Their rest seemed as eternal as the snows.

It would take an earthquake to burst those stones asunder and thrust the coffins up from the earth. The boy wondered why people hadn't made it easier for the dead to rise. They were so securely entombed that it appeared as though no one really wanted them to get out.

'God has need of your father . . .' With those words a well-meaning missionary had tried to console him.

And had God, in the same way, laid claim to the thousands of men, women and children who had been put to rest here in these neat and serried rows? What could he have wanted them for? Of what use are we to God when we are dead, wondered the boy.

The cemetery gate stood open but the boy leant against the old stone wall and stared down at the mourners as they shuffled about with the unease of a batsman about to face a very fast bowler. Only this bowler was invisible and would come up stealthily and from behind.

Padre Lal's voice droned on through the funeral service and then the coffin was lowered—down, deep down—the boy was surprised at how far down it seemed to go! Was that other, better world down in the depths of the earth? How could anyone, even a Samson, push his way back to the surface again? Superman did it in comics but his father was a gentle soul who wouldn't fight too hard against the earth and the grass and the roots of tiny trees. Or perhaps he'd grow into a tree and escape that way! 'If ever I'm put away like this,' thought the boy, 'I'll get into the root of a plant and then I'll become a flower and then maybe a bird will come and carry my seed away . . . I'll get out somehow!'

A few more words from the Padre and then some of those present threw handfuls of earth over the coffin before moving away.

Slowly, in twos and threes, the mourners departed. The mist swallowed them up. They did not see the boy behind the wall. They were getting hungry.

He stood there until they had all gone. Then he noticed that the gardeners or caretakers were filling in the grave. He did not know whether to go forward or not. He was a little afraid. And it was too late now. The grave was almost covered.

He turned and walked away from the cemetery. The road stretched ahead of him, empty, swathed in mist. He was alone. What had his father said to him once? 'The strongest man in the world is he who stands alone.'

Well, he was alone, but at the moment he did not feel very strong.

For a moment he thought his father was beside him, that they were together on one of their long walks. Instinctively, he put out his hand, expecting his father's warm, comforting touch. But there was nothing there, nothing, no one . . .

He clenched his fists and pushed them deep down into his pockets. He lowered his head so that no one would see his tears. There were people in the mist but he did not want to go near them for they had put his father away.

'He'll find a way out,' the boy said fiercely to himself. 'He'll get out somehow!'

All Creatures Great and Small

INSTEAD OF HAVING brothers and sisters to grow up with in India, I had as my companions an odd assortment of pets, which included a monkey, a tortoise, a python and a Great Indian Hornbill. The person responsible for all this wildlife in the home was my grandfather. As the house was his own, other members of the family could not prevent him from keeping a large variety of pets, though they could certainly voice their objections; and as most of the household consisted of women— my grandmother, visiting aunts and occasional in-laws (my parents were in Burma at the time)—Grandfather and I had to be alert and resourceful in dealing with them. We saw eye to eye on the subject of pets, and whenever Grandmother decided it was time to get rid of a tame white rat or a squirrel, I would conceal them in a hole in the jackfruit tree; but unlike my aunts, she was generally tolerant of Grandfather's hobby, and even took a liking to some of our pets.

Grandfather's house and menagerie were in Dehra and I remember travelling there in a horse-drawn buggy. There were cars in those days—it was just over twenty years ago—but in the foothills a tonga was just as good, almost as fast, and certainly more dependable when it came to getting across the swift little Tons river.

During the rains, when the river flowed strong and deep, it was impossible to get across except on a hand-operated ropeway; but in the dry months, the horse went splashing through, the carriage wheels churning through clear mountain water. If the horse found the going difficult, we removed our shoes, rolled up our skirts or trousers, and waded across.

When Grandfather first went to stay in Dehra, early in the century, the only way of getting there was by the night mailcoach. Mail ponies, he told me, were difficult animals, always attempting to turn around and get into the coach with the passengers. It was only when the coachman used his whip liberally, and reviled the ponies' ancestors as far back as their third and fourth generations, that the beasts could be persuaded to move. And once they started, there was no stopping them. It was a gallop all the way to the first stage, where the ponies were changed to the accompaniment of a bugle blown by the coachman.

At one stage of the journey, drums were beaten; and if it was night, torches were lit to keep away the wild elephants who, resenting the approach of this clumsy caravan, would sometimes trumpet a challenge and throw the ponies into confusion.

Grandfather disliked dressing up and going out, and was only too glad to send everyone shopping or to the pictures—Harold Lloyd and Eddie Cantor were the favourites at Dehra's small cinema—so that he could be left alone to feed his pets and potter about in the garden. There were a lot of animals to be fed, including, for a time, a pair of great Danes who had such enormous appetites that we were forced to give them away to a more affluent family.

The Great Danes were gentle creatures, and I would sit astride one of them and go for rides round the garden. In spite of their size, they were very sure-footed and never knocked over people or chairs. A little monkey, like Toto, did much more damage.

Grandfather bought Toto from a tonga-owner for the sum of five rupees. The tonga-man used to keep the little red monkey tied to a feeding-trough, and Toto looked so out of place there—almost conscious of his own incongruity—that Grandfather immediately decided to add him to our menagerie. Toto was really a pretty little monkey. His bright eyes sparkled with mischief beneath deep-set eyebrows, and his teeth, a pearly-white, were often on display in a smile that frightened the life out of elderly Anglo-Indian ladies. His hands were not those of a Tallulah Bankhead (Grandfather's only favourite actress), but were shrivelled and dried-up, as though they had been pickled in the sun for many years. But his fingers were quick and restless; and his tail, while adding to his good looks—Grandfather maintained that a tail would add to anyone's good looks—often performed the service of a third hand. He could use it to hang from a branch; and it was capable of scooping up any delicacy that might be out of reach of his hands.

Grandmother, anticipating an outcry from other relatives, always raised objections when Grandfather brought home some new bird or animal, and so for a while we managed to keep Toto's presence a secret by lodging him in a little closet opening into my bedroom wall. But in a few hours he managed to dispose of Grandmother's ornamental wallpaper and the better part of my school blazer. He was transferred to the stables for a day or two, and then Grandfather had to make a trip to neighbouring Saharanpur to collect his railway pension and, anxious to keep Toto out of trouble, he decided to take the monkey along with him.

Unfortunately, I could not accompany Grandfather on this trip, but he told me about it afterwards.

A black kit-bag was provided for Toto. When the strings of the bag were tied, there was no means of escape from within, and the canvas was too strong for Toto to bite his way through. His initial efforts to get out only had the effect of making the bag roll about on the floor, or occasionally jump in the air—an exhibition that attracted a curious crowd of onlookers on the Dehra railway platform.

Toto remained in the bag as far as Saharanpur, but while Grandfather was producing his ticket at the railway turnstile, Toto managed to get his hands through the aperture where the bag was tied, loosened the strings, and suddenly thrust his head through the opening.

The poor ticket-collector was visibly alarmed; but with great presence of mind, and much to the annoyance of

Grandfather, he said, 'Sir, you have a dog with you. You'll have to pay for it accordingly.'

In vain did Grandfather take Toto out of the bag to prove that a monkey was not a dog or even a quadruped. The ticket-collector, now thoroughly annoyed, insisted on classing Toto as a dog; and three rupees and four annas had to be handed over as his fare. Then Grandfather, out of sheer spite, took out from his pocket a live tortoise that he happened to have with him, and said, 'What must I pay for this, since you charge for all animals?'

The ticket-collector retreated a pace or two; then advancing again with caution, he subjected the tortoise to a grave and knowledgeable stare.

'No ticket is necessary, sir,' he finally declared. 'There is no charge for insects.'

When we discovered that Toto's favourite pastime was catching mice, we were able to persuade Grandmother to let us keep him. The unsuspecting mice would emerge from their holes at night to pick up any corn left over by our pony; and to get at it they had to run the gauntlet of Toto's section of the stable. He knew this, and would pretend to be asleep, keeping, however, one eye open. A mouse would make a rush—in vain; Toto, as swift as a cat, would have his paws upon him . . . Grandmother decided to put his talents to constructive use by tying him up one night in the larder, where a guerrilla band of mice were playing havoc with our food supplies.

Toto was removed from his comfortable bed of straw in the stable, and chained up in the larder, beneath shelves of jam pots and other delicacies. The night was a long and miserable one for Toto, who must have wondered what he had done to deserve such treatment. The mice scampered about the place, while he, most uncatlike, lay curled up in a soup tureen, trying to snatch some sleep. At dawn, the mice returned to their holes; Toto awoke, scratched himself, emerged from the soup tureen, and looked about for something to eat. The jam pots attracted his notice, and it did not take him long to prise open the covers. Grandmother's treasured jams—she had made most of them herself—disappeared in an amazingly short time. I was present when she opened the door to see how many mice Toto had caught. Even the rain god Indra could not have looked more terrible when planning a thunderstorm; and the imprecations Grandmother hurled at Toto were surprising coming from someone who had been brought up in the genteel Victorian manner.

The monkey was later reinstated in Grandmother's favour. A great treat for him on cold winter evenings was the large bowl of warm water provided by Grandmother for his bath. He would bathe himself, first of all gingerly testing the temperature of the water with his fingers. Leisurely, he would step into the bath, first one foot, then the other, as he had seen me doing, until he was completely sitting down in it. Once comfortable, he would take the soap in his hands or feet, and rub himself all over. When he found the water becoming cold, he would get out and run as quickly as he could to the fire, where his coat soon dried. If anyone laughed at him during this performance, he would look extremely hurt, and refuse to go on with his ablutions.

One day Toto nearly succeeded in boiling himself to death.

The large kitchen kettle had been left on the fire to boil for tea; and Toto, finding himself for a few minutes alone with it, decided to take the lid off. On discovering that the water inside was warm, he got into the kettle with the intention of having a bath, and sat down with his head protruding from the opening. This was very pleasant for some time, until the water began to simmer. Toto raised himself a little, but finding it cold outside, sat down again. He continued standing and sitting for some time, not having the courage to face the cold air. Had it not been for the timely arrival of Grandmother, he would have been cooked alive.

If there is a part of the brain specially devoted to mischief, that part must have been largely developed in Toto. He was always tearing things to bits, and whenever one of my aunts came near him, he made every effort to get hold of her dress and tear a hole in it. A variety of aunts frequently came to stay with my grandparents, but during Toto's stay they limited their visits to a day or two, much to Grandfather's relief and Grandmother's annoyance.

Toto, however, took a liking to Grandmother, in spite of the beatings he often received from her. Whenever she allowed him the liberty, he would lie quietly in her lap instead of scrambling all over her as he did on most people.

Toto lived with us for over a year, but the following winter, after too much bathing, he caught pneumonia. Grandmother wrapped him in flannel, and Grandfather gave him a diet of chicken soup and Irish stew; but Toto did not recover. He was buried in the garden, under his favourite mango tree.

Perhaps it was just as well that Toto was no longer with us when Grandfather brought home the python, or his demise might have been less conventional. Small monkeys are a favourite delicacy with pythons.

Grandmother was tolerant of most birds and animals, but she drew the line at reptiles. She said they made her blood run cold. Even a handsome, sweet-tempered chameleon had to be given up. Grandfather should have known that there was little chance of his being allowed to keep the python. It was about four feet long, a young one, when Grandfather bought it from a snake charmer for six rupees, impressing the bazaar crowd by slinging it across his shoulders and walking home with it. Grandmother nearly fainted at the sight of the python curled round Grandfather's throat.

'You'll be strangled!' she cried. 'Get rid of it at once!'

'Nonsense,' said Grandfather. 'He's only a young fellow. He'll soon get used to us.'

'Will he, indeed?' said Grandmother. 'But I have no intention of getting used to him. You know quite well that your cousin Mabel is coming to stay with us tomorrow. She'll leave us the minute she knows there's a snake in the house.'

'Well, perhaps we ought to show it to her as soon as she arrives,' said Grandfather, who did not look forward to fussy Aunt Mabel's visits any more than I did.

'You'll do no such thing,' said Grandmother.

'Well, I can't let it loose in the garden,' said Grandfather with an innocent expression. 'It might find its way into the poultry house, and then where would we be?'

'How exasperating you are!' grumbled Grandmother. 'Lock the creature in the bathroom, go back to the bazaar and find the man you bought it from, and get him to come and take it back.'

In my awestruck presence, Grandfather had to take the python into the bathroom, where he placed it in a steep-sided tin tub. Then he hurried off to the bazaar to look for the snake charmer, while Grandmother paced anxiously up and down the veranda. When he returned looking crestfallen, we knew he hadn't been able to find the man.

'You had better take it away yourself,' said Grandmother, in a relentless mood. 'Leave it in the jungle across the riverbed.'

'All right, but let me give it a feed first,' said Grandfather; and producing a plucked chicken, he took it into the bathroom, followed, in single file, by me, Grandmother, and a curious cook and gardener.

Grandfather threw open the door and stepped into the bathroom. I peeped round his legs, while the others remained well behind. We couldn't see the python anywhere.

'He's gone,' announced Grandfather. 'He must have felt hungry.'

'I hope he isn't too hungry,' I said.

'We left the window open,' said Grandfather, looking embarrassed.

A careful search was made of the house, the kitchen,

the garden, the stable and the poultry shed; but the python couldn't be found anywhere.

'He'll be well away by now,' said Grandfather reassuringly.

'I certainly hope so,' said Grandmother, who was half way between anxiety and relief.

Aunt Mabel arrived next day for a three-week visit, and for a couple of days Grandfather and I were a little apprehensive in case the python made a sudden reappearance; but on the third day, when he didn't show up, we felt confident that he had gone for good.

And then, towards evening, we were startled by a scream from the garden. Seconds later, Aunt Mabel came flying up the veranda steps, looking as though she had seen a ghost.

'In the guava tree!' she gasped. 'I was reaching for a guava, when I saw it staring at me. The *look* in its eyes! As though it would *devour* me—'

'Calm down, my dear,' urged Grandmother, sprinkling her with eau-de-Cologne. 'Calm down and tell us what you saw.'

'A snake!' sobbed Aunt Mabel. 'A great boa-constrictor. It must have been twenty feet long! In the guava tree. Its eyes were terrible. It looked at me in such a *queer* way . . .'

My grandparents looked significantly at each other, and Grandfather said, 'I'll go out and kill it,' and sheepishly taking hold of an umbrella, sallied out into the garden. But when he reached the guava tree, the python had disappeared.

'Aunt Mabel must have frightened it away,' I said.

'Hush,' said Grandfather. 'We mustn't speak of your aunt in that way.' But his eyes were alive with laughter.

After this incident, the python began to make a series of appearances, often in the most unexpected places. Aunt Mabel had another fit of hysterics when she saw him admiring her from under a cushion. She packed her bags, and Grandmother made us intensify the hunt.

Next morning, I saw the python curled up on the dressing table, gazing at his reflection in the mirror. I went for Grandfather, but by the time we returned, the python had moved elsewhere. A little later he was seen in the garden again. Then he was back on the dressing table, admiring himself in the mirror. Evidently, he had become enamoured of his own reflection. Grandfather observed that perhaps the attention he was receiving from everyone had made him a little conceited.

'He's trying to look better for Aunt Mabel,' I said; a remark that I instantly regretted, because Grandmother overheard it, and brought the flat of her broad hand down on my head.

'Well, now we know his weakness,' said Grandfather.

'Are you trying to be funny too?' demanded Grandmother, looking her most threatening.

'I only meant he was becoming very vain,' said Grandfather hastily. 'It should be easier to catch him now.'

He set about preparing a large cage with a mirror at one end. In the cage he left a juicy chicken and various other delicacies, and fitted up the opening with a trapdoor. Aunt Mabel had already left by the time we had this trap ready, but we had to go on with the project because we couldn't have the python prowling about the house indefinitely.

For a few days nothing happened, and then, as I was leaving for school one morning, I saw the python curled up in the cage. He had eaten everything left out for him, and was relaxing in front of the mirror with something resembling a smile on his face—if you can imagine a python smiling . . . I lowered the trapdoor gently, but the python took no notice; he was in raptures over his handsome reflection. Grandfather and the gardener put the cage in the ponytrap, and made a journey to the other side of the riverbed. They left the cage in the jungle, with the trapdoor open.

'He made no attempt to get out,' said Grandfather later. 'And I didn't have the heart to take the mirror away. It's the first time I've seen a snake fall in love.'

And the frogs have sung their old song in the mud . . . This was Grandfather's favourite quotation from Virgil, and he used it whenever we visited the rain-water pond behind the house where there were quantities of mud and frogs and the occasional water buffalo. Grandfather had once brought a number of frogs into the house. He had put them in a glass jar, left them on a window sill, and then forgotten all about them. At about four o'clock in the morning the entire household was awakened by a loud and fearful noise, and Grandmother and several nervous relatives gathered in their nightclothes on the veranda. Their timidity changed to fury when they discovered that the ghastly sounds had come from Grandfather's frogs. Seeing the dawn breaking, the frogs had with one accord begun their morning song.

Grandmother wanted to throw the frogs, bottle and all,

out of the window; but Grandfather said that if he gave the bottle a good shaking, the frogs would remain quiet. He was obliged to keep awake, in order to shake the bottle whenever the frogs showed any inclination to break into song. Fortunately for all concerned, the next day a servant took the top off the bottle to see what was inside. The sight of several big frogs so startled him that he ran off without replacing the cover; the frogs jumped out and presumably found their way back to the pond.

It became a habit with me to visit the pond on my own, in order to explore its banks and shallows. Taking off my shoes, I would wade into the muddy water up to my knees, to pluck the water lilies that floated on the surface.

One day I found the pond already occupied by several buffaloes. Their keeper, a boy a little older than me, was swimming about in the middle. Instead of climbing out on to the bank, he would pull himself up on the back of one of his buffaloes, stretch his naked brown body out on the animal's glistening wet hide, and start singing to himself.

When he saw me staring at him from across the pond, he smiled, showing gleaming white teeth in a dark, sun-burnished face. He invited me to join him in a swim. I told him I couldn't swim, and he offered to teach me. I hesitated, knowing that Grandmother held strict and old-fashioned views about mixing with village children; but, deciding that Grandfather—who sometimes smoked a hookah on the sly—would get me out of any trouble that might occur, I took the bold step of accepting the boy's offer. Once taken, the step did not seem so bold.

He dived off the back of his buffalo, and swam across to me. And I, having removed my clothes, followed his instructions until I was floundering about among the water lilies. His name was Ramu, and he promised to give me swimming lessons every afternoon; and so it was during the afternoons—specially summer afternoons when everyone was asleep—that we usually met. Before long I was able to swim across the pond to sit with Ramu astride a contented buffalo, the great beast standing like an island in the middle of a muddy ocean.

Sometimes we would try racing the buffaloes, Ramu and I sitting on different mounts. But they were lazy creatures, and would leave one comfortable spot only to look for another; or, if they were in no mood for games, would roll over on their backs, taking us with them into the mud and green slime of the pond. Emerging in shades of green and khaki, I would slip into the house through the bathroom and bathe under the tap before getting into my clothes.

One afternoon Ramu and I found a small tortoise in the mud, sitting over a hole in which it had laid several eggs. Ramu kept the eggs for his dinner, and I presented the tortoise to Grandfather. He had a weakness for tortoises, and was pleased with this addition to his menagerie, giving it a large tub of water all to itself, with an island of rocks in the middle. The tortoise, however, was always getting out of the tub and wandering about the house. As it seemed able to look after itself quite well, we did not interfere. If one of the dogs bothered it too much, it would draw its head and legs into its shell and defy all their attempts at rough play.

Ramu came from a family of bonded labourers, and had received no schooling. But he was well versed in folklore, and knew a great deal about birds and animals.

'Many birds are sacred,' said Ramu, as we watched a bluejay swoop down from a peepul tree and carry off a grasshopper. He told me that both the bluejay and the god Shiva were called Nilkanth. Shiva had a blue throat, like the bird, because out of compassion for the human race he had swallowed a deadly poison which was intended to destroy the world. Keeping the poison in his throat, he did not let it go any further.

'Are squirrels sacred?' I asked, seeing one sprint down the trunk of the peepul tree.

'Oh yes, Lord Krishna loved squirrels,' said Ramu. 'He would take them in his arms and stroke them with his long fingers. That is why they have four dark lines down their backs from head to tail. Krishna was very dark, and the lines are the marks of his fingers.'

Both Ramu and Grandfather were of the opinion that we should be more gentle with birds and animals and should not kill so many of them.

'It is also important that we respect them,' said Grandfather. 'We must acknowledge their rights. Everywhere, birds and animals are finding it more difficult to survive, because we are trying to destroy both them and their forests. They have to keep moving as the trees disappear.'

This was specially true of the forests near Dehra, where the tiger and the pheasant and the spotted deer were beginning to disappear.

Ramu and I spent many long summer afternoons at the pond. I still remember him with affection, though we never saw each other again after I left Dehra. He could not read or write, so we were unable to keep in touch. And neither his people, nor mine, knew of our friendship. The buffaloes and frogs had been our only confidants. They had accepted us as part of their own world, their muddy but comfortable pond. And when I left Dehra, both they and Ramu must have assumed that I would return again like the birds.

Coming Home to Dehra

THE FAINT QUEASINESS I always feel towards the end of a journey probably has its origin in that first homecoming after my father's death.

It was the winter of '44—yes, a long time ago—and the train was running through the thick sal forests near Dehra, bringing me at every click of the rails nearer to the mother I hadn't seen for four years and the stepfather I had seen just once or twice before my parents were divorced.

I was eleven and I was coming home to Dehra.

Three years earlier, after the separation, I had gone to live with my father. We were very happy together. He was serving in the RAF, at New Delhi, and we lived in a large tent somewhere near Humayun's tomb. The area is now a very busy part of urban Delhi, but in those days it was still a wilderness of scrub jungle where black buck and nilgai roamed freely. We took long walks together, exploring the ruins of old tombs and forts; went to the pictures (George Formby comedies were special favourites of mine); collected stamps; bought books (my father had taught me to read and write before I started going to school); and made plans for going to England when the war was over.

Six months of bliss, even though it was summer and there weren't any fans, only a thick khus reed curtain which had to be splashed with water every hour by a bhisti (water-carrier) who did the rounds of similar tents with his goatskin water bag. I remember the tender refreshing fragrance of the khus, and also the smell of damp earth outside, where the water had spilt.

A happy time. But it had to end. My father's periodic bouts of malarial fever resulted in his having to enter hospital for a week. The bhisti's small son came to stay with me at night, and during the day I took my meals with an Anglo-Indian family across the road.

I would have been quite happy to continue with this arrangement whenever my father was absent, but someone at Air Headquarters must have advised him to put me in a boarding school.

Reluctantly, he came to the decision that this would be the best thing—'until the war is over'—and in the June of '43 he took me to Simla, where I was incarcerated in a preparatory school for boys.

This is not the story of my life at boarding school. It might easily have been a public school in England; it did in fact pride itself on being the 'Eton of the East'. The traditions—such as ragging and flogging, compulsory games and chapel attendance, prefects larger than life, and Honour Boards for everything from school captaincy to choir membership—had all apparently been borrowed from *Tom Brown's Schooldays.*

My father wrote to me regularly, and his letters were the things I looked forward to more than anything else. I went to him for the winter holidays, and the following summer he came to Simla during my mid-term break and took me out for the duration of the holidays. We stayed in a hotel called Craig-Dhu, on a spur north of Jacko Hill. It was an idyllic week; long walks; stories about phantom rickshaws; ice creams in the sun; browsings in bookshops; more plans, 'We will go to England next year.'

School seemed a stupid and heartless place after my father had gone away. He had been transferred to Calcutta and he wasn't keeping well there. Malaria again. And then jaundice. But his last letter sounded quite cheerful. He'd been selling part of his valuable stamp collection so as to have enough money for the fares to England.

One day my class teacher sent for me.

'I want to talk to you, Bond,' he said. 'Let's go for a walk.' I knew immediately that something was wrong.

We took the path that went through the deodar forest, past Council Rock where Scout meetings were held. As soon as my unfortunate teacher (no doubt cursing the Headmaster for having given him this unpleasant task) started on the theme of 'God wanting your father in a higher and better place', as though there could be any better place than Jacko Hill in mid-summer, I knew my father was dead, and burst into tears.

They let me stay in the school hospital for a few days until I felt better. The Headmaster visited me there and took away the pile of my father's letters that I'd kept beside me.

'Your father's letters. You might lose them. Why not leave them with me? Then at the end of the year, before you go home, you can come and collect them.'

Unwillingly, I gave him the letters. He told me he'd heard from my mother that I would be going home to her at the end of the year. He seemed surprised that I evinced no interest in this prospect.

At the end of the year, the day before school closed, I went to the HM's office and asked for my letters.

'What letters?' he said. His desk was piled with papers and correspondence, and he was irritated by my interruption.

'My father's letters,' I explained. 'I gave them to you to keep for me, Sir—when he died . . .'

'Letters. Are you sure you gave them to me?'

He grew more irritated. 'You must be mistaken, Bond. Why should I want to keep your father's letters?'

'I don't know, sir. You said I could collect them before going home.'

'Look, I don't remember any letters and I'm very busy just now, so run along. I'm sure you're mistaken, but if I find your letters, I'll send them to you.'

I don't suppose he meant to be unkind, but he was the first man who aroused in me feelings of hate . . .

As the train drew into Dehra, I looked out of the window to see if there was anyone on the platform waiting to receive me. The station was crowded enough, as most railway stations are in India, with overloaded travellers, shouting coolies, stray dogs, stray stationmasters . . . Pandemonium broke loose as the train came to a halt and people debouched from the carriages. I was thrust on the platform with my tin trunk and small attache case. I sat on the trunk and waited for someone to find me.

Slowly, the crowd melted away. I was left with one elderly coolie who was too feeble to carry heavy luggage and had decided that my trunk was just the right size and weight for his head and shoulders. I waited another ten minutes, but no representative of my mother or stepfather appeared. I permitted the coolie to lead me out of the station to the tonga stand.

Those were the days when everyone, including high-ranking officials, went about in tongas. Dehra had just one taxi. I was quite happy sitting beside a rather smelly, paan-spitting tonga driver, while his weary, underfed pony clip-clopped along the quiet tree-lined roads.

Dehra was always a good place for trees. The valley soil is very fertile, the rainfall fairly heavy; almost everything grows there, if given the chance. The roads were lined with neem and mango trees, eucalyptus, Persian lilac, jacaranda, amaltas (laburnum) and many others. In the gardens of the bungalows were mangoes, litchis and guavas; sometimes jackfruit and papaya. I did not notice all these trees at once; I came to know them as time passed.

The tonga first took me to my grandmother's house. I was under the impression that my mother still lived there.

A lovely, comfortable bungalow that spread itself about

the grounds in an easygoing, old-fashioned way. There was even smoke coming from the chimneys, reminding me of the smoke from my grandfather's pipe. When I was eight, I had spent several months there with my grandparents. In retrospect, it had been an idyllic interlude. But Grandfather was dead. Grandmother lived alone.

White-haired, but still broad in the face and even broader behind, she was astonished to see me getting down from the tonga.

'Didn't anyone meet you at the station?' she asked.

I shook my head. Grandmother said: 'Your mother doesn't live here any more. You can come in and wait, but she may be worried about you, so I'd better take you to her place. Come on, help me up into the tonga ... I might have known it would be a white horse. It always makes me nervous sitting in a tonga behind a white horse.'

'Why, Granny?'

'I don't know, I suppose white horses are nervous, too. Anyway, they are always trying to topple me out. Not so fast, driver!' she called out, as the tonga-man cracked his whip and the pony changed from a slow shuffle to a brisk trot.

It took us about twenty-five minutes to reach my stepfather's house which was in the Dalanwala area, not far from the dry bed of the seasonal Rispana river. My grandmother, seeing that I was in need of moral support, got down with me, while the tonga-driver carried my bedding-roll and tin trunk on to the veranda. The front door was bolted from inside. We had to knock on it repeatedly and call out before it was opened by a servant who did not look pleased at being disturbed. When he saw my grandmother, he gave her a deferential salaam, then gazed at me with open curiosity.

'Where's the memsahib?' asked Grandmother.

'Out,' said the servant.

'I can see that, but where have they gone?'

'They went yesterday to Motichur, for shikar. They will be back this evening.'

Grandmother looked upset, but motioned to the servant to bring in my things. 'Weren't they expecting the boy?' she asked.

'Yes,' he said looking at me again. 'But they said he would be arriving tomorrow.'

'They'd forgotten the date,' said Grandmother in a huff. 'Anyway, you can unpack and have a wash and change your clothes.'

Turning to the servant, she asked, 'Is there any lunch?'

'I will make lunch,' he said. He was staring at me again, and I felt uneasy with his eyes on me. He was tall and swarthy, with oily, jet-back hair and a thick moustache. A heavy scar ran down his left cheek, giving him a rather sinister appearance. He wore a torn shirt and dirty pyjamas. His broad, heavy feet were wet. They left marks on the uncarpeted floor.

A baby was crying in the next room, and presently a woman (who turned out to be the cook's wife) appeared in the doorway, jogging the child in her arms.

'They've left the baby behind, too,' said Grandmother,

becoming more and more irate. 'He is your young brother. Only six months old.' I hadn't been told anything about a younger brother. The discovery that I had one came as something of a shock. I wasn't prepared for a baby brother, least of all a baby half-brother. I examined the child without much enthusiasm. He looked healthy enough and he cried with gusto.

'He's a beautiful baby,' said Grandmother. 'Well, I've got work to do. The servants will look after you. You can come and see me in a day or two. You've grown since I last saw you. And you're getting pimples.'

This reference to my appearance did not displease me as Grandmother never indulged in praise. For her to have observed my pimples indicated that she was fond of me.

The tonga-driver was waiting for her. 'I suppose I'll have to use the same tonga,' she said. 'Whenever I need a tonga, they disappear, except for the ones with white ponies . . . When your mother gets back, tell her I want to see her. Shikar, indeed. An infant to look after, and they've gone shooting.'

Grandmother settled herself in the tonga, nodded in response to the cook's salaam, and took a tight grip of the armrests of her seat. The driver flourished his whip and the pony set off at the same listless, unhurried trot, while my grandmother, feeling quite certain that she was going to be hurtled to her doom by a wild white pony, set her teeth and clung tenaciously to the tonga seat. I was sorry to see her go.

My mother and stepfather returned in the evening from their hunting trip with a pheasant which was duly handed over to the cook, whose name was Mangal Singh. My mother gave me a perfunctory kiss. I think she was pleased to see me, but I was accustomed to a more intimate caress from my father, and the strange reception I had received made me realize the extent of my loss. Boarding school life had been routine. Going home was something that I had always looked forward to. But going home had meant my father, and now he had vanished and I was left quite desolate.

I suppose if one is present when a loved one dies, or sees him dead and laid out and later buried, one is convinced of the finality of the thing and finds it easier to adapt to the changed circumstances. But when you hear of a death, a father's death, and have only the faintest idea of the manner of his dying, it is rather a lot for the imagination to cope with—specially when the imagination is a small boy's. There being no tangible evidence of my father's death, it was, for me, not a death but a vanishing. And although this enabled me to remember him as a living, smiling, breathing person, it meant that I was not wholly reconciled to his death, and subconsciously expected him to turn up (as he often did, when I most needed him) and deliver me from an unpleasant situation.

My stepfather barely noticed me. The first thing he did on coming into the house was to pour himself a whisky and soda. My mother, after inspecting the baby, did likewise. I was left to unpack and settle in my room.

I was fortunate in having my own room. I was as desirous of my own privacy as much as my mother and stepfather were desirous of theirs. My stepfather, a local businessman, was ready to put up with me provided I did not get in the way. And, in a different way, I was ready to put up with him, provided he left me alone. I was even willing that my mother should leave me alone.

There was a big window to my room, and I opened it to the evening breeze, and gazed out on to the garden, a rather unkempt place where marigolds and a sort of wild blue everlasting grew rampant among the litchi trees.

What's Your Dream?

AN OLD MAN, a beggar bent double, with a flowing, white beard and piercing grey eyes, stopped on the road on the other side of the garden wall and looked up at me, where I perched on the branch of a litchi tree.

'What's your dream?' he asked.

It was a startling question coming from that raggedy old man on the street. Even more startling that it should have been made in English. English-speaking beggars were a rarity in those days.

'What's your dream?' he repeated.

'I don't remember,' I said. 'I don't think I had a dream last night.'

'That's not what I mean. You know it isn't what I mean. I can see you're a dreamer. It's not the litchi season, but you sit in that tree all afternoon, dreaming.'

'I just like sitting here,' I said. I refused to admit that I

was a dreamer. Other boys didn't dream, they had catapults.

'A dream, my boy, is what you want most in life. Isn't there something that you want more than anything else?'

'Yes,' I said promptly. 'A room of my own.'

'Ah! A room of your own, a tree of your own, it's the same thing. Not many people can have their own rooms, you know. Not in a land as crowded as ours.'

'Just a small room.'

'And what kind of room do you live in at present?'

'It's a big room, but I have to share it with my brothers and sisters and even my aunt when she visits.'

'I see. What you really want is freedom. Your own tree, your own room, your own small place in the sun.'

'Yes, that's all.'

'That's all? That's everything! When you have all that, you'll have found your dream.'

'Tell me how to find it!'

'There's no magic formula, my friend. If I was a godman, would I be wasting my time here with you? You must work for your dream and move towards it all the time, and discard all those things that come in the way of finding it. And then, if you don't expect too much too quickly, you'll find your freedom, a room of your own. The difficult time comes afterwards.'

'Afterwards?'

'Yes, because it's so easy to lose it all, to let someone take it away from you. Or you become greedy, or careless, and start taking everything for granted and—poof!—suddenly the dream has gone, vanished!'

'How do you know all this?' I asked.

'Because I had my dream and lost it.'

'Did you lose everything?'

'Yes, just look at me now, my friend. Do I look like a king or a godman? I had everything I wanted, but then I wanted more and more . . . You get your room, and then you want a building, and when you have your building, you want your own territory, and when you have your own territory, you want your own kingdom—and all the time it's getting harder to keep everything. And when you lose it—in the end, all kingdoms are lost—you don't even have your room any more.'

'Did you have a kingdom?'

'Something like that . . . Follow your own dream, boy, but don't take other people's dreams, don't stand in anyone's way, don't take from another man his room or his faith or his song.' And he turned and shuffled away, intoning the following verse which I have never heard elsewhere, so it must have been his own—

> Live long, my friend, be wise and strong,
> But do not take from any man his song.

I remained in the litchi tree, pondering his wisdom and wondering how a man so wise could be so poor. Perhaps he became wise afterwards. Anyway, he was free, and I was free, and I went back to the house and demanded (and got) a room of my own. Freedom, I was beginning to realize, is something you have to insist upon.

Life with Uncle Ken

Granny's fabulous kitchen

AS KITCHENS WENT, it wasn't all that big. It wasn't as big as the bedroom or the living room, but it was big enough, and there was a pantry next to it. What made it fabulous was all that came out of it: good things to eat like cakes and curries, chocolate fudge and peanut toffee, jellies and jam tarts, meat pies, stuffed turkeys, stuffed chickens, stuffed eggplants, and hams stuffed with stuffed chickens.

As far as I was concerned, Granny was the best cook in the whole wide world.

Two generations of Clerkes had lived in India and my maternal grandmother had settled in a small town in the foothills, just where the great plain ended and the Himalayas began. The town was called Dehra Dun. It's still there, though much bigger and busier now. Granny had a house, a large rambling bungalow, on the outskirts of the town, on Old Survey Road. In the grounds were many trees, most of them fruit trees. Mangoes, litchis, guavas, bananas, papayas, lemons—there was room for all of them, including a giant jackfruit tree casting its shadow on the walls of the house.

> Blessed is the house upon whose walls
> The shade of an old tree softly falls.

I remember those lines of Granny's. They were true words, because it was a good house to live in, specially for a nine-year-old with a tremendous appetite. If Granny was the best cook in the world, I must have been the boy with the best appetite.

Every winter, when I came home from boarding school, I would spend about a month with Granny before going on to spend the rest of the holidays with my mother and stepfather. My parents couldn't cook. They employed a khansama—a professional cook—who made a good mutton curry but little else. Mutton curry for lunch and mutton curry for dinner can be a bit tiring, specially for a boy who liked to eat almost everything.

Granny was glad to have me because she lived alone most of the time. Not entirely alone, though . . . There was a gardener, Dukhi, who lived in an outhouse. And he had a son called Mohan, who was about my age. And there was Ayah, an elderly maidservant, who helped with the household work. And there was a Siamese cat with bright blue eyes, and a mongrel dog called Crazy because he ran in circles round the house.

And, of course, there was Uncle Ken, Granny's nephew, who came to stay whenever he was out of a job (which was quite often) or when he felt like enjoying some of Granny's cooking.

So Granny wasn't really alone. All the same, she was glad to have me. She didn't enjoy cooking for herself, she said; she had to cook for *someone*. And although the cat and the dog and sometimes Uncle Ken appreciated her efforts, a good cook likes to have a boy to feed, because boys are adventurous and ready to try the most unusual dishes.

Whenever Granny tried out a new recipe on me, she would wait for my comments and reactions, and then make a note in one of her exercise books. These notes were useful when she made the dish again, or when she tried it out on others.

'Do you like it?' she'd ask, after I'd taken a few mouthfuls.

'Yes, Gran.'

'Sweet enough?'

'Yes, Gran.'

'Not *too* sweet?'

'No, Gran.'

'Would you like some more?'

'Yes, please, Gran.'

'Well, finish it off.'

'If you say so, Gran.'

Roast Duck. This was one of Granny's specials. The first time I had roast duck at Granny's place, Uncle Ken was there too.

He'd just lost a job as a railway guard, and had come to stay with Granny until he could find another job. He always stayed as long as he could, only moving on when Granny offered to get him a job as an assistant master in Padre Lal's Academy for Small Boys. Uncle Ken couldn't stand small boys. They made him nervous, he said. I made him nervous too, but there was only one of me, and there was always Granny to protect him. At Padre Lal's, there were over a hundred small boys.

Although Uncle Ken had a tremendous appetite, and ate just as much as I did, he never praised Granny's dishes. I think this is why I was annoyed with him at times, and why sometimes I enjoyed making him feel nervous.

Uncle Ken looked down at the roast duck, his glasses slipping down to the edge of his nose.

'Hm . . . Duck again, Aunt Ellen?'

'What do you mean, duck again? You haven't had duck since you were here last month.'

'That's what I mean,' said Uncle Ken. 'Somehow, one expects more variety from you, Aunt.'

All the same, he took two large helpings and ate most of the stuffing before I could get at it. I took my revenge by emptying all the apple sauce onto my plate. Uncle Ken knew I loved the stuffing; and I knew he was crazy about Granny's apple sauce. So we were even.

'When are you joining your parents?' he asked hopefully, over the jam tart.

'I may not go to them this year,' I said. 'When are you getting another job, Uncle?'

'Oh, I'm thinking of taking a rest for a couple of months.'

I enjoyed helping Granny and Ayah with the washing up. While we were at work, Uncle Ken would take a siesta on the veranda or switch on the radio to listen to dance music. Glenn Miller and his swing band was all the rage then.

'And how do you like your Uncle Ken?' asked Granny one day, as she emptied the bones from his plate into the dog's bowl.

'I wish he was someone else's uncle,' I said. 'He's not so bad, really. Just eccentric.'

'What's eccentric?'

'Oh, just a little crazy.'

'At least Crazy runs round the house,' I said. 'I've never seen Uncle Ken running.'

But I did one day.

Mohan and I were playing marbles in the shade of the mango grove when we were taken aback by the sight of Uncle Ken charging across the compound, pursued by a swarm of bees. He'd been smoking a cigar under a silk cotton tree, and the fumes had disturbed the wild bees in their hive, directly above him. Uncle Ken fled indoors and leapt into a tub of cold water. He had received a few stings and decided to remain in bed for three days. Ayah took his meals to him on a tray.

'I didn't know Uncle Ken could run so fast,' I said, later that day.

'It's nature's way of compensating,' said Granny.

'What's compensating?'

'Making up for things . . . Now at least Uncle Ken knows that he can run. Isn't that wonderful?'

Whenever Granny made vanilla or chocolate fudge, she gave me some to take to Mohan, the gardener's son. It was no use taking him roast duck or curried chicken because in his house no one ate meat. But Mohan liked sweets—Indian sweets, which were made with lots of milk and lots of sugar, as well as Granny's home-made English sweets.

We would climb into the branches of the jackfruit tree and eat fudge or peppermints or sticky toffee. We couldn't eat the jackfruit, except when it was cooked as a vegetable or made into a pickle. But the tree itself was wonderful for climbing. And some wonderful creatures lived in it—squirrels and fruit bats and a pair of green parrots. The squirrels were friendly and soon got into the habit of eating from our hands. They, too, were fond of chocolate fudge. One young squirrel would even explore my pockets to see if I was keeping anything from him.

Mohan and I could climb almost any tree in the garden, and if Granny was looking for us, she'd call from the front veranda and then from the back veranda and then from the pantry at the side of the house and, finally, from her bathroom window on the other side of the house. There were trees on all sides and it was impossible to tell which one we were in until we answered her call. Sometimes Crazy would give us away by barking beneath our tree.

When there was fruit to be picked, Mohan did the picking.

The mangoes and litchis came into season during the summer, when I was away at boarding school, so I couldn't help with the fruit gathering. The papayas were in season during the winter, but you don't climb papaya trees, they are too slender and wobbly. You knock the papayas down with a long pole.

Mohan also helped Granny with the pickling. She was justly famous for her pickles. Green mangoes, pickled in oil, were always popular. So was her hot lime pickle. And she was equally good at pickling turnips, carrots, cauliflowers, chillies and other fruits and vegetables. She could pickle almost anything, from a nasturtium seed to a jackfruit. Uncle Ken didn't care for pickles, so I was always urging Granny to make more of them.

My own preference was for sweet chutneys and sauces, but I ate pickles too, even the very hot ones.

One winter, when Granny's funds were low, Mohan and I went from house to house, selling pickles for her.

In spite of all the people and pets she fed, Granny wasn't rich. The house had come to her from Grandfather, but there wasn't much money in the bank. The mango crop brought in a fair amount every year, and there was a small pension from the Railways (Grandfather had been one of the pioneers who'd helped bring the railway line to Dehra at the turn of the century), but there was no other income. And now that I come to think of it, all those wonderful meals consisted only of the one course, followed by a sweet dish. It was Granny's cooking that turned a modest meal into a feast.

I wasn't ashamed to sell pickles for Granny. It was great fun. Mohan and I armed ourselves with baskets filled with pickle bottles, then set off to cover all the houses in our area.

Major Wilkie, across the road, was our first customer. He had a red beard and bright blue eyes and was almost always good-humoured.

'And what have you got there, young Bond?' he asked.

'Pickles, sir.'

'Pickles! Have you been making them?'

'No, sir, they're my grandmother's. We're selling them, so we can buy a turkey for Christmas.'

'Mrs Clerke's pickles, eh? Well, I'm glad mine is the first house on your way because I'm sure that basket will soon be empty. There is no one who can make a pickle like your grandmother, son. I've said it before and I'll say it again, she's God's gift to a world that's terribly short of good cooks. My wife's gone shopping, so I can talk quite freely, you see . . . What have you got this time? Stuffed chillies, I trust. She knows they're my favourite. I shall be deeply wounded if there are no stuffed chillies in that basket.'

There were, in fact, three bottles of stuffed red chillies in the basket, and Major Wilkie took all of them.

Our next call was at Miss Kellner's house. Miss Kellner couldn't eat hot food, so it was no use offering her pickles. But she bought a bottle of preserved ginger. And she gave me a little prayer book. Whenever I went to see her, she gave me a new prayer book. Soon, I had quite a collection of prayer books. What was I to do with them? Finally, Uncle Ken took them off me, and sold them to the Children's Academy.

Further down the road, Dr Dutt, who was in charge of the hospital, bought several bottles of lime pickles, saying it was good for his liver. And Mr Hari, who owned a garage at the end of the road and sold all the latest cars, bought two bottles of pickled onions and begged us to bring him another two the following month.

By the time we got home, the basket would usually be empty, and Granny richer by twenty or thirty rupees—enough, in those days, for a turkey.

'It's high time you found a job,' said Granny to Uncle Ken one day.

'There are no jobs in Dehra,' complained Uncle Ken.

'How can you tell? You've never looked for one. And anyway, you don't have to stay here for ever. Your sister Emily is headmistress of a school in Lucknow. You could go to her. She said before that she was ready to put you in charge of a dormitory.'

'Bah!' said Uncle Ken. 'Honestly, Aunt, you don't expect me to look after a dormitory seething with forty or fifty demented small boys?'

'What's demented?' I asked.

'Shut up,' said Uncle Ken.

'It means crazy,' said Granny.

'So many words mean crazy,' I complained. 'Why don't we just say crazy? We have a crazy dog, and now Uncle Ken is crazy too.'

Uncle Ken clipped me over my ear, and Granny said, 'Your Uncle isn't crazy, so don't be disrespectful. He's just lazy.'

'And eccentric,' I said. 'I heard he was eccentric.'

'Who said I was eccentric?' demanded Uncle Ken.

'Miss Leslie,' I lied. I knew Uncle Ken was fond of Miss Leslie, who ran a beauty parlour in Dehra's smart shopping centre, Astley Hall.

'I don't believe you,' said Uncle Ken. 'Anyway, when did you see Miss Leslie?'

'We sold her a bottle of mint chutney last week. I told her you liked mint chutney. But she said she'd bought it for Mr Brown who's taking her to the pictures tomorrow.'

'Eat well, but don't overeat,' Granny used to tell me. 'Good food is a gift from God and like any other gift, it can be misused.'

She'd made a list of kitchen proverbs and pinned it to the pantry door—not so high that I couldn't read it either.

These were some of the proverbs:

LIGHT SUPPERS MAKE LONG LIVES.

BETTER A SMALL FISH THAN AN EMPTY DISH.

THERE IS SKILL IN ALL THINGS, EVEN IN MAKING PORRIDGE.

EATING AND DRINKING SHOULD NOT KEEP MEN FROM THINKING.

DRY BREAD AT HOME IS BETTER THAN ROAST MEAT ABROAD.

A GOOD DINNER SHARPENS THE WIT AND SOFTENS THE HEART.

LET NOT YOUR TONGUE CUT YOUR THROAT.

Uncle Ken does nothing

To our surprise, Uncle Ken got a part-time job as a guide, showing tourists the 'sights' around Dehra.

There was an old fort near the riverbed; and a seventeenth-century temple; and a jail where Pandit Nehru had spent some time as a political prisoner; and, about ten miles into the foothills, the hot sulphur springs.

Uncle Ken told us he was taking a party of six American tourists, husbands and wives, to the sulphur springs. Granny was pleased. Uncle Ken was busy at last! She gave him a hamper filled with ham sandwiches, home-made biscuits and a dozen oranges—ample provision for a day's outing.

The sulphur springs were only ten miles from Dehra, but we didn't see Uncle Ken for three days.

He was a sight when he got back. His clothes were dusty and torn; his cheeks were sunken; and the little bald patch on top of his head had been burnt a bright red.

'What have you been doing to yourself?' asked Granny.

Uncle Ken sank into the armchair on the veranda. 'I'm starving, Aunt Ellen. Give me something to eat.'

'What happened to the food you took with you?'

'There were seven of us, and it was all finished on the first day.'

'Well it was only supposed to last a day. You said you were going to the sulphur springs.'

'Yes, that's where we were going,' said Uncle Ken. 'But we never reached them. We got lost in the hills.'

'How could you possibly have got lost in the hills? You

had only to walk straight along the riverbed and up the valley . . . *You* ought to know, you were the guide and you'd been there before, when my husband was alive.'

'Yes, I know,' said Uncle Ken, looking crestfallen. 'But I forgot the way. That is, I forgot the valley. I mean, I took them up the wrong valley. And I kept thinking the springs would be at the same river, but it wasn't the same river . . . So we kept walking, until we were in the hills, and then I looked down and saw we'd come up the wrong valley. We had to spend the night under the stars. It was very, very cold. And next day I thought we'd come back a quicker way, through Mussoorie, but we took the wrong path and reached Kempti instead . . . And then we walked down to the motor road and caught a bus.'

I helped Granny put Uncle Ken to bed, and then helped her make him a strengthening onion soup. I took him the soup on a tray, and he made a face while drinking it and then asked for more. He was in bed for two days, while Ayah and I took turns taking him his meals. He wasn't a bit graceful.

When Uncle Ken complained he was losing his hair and that his bald patch was increasing in size, Granny looked up her book of old recipes and said there was one for baldness which Grandfather had used with great success. It consisted of a lotion made with gherkins soaked in brandy. Uncle Ken said he'd try it.

Granny soaked some gherkins in brandy for a week, then gave the bottle to Uncle Ken with instructions to rub a little into his scalp mornings and evenings.

Next day, when she looked into his room, she found only gherkins in the bottle. Uncle Ken had drunk all the brandy.

Uncle Ken liked to whistle.

Hands in his pockets, nothing to do, he would stroll about the house, around the garden, up and down the road, whistling feebly to himself.

It was always the same whistle, tuneless to everyone except my uncle.

'What are you whistling today, Uncle Ken?' I'd ask.

'"Ol' Man River". Don't you recognize it?'

And the next time around he'd be whistling the same notes, and I'd say, 'Still whistling "Ol' Man River", Uncle?'

'No, I'm not. This is "Danny Boy". Can't you tell the difference?'

And he'd slouch off, whistling tunelessly. Sometimes it irritated Granny.

'Can't you stop whistling, Ken? It gets on my nerves. Why don't you try singing for a change?'

'I can't. It's "The Blue Danube", there aren't any words,' and he'd waltz around the kitchen, whistling.

'Well, you can do your whistling and waltzing on the veranda,' Granny would say. 'I won't have it in the kitchen. It spoils the food.'

When Uncle Ken had a bad tooth removed by our dentist, Dr Kapadia, we thought his whistling would stop. But it only became louder and shriller.

One day, while he was strolling along the road, hands

in his pockets, doing nothing, whistling very loudly, a girl on a bicycle passed him. She stopped suddenly, got off the bicycle, and blocked his way.

'If you whistle at me every time I pass, Kenneth Clerke,' she said, 'I'll wallop you!'

Uncle Ken went red in the face. 'I wasn't whistling at you,' he said.

'Well, I don't see anyone else on the road.'

'I was whistling "God Save The King". Don't you recognize it?'

Uncle Ken on the job

'We'll have to do something about Uncle Ken,' said Granny to the world at large.

I was in the kitchen with her, shelling peas and popping a few into my mouth now and then. Suzie, the Siamese cat, sat on the sideboard, patiently watching Granny prepare an Irish stew. Suzie liked Irish stew.

'It's not that I mind him staying,' said Granny, 'and I don't want any money from him either. But it isn't healthy for a young man to remain idle for so long.'

'Is Uncle Ken a young man, Gran?'

'He's forty. Everyone says he'll improve as he grows up.'

'He could go and live with Aunt Mabel.'

'He *does* go and live with Aunt Mabel. He also lives with Aunt Emily and Aunt Beryl. That's his trouble—he has too many doting sisters ready to put him up and put up with him . . . Their husbands are all quite well-off and can afford to have him now and then. So our Ken spends three months with Mabel, three months with Beryl, three months with me. That way he gets through the year as everyone's guest and doesn't have to worry about making a living.'

'He's lucky in a way,' I said.

'His luck won't last for ever. Already Mabel is talking of going to New Zealand. And once India is free—in just a year or two from now—Emily and Beryl will probably go off to England, because their husbands are in the army and all the British officers will be leaving.'

'Can't Uncle Ken follow them to England?'

'He knows he'll have to start working if he goes there. When your aunts find they have to manage without servants, they won't be ready to keep Ken for long periods. In any case, who's going to pay his fare to England or New Zealand?'

'If he can't go, he'll stay here with you, Granny. You'll be here, won't you?'

'Not for ever. Only while I live.'

'You won't go to England?'

'No, I've grown up here. I'm like the trees. I've taken root, I won't be going away—not until, like an old tree, I'm without any more leaves . . . You'll go, though, when you are bigger. You'll probably finish your schooling abroad.'

'I'd rather finish it here. I want to spend all my holidays with you. If I go away, who'll look after you when you grow old?'

'I'm old already. Over sixty.'

'Is that very old? It's only a little older than Uncle Ken. And how will you look after him when you're *really* old?'

'He can look after himself if he tries. And it's time he started. It's time he took a job.'

I pondered on the problem. I could think of nothing that would suit Uncle Ken—or rather, I could think of no one who would find him suitable. It was Ayah who made a suggestion.

'The Maharani of Jetpur needs a tutor for her children,' she said. 'Just a boy and a girl.'

'How do you know?' asked Granny.

'I heard it from their ayah. The pay is two hundred rupees a month, and there is not much work—only two hours every morning.'

'That should suit Uncle Ken,' I said.

'Yes, it's a good idea,' said Granny. 'We'll have to talk him into applying. He ought to go over and see them. The maharani is a good person to work for.'

Uncle Ken agreed to go over and inquire about the job. The maharani was out when he called, but he was interviewed by the maharaja.

'Do you play tennis?' asked the maharaja.

'Yes,' said Uncle Ken, who remembered having played a bit of tennis when he was a schoolboy.

'In that case, the job's yours. I've been looking for a fourth player for a doubles match . . . By the way, were you at Cambridge?'

'No, I was at Oxford,' said Uncle Ken.

The maharaja was impressed. An Oxford man who could play tennis was just the sort of tutor he wanted for his children.

When Uncle Ken told Granny about the interview, she said, 'But you haven't been to Oxford, Ken. How could you say that!'

'Of course I have been to Oxford. Don't you remember? I spent two years there with your brother Jim!'

'Yes, but you were helping him in his pub in the town. You weren't at the University.'

'Well, the maharaja never asked me if I had been to University. He asked me if I was at Cambridge, and I said no, I was at Oxford, which was perfectly true. He didn't ask me what I was doing at Oxford. What difference does it make?' And he strolled off, whistling.

To our surprise, Uncle Ken was a great success in his job. In the beginning, anyway.

The maharaja was such a poor tennis player that he was delighted to discover that there was someone who was even worse. So, instead of becoming a doubles partner for the maharaja, Uncle Ken became his favourite singles opponent. As long as he could keep losing to His Highness, Uncle Ken's job was safe.

In between tennis matches and accompanying his employer on duck shoots, Uncle Ken squeezed in a few lessons for the children, teaching them reading, writing and arithmetic. Sometimes he took me along, so that I could tell him when he got his sums wrong. Uncle Ken wasn't very good at subtraction, although he could add fairly well.

The maharaja's children were smaller than me. Uncle Ken would leave me with them, saying, 'Just see that they do their sums properly, Ruskin,' and he would stroll off to the tennis courts, hands in his pockets, whistling tunelessly.

Even if his pupils had different answers to the same sum, he would give both of them an encouraging pat, saying, 'Excellent, excellent. I'm glad to see both of you trying so hard. One of you is right and one of you is wrong, but as I don't want to discourage either of you, I won't say who's right and who's wrong!'

But afterwards, on the way home, he'd ask me, 'Which was the right answer, Ruskin?'

Uncle Ken always maintained that he would never have lost his job if he hadn't beaten the maharaja at tennis.

Not that Uncle Ken had any intention of winning. But by playing occasional games with the maharaja's secretaries and guests, his tennis had improved and so, try as hard as he might to lose, he couldn't help winning a match against his employer.

The maharaja was furious.

'Mr Clerke,' he said sternly, 'I don't think you realize the importance of losing. We can't all win, you know. Where would the world be without losers?'

'I'm terribly sorry,' said Uncle Ken. 'It was just a fluke, Your Highness.'

The maharaja accepted Uncle Ken's apologies; but a

week later it happened again. Kenneth Clerke won and the maharaja stormed off the court without saying a word. The following day he turned up at lesson time. As usual Uncle Ken and the children were engaged in a game of noughts and crosses.

'We won't be requiring your services from tomorrow, Mr Clerke. I've asked my secretary to give you a month's salary in lieu of notice.'

Uncle Ken came home with his hands in his pockets, whistling cheerfully.

'You're early,' said Granny.

'They don't need me any more,' said Uncle Ken. 'Oh well, never mind. Come in and have your tea.'

Granny must have known the job wouldn't last very long. And she wasn't one to nag. As she said later, 'At least he tried. And it lasted longer than most of his jobs—two months.'

Uncle Ken at the wheel

On my next visit to Dehra, Mohan met me at the station. We got into a tonga with my luggage and we went rattling and jingling along Dehra's quiet roads to Granny's house.

'Tell me all the news, Mohan.'

'Not much to tell. Some of the sahibs are selling their houses and going away. Suzie has had kittens.'

Granny knew I'd been in the train for two nights, and she had a huge breakfast ready for me. Porridge, scrambled eggs on toast. Bacon with fried tomatoes. Toast and marmalade. Sweet milky tea.

She told me there'd been a letter from Uncle Ken.

'He says he's the assistant manager at Firpo's hotel in Simla,' she said. 'The salary is very good, and he gets free board and lodging. It's a steady job and I hope he keeps it.'

Three days later Uncle Ken was on the veranda steps with his bedding roll and battered suitcase.

'Have you given up the hotel job?' asked Granny.

'No,' said Uncle Ken. 'They have closed down.'

'I hope it wasn't because of you.'

'No, Aunt Ellen. The bigger hotels in the hill stations are all closing down.'

'Well, never mind. Come along and have your tiffin. There is a kofta curry today. It's Ruskin's favourite.'

'Oh, is he here too? I have far too many nephews and nieces. Still he's preferable to those two girls of Mabel's. They made life miserable for me all the time I was with them in Simla.'

Over tiffin (as lunch was called in those days), Uncle Ken talked very seriously about ways and means of earning a living. 'There is only one taxi in the whole of Dehra,' he mused.

'Surely there is business for another?'

'I'm sure there is,' said Granny. 'But where does it get you? In the first place, you don't have a taxi. And in the second place, you can't drive.'

'I can soon learn. There's a driving school in town. And I can use Uncle's old car. It's been gathering dust in the garage for years.' (He was referring to Grandfather's vintage Hillman Roadster. It was a 1926 model, about twenty years old.)

'I don't think it will run now,' said Granny.

'Of course it will. It just needs some oiling and greasing and a spot of paint.'

'All right, learn to drive. Then we will see about the Roadster.'

So Uncle Ken joined the driving school.

He was very regular, going for his lessons for an hour in the evening. Granny paid the fee.

After a month, Uncle Ken announced that he could drive and that he was taking the Roadster out for a trial run.

'You haven't got your licence yet,' said Granny.

'Oh, I won't take her far,' said Uncle Ken. 'Just down the road and back again.'

He spent all morning cleaning up the car. Granny gave him money for a can of petrol.

After tea, Uncle Ken said, 'Come along, Ruskin, hop in and I will give you a ride. Bring Mohan along too.'

Mohan and I needed no urging. We got into the car beside Uncle Ken.

'Now don't go too fast, Ken,' said Granny anxiously. 'You are not used to the car as yet.'

Uncle Ken nodded and smiled and gave two sharp toots on the horn. He was feeling pleased with himself.

Driving through the gate, he nearly ran over Crazy.

Miss Kellner, coming out for her evening rickshaw ride, saw Uncle Ken at the wheel of the Roadster and went indoors again.

Uncle Ken drove straight and fast, tootling the horn without a break.

At the end of the road there was a roundabout.

'We'll turn here,' said Uncle Ken, 'and then drive back again.'

He turned the steering wheel; we began going round the roundabout; but the steering wheel wouldn't turn all the way, not as much as Uncle Ken would have liked it to . . . So, instead of going round, we took a right turn and kept going, straight on—and straight through the Maharaja of Jetpur's garden wall.

It was a single-brick wall, and the Roadster knocked it down and emerged on the other side without any damage to the car or any of its occupants. Uncle Ken brought it to a halt in the middle of the maharaja's lawn.

Running across the grass came the maharaja himself, flanked by his secretaries and their assistants.

When he saw that it was Uncle Ken at the wheel, the maharaja beamed with pleasure.

'Delighted to see you, old chap!' he exclaimed. 'Jolly decent of you to drop in again. How about a game of tennis?'

Uncle Ken at the wicket

Although restored to the maharaja's favour, Uncle Ken was still without a job.

Granny refused to let him take the Hillman out again and so he decided to sulk. He said it was all Grandfather's fault for not seeing to the steering wheel ten years ago, while he was still alive. Uncle Ken went on a hunger strike for two hours (between tiffin and tea), and we did not hear him whistle for several days.

'The blessedness of silence,' said Granny.

And then he announced that he was going to Lucknow to stay with Aunt Emily.

'She has three children and a school to look after,' said Granny. 'Don't stay too long.'

'She doesn't mind how long I stay,' said Uncle Ken and off he went.

His visit to Lucknow was a memorable one, and we only heard about it much later.

When Uncle Ken got down at Lucknow station, he found himself surrounded by a large crowd, every one waving to him and shouting words of welcome in Hindi, Urdu and English. Before he could make out what it was all about, he was smothered by garlands of marigolds. A young man came forward and announced, 'The Gomti Cricketing Association welcomes you to the historical city of Lucknow,' and promptly led Uncle Ken out of the station to a waiting car.

It was only when the car drove into the sports' stadium that Uncle Ken realized that he was expected to play in a cricket match.

This is what had happened.

Bruce Hallam, the famous English cricketer, was touring India and had agreed to play in a charity match at Lucknow. But the previous evening, in Delhi, Bruce had gone to bed with an upset stomach and hadn't been able to get up in time to catch the train. A telegram was sent to the organizers of the match in Lucknow but like many a telegram, it did not reach its destination. The cricket fans of Lucknow had arrived at the station in droves to welcome the great cricketer. And by a strange coincidence, Uncle Ken bore a startling resemblance to Bruce Hallam; even the bald patch on the crown of his head was exactly like Hallam's. Hence the muddle. And, of course, Uncle Ken was always happy to enter into the spirit of a muddle.

Having received from the Gomti Cricketing Association a rousing reception and a magnificent breakfast at the stadium, he felt that it would be very unsporting on his part if he refused to play cricket for them. 'If I can hit a tennis ball,' he mused, 'I ought to be able to hit a cricket ball.' And luckily there was a blazer and a pair of white flannels in his suitcase.

The Gomti team won the toss and decided to bat. Uncle Ken was expected to go in at number three, Bruce Hallam's normal position. And he soon found himself walking to the wicket, wondering why on earth no one had as yet invented a more comfortable kind of pad.

The first ball he received was short-pitched, and he was able to deal with it in tennis fashion, swatting it to the mid-wicket boundary. He got no runs, but the crowd cheered.

The next ball took Uncle Ken on the pad. He was right in front of his wicket and should have been given out lbw. But the umpire hesitated to raise his finger. After all, hundreds of people had paid good money to see Bruce Hallam play, and it would have been a shame to disappoint them. 'Not out,' said the umpire.

The third ball took the edge of Uncle Ken's bat and sped through the slips.

'Lovely shot!' exclaimed an elderly gentleman in the pavilion. 'A classic late cut,' said another.

The ball reached the boundary and Uncle Ken had four runs to his name. Then it was 'over', and the other batsman had to face the bowling. He took a run off the first ball and called for a second run. Uncle Ken thought one run was more than enough. Why go charging up and down the wicket like a mad man? However, he couldn't refuse to run, and he was half-way down the pitch when the fielder's throw hit the wicket. Uncle Ken was run-out by yards. There could be no doubt about it this time.

He returned to the pavilion to the sympathetic applause of the crowd.

'Not his fault,' said the elderly gentleman. 'The other chap shouldn't have called. There wasn't a run there. Still, it was worth coming here all the way from Kanpur if only to see that superb late cut . . .'

Uncle Ken enjoyed a hearty tiffin-lunch (taken at noon), and then, realizing that the Gomti team would probably have to be in the field for most of the afternoon—more running about!—he slipped out of the pavilion, left the stadium, and took a tonga to Aunt Emily's house in the cantonment.

He was just in time for a second lunch (taken at one o'clock) with Aunt Emily's family: and it was presumed at the stadium that Bruce Hallam had left early to catch the train to Allahabad, where he was expected to play in another charity match.

Aunt Emily, a forceful woman, fed Uncle Ken for a

week, and then put him to work in the boys' dormitory of her school. It was several months before he was able to save up enough money to run away and return to Granny's place.

But he had the satisfaction of knowing that he had helped the great Bruce Hallam to add another four runs to his grand aggregate. The scorebook of the Gomti Cricketing Association had recorded his feat for all time:

'B. Hallam, run-out, 4'

The Gomti team lost the match. But, as Uncle Ken would readily admit, where would we be without losers?

The Crooked Tree

*'You must pass your exams and go to college, but do
not feel that if you fail, you will be able to do nothing.'*

MY ROOM IN Shahganj was very small. I had paced about
in it so often that I knew its exact measurements: twelve
feet by ten. The string of my cot needed tightening. The
dip in the middle was so pronounced that I invariably woke
up in the morning with a backache; but I was hopeless at
tightening charpoy strings.

Under the cot was my tin trunk. Its contents ranged
from old, rejected manuscripts to clothes and letters and
photographs. I had resolved that one day, when I had
made some money with a book, I would throw the trunk
and everything else out of the window, and leave Shahganj
forever. But until then I was a prisoner. The rent was nominal,

the window had a view of the bus stop and rickshaw-stand, and I had nowhere else to go.

I did not live entirely alone. Sometimes a beggar spent the night on the balcony; and, during cold or wet weather, the boys from the tea shop, who normally slept on the pavement, crowded into the room.

Usually I woke early in the mornings, as sleep was fitful, uneasy, crowded with dreams. I knew it was five o'clock when I heard the first upcountry bus leaving its shed. I would then get up and take a walk in the fields beyond the railroad tracks.

One morning, while I was walking in the fields, I noticed someone lying across the pathway, his head and shoulders hidden by the stalks of young sugar cane. When I came near, I saw he was a boy of about sixteen. His body was twitching convulsively, his face was very white, except where a little blood had trickled down his chin. His legs kept moving, and his hands fluttered restlessly, helplessly.

'What's the matter with you?' I asked, kneeling down beside him.

But he was still unconscious and could not answer me.

I ran down the footpath to a well and, dipping the end of my shirt in a shallow trough of water, ran back and sponged the boy's face. The twitching ceased and, though he still breathed heavily, his hands were still and his face calm. He opened his eyes and stared at me, without any immediate comprehension.

'You have bitten your tongue,' I said, wiping the blood from his mouth. 'Don't worry. I'll stay with you until you feel better.'

He sat up now, and said, 'I'm all right, thank you.'

'What happened?' I asked, sitting down beside him.

'Oh, nothing much. It often happens, I don't know why. But I cannot control it.' 'Have you seen a doctor?'

'I went to the hospital in the beginning. They gave me some pills, which I had to take every day. But the pills made me so tired and sleepy that I couldn't work properly. So I stopped taking them. Now this happens once or twice a month. But what does it matter? I'm all right when it's over, and I don't feel anything while it is happening.'

He got to his feet, dusting his clothes and smiling at me. He was slim, long-limbed and bony. There was a little fluff on his cheeks and the promise of a moustache.

'Where do you live?' I asked. 'I'll walk back with you.'

'I don't live anywhere,' he said. 'Sometimes I sleep in the temple, sometimes in the gurdwara. In summer months, I sleep in the municipal gardens.'

'Well, then let me come with you as far as the gardens.' He told me that his name was Kamal, that he studied at the Shahganj High School, and that he hoped to pass his examinations in a few months' time. He was studying hard and, if he passed with a good division, he hoped to attend a college. If he failed, there was only the prospect of continuing to live in the municipal gardens . . .

He carried with him a small tray of merchandise, supported by straps that went round his shoulders. In it were combs and buttons and cheap toys and little vials of perfume. All day he walked about Shahganj, selling odds and ends to people in the bazaar or at their houses. He made, on an average, two rupees a day, which was enough for his food and his school fees.

He told me all this while we walked back to the bus stand. I returned to my room, to try and write something, while Kamal went on to the bazaar to try and sell his wares.

There was nothing very unusual about Kamal's being an orphan and a refugee. During the communal holocaust of 1947, thousands of homes had been broken up, and women and children had been killed. What was unusual in Kamal was his sensitivity, a quality I thought rare in a Punjabi youth who had grown up in the Frontier provinces during a period of hate and violence. And it was not so much his positive attitude to life that appealed to me (most people in Shahganj were completely resigned to their lot) as his gentleness, his quiet voice and the smile that flickered across his face regardless of whether he was sad or happy.

In the morning, when I opened my door, I found Kamal asleep at the top of the steps. His tray lay a few feet away. I shook him gently, and he woke at once.

'Have you been sleeping here all night?' I asked. 'Why didn't you come inside?'

'It was very late,' he said. 'I didn't want to disturb you.'

'Someone could have stolen your things while you slept.'

'Oh, I sleep quite lightly. Besides, I have nothing of special value. But I came to ask you something.' 'Do you need any money?'

'No. I want you to take your meal with me tonight.'

'But where? You don't have a place of your own. It will be too expensive in a restaurant.'

'In your room,' said Kamal. 'I will bring the food and cook it here. You have a stove?'

'I think so,' I said. 'I will have to look for it.'

'I will come at seven,' said Kamal, strapping on his tray. 'Don't worry. I know how to cook!'

He ran down the steps and made for the bazaar. I began to look for the oil stove, found it at the bottom of my tin trunk, and then discovered I hadn't any pots or pans or dishes. Finally, I borrowed these from Deep Chand, the barber.

Kamal brought a chicken for our dinner. This was a costly luxury in Shahganj, to be taken only two or three times a year. He had bought the bird for three rupees, which was cheap, considering it was not too skinny. While Kamal set about roasting it, I went down to the bazaar and procured a bottle of beer on credit, and this served as an appetizer.

'We are having an expensive meal,' I observed. 'Three rupees for the chicken and three rupees for the beer. But I wish we could do it more often.'

'We should do it at least once a month,' said Kamal. 'It should be possible if we work hard.'

'You know how to work. You work from morning to night.'

'But you are a writer, Rusty. That is different. You have to wait for a mood.'

'Oh, I'm not a genius that I can afford the luxury of moods. No, I'm just lazy, that's all.'

'Perhaps you are writing the wrong things.'

'I know I am. But I don't know how I can write anything else.'

'Have you tried?'

'Yes, but there is no money in it. I wish I could make a living in some other way. Even if I repaired cycles, I would make more money.'

'Then why not repair cycles?'

'No, I will not repair cycles. I would rather be a bad writer than a good repairer of cycles. But let us not think of work. There is time enough for work. I want to know more about you.'

Kamal did not know if his parents were alive or dead. He had lost them, literally, when he was six. It happened at the Amritsar Railroad Station, where trains coming across the border disgorged thousands of refugees, or pulled into the station half-empty, drenched with blood and littered with corpses.

Kamal and his parents were lucky to escape the massacre. Had they travelled on an earlier train (they had tried desperately to get into one), they might well have been killed; but circumstances favoured them then, only to trick them later.

Kamal was clinging to his mother's sari, while she remained close to her husband, who was elbowing his way through the frightened, bewildered throng of refugees. Glancing over his shoulder at a woman who lay on the ground, wailing and beating her breasts, Kamal collided with a burly Sikh and lost his grip of his mother's sari.

The Sikh had a long curved sword at his waist; and Kamal stared up at him in awe and fascination—at his long hair, which had fallen loose, and his wild black beard, and the bloodstains on his white shirt. The Sikh pushed him out of the way and when Kamal looked around for his mother, she was not to be seen. She was hidden from him by a mass of restless bodies, pushed in different directions. He could hear her calling, 'Kamal, where are you, Kamal?' He tried to force his way through the crowd, in the direction of the voice, but he was carried the other way . . .

At night, when the platform was empty, he was still searching for his mother. Eventually, some soldiers took him away. They looked for his parents, but without success, and, finally, they sent Kamal to a refugee camp. From there he went to an orphanage. But when he was eight, and felt himself a man, he ran away.

He worked for some time as a helper in a tea shop; but when he started getting epileptic fits, the shopkeeper asked him to leave, and he found himself on the streets, begging for a living. He begged for a year, moving from one town to another, and ending up finally at Shahganj. By then he was twelve and too old to beg; but he had saved some money, and with it he bought a small stock of combs, buttons, cheap perfumes and bangles; and, converting himself into a mobile shop, went from door to door, selling his wares.

Shahganj was a small town, and there was no house which Kamal hadn't visited. Everyone recognized him, and there were some who offered him food and drink; the children knew him well, because he played on a small flute whenever he made his rounds, and they followed him to listen to the flute.

I began to look forward to Kamal's presence. He dispelled some of my own loneliness. I found I could work better, knowing that I did not have to work alone. And Kamal came to me, perhaps because I was the first person to have taken a personal interest in his life, and because I saw nothing frightening in his sickness. Most people in Shahganj thought epilepsy was infectious; some considered it a form of divine punishment for sins committed in a former life. Except for children, those who knew of his condition generally gave him a wide berth.

At sixteen, a boy grows like young wheat, springing up so fast that he is unaware of what is taking place within him. His mind quickens, his gestures are more confident. Hair sprouts like young grass on his face and chest, and his muscles begin to mature. Never again will he experience so much change and growth in so short a time. He is full of currents and countercurrents.

Kamal combined the bloom of youth with the beauty of the short-lived. It made me sad even to look at his pale, slim body. It hurt me to look into his eyes. Life and death were always struggling in their depths.

'Should I go to Delhi and take up a job?' I asked. 'Why not? You are always talking about it.'

'Why don't you come too? Perhaps they can stop your fits.'

'We will need money for that. When I have passed my examinations, I will come.'

'Then I will wait,' I said. I was twenty-two, and there was world enough and time for everything.

We decided to save a little money from his small earnings and my occasional payments. We would need money to go to Delhi, money to live there until we could earn a living. We put away twenty rupees one week, but lost it the next, when we lent it to a friend who owned a cycle rickshaw. But this gave us the occasional use of his cycle, and early one morning, with Kamal sitting on the crossbar, I rode out of Shahganj.

After cycling for about two miles, we got down and pushed the cycle off the road, taking a path through a paddy field and then through a field of young maize, until in the distance we saw a tree, a crooked tree, growing beside an old well.

I do not know the name of that tree. I had never seen one like it before. It had a crooked trunk and crooked branches, and was clothed in thick, broad, crooked leaves, like the leaves on which food is served in the bazaar.

In the trunk of the tree there was a hole, and, when we set the bicycle down with a crash, a pair of green parrots flew out, and went dipping and swerving across the fields. There was grass around the well, cropped short by grazing cattle.

We sat in the shade of the crooked tree, and Kamal untied the red cloth in which he had brought our food. When we had eaten, we stretched ourselves out on the grass. I closed my eyes, and became aware of a score of different sensations. I heard a cricket singing in the tree, the cooing of pigeons from the walls of the old well, the quiet breathing of Kamal, the parrots returning to the tree, the distant hum of an airplane. I smelled the grass and the old bricks round the well and the promise of rain. I felt Kamal's fingers against

my arm, and the sun creeping over my cheek. And, when I opened my eyes, there were clouds on the horizon, and Kamal was asleep, his arm thrown across his face to keep out the glare.

I went to the well and, putting my shoulders to the ancient handle, turned the wheel, moving around while cool, clean water gushed out over the stones and along the channel to the fields. The discovery that I could water a field, that I had the power to make things grow, gave me a thrill of satisfaction; it was like writing a story that had the ring of truth. I drank from one of the trays; the water was sweet with age.

Kamal was sitting up, looking at the sky. 'It's going to rain,' he said.

We began cycling homeward; but we were still some way out of Shahganj when it began to rain. A lashing wind swept the rain across our faces, but we exulted in it, and sang at the top of our voices until we reached the Shahganj bus stop.

Across the railroad tracks and the dry riverbed, fields of maize stretched away, until there came a dry region of thorn bushes and lantana scrub, where the earth was cut into jagged cracks, like a jigsaw puzzle. Dotting the landscape were old abandoned brick kilns. When it rained heavily, the hollows filled up with water.

Kamal and I came to one of these hollows to bathe and swim. There was an island in the middle of it, and on this small mound lay the ruins of a hut where a night watchman had once lived, looking after the brick kilns. We would swim out to the island, which was only a few yards from the banks of the hollow. There was a grassy patch in front of the hut, and early in the mornings, before it got too hot, we would wrestle on the grass.

Though I was heavier than Kamal, my chest as sound as a new drum, he had strong, wiry arms and legs, and would often pinion me around the waist with his bony knees. Now, while we wrestled on the new monsoon grass, I felt his body go tense. He stiffened, his legs jerked against my body, and a shudder passed through him. I knew that he had a fit coming on but I was unable to extricate myself from his arms.

He gripped me more tightly as the fit took possession of him. Instead of struggling, I lay still, tried to absorb some of his anguish, tried to draw some of his agitation to myself. I had a strange fancy that by identifying myself with his convulsions, I might alleviate them.

I pressed against Kamal, and whispered soothingly into his ear; and then, when I noticed his mouth working, I thrust my fingers between his teeth to prevent him from biting his tongue. But so violent was the convulsion that his teeth bit into the flesh of my palm and ground against my knuckles. I shouted with the pain and tried to jerk my hand away, but it was impossible to loosen the grip of his jaws. So I closed my eyes and counted—counted till seven—until consciousness returned to him, and his muscles relaxed.

My hand was shaking and covered with blood. I bound it in my handkerchief, and kept it hidden from Kamal.

We walked back to the room without talking much.

Kamal looked depressed and weak. I kept my hand beneath my shirt, and Kamal was too dejected to notice anything. It was only at night, when he returned from his classes, that he noticed the cuts, and I told him I had slipped in the road, cutting my hand on some broken glass.

Rain upon Shahganj. And, until the rain stops, Shahgani is fresh and clean and alive. The children run out of their houses, glorying in their nakedness. The gutters choke, and the narrow street becomes a torrent of water, coursing merrily down to the bus stop. It swirls over the trees and the roofs of the town, and the parched earth soaks it up, exuding a fragrance that comes only once in a year, the fragrance of quenched earth, that most exhilarating of smells.

The rain swept in through the door and soaked the cot. When I had succeeded in closing the door, I found the roof leaking, the water trickling down the walls and forming new pictures on the cracking plaster. The door flew open again, and there was Kamal standing on the threshold, shaking himself like a wet dog. Coming in, he stripped and dried himself, and then sat shivering on the bed while I made frantic efforts to close the door again.

'You need some tea,' I said.

He nodded, forgetting to smile for once, and I knew his mind was elsewhere, in one of a hundred possible places from his dreams.

'One day I will write a book,' I said, as we drank strong tea in the fast fading twilight. 'A real book, about real people. Perhaps it will be about you and me and Shahganj. And then we will run away from Shahganj, fly on the wings of

Garuda, and all our troubles will be over and fresh troubles will begin. Why should we mind difficulties, as long as they are new difficulties?'

'First, I must pass my exams,' said Kamal. 'Otherwise, I can do nothing, go nowhere.'

'Don't take exams too seriously. I know that in India they are the passport to any kind of job, and that you cannot become a clerk unless you have a degree. But do not forget that you are studying for the sake of acquiring knowledge, and not for the sake of becoming a clerk. You don't want to become a clerk or a bus conductor, do you? You must pass your exams and go to college, but do not feel that if you fail, you will be able to do nothing. Why, you can start making your own buttons instead of selling other people's!'

'You are right,' said Kamal. 'But why not be an educated button manufacturer?'

'Why not, indeed? That's just what I mean. And while you are studying for your exams, I will be writing my book. I will start tonight! It is an auspicious night, the beginning of the monsoon.'

The light did not come on. A tree must have fallen across the wires. I lit a candle and placed it on the window sill and, while the candle spluttered in the steamy air, Kamal opened his books and, with one hand on a book and the other hand playing with his toes—this attitude helped him to concentrate—he devoted his attention to algebra.

I took an ink bottle down from a shelf and, finding it empty, added a little rainwater to the crusted contents. Then I sat down beside Kamal and began to write; but the pen was useless and made blotches all over the paper, and I had no idea what I should write about, though I was full of writing just then. So I began to look at Kamal instead; at his eyes, hidden in shadow, and his hands, quiet in the candlelight; and I followed his breathing and the slight movement of his lips as he read softly to himself.

And, instead of starting my book, I sat and watched Kamal.

Sometimes Kamal played the flute at night, while I was lying awake; and, even when I was asleep, the flute would play in my dreams. Sometimes he brought it to the crooked tree, and played it for the benefit of the birds; but the parrots only made harsh noises and flew away.

Once, when Kamal was playing his flute to a group of children, he had a fit. The flute fell from his hands, and he began to roll about in the dust on the roadside. The children were frightened and ran away. But the next time they heard Kamal play his flute, they came to listen as usual.

That Kamal was gaining in strength I knew from the way he was able to pin me down whenever we wrestled on the grass near the old brick kilns. It was no longer necessary for me to yield deliberately to him. And, though his fits still recurred from time to time—as we knew they would continue to do—he was not so depressed afterwards. The anxiety and the death had gone from his eyes.

His examinations were nearing, and he was working hard. (I had yet to begin the first chapter of my book.) Because of the necessity of selling two or three rupees' worth of articles every day, he did not get much time for studying;

but he stuck to his books until past midnight, and it was seldom that I heard his flute.

He put aside his tray of odds and ends during the examinations, and walked to the examination centre instead. And after two weeks, when it was all over, he took up his tray and began his rounds again. In a burst of creativity, I wrote three pages of my novel.

On the morning the results of the examination were due, I rose early, before Kamal, and went down to the news agency. It was five o'clock and the newspapers had just arrived. I went through the columns relating to Shahganj, but I couldn't find Kamal's roll number on the list of successful candidates. I had the number written down on a slip of paper, and I looked at it again to make sure that I had compared it correctly with the others; then I went through the newspaper once more.

When I returned to the room, Kamal was sitting on the doorstep. I didn't have to tell him he had failed. He knew by the look on my face. I sat down beside him, and we said nothing for some time.

'Never mind,' said Kamal, eventually. 'I will pass next year.'

I realized that I was more depressed than he was, and that he was trying to console me.

'If only you'd had more time,' I said.

'I have plenty of time now. Another year. And you will have time in which to finish your book; then we can both go away. Another year of Shahganj won't be so bad. As long

346

as I have your friendship, almost everything else can be tolerated, even my sickness.'

And then, turning to me with an expression of intense happiness, he said, 'Yesterday I was sad, and tomorrow I may be sad again, but today I know that I am happy. I want to live on and on. I feel that life isn't long enough to satisfy me.'

He stood up, the tray hanging from his shoulders.

'What would you like to buy?' he said. 'I have everything you need.'

At the bottom of the steps he turned and smiled at me, and I knew then that I had written my story.

Untouchable

THE SWEEPER BOY splashed water over the khus matting that hung in the doorway and for a while the air was cooled.

I sat on the edge of my bed, staring out of the open window, brooding upon the dusty road shimmering in the noonday heat. A car passed and the dust rose in billowing clouds.

Across the road lived the people who were supposed to look after me while my father lay in hospital with malaria. I was supposed to stay with them, sleep with them. But except for meals, I kept away. I did not like them and they did not like me.

For a week, longer probably, I was going to live alone in the red-brick bungalow on the outskirts of the town, on the fringe of the jungle. At night, the sweeper boy would keep guard, sleeping in the kitchen. Apart from him, I had no company; only the neighbours' children, and I did not like them and they did not like me.

Their mother said, 'Don't play with the sweeper boy, he is unclean. Don't touch him. Remember, he is a servant. You must come and play with my boys.'

Well, I did not intend playing with the sweeper boy; but neither did I intend playing with her children. I was going to sit on my bed all week and wait for my father to come home.

Sweeper boy . . . all day he pattered up and down between the house and the water tank, with the bucket clanging against his knees.

Back and forth, with a wide, friendly smile. I frowned at him.

He was about my age, ten. He had short cropped hair, very white teeth, and muddy feet, hands, and face. All he wore was an old pair of khaki shorts; the rest of his body was bare, burnt a deep brown.

On every trip to the water tank he bathed, and returned dripping and glistening from head to toe.

I dripped with sweat.

It was supposedly below my station to bathe at the tank, where the gardener, water-carrier, cooks, ayahs, sweepers, and their children all collected. I was the son of a 'sahib' and convention ruled that I did not play with servant children.

But I was just as determined not to play with the other sahibs' children, for I did not like them and they did not like me.

I watched the flies buzzing against the windowpane, the

lizards scuttling across the rafters, the wind scattering petals of scorched, long-dead flowers.

The sweeper boy smiled and saluted in play. I avoided his eyes and said, 'Go away.'

He went into the kitchen.

I rose and crossed the room, and lifted my sun helmet off the hatstand.

A centipede ran down the wall, across the floor.

I screamed and jumped on the bed, shouting for help.

The sweeper boy darted in. He saw me on the bed, the centipede on the floor; and picking a large book off the shelf, slammed it down on the repulsive insect.

I remained standing on my bed, trembling with fear and revulsion.

He laughed at me, showing his teeth, and I blushed and said, 'Get out!'

I would not, could not, touch or approach the hat or hatstand. I sat on the bed and longed for my father to come home.

A mosquito passed close by me and sang in my ear. Half-heartedly, I clutched at it and missed; and it disappeared behind the dressing table.

That mosquito, I reasoned, gave malaria to my father.

And now it was trying to give it to me!

The next-door lady walked through the compound and smiled thinly from outside the window. I glared back at her.

The sweeper boy passed with the bucket, and grinned. I turned away.

In bed at night, with the lights on, I tried reading. But even books could not quell my anxiety.

The sweeper boy moved about the house, bolting doors, fastening windows. He asked me if I had any orders.

I shook my head.

He skipped across to the electric switch, turned off the light, and slipped into his quarters. Outside, inside, all was dark; only one shaft of light squeezed in through a crack in the sweeper boy's door, and then that, too, went out.

I began to wish I had stayed with the neighbours. The darkness worried me—silent and close—silent, as if in suspense. Once a bat flew flat against the window, falling to the ground outside; once an owl hooted. Sometimes a dog barked. And I tautened as a jackal howled hideously in the jungle behind the bungalow. But nothing could break the overall stillness, the night's silence . . . Only a dry puff of wind . . .

It rustled in the trees, and put me in mind of a snake slithering over dry leaves and twigs. I remembered a tale I had been told not long ago, of a sleeping boy who had been bitten by a cobra.

I would not, could not, sleep. I longed for my father . . .

The shutters rattled, the doors creaked. It was a night for ghosts.

Ghosts!

God, why did I have to think of them?

My God! There, standing by the bathroom door . . .

My father! My father dead from malaria, and come to see me!

I threw myself at the switch. The room lit up. I sank down on the bed in complete exhaustion, the sweat soaking my nightclothes.

It was not my father I had seen. It was his dressing gown hanging on the bathroom door. It had not been taken with him to the hospital.

I turned off the light.

The hush outside seemed deeper, nearer. I remembered the centipede, the bat, thought of the cobra and the sleeping boy; pulled the sheet tight over my head. If I could see nothing, well then, nothing could see me.

A thunderclap shattered the brooding stillness.

A streak of lightning forked across the sky, so close that even through the sheet I saw a tree and the opposite house silhouetted against the flashing canvas of gold.

I dived deeper beneath the bedclothes, gathered the pillow about my ears.

But at the next thunderclap, louder this time, louder than I had ever heard, I leapt from my bed. I could not stand it. I fled, blundering into the sweeper boy's room.

The boy sat on the bare floor. 'What is happening?' he asked.

The lightning flashed, and his teeth and eyes flashed with it. Then he was a blur in the darkness.

'I am afraid,' I said.

I moved towards him and my hand touched a cold shoulder. 'Stay here,' he said. 'I, too, am afraid.'

I sat down, my back against the wall; beside the untouchable, the outcaste . . . and the thunder and lightning ceased, and the rain came down, swishing and drumming on the corrugated roof.

'The rainy season has started,' observed the sweeper boy, turning to me. His smile played with the darkness, and then he laughed. And I laughed too, but feebly.

But I was happy and safe. The scent of the wet earth blew in through the skylight and the rain fell harder.

A Crow for All Seasons

EARLY TO BED and early to rise makes a crow healthy, wealthy and wise.

They say it's true for humans too. I'm not so sure about that. But for crows, it's a must.

I'm always up at the crack of dawn, often the first crow to break the night's silence with a lusty caw. My friends and relatives, who roost in the same tree, grumble a bit and mutter to themselves, but they are soon cawing just as loudly. Long before the sun is up, we set off on the day's work.

We do not pause even for the morning wash. Later in the day, if it's hot and muggy, I might take a dip in some human's bathwater; but early in the morning we like to be up and about before everyone else. This is the time when trash cans and refuse dumps are overflowing with goodies, and we like to sift through them before the dustmen arrive in their disposal trucks.

Not that we are afraid of a famine in refuse. As human beings multiply, so does their rubbish.

Only yesterday I rescued an old typewriter ribbon from the dustbin, just before it was emptied. What a waste that would have been! I had no use for it myself, but I gave it to one of my cousins who got married recently, and she tells me it's just right for her nest, the one she's building on a telegraph pole. It helps her bind the twigs together, she says.

My own preference is for toothbrushes. They're just a hobby, really, like stamp collecting with humans. I have a small but select collection which I keep in a hole in the garden wall. Don't ask me how many I've got—crows don't believe there's any point in counting beyond *two*—but I know there's more than one, that there's a whole lot of them in fact, because there isn't anyone living on this road who hasn't lost a toothbrush to me at some time or another.

We crows living in the jackfruit tree have this stretch of road to ourselves, but so that we don't quarrel or have misunderstandings, we've shared the houses out. I picked the bungalow with the orchard at the back. After all, I don't eat rubbish and throwaways all the time. Just occasionally I like a ripe guava or the soft flesh of a papaya. And sometimes I like the odd beetle as an hors d'oeuvre. Those humans in the bungalow should be grateful to me for keeping down the population of fruit-eating beetles, and even for recycling their refuse; but no, humans are never grateful. No sooner do I settle in one of their guava trees than stones are whizzing past me. So I return to the dustbin on the back veranda steps. They don't mind my being there.

One of my cousins shares the bungalow with me, but he's a lazy fellow and I have to do most of the foraging. Sometimes I get him to lend me a claw; but most of the time he's preening his feathers and trying to look handsome for a pretty young thing who lives in the banyan tree at the next turning.

When he's in the mood, he can be invaluable, as he proved recently when I was having some difficulty getting at the dog's food on the veranda.

This dog who is fussed over so much by the humans I've adopted is a great big fellow, a mastiff who pretends to a pedigree going back to the time of Genghis Khan—he likes to pretend one of his ancestors was the great Khan's watchdog—but, as often happens in famous families, animal or human, there is a falling off in quality over a period of time, and this huge fellow—Tiger, they call him—is a case in point. All brawn and no brain. Many a time I've removed a juicy bone from his plate or helped myself to pickings from under his nose.

But of late he's been growing canny and selfish. He doesn't like to share any more. And the other day I was almost in his jaws when he took a sudden lunge at me. Snap went his great teeth; but all he got was one of my tail feathers. He spat it out in disgust. Who wants crow's meat, anyway?

All the same, I thought, I'd better not be too careless. It's not for nothing that a crow's IQ is way above that of all other birds. And it's higher than a dog's, I bet.

I woke Cousin Slow from his midday siesta and said, 'Hey, Slow, we've got a problem. If you want any of that delicious tripe today, you've got to lend a claw—or a beak. That dog's getting snappier day by day.'

Slow opened one eye and said, 'Well, if you insist. But you know how I hate getting into a scuffle. It's bad for the gloss on my feathers.'

'I don't insist,' I said politely, 'but I'm not foraging for both of us today. It's every crow for himself.'

'Okay, okay, I'm coming,' said Slow, and with barely a flap he dropped down from the tree to the wall.

'What's the strategy?' I asked.

'Simple. We'll just give him the old one-two.'

We flew across to the veranda. Tiger had just started his meal. He was a fast, greedy eater who made horrible slurping sounds while he guzzled his food. We had to move fast if we wanted to get something before the meal was over.

I sidled up to Tiger and wished him good afternoon. He kept on gobbling—but quicker now.

Slow came up from behind and gave him a quick peck near the tail—a sensitive spot—and, as Tiger swung round snarling, I moved in quickly and snatched up several tidbits.

Tiger went for me, and I flew freestyle for the garden wall. The dish was untended, so Slow helped himself to as many scraps as he could stuff in his mouth.

He joined me on the garden wall, and we sat there feasting, while Tiger barked himself hoarse below.

'Go catch a cat,' said Slow, who is given to slang. 'You're in the wrong league, big boy.'

The great sage Pratyasataka—ever heard of him? I guess not—once said, 'Nothing can improve a crow.'

Like most human sages, he wasn't very clear in his thinking, so there has been some misunderstanding about what he meant. Humans like to think that what he really meant was that crows were so bad as to be beyond improvement. But we crows know better. We interpret the saying as meaning that the crow is so perfect that no improvement is possible.

It's not that we aren't human—what I mean is, there are times when we fall from our high standards and do rather foolish things. Like at lunch time the other day.

Sometimes, when the table is laid in the bungalow, and before the family enters the dining room, I nip in through the open window and make a quick foray among the dishes. Sometimes I'm lucky enough to pick up a sausage or a slice of toast, or even a pat of butter, making off before someone enters and throws a bread knife at me. But on this occasion, just as I was reaching for the toast, a thin slouching fellow— Junior sahib they call him—entered suddenly and shouted at me. I was so startled that I leapt across the table, seeking shelter. Something flew at me and in an effort to dodge the missile I put my head through a circular object and then found it wouldn't come off.

It wasn't safe to hang around there, so I flew out of the window with this dashed ring still round my neck.

Serviette or napkin rings, that's what they are called. Quite unnecessary objects, but some humans—particularly the well-to-do sort—seem to like having them on their tables, holding bits of cloth in place. The cloth is used for wiping the mouth. Have you ever heard of such nonsense?

Anyway, there I was with a fat napkin ring round my neck, and as I perched on the wall trying to get it off, the entire human family gathered on their veranda to watch me.

There was the Colonel sahib and his wife, the memsahib; there was the scrawny Junior sahib (worst of the lot); there was a mischievous boy (the Colonel sahib's grandson) known as the Baba; and there was the cook (who usually flung orange peels at me) and the gardener (who once tried to decapitate me with a spade), and the dog Tiger who, like most dogs, tries unsuccessfully to be a human.

Today, they weren't cursing and shaking their fists at me; they were just standing and laughing their heads off. What's so funny about a crow with its head stuck in a napkin ring?

Worse was to follow.

The noise had attracted the other crows in the area, and if there's one thing crows detest, it's a crow who doesn't look like a crow.

They swooped low and dived on me, hammering at the wretched napkin ring, until they had knocked me off the wall and into a flower bed. Then six or seven toughs landed on me with every intention of finishing me off.

'Hey, boys!' I cawed. 'This is me, Speedy! What are you trying to do—kill me?'

'That's right! You don't look like Speedy to us. What have you done with him, hey?'

And they set upon me with even greater vigour.

'You're just like a bunch of lousy humans!' I shouted.

'You're no better than them—this is just the way they carry on amongst themselves!'

That brought them to a halt. They stopped trying to peck me to pieces, and stood back, looking puzzled. The napkin ring had been shattered in the onslaught and had fallen to the ground.

'Why, it's Speedy!' said one of the gang. 'None other!'

'Good old Speedy—what are you doing here? And where's the guy we were hammering just now?'

There was no point in trying to explain things to them. Crows are like that. There're all good pals—until one of them tries to look different. Then he could be just another bird.

'He took off for Tibet,' I said. 'It was getting unhealthy for him around here.'

Summertime is here again. And although I'm a crow for all seasons, I must admit to a preference for the summer months.

Humans grow lazy and don't pursue me with so much vigour. Garbage cans overflow. Food goes bad and is constantly being thrown away. Overripe fruit gets tastier by the minute. If fellows like me weren't around to mop up all these unappreciated riches, how would humans manage?

There's one character in the bungalow, the Junior sahib, who will never appreciate our services it seems. He simply hates crows. The small boy may throw stones at us occasionally, but then, he's the sort who throws stones at almost anything. There's nothing personal about it. He just throws stones on principle.

The memsahib is probably the best of the lot. She often throws me scraps from the kitchen—onion-skins, potato peels, crusts, and leftovers—and even when I nip in and make off with something not meant for me (like a jam tart or a cheese pakora) she is quite sporting about it. The Junior sahib looks outraged, but the lady of the house says, 'Well, we've all got to make a living somehow, and that's how crows make theirs. It's high time you thought of earning a living.' Junior sahib's her nephew—that's his occupation. He has never been known to work.

The Colonel sahib has a sense of humour but it's often directed at me. He thinks I'm a comedian.

He discovered I'd been making off with the occasional egg from the egg basket on the veranda, and one day, without my knowledge, he made a substitution.

Right on top of the pile I found a smooth, round egg, and before anyone could shout 'Crow!', I'd made off with it. It was abnormally light. I put it down on the lawn and set about cracking it with my strong beak; but it would keep slipping away or bouncing off into the bushes. Finally, I got it between my feet and gave it a good hard whack. It burst open. To my utter astonishment there was nothing inside!

I looked up and saw the old man standing on the veranda, doubled up with laughter.

'What are you laughing at?' asked the memsahib, coming out to see what it was all about.

'It's that ridiculous crow!' guffawed the Colonel,

pointing at me. 'You know he's been stealing our eggs. Well, I placed a ping-pong ball on top of the pile, and he fell for it! He's been struggling with that ball for twenty minutes! That will teach him a lesson.'

It did. But I had my revenge later, when I pinched a brand new toothbrush from the Colonel's bathroom.

The Junior sahib has no sense of humour at all. He idles about the house and grounds all day, whistling or singing to himself.

'Even that crow sings better than Uncle,' said the boy.

A truthful boy; but all he got for his honesty was a whack on the head from his uncle.

Anyway, as a gesture of appreciation, I perched on the garden wall and gave the family a rendering of my favourite crow song, which is my own composition. Here it is, translated for your benefit:

Oh, for the life of a crow!
A bird who's in the know,
Although we are cursed,
We are never dispersed—
We're always on the go!

I know I'm a bit of a rogue
(And my voice wouldn't pass for a brogue),
But there's no one as sleek
Or as neat with his beak—
So they're putting my picture in *Vogue*!

Oh, for the life of a crow!
I reap what I never sow,
They call me a thief—
Pray I'll soon come to grief—
But there's no getting rid of a crow!

I gave it everything I had, and the humans—all of them on the lawn to enjoy the evening breeze, listened to me in silence, struck with wonder at my performance.

When I had finished, I bowed and preened myself, waiting for the applause.

They stared at each other for a few seconds. Then the Junior sahib stooped, picked up a bottle opener, and flung it at me.

Well, I ask you!

What can one say about humans? I do my best to defend them from all kinds of criticism, and this is what I get for my pains.

Anyway, I picked up the bottle opener and added it to my collection of odds and ends.

It was getting dark, and soon everyone was stumbling around, looking for another bottle opener. Junior sahib's popularity was even lower than mine.

One day Junior sahib came home carrying a heavy shotgun. He pointed it at me a few times and I dived for cover. But he didn't fire. Probably, I was out of range.

'He's only threatening you,' said Slow, from the safety of the jamun tree, where he sat in the shadows. 'He probably doesn't know how to fire the thing.'

But I wasn't taking any chances. I'd seen a sly look on Junior sahib's face, and I decided that he was trying to make me careless. So I stayed well out of range.

Then one evening I received a visit from my cousin brother, Charm. He'd come to me for a loan. He wanted some new bottle caps for his collection and brought me a mouldy old toothbrush in exchange.

Charm landed on the garden wall, toothbrush in his beak, and was waiting for me to join him there, when there was a flash and a tremendous bang. Charm was sent several feet into the air, and landed limp and dead in a flower bed.

'I've got him, I've got him!' shouted Junior sahib. 'I've shot that blasted crow!'

Throwing away the gun, Junior sahib ran out into the garden, overcome with joy. He picked up my fallen relative, and began running around the bungalow with his trophy.

The rest of the family had collected on the veranda.

'Drop that thing at once!' called the memsahib.

'Uncle is doing a war dance,' observed the boy.

'It's unlucky to shoot a crow,' said the Colonel.

I thought it was time to take a hand in the proceedings and let everyone know that the *right* crow—the one and only Speedy—was alive and kicking. So I swooped down the jackfruit tree, dived through Junior sahib's window and emerged with one of his socks.

Triumphantly flaunting his dead crow, Junior sahib came dancing up the garden path, then stopped dead when he saw me perched on the window sill, a sock in my beak. His jaw fell, his eyes bulged; he looked like the owl in the banyan tree.

'You shot the wrong crow!' shouted the Colonel, and everyone roared with laughter.

Before Junior sahib could recover from the shock, I took off in a leisurely fashion and joined Slow on the wall.

Junior sahib came rushing out with the gun, but by now it was too dark to see anything, and I heard the memsahib telling the Colonel, 'You'd better take that gun away before he does himself a mischief.' So the Colonel took Junior indoors and gave him a brandy.

I composed a new song for Junior sahib's benefit and sang it to him outside his window early next morning:

I understand you want a crow
To poison, shoot or smother;
My fond salaams, but by your leave
I'll substitute another:
Allow me then, to introduce
My most respected brother.

Although I was quite understanding about the whole tragic mix-up—I was, after all, the family's very own house-crow—my fellow crows were outraged at what happened to Charm, and swore vengeance on Junior sahib.

'*Corvus splendens!*' they shouted with great spirit, forgetting that this title had been bestowed on us by a human.

In times of war, we forget how much we owe to our enemies.

Junior sahib had only to step into the garden, and several crows would swoop down on him, screeching and swearing and aiming lusty blows at his head and hands. He took to coming out wearing a sola-topee, and even then they knocked it off and drove him indoors. Once he tried lighting a cigarette on the veranda steps, when Slow swooped low across the porch and snatched it from his lips.

Junior sahib shut himself up in his room, and smoked countless cigarettes—a sure sign that his nerves were going to pieces.

Every now and then the memsahib would come out and shoo us off; and because she wasn't an enemy, we obliged by retreating to the garden wall. After all, Slow and I depended on her for much of our board if not for our lodging. But Junior sahib had only to show his face outside the house, and all the crows in the area would be after him like avenging furies.

'It doesn't look as though they are going to forgive you,' said the memsahib.

'Elephants never forget, and crows never forgive,' said the Colonel.

'Would you like to borrow my catapult, Uncle?' asked the boy. 'Just for self-protection, you know.'

'Shut up,' said Junior sahib and went to bed.

One day he sneaked out of the back door and dashed across to the garage. A little later, the family's old car, seldom used, came out of the garage with Junior sahib at the wheel. He'd decided that if he couldn't take a walk in safety, he'd go for a drive. All the windows were up.

No sooner had the car turned into the driveway than about a dozen crows dived down on it, crowding the bonnet

367

and flipping in front of the windscreen. Junior sahib couldn't see a thing. He swung the steering wheel left, right and centre, and the car went off the driveway, ripped through a hedge, crushed a bed of sweet peas and came to a stop against the trunk of a mango tree.

Junior sahib just sat there, afraid to open the door. The family had to come out of the house and rescue him. 'Are you all right?' asked the Colonel.

'I've bruised my knees,' said Junior sahib.

'Never mind your knees,' said the memsahib, gazing around at the ruin of her garden. 'What about my sweet peas?'

'I think your uncle is going to have a nervous breakdown,' I heard the Colonel saying.

'What's that?' asked the boy. 'Is it the same as a car having a breakdown?'

'Well—not exactly . . . But you could call it a mind breaking up.'

Junior sahib had been refusing to leave his room or take his meals. The family was worried about him. I was worried, too. Believe it or not, we crows are among the very few who sincerely desire the preservation of the human species.

'He needs a change,' said the memsahib.

'A rest cure,' said the Colonel sarcastically. 'A rest from doing nothing.'

'Send him to Switzerland,' suggested the boy.

'We can't afford that. But we can take him up to a hill station.'

The nearest hill station was some fifty miles as the

human drives (only ten as the crow flies). Many people went up during the summer months. It wasn't fancied much by crows.

For one thing, it was a tidy sort of place, and people lived in houses that were set fairly far apart. Opportunities for scavenging were limited. Also, it was rather cold and the trees were inconvenient and uncomfortable. A friend of mine who had spent a night in a pine tree said he hadn't been able to sleep because of prickly pine needles and the wind howling through the branches.

'Let's all go up for a holiday,' said the memsahib. 'We can spend a week in a boarding house. All of us need a change.'

A few days later the house was locked up, and the family piled into the old car and drove off to the hills.

I had the grounds to myself.

The dog had gone too, and the gardener spent all day dozing in his hammock. There was no one around to trouble me.

'We've got the whole place to ourselves,' I told Slow.

'Yes, but what good is that? With everyone gone, there are no throwaways, giveaways and takeaways!'

'We'll have to try the house next door.'

'And be driven off by the other crows? That's not our territory, you know. We can go across to help them, or to ask for their help, but we're not supposed to take their pickings. It just isn't cricket, old boy.'

We could have tried the bazaar or the railway station, where there is always a lot of rubbish to be found, but there is also a lot of competition in those places. The station crows are gangsters. The bazaar crows are bullies. Slow and I had grown soft. We'd have been no match for the bad boys.

'I've just realized how much we depend on humans, I said. 'We could go back to living in the jungle,' said Slow.

'No, that would be too much like hard work. We'd be living on wild fruit most of the time. Besides, the jungle crows won't have anything to do with us now. Ever since we took up with humans, we became the outcasts of the bird world.'

'That means we're almost human.'

'You might say we have all their vices and none of their virtues.'

'Just a different set of values, old boy.'

'Like eating hens' eggs instead of crows' eggs. That's something in their favour. And while you're hanging around here waiting for the mangoes to fall, I'm off to locate our humans.'

Slow's beak fell open. He looked like—well, a hungry crow.

'Don't tell me you're going to follow them up to the hill station? You don't even know where they are staying.'

'I'll soon find out,' I said, and took off for the hills.

You'd be surprised at how simple it is to be a good detective, if only you put your mind to it. Of course, if Ellery Queen had been able to fly, he wouldn't have required fifteen chapters and his father's assistance to crack a case.

Swooping low over the hill station, it wasn't long before I spotted my humans' old car. It was parked outside a boarding house called the Climber's Rest. I hadn't seen anyone climbing, but, dozing in an armchair in the garden, was my favourite human.

I perched on top of a colourful umbrella and waited for Junior sahib to wake up. I decided it would be rather inconsiderate of me to disturb his sleep, so I waited patiently on the brolly, looking at him with one eye and keeping one eye on the house. He stirred uneasily, as though he'd suddenly had a bad dream; then he opened his eyes. I must have been the first thing he saw.

'Good morning,' I cawed, in a friendly tone—always ready to forgive and forget, that's Speedy!

He leapt out of the armchair and ran into the house, hollering at the top of his voice.

I supposed he hadn't been able to contain his delight at seeing me again. Humans can be funny that way. They'll hate you one day and love you the next.

Well, Junior sahib ran all over the boarding house, screaming, 'It's that crow, it's that crow! He's following me everywhere!'

Various people, including the family, ran outside to see what the commotion was about, and I thought it would be better to make myself scarce. So I flew to the top of a spruce tree and stayed very still and quiet.

'Crow! What crow?' said the Colonel.

'Our crow!' cried Junior sahib. 'The one that persecutes me. I was dreaming of it just now, and when I opened my eyes, there it was, on the garden umbrella!'

'There's nothing there now,' said the memsahib. 'You probably hadn't woken up completely.'

'He is having illusions again,' said the boy. 'Delusions,' corrected the Colonel.

'Now look here,' said the memsahib. 'You'll have to pull yourself together. You'll take leave of your senses if you don't.'

'I tell you, it's here!' sobbed Junior sahib. 'It's following me everywhere.'

'It's grown fond of Uncle,' said the boy. 'And it seems Uncle can't live without crows.'

Junior sahib looked up with a wild glint in his eye.

'That's it!' he cried. 'I can't live without them. That's the answer to my problem. I don't hate crows—I love them!'

Everyone just stood around, goggling at Junior sahib.

'I'm feeling fine now,' he carried on. 'What a difference it makes if you can just do the opposite to what you've been doing before!' And flapping his arms, and trying to caw like a crow, he went prancing about the garden.

'Now he thinks he's a crow,' said the boy. 'Is he still having delusions?'

'That's right,' said the memsahib. 'Delusions of grandeur.'

After that, the family decided that there was no point in staying on in the hill station any longer. Junior sahib had completed his rest cure. And even if he was the only one who believed himself cured, that was all right, because after all he was the one who mattered . . . If you're feeling fine, can there be anything wrong with you?

No sooner was everyone back in the bungalow than Junior sahib took to hopping barefoot on the grass early every morning, all the time scattering food about for the crows. Bread, chapatties, cooked rice, curried eggplants, the memsahib's home-made toffee—you name it, we got it!

Slow and I were the first to help ourselves to these dawn offerings, and soon the other crows had joined us on the lawn. We didn't mind. Junior sahib brought enough for everyone.

'We ought to honour him in some way,' said Slow.

'Yes, why not?' said I. 'There was someone else, hundreds of years ago, who fed the birds. They followed him wherever he went.'

'That's right. They made him a saint. But as far as I know, he didn't feed any crows. At least, you don't see any crows in the pictures—just sparrows and robins and wagtails.'

'Small fry. *Our* human is dedicated exclusively to crows. Do you realize that, Slow?'

'Sure. We ought to make him the patron saint of crows. What do you say, fellows?'

'Caw, caw, caw!' All the crows were in agreement.

'St Corvus!' said Slow, as Junior sahib emerged from the house, laden with good things to eat.

'Corvus, corvus, corvus!' we cried.

And what a pretty picture he made—a crow eating from his hand, another perched on his shoulder, and about a dozen of us on the grass, forming a respectful ring around him.

From persecutor to protector; from beastliness to saintliness. And sometimes it can be the other way round: you never know with humans!

Upon an Old Wall Dreaming

IT IS TIME to confess that at least half my life has been spent in idleness. My old school would not be proud of me. Nor would my Aunt Muriel.

'You spend most of your time sitting on that wall, doing nothing,' scolded Aunt Muriel, when I was seven or eight. 'Are you *thinking* about something?'

'No, Aunt Muriel.'

'Are you *dreaming*?' 'I'm awake!'

'Then what on earth are you doing there?' 'Nothing, Aunt Muriel.'

'He'll come to no good,' she warned the world at large. 'He'll spend all his life sitting on walls, doing nothing.'

And how right she proved to be! Sometimes I bestir myself, and bang out a few sentences on my old typewriter, but most of the time I'm still sitting on that wall, preferably in the winter sunshine. Thinking? Not very deeply. Dreaming?

But I've grown too old to dream. Meditation, perhaps. That's been fashionable for some time. But it isn't that either. Contemplation might come closer to the mark.

Was I born with a silver spoon in my mouth that I could afford to sit in the sun for hours, doing nothing? Far from it; I was born poor and remained poor, as far as worldly riches went. But one has to eat and pay the rent. And there have been others to feed too. So I have to admit that between long bouts of idleness, there have been short bursts of creativity. My typewriter, after more than thirty years of loyal service, has finally collapsed, proof enough that it has not lain idle all this time.

Sitting on walls, apparently doing nothing, has always been my favourite form of inactivity. But for these walls, and the many idle hours I have spent upon them, I would not have written even a fraction of the hundreds of stories, essays and other diversions that have been banged out on the typewriter over the years. It is not the walls themselves that set me off or give me ideas, but a personal view of the world that I receive from sitting there.

Creative idleness, you could call it. A receptivity to the world around me—the breeze, the warmth of the old stone, the lizard on the rock, a raindrop on a blade of grass—these and other impressions impinge upon me as I sit in that passive, benign condition that makes people smile tolerantly at me as they pass. 'Eccentric writer,' they remark to each other as they drive on, hurrying in a heat of hope, towards the pot of gold at the end of their personal rainbows.

It's true that I am eccentric in many ways, and old walls bring out the essence of my eccentricity.

I do not have a garden wall. This shaky tumbledown house in the hills is perched directly above a motorable road, making me both accessible and vulnerable to casual callers of all kinds—inquisitive tourists, local busybodies, schoolgirls with their poems, hawkers selling candy-floss, itinerant sadhus, scrap merchants, potential Nobel Prize winners . . .

To escape them, and to set my thoughts in order, I walk a little way up the road, cross it, and sit down on a parapet wall overlooking the Woodstock spur. Here, partially shaded by an overhanging oak, I am usually left alone. I look suitably down and out, shabbily dressed, a complete nonentity—not the sort of person you would want to be seen talking to!

Stray dogs sometimes join me here. Having been a stray dog myself at various periods of my life, I can empathize with these friendly vagabonds of the road. Far more intelligent than your inbred Pom or Peke, they let me know by their silent companionship that they are on the same wavelength. They sport about on the road, but they do not yap at all and sundry.

Left to myself on the wall, I am soon in the throes of composing a story or poem. I do not write it down—that can be done later—I just work it out in my mind, memorize my words, so to speak, and keep them stored up for my next writing session.

Occasionally, a car will stop, and someone I know will stick his head out and say, 'No work today, Mr Bond? How I envy you! Not a care in the world!'

I travel back in time some fifty years to Aunt Muriel asking me the same question. The years melt away, and I am a child again, sitting on the garden wall, doing nothing.

'Don't you get bored sitting there?' asks the latest passing motorist, who has one of those half beards which are in vogue with TV newsreaders. 'What are you doing?'

'Nothing, Aunty,' I reply.

He gives me a long hard stare.

'You must be dreaming. Don't you recognize me?'

'Yes, Aunt Muriel.'

He shakes his head sadly, steps on the gas, and goes roaring up the hill in a cloud of dust.

'Poor old Bond,' he tells his friends over evening cocktails. 'Must be going round the bend. This morning he called me Aunty.'

Remember This Day

IF YOU CAN get a year off from school when you are nine, and can have a memorable time with a great father, then that year has to be the best time of your life, even if it is followed by sorrow and insecurity. It was the result of my parents' separation at a time when my father was on active service in the RAF during World War II. He kept me with him that summer and winter, at various locations in New Delhi—Hailey Road, Atul Grove Lane, Scindia House—in rented apartments, as he was not permitted to keep a child in the service personnel quarters. This suited me perfectly, and I had a wonderful year in Delhi, going to the cinema, quaffing milk shakes, helping my father with his stamp collection; but this idyllic situation could not continue forever, and when my father was transferred to Karachi, he had no option but to put me in a boarding school.

This was the Bishop Cotton Preparatory School in

Simla—or rather, Chotta Simla—where boys studied up to Class 5, after which they moved on to the senior school. Although I was a shy boy, I had settled down quite well in the friendly atmosphere of this little school, but I did miss my father's companionship, and I was overjoyed when he came up to see me during the midsummer break. He had only a couple of days' leave, and he could only take me out for a day, bringing me back to school in the evening.

I was so proud of him when he turned up in his dark blue RAF uniform, a flight lieutenant's stripes in evidence, as he had just been promoted. He was already forty, engaged in codes and ciphers and not flying much. He was short and stocky, getting bald, but smart in his uniform. I gave him a salute—I loved giving salutes—and he returned the salutation and followed it up with a hug and a kiss on my forehead. 'And what would you like to do today, son?'

'Let's go to Davico's,' I said. Davico's was the best restaurant in town, famous for its meringues, marzipans, curry puffs and pastries. So to Davico's we went, where I gorged myself on confectionery as only a schoolboy can do.

'Lunch is still a long way off, so let's take a walk,' suggested my father. And provisioning ourselves with more pastries, we left the mall and trudged up to the Monkey Temple at the top of Jakko Hill. Here we were relieved of the pastries by the monkeys, who simply snatched them away from my unwilling hands, and we came downhill in a hurry before I could get hungry again. Small boys and monkeys have much in common.

My father suggested a rickshaw ride around Elysium

Hill, and this we did in style, swept along by four sturdy young rickshaw pullers. My father took the opportunity of relating the story of Kipling's 'Phantom Rickshaw' (this was before I discovered it in print) and a couple of other ghost stories designed to build up my appetite for lunch.

We ate at Wenger's (or was it Clark's) and then— 'Enough of ghosts, Ruskin. Let's go to the pictures.' I loved going to the pictures. I knew the Delhi cinemas intimately, and it hadn't taken me long to discover the Simla cinemas. There were three—the Regal, the Ritz, and the Rivoli.

We went to the Rivoli. It was down near the ice-skating rink and the old Blessington hotel. The film was about an ice-skater and starred Sonja Hemé, a pretty young Norwegian Olympic champion, who appeared in a number of Hollywood musicals. All she had to do was skate and look pretty, and this she did to perfection. I decided to fall in love with her. But by the time I'd grown up and finished school, she'd stopped skating and making films! Whatever happened to Sonja Hemé? After the picture, it was time to return to school. We walked all the way to Chotta Simla, talking about what we'd do during the winter holidays, and where we would go when the war was over. 'I'll be in Calcutta now,' said my father. 'There are good bookshops there. And cinemas. And Chinese restaurants. And we'll buy more gramophone records and add to the stamp collection.'

It was dusk when we walked down the path to the school gate and playing field. Two of my friends, Bimal and Riaz, were waiting for me. My father spoke to them and asked about their homes. A bell started ringing and we said goodbye.

'Remember this day, Ruskin,' said my father. He patted me gently on the head and walked away. I never saw him again. Three months later I heard that he had passed away in the military hospital in Calcutta.

I dream of him sometimes, and in my dreams he is always the same, caring for me and leading me by the hand along old familiar roads. And, of course, I remember that day. Over sixty-five years have passed, but it's as fresh as yesterday.

The Big Race

I WAS AWAKENED by the sound of a hornbill honking in the banyan tree. I lay in bed, looking through the open window as the early morning sunshine crept up the wall. I knew it was a holiday, and that there was something important to be done that day, but for some time I couldn't quite remember what it was. Then, as the room got brighter, and the hornbill stopped his noise, I remembered.

It was the day of the big race.

I leapt out of bed, pulled open a dressing table drawer and brought out a cardboard box punctured with little holes. I opened the lid to see if Maharani was all right.

Maharani, my bamboo beetle, was asleep on the core of an apple. I had given her a week's rigorous training for the monsoon beetle race, and she was enjoying a well-earned rest before the big event. I did not disturb her.

Closing the box, I crept out of the house by the back

door. I did not want my parents to see me sneaking off to the municipal park at that early hour.

When I reached the gardens, the early morning sun was just beginning to make emeralds of the dewdrops, and the grass was cool and springy to my bare feet. A group of boys had gathered in a corner of the gardens, and among them were Kamal and Anil.

Anil's black rhino beetle was the favourite. It was a big beetle, with an aggressive forehead rather like its owner's. It was called Black Prince. Kamal's beetle was quite ordinary in size, but it possessed a long pair of whiskers (I suspected it belonged to the cockroach rather than the beetle family), and was called Moochha, which is Hindi for moustache.

There were one or two other entries, but none of them looked promising and interest centred on Black Prince, Moochha, and my own Maharani who was still asleep on her apple core. A few bets were being made, in coins or marbles, and a prize for the winner was on display; a great stag-beetle, quite dangerous to look at, which would enable the winner to start a stable and breed beetles on a large scale.

There was some confusion when Kamal's Moochha escaped from his box and took a preliminary canter over the grass, but he was soon caught and returned to his paddock. Moochha appeared to be in good form, and several boys put their marbles on him.

The course was about six feet long, the tracks six inches wide. The tracks were fenced with strips of cardboard so that the contestants would not move over to each other's path or leave the course altogether. They could only go forwards or backwards. They were held at the starting point by another piece of cardboard, which would be placed behind them as soon as the race began.

A little Sikh boy in a yellow pyjama suit was acting as starter, and he kept blowing his whistle for order and attention. Eventually he gained enough silence in which to announce the rules of the race: the contesting beetles were not allowed to be touched during the race, or blown at from behind, or bribed forward with bits of food. Only moral assistance was allowed, in the form of cheering and advice.

Moochha and Black Prince were already at the starting point, but Maharani seemed unwilling to leave her apple core, and I had to drag her to the starting post. There was further delay when Moochha got his whiskers entangled in the legs of a rival, but they were soon separated and the beetles placed in separate lanes. The race was about to start.

Kamal sat on his haunches, very quiet and serious, looking from Moochha to the finishing line and back again. I was biting my nails. Anil's bushy eyebrows were bunched together in a scowl. There was a tense hush amongst the spectators.

'Pee-ee-eep!' went the whistle. And they were off!

Or rather, Moochha and Black Prince were off because Maharani was still at the starting post, wondering what had happened to her apple core.

Everyone was cheering madly, Anil was jumping about, and Kamal was shouting himself hoarse.

Moochha was going at a spanking rate. Black Prince really wasn't taking much interest in the proceedings, but at least he was moving, and everything could happen in a race of this nature. I was in a furious temper. All the coaching I had given Maharani appeared to be of no use. She was still looking confused and a little resentful at having been deprived of her apple.

Then Moochha suddenly stopped, about two feet from the finishing line. He seemed to be having trouble with his whiskers, and kept twitching them this way and that. Black Prince was catching up inch by inch, and both Anil and Kamal were hopping about with excitement. Nobody was paying any attention to Maharani, who was looking suspiciously at the other beetles in the rear. No doubt she suspected them of having something to do with the disappearance of her apple. I begged her to make an effort. It was with difficulty that I prevented myself from giving her a push, but that would have meant disqualification.

As Black Prince drew level with Moochha, he stopped and appeared to be enquiring about his rival's whiskers. Anil and Kamal now became even more frantic in their efforts to encourage their racers, and the cheering on all sides was deafening.

Maharani, enraged at having been deprived of her apple core, now decided to make a bid for liberty and rushed forward in great style.

I gave a cry of joy, but the others did not notice this new challenge until Maharani had drawn level with her rivals. There was a gasp of surprise from the spectators, and Maharani dashed across the finishing line in record time.

Everyone cheered the gallant outsider. Anil and Kamal

very sportingly shook my hand and congratulated me on my methods. Coins and marbles passed from hand to hand. The little Sikh boy blew his whistle for silence and presented me with the first prize.

I examined the new beetle with respect and gently stroked its hard, smooth back. Then, in case Maharani should feel jealous, I put away the prize beetle and returned Maharani to her apple core. I was determined that I would not indulge in any favouritism.

Read More in Puffin

Hip-Hop Nature Boy and Other Poems
Ruskin Bond

*If a tortoise could run
And losses be won,
And bullies be buttered on toast;
If a song brought a shower
And a gun grew a flower,
This world would be nicer than most!*

Beautiful, poignant and funny, Ruskin Bond's verses for children are a joy to read to yourself on a lazy summer afternoon or to recite in school among friends. For the first time, his poems for children, old and new, come together in this illustrated volume. Nature, love, friends, school, books—all find a place in the poetry of India's favourite children's writer.

Read More in Puffin

Thick as Thieves: Tales of Friendship
Ruskin Bond

Somewhere in life
There must be someone
To take your hand
And share the torrid day.
Without the touch of friendship
There is no life and we must fade away.

Discover a hidden pool with three young boys, laugh out loud as a little mouse makes demands on a lonely writer, follow the mischievous 'four feathers' as they discover a baby lost in the hills and witness the bond between a tiger and his master. Some stories will make you smile, some will bring tears to your eyes, some may make your heart skip a beat but all of them will renew your faith in the power of friendship.

Read More in Puffin

Uncles, Aunts and Elephants:
Tales from your Favourite Storyteller
Ruskin Bond

I know the world's a crowded place,
And elephants do take up space,
But if it makes a difference, Lord,
I'd gladly share my room and board.
A baby elephant would do...
But, if he brings his mother too,
There's Dad's garage. He wouldn't mind.
To elephants, he's more than kind.
But I wonder what my Mum would say
If their aunts and uncles came to stay!

Ruskin Bond has entertained generations of readers for many decades. This delightful collection of poetry, prose and non-fiction brings together some of his best work in a single volume. Sumptuously illustrated, *Uncles, Aunts and Elephants* is a book to treasure for all times.